WARRANT FOR X

WARRANT
FOR
X

BY PHILIP
MACDONALD

VINTAGE BOOKS
A DIVISION OF RANDOM HOUSE
NEW YORK

Library of Congress Cataloging in Publication Data
MacDonald, Philip.
Warrant for X.
Reprint. Originally published:
Garden City, N.Y. : Doubleday, Doran, 1938.
I. Title.
PR6025.A2218W3 1983   823'.912   83-5732
ISBN 0-394-71660-4

Manufactured in the United States of America

CHAPTER I

The fact that Sheldon Garrett was an American makes it comprehensible that, although a widely travelled and widely read person, it was not until his thirty-fourth birthday that he made acquaintance with any of the work of Mr. G. K. Chesterton. This birthday fell, in the year with which we are concerned, upon a September Friday and coincided happily enough with the first night of the London production of his play, *Wise Man's Holiday*. It being clear by 11:45 P.M. that the play was going to be a success, the party given after the show by Brooks-Carew was a decisively alcoholic affair. It is instructive to think that had it not been, Sheldon Garrett would not have spent the most of Saturday reading the *Napoleon of Notting Hill* and would not, therefore, have been himself in the vicinity of Notting Hill upon Sunday afternoon. For, if Brooks-Carew's drinks had been fewer and smaller, neither Sheldon Garrett nor Manvers, of the *Telegram*, would have reached that solemn stage of insobriety which led them, neither knowing the other from Adam or even Eve, to a ponderous literary discussion conducted in Brooks-Carew's bathroom; and then Garrett, looking over the Savoy bookstall on the following night, would not have purchased a cheap edition of what is, after all, perhaps the best of all Mr. Chesterton's good work.

He read from one o'clock upon Sunday morning until, at just before five, he had finished with the histories of Adam Wayne and Auberon. And then he slept, to wake at the awkward hour of 1 P.M. This tardiness necessitated the mendacious cancellation of a luncheon appointment and, further, left the liar with nothing to do in London

5

upon a grey autumnal Sunday afternoon. He lunched in belated solitude and in his own sitting room. Over the meal he dipped again into *Napoleon*—and by half-past three was descending from a scarlet omnibus opposite the depressing façade of Notting Hill underground station.

He then walked—led, as it were, by Chance and Chesterton. At first unable to reconcile even the Sunday afternoon quietude of the main thoroughfare with the brave sombreness of the streets down which Adam Wayne had walked and wondered, he found himself, by a lucky turn to his left, at once in an atmosphere where indeed the railings were like spears.

London was very grey that day and, summertime having undergone its annual destruction three days before, the blue dimness of early evening soon began to blend with the steely light which had been all that told of a sun somewhere above smooth, unending clouds.

He had, he thought, been walking for some thirty minutes before he glanced at his watch and found, not without surprise, that it was a little more than double that time since he had alighted from the bus. He was in some sort of Ladbrookish square whose tall, grey-fronted, be-pillared houses frowned down with ugly and angular dignity upon an iron-surrounded oval of bright green grass and dusty, dark green bushes.

The place seemed dead and Garrett felt himself on a sudden very tired and—yes!—faintly afraid. He did up the top button of his overcoat, squared his admirable shoulders and set off at a brisk pace designed to assure himself that he was moving somewhere of set purpose.

He was unashamedly relieved when, coming to a side turning, he met another wayfarer in this dead place of glowering brick—a grimy man who carried over his shoulder a slender, laden sack.

They met almost face to face, so that the sack bearer was forced to step aside.

"Evening!" said Sheldon Garrett, who felt the need for speech.

"Eh?" said the sack bearer.

"Er," said Sheldon Garrett and hastily produced a cigarette case. "Got a match?"

The sack bearer searched in pockets with his right hand,

balancing his sack with his left. Without a word he produced matches and proffered them.

"Thanks!" said Garrett and lit a cigarette which he did not want. He held out the still-open case. "Have one?"

The sack bearer shook his head. Garrett closed the case, put it back in his pocket and returned the box of matches. "Thanks," he said.

The sack bearer returned box to pocket, shifted his burden from the left shoulder to the right, took a step sideways to avoid his accoster and marched off into the gathering gloom.

Young Garrett looked after him, feeling a violent and ridiculous urge to run in pursuit and—as he had seen in English newspaper reportings—"commit assault with intent to do grievous bodily harm." But Mr. Sheldon Garrett, traveller and man of substance and author of the successful play, *Wise Man's Holiday,* merely threw away a newly lighted cigarette and strode off in the opposite direction.

Now it was really dark. Behind curtains lights began to show in windows which hitherto had been blankly frowning eyes and every here and there, on high, the distorted rectangles of street lamps sent out feeble yellow radiance. Garrett tried to remember the course of his meanderings and came to the conclusion that if he kept bearing to his right he would once more reach the thoroughfare along whose bosom he had been borne from the Savoy and the haunts of men. He turned to his right and was in a street which was like many others along which he had walked. Halfway down it he saw a boy with a dog but he did not speak to the boy. He came to the end of the street and found forward progress barred. He turned left—and it seemed to him that he was in the same street yet again. He saw a woman with a dog. He did not speak to the woman. He walked on, unconsciously both lengthening and quickening his stride rather in the way in which a man lost in the bush will lengthen and quicken his stride before allowing his mind to tell him that he doesn't know, after all, where he is.

He turned to his right. And now he was clearly in a different street. It was narrower and the houses which lined it, although they, too, frowned, were shorter and dingier and behind their railings (which did not look in the least

7

like spears) seemed to give out into the chill dank air an abstract miasma of decay. Onto a low wall dividing the pavement along which he walked from the dark shadows of the houses behind it jumped a long, gaunt cat. It stared at him with shiny yellow eyes and was gone.

He became aware now of physical as well as spiritual discomfort. His legs ached and his feet were resenting the pounding of paving stones. The chill air stung his face but beneath his clothes his body was uncomfortably warm.

He came to a turning upon his right and took it and found himself, by means of one of those sulky conjuring tricks which London so often performs, in a different world. Gone was the sense of decay. Now there surrounded him, like an uncomfortable cloak, that air of chilly, black-gloved rectitude which, owing to the lingering slaughter of the English language, must be expressed in the word "respectability." The houses were neat. The brass of letter boxes and knockers shone bright. The very street lamps seemed to have cleaner panes to their windows. The railings, though certainly not spears again, were yet frigid guardians of a privacy which needed no guard.

And then, though direfully discreet, came small shops, all but the last having barred doors and blank, shaded windows which offered nothing save unfriendliness.

Garrett strode on; but at the next corner suddenly halted. For the last shop was not, strictly speaking, a shop at all. Over its door hung a lantern encased in fancifully patterned wrought iron which tried to look old. And behind the glass panes of the lantern shone a yellow light and on the panes of the lantern appeared the words, in tortured Gothic script, Ye Willow-Pattern Tea Shoppe.

"Ah!" said Garrett aloud.

Most untraditionally he liked tea. And he was tired and footsore and too hot for more walking and his throat was parched. He pressed the handle of the muslin-curtained door and from somewhere in dim recesses came the tinkle of a mournful bell.

2

Inside the place was dimly lighted and larger than he had expected. Along one wall were ranged, to face each other, high-backed settles of deal stained to look like oak.

On the walls were hanging plates and dishes of cheap earthenware painted to look like willow pattern. Such light as there was came from a central hanging lamp of brass designed to look as if it were old and from a few weakly powered and faintly pink bulbs held to the walls by iron brackets which tried to look like candlesticks. Ye Willow-Pattern Tea Shoppe was, in other words, own brother to a hundred other Tea Shoppes.

It was empty. For a moment Garrett looked about him, considering flight, but then there appeared—silently and as if by some dreary magic—the usual handmaiden. She was tall and willowy and fatigued. She was clad in the sort of long and shapeless garment which invariably goes with Tea Shoppes and had about her, as inevitably, an air of aggressive gentility. She did not speak to Garrett; she merely looked at him with a glitter of pince-nez.

Garrett said: "Tea. Could I have some tea, please?" and presently found himself seated, to face the door, in the last and darkest of the booths made by the settles.

He ordered China tea and, because it seemed expected of him, scones and jam. The neophyte drifted silently away to be lost in the shadows at the far end of the room. There came to Garrett's ears the sound of a door opening and shutting and then, from somewhere presumably behind this door, a faint chinking of china. He lit a cigarette and disposed himself as comfortably as the unfriendly settle would let him. He found himself still too warm and rose and took off his overcoat and put this down with his hat upon the settle facing him.

He had finished his cigarette when his tea came. Strangely enough it was good. He drank two cups and ate two pieces of one tasteless scone. He poured himself the third cup and lit another cigarette and sat back in his corner and wondered what he was thinking about and found that he did not know.

The street door opened with a faint squeaking followed by the dim tinkling of the bell. It closed again and the bell stopped ringing and Garrett heard footsteps and the voices of women. He was sitting in the angle formed by the wall and the back of his booth and he did not move. He felt, indeed, vaguely annoyed at the intrusion in the way that a man does when suddenly aroused from the pleasant state of musing heavily upon nothing. He heard another faint sound from the door in the black shadows at the far end of the shop and then, a moment later, another murmur of voices as the languid ancilla spoke with the newcomers. Then there came a sudden marching of feet and persons disposed themselves in the booth immediately next to his. He still had not moved forward, so that he did not see them nor they him; but his ears told him that there were two.

Followed murmurs, rustles, the clearing of a throat, clatters as umbrellas were laid down and creakings as bodies were disposed upon the deal seats. The neophyte came, swimming for a moment across Garrett's little field of vision, then departed with orders. The voice that gave the order was beyond doubt a woman's; but it was curiously deep and had in its tone a decisive and masculine quality which interested Garrett despite himself.

His cigarette had been finished before the new entry and now he idly debated with himself as to whether the trouble of reaching to a hip pocket for his case were worth the dubious solace of more tobacco. He decided that it was not and thereby irretrievably involved himself.

He looked at the watch upon his wrist. Its hands stood at twenty minutes to six. He had not realized that it was so late. He must be back at the Savoy and changing by half-past six. Without otherwise moving he put a hand to his breast pocket for his notecase, remembering that he had no change. He pulled out the soft leather wallet with fingers so idle that the thing slipped from them, struck softly against his knee and slid noiselessly to the floor. He bent to retrieve it. His groping hand did not find it at first, so that he was forced to sink to one knee and continue his fumbling over a wider area.

Curiously—because he was not particularly endeavouring to be quiet—it so happened that over the whole of this operation he made no noise at all.

His searching fingers had just found the edge of the wallet when there came to his ear, echoing curiously by reason of his nearness to the floor, the sound of voices from the next booth. The first voice was the deep one but the second voice was its very antithesis: high pitched yet soft; youthful yet pleasantly modulated; delightful yet somehow strange in accent to Garrett's ear. And it managed to convey, without tremolo, a suggestion of fear.

10

The first voice said: "I told you so. Not a soul in the place."

The second voice said: "Except the waitress . . . and . . . did you look in the booth behind me?"

The deep voice said: "Not a soul, I tell you! Don't be——"

The gentle voice said: "I'll look . . . just to make sure. . . . There's no harm . . ." It died away. Like the other voice it had not whispered and yet, like the other voice, it somehow conveyed to Garrett's ear a suggestion of furtiveness. The wallet now in his fingers, he remained—quite why he could not have told you at the moment—utterly immobile. He even held his breath. He heard through the pounding of the blood through his ears the sounds of someone rising; then a scraping upon the boards and then, following the sound of this one seating herself again, the second or gentle voice. It said:

"No. There isn't anybody." It was noticeably louder. It was, also, *surer*.

The deep voice said: "What did I tell you! Never talk secrets in a private house. Never talk secrets in a public park. If you must talk secrets, talk 'em in a teashop."

A muffled bubble of laughter, not conveying much of mirth, came from the other throat and the gentle voice said: "You do say such *things!*"

"What I say," said the deep voice, "always means something. . . . Now then, miss, what's your answer? Are you going to see it through? Or not?"

The gentle voice said: "I—I—can't make up my mind. It sort of frightens me. I—you see—I——"

To the ears of Sheldon Garrett, conscious not only of the slightly ludicrous indignity of his position but of certain views of his own upon eavesdroppers, came the sound of the service door opening and a faint rattling which told of the bearing of a laden tray. In one swift movement, cleverly noiseless, he was up from the floor and in his seat again.

The deep voice said in a harsh, savage half whisper which only just carried to Garrett's ear:

"Shut up!" And then, in a louder and commendably natural tone: "Good! Here's our tea!"

It came and its bearer went. Sheldon Garrett found himself relieved that not once did the languid servitor so

11

much as glance in his direction. He sat back and played with the notecase, telling himself mendaciously that he was about to go. But he played with a deliberate absence of sound. And he did not go. Nor did he move.

The deep voice said roughly: "Now she's gone! Take that moony look off your face and answer up. On or off?"

"I—I—I tell you I'm . . ." stammered the gentle voice.

"Don't tell me you're afraid. You said that before."

"But I . . . but I . . ."

"You sound like a gramophone record that's stuck. I told you last time, and I'm telling you again today, that there's nothing to be afraid of!"

The gentle voice said after a noticeable pause:

"But I *am* afraid! Sometimes I want to do it and then I think perhaps that if I do terrible things will happen to me. Because after all it's—it's not *right!*" The words had come fast this time: only once, and that towards the end of the sentence, had there been any of the hesitation of the previous periods. But the speed had been the speed of agitation.

There followed a silence, broken by the chinking of china as, probably, the spout of a teapot clinked against a cup edge. Garrett took opportunity to remonstrate with himself. Why should he sit here, in deliberate hiding, and listen to the confidences of two women who imagined themselves alone? Why, because he was a stranger to London and had found a part of London which was inimical as the jungle, should he have this queer sense of disaster to come? Why, even if he were weak minded enough to allow climate and surroundings so to impress him, should he imagine that what was probably the beginning of some sordid discussion, abortive in all senses of the word, was a dark and hideous sidelight upon some facet of abomination? Why, in short, did he not cough and rattle crockery and get to his feet and stamp towards the door and pay his bill and go away from here? . . .

Four whys, and not an answer. He sat still.

The deep voice said—and it was harsher even than before: "So you're *frightened!* Frightened of doing something which couldn't possibly get you into any trouble! Frightened of living in comfort for a while and then getting a lump of money which'll keep you in a damn sight more than comfort for the rest of your life if you live to be a hundred! *Frightened!*" The voice suddenly altered its tone; with its next words it kept all the harshness but seemed to take on a sort of musing quality most unpleasing to the ear; a quality which was in itself a threat. It said: "Well, I'll have to go back and tell Evans. I don't suppose he'll like it, with you knowing all about things. But there we are."

"Oh!" said the gentle voice suddenly, itself on a new note. "Don't talk like that! I—I—I didn't say I wouldn't. I was just saying that I was———"

"Frightened! I know. Well, forget it and don't be a silly fool. Think of that money. God knows, you must want money or you'd never———"

"You don't understand! Of course I want the money!" The gentle voice was lower now; but still, by leaning a little forward, Sheldon Garrett could catch its words. "And I know *I* shan't get into trouble—at least if everything is as you and he said it would be ... but it isn't that at all! It's—it's—well, I might get fond ..." Here the gentle voice dropped so low that for the first time Garrett could not hear its words; only a little murmur reached his ear at the end of this sentence.

"You make me tired!" The deep voice was contemptuous. "Nobody's going to hurt it."

The note of sneering ire seemed to sting the owner of the gentle voice into some loss of temper herself. She said with a rather astonishing acerbity in her soft tones:

"Well, suppose they don't. It's still ... not right! And anyhow, what about *him!*" The gentle voice paused on an upward and, as it were, temporarily triumphant inflection.

"Eh?" said the harsh voice quickly, and even in the tone of this one ejaculation Garrett could detect a sudden and intense interest. "What you talking about?"

"You know very well what I'm talking about. Suppose I *was* willing to take the position and then do what I'm told and then get the money. That's all right. But it doesn't mean that on top of that I'm willing to be mixed up in what's nothing more nor less than———"

Garrett did not hear the end of this sentence for the excellent reason that it was never finished. Instead of words there came a sudden violent creaking of the settle; a soft thud as something struck the edge of the table; a rattling of overturned crockery.

13

And then a whispered little scream of protest—from the gentle voice. It said:

"Oh, *don't!* You're hurting!"

Another creaking as someone resumed a seat. Then the deep voice again. It said in a tone much lower than it had used before and with a slowness which gave to it—at least to Garrett's ear—a quality of increased menace:

"You must be crazy!"

A little stifled sound which might be a sob. And then:

"You're rough! You hurt my wrist."

"Damn your wrist!"

Two stifled sounds, definitely sobs.

"You're—you're—horrible today!"

"You're mad today. . . . Will you tell me, *now,* what crazy bee's buzzing round in your bonnet?"

"I—I—I didn't mean anything. . . ."

"You don't say!"

"Don't look at me like that! You know I—I—why, you know I wouldn't ever—ever *say* anything."

The deep voice said: "You might not get the chance! . . . And don't sit there and snivel! Tell me, *now,* what crazy idea you've got in your head. *And* where you got it from. Come on, now!"

"I—I—oh dear! . . . I didn't mean anything. . . . It was something I heard the other——"

The deep voice interrupted in a savage half whisper. "Something you *heard?*" said the deep voice on a note of restrained fury. "Where did you hear it? When? What was it? Come on, tell me now or we'll go straight round and see Evans." The words came very fast and the voice was so low that Garrett only just caught them.

"The last time I was at the house. I was in the parlour there; and you and——"

"Keyhole work, eh!" said the deep voice. There was a muffled note to its clearness now, as if the words had been said without the speaker opening her teeth.

"No! No! I wasn't listening. Really I wasn't! I mean, not on purpose. I went over to that corner table there by the door to get a paper and the other man was talking very loud. I couldn't help hearing. I——"

"What—did—you—hear?"

"Please don't look at me like that. I didn't hear anything, really. I mean it wasn't—wasn't sort of definite. It

14

only gave me a sort of idea and then when I was thinking . . . I suppose I'm really very stupid. . . ."

"You are! Go on."

"Well, I—I—when you got angry at me just now I was very silly and got sort of angry too. And then—well, I suppose I said more than I really meant. But I didn't say anything really. Did I?"

The harsh voice said: "You *should* be good for the job. You're just like a kid yourself. But sometimes kids get silly ideas. And very often kids wag their tongues a lot too much."

"I didn't mean to say anything, really I didn't. It was just that I got angry a little because I thought you were angry at me."

"Hmm! It doesn't matter what you meant to say. What does matter is what you think."

"I don't think anything. Really I don't. . . . I—I was just being silly." There was a dreadful note of eagerness in the soft voice.

The deep voice said less harshly: "That's all right, then—*if* you're on."

"You mean if I——"

"If you take the job. *And* do exactly as you're told. And remember, for your own damn fool sake, that nobody—is—going—to—get—hurt."

Pause.

The gentle voice said then with a tremulous but definite decision: "I'll do it."

The deep voice laughed; a musical and paradoxical sound at once genial and humourless. "You may seem a fool but you're a sensible girl really. That amount of money, *and* a possible extra cut, isn't bad for a few months work. Especially when the work's what *they'd* call a cinch."

The gentle voice said: "How long will it be?"

"You know enough not to ask silly questions like that. I can tell you how long it *won't* be. It won't be longer than six months."

"But it might be shorter. Do say it might be shorter."

The harsh voice chuckled again. "It not only *might* be shorter, it probably will be. And a damn sight shorter. . . . Here, let's get out of this."

Sheldon Garrett stiffened in his corner. Instinctively he

15

drew his body back, pressing it against the wall and the back of his settle as if he would merge himself into the wood and plaster. To his strained ears the sound of a teaspoon rattling against a cup in traditional demand for attention sounded loud as gunfire. He started. Behind his right shoulder the deal boards creaked. He sat motionless, holding his breath and expecting every moment sounds from the other side of the far partition which would tell that his presence had been heard.

But it had not. The teacup was rattled again, furiously. In answer to it came first the creaking of the service door and then, more languid than ever, the genteel servitor. For a moment she crossed Garrett's line of vision again but again she did not look at him. He heard her beside the next booth; heard the harsh voice ask the amount owing and heard the mincing tones which answered her. . . .

And here Garrett made a mistake. He sat where he was. From behind the thin partition he could hear the chinking of money. Then came the inevitable "Thenk yew" of all Olde Tea Shoppes and the scraping bustle of departure.

Ancilla drifted once more away. Feminine heels clattered on the boards as his two neighbours went towards the door. Careful to be silent, Garrett leaned swiftly forward, propping his body on a hand placed at the very outside edge of his settle. He caught one glimpse of them as they opened the door. Their backs were as unlike as their voices—one short and solid and square, very erect, with a subtle suggestion of unperverted masculinity about it; the other tall, slender and with that charm which makes a man want to see the face.

They looked, somewhat, just as he had imagined they would look. The short thick one—Deep Voice evidently—was clad in some dark, "respectable" clothing (the strange words *sub fusc* flooded into Garrett's mind). But the tall slim Gentle Voice had subdued touches of colour about her. Her hat, certainly, was red; and the fur about her neck was of a delightful blue-y grey. And he thought there had been a coloured belt to the dark overcoat.

He jerked himself back into hiding as they reached the door and one of them set fingers to its handle.

The bell clinked dismally as the door opened and then was silent as it shut behind the outgoers. Its opening brought with it, for a flash of time, a ghostly eddy of cold, dank air.

Garrett jumped to his feet, knocking the table with his knee so that cup and saucer and teapot rattled violently in the dusty silence. He was out of the booth and reaching for his coat and struggling into it in one continuous movement. He became aware, without time for surprise, that his heart was thudding as if he had been running. It is to be believed—though he is not quite sure upon the point himself—that in this dim sanctuary of the drear he even shouted for his bill. But no answer came and the service door did not creak and already the two women whose course he knew he must follow had been gone for many seconds.

He rammed on his hat, fumbled in his pocket, remembered that he had no change and in two bounds was at the door. He wrenched it open and plunged into outer air.

3

For a moment, with a most curious mixture of relief and disappointment, he thought he had lost them. And then, by the grace of God and a street lamp under which they passed, he saw them. They were to his right as he stood with his back to the door. They were some thirty yards away. There was no mistaking the backs.

He set off in pursuit. He wanted to run but restrained himself, for the sound of running feet in this brick solitude might well make his quarry turn to look. By dint of long and furious strides he was soon at a reasonable distance. The night was very still and he could hear the murmur of the women's voices as they talked ahead of him. He crossed the road lest they should have any feeling of pursuit. He walked along upon the far pavement only a few yards behind them.

But by having crossed the road he very nearly lost them again. For suddenly they went into a narrow, dark-mouthed turning to their right; a turning which, from his far side of the street, he had neither seen nor suspected. He plunged after them, again barely restraining himself from running.

It was an alleyway between two houses into which they had gone—probably, Garrett thought with dim memories

17

of the peculiarities of English law, some ancient right of way which must be preserved. It was a dark narrow place with high walls and the tapping of their heels was flung back to him twentyfold by dismal, long-drawn echoes. He walked like Agag. He had lost way and was now some fifteen yards behind. He would have liked to shorten this distance but with the necessity here for tiptoed progress he could not.

The gloom lessened. At the far end of the alleyway there were lights and from the direction of the lights a steadily increasing rumble of traffic.

Garrett diagnosed a main road. Fearful lest once in a busy thoroughfare he should lost the quarry, he threw part of discretion to the winds and ran with loping but still tiptoed strides until he was only some twenty-five feet behind them.

They did not look round. He could hear their voices plainly now; could even catch some of the words. It was the deep voice which was speaking. He caught a mumble and then one or two half words and then, quite clearly:

" ... if he can see you tomorrow. Then we can go ahead. You should be there in under a fortnight."

The end of this sentence brought the women to the end of the alleyway. They turned to their right and were, therefore, for a few seconds hidden from Garrett's eyes. He covered the last yards that he had to travel in leaping strides.

He emerged from the mouth of the alleyway like a halfback getting away from the scrum. His right shoulder caught a man's chest and his left arm a woman's ribs. Even as he recovered himself he glared wildly to his right; then breathed relief. Not only were they in sight, but they were stationary.

"Reely!" said the woman he had struck. But she sniffed and passed on. Garrett raised his hat to a departing back. He began to say:

"You must pardon me, mad ..." but was cut short by his other victim.

This was a burly person in neckerchief and corduroy. He said, catching Garrett by the shoulder and swinging him round:

" 'Ere, 'ere! Wot's the bleedin' 'urry?"

"So sorry! So sorry!" Garrett said feverishly. He stared

18

anxiously over his victim's shoulder. . . . Yes: they were still there. They were pretending to look into a shop window but probably they were still talking. If only he could be behind them, listening. Then he might . . .

"I said, wot's the bloody 'urry?" The hoarse voice recalled him to himself.

He said desperately: "I'm very sorry. I was trying to catch a friend of mine."

Over the man's shoulder he saw his quarry moving; and moving away from him! He looked for the first time closely at his interlocutor, gauging the man's age as ten years more than his and his weight at only a few pounds more. He said briskly:

"I've apologized. I'm busy. Get the hell out of it!" He wrenched his shoulder free from the calloused hand which still held it, put his own right hand flat against the spotted neckerchief—and thrust. The attacked staggered back, to come with a resounding thud against the end of the alley wall. He coughed and gasped and then lurched forward.

But his adversary was gone. Threading syncopated way across the bus-ridden road were the short, square, swaggering back and the slim, tall, very feminine back, and close behind them, twice narrowly missing death, went Sheldon Garrett.

The women reached the far curb. A violent hooting and a hoarse cry made Garrett leap back. A vast omnibus surged between him and the pavement. He ran round its tail and reached the curb. There were many people upon the pavement. They were all bent, it seemed to him, upon obstructing him. And they all were surging towards a great arched doorway. He reared himself to the full of his height and looked wildly over as many heads as he could. Ah! There they were. He had caught sight of the red hat. He began to plough his way through the crowd, heedless of glares and objurgation, and found himself in what he had sufficient knowledge of London to know was the booking hall of an underground station.

Ah! There was the slim back beneath the red hat. It was before a ticket machine. He moved towards it.

Ah! There was the square back, beside the other one. They moved away, walking towards a corner where showed the grilled gates of four lifts.

Garrett followed; then remembered that he must have a

19

ticket before he could pass the man at the door of what he called the elevator.

In his own land he would have chanced the possibility of pushing by a ticket clipper, thrusting a note into the man's hand, but, rightly or wrongly, he decided that a servant of London Railways was unlikely to permit this. He pulled out his notecase and ran wildly back, bumping oncoming passengers, towards the window of the booking office. Mercifully no one was at it. He slammed down a note, shouted, "Piccadilly Circus," snatched the yellow pasteboard shot towards him and ran off without his change.

As he crossed the hall people were still streaming into what he knew was the first liftful. He sighed relief and ran on, reaching the doors of the entrance to the lift behind a last thin rank.

Over a fat, seal-covered shoulder he peered into the packed interior.

Thank God! There they were, still with their backs towards him.

The man before him moved forward, had his ticket clipped and stepped in.

Garrett moved forward but was held back by a blue official arm. In his ear a hoarse cry sounded. "Next lift, please!" and across his face, barely an inch from it, shot the extending grille of the lift gate as it shut with a roaring clang.

"God damn the luck to hell!" said Sheldon Garrett.

With a gargantuan sigh the lift descended. Hopelessly he went to the next and, when it was full, descended to tubular warrens which for a long and entirely fruitless while he searched. . . .

4

Despondent, he came up to ground level again and pushed his way out to the street and found a taxi and gave its driver vague orders. Eventually—perhaps half an hour later—he entered for the second time Ye Willow-Pattern Tea Shoppe. He stood just inside the door and waited. The service door creaked. Ancilla floated drearily towards him. As she drew near a spasm of something like human feeling flitted across her face beneath the pince-nez. But before she could speak Garrett had his notecase out. He said hurriedly:

"I left without paying my check."

A spasm which might have been a smile had crossed the woman's pale lips at the sight of the notecase, but at Garrett's speech this was replaced by something like a frown. She said:

"Cheque? Ay'm afraid we cannot ..."

Garrett said: "I beg your pardon. I meant my *bill*. I had tea here. I rushed out without paying, so I thought I'd ..." He let his speech tail off but he took from the wallet a ten-shilling note and proffered it.

It was taken, with an action most genteel, from between his fingers. The woman said:

"Ay'm mech oblayged, Ay'm sewer."

Garrett, though he did not understand a word of this, took it correctly enough to be thanks. He hurried on to his purpose. He said, with a laugh which he meant to be genial but which frightened his own ears by its appalling artificiality:

"Very strange thing! Those two ladies who sat in the booth next to mine ..."

"Booth?" Ancilla repeated.

Garrett repressed an urgent desire to take the thin neck between his hands and squeeze. He turned and pointed. He said: "At the next table."

"Oh yais. Ay believe Ay remember. Two ladies. Yais."

Garrett smiled. He would like to have risked the jovial laugh again but feared it. He said, still smiling:

"I knew them. But I didn't realize it until I saw them go. I suppose I must have been thinking of something else. When I saw them go, and recognized them—or rather, one of them—I had to run after them."

Ancilla said: "Ay quate understand. . . . Bay the way, one of your friends left a glev. . . . Ay wonder ..."

Garrett's heart leapt. So he *was* going to find something tangible. But what was it? He said:

"I beg your pardon!"

Ancilla said: "One of your friends—one left a glev."

"Indeed!" said Garrett, hoping that time would show.

It did. Ancilla swam away from him, was lost in dim shadows near the service door and swam back.

"Oh!" said Garrett. "A glove."

Ancilla said, "Yais. One of your friends mest hev dropped it."

She handed it to him. Garrett took it. He did not want to betray too much interest so folded it with as careless an air as he could manage and thrust it into a side pocket. It was a very ordinary glove, for a very ordinary-sized hand. It was of black kid and had white stitching on the backs of the hands and white mother-of-pearl buttons.

"Thank you!" said Garrett and then, carried away by a passion for his part: "Doris *will* be glad to have it back."

"Deon't mention it," Ancilla said. "Gled to hev been of service, Ay'm sewer. . . . End yewer bill—one and nane." She looked down at the note in her fingers. "Ay will procure change."

She melted away from Garrett's sight. So soon as she had gone he took the glove from his pocket and turned it this way and that. He wished that he were Dr. Thorndyke—and then, with an excitement such as he had not felt for years, felt suddenly, if not like Dr. Thorndyke, at least like Inspector French.

For as he held the glove in his hand, feeling its cheap texture, he felt something else. In the palm of the glove it was.

With fingers which he noted with surprise to be not quite steady he searched it.

He found a bus ticket and a little slip of paper.

CHAPTER II

He was very late for dinner. After it he spoke for a moment with a pacified hostess. He said:

"It was unpardonable. But a most curious affair was the cause of it. I'm certain I overheard two people planning a—well, a crime. I——"

"*Terribly* interesting!" his hostess said. "How *fasc*inating! I'm so frightfully keen on criminology, aren't you! So—so *real!* I wish Roger were here. You and he really ought to get together. Yes, you and Roger would have such a *lot* in common. . . . Oh, you *must* meet Adela properly, you and she were so far apart at dinner. . . . Adela! Adela! Come over here a minute. . . . Adela Pomfret, you know. Written all *sorts* of things, including that thing everybody was *raving* about last year or something; that thing, Mr. Somebody's Whatd'youcallit or something. . . . Oh, Adela darling, I thought you and Mr. Sheldon should talk to each other. The bad man was so late there were no proper introductions before dinner. Mr. Sheldon's an expert on criminology, aren't you, Mr. Sheldon? And *have* you seen his play at the Apollo, *Fools Rush In?* Of course you have. . . . Now I *must* go and talk to Tommy. . . ."

Mr. Sheldon Garrett looked at Miss Adela Pomfret. She was shaped like a tarantella dancer but her face was that of an egocentric and ill-tempered horse. He said:

"My name's Garrett. Sheldon Garrett. . . ."

She nodded. "I know. And the play's called *Wise Man's Holiday.* I haven't seen it."

"Er—yes," Garrett said. "Or no, I should say."

"I never go to the theatre!" said Adela Pomfret. "I never read. I hardly ever go out. I am not interested in

23

criminology. Have you heard Pandomano's lectures? I don't suppose so. No. Do I see drinks on that table over there? You could get me one."

"Certainly," said Garrett and bowed and left her and was at pains not to return.

He was introduced to a man whose name he did not catch; a tall, heavily built person with a face which seemed made for a K.C.'s wig. They chatted. After a while Garrett said:

"What would you do if you knew some sort of a—well, crime was going to be committed and——"

The heavy face gave forth sonorous laughter. "Tell the criminals how to do it, make sure there was a loophole and get briefed for the defence. What d'you think of that? Eh? What?"

Garrett screwed his face into a polite semblance of mirth. He said after due protraction of the spasm:

"I meant it seriously, though. If you *knew* that a serious crime was going to be committed——"

"What sort of a crime?" said Vaughan Critchley, who was indeed a K.C. "Murder? Arson? Rape? Criminal libel? Theft? Blackmail? Treason, Fraud? Abduction? . . . There are many."

"Yes," Garrett said with an iron patience. "I know there are a lot of headings under the word 'crime.' I——"

He was interrupted. His hostess was at his elbow. Words came from her. They seemed to say:

"Oh, there you are, Mr. Sheldon. . . . Vaughan, do you know Mr. Garrett Sheldon? Oh, of course . . . I see you do. I heard what you were saying, Mr. Sheldon. . . . Vaughan, do you know that Mr. Sheldon's an expert criminologist? . . . You two should have a lot in common. . . . Oh, I must go and talk to Adela. . . . I'll leave you to your talk . . . so interesting. . . ."

It seemed to Garrett that Vaughan Critchley's eyes rested upon him with something of disfavour. Vaughan Critchley said:

"So you're interested in criminology?"

Garrett shook his head. "No," he said firmly. "Not at all."

"Oh," said Vaughan Critchley and then, catching sight of an acquaintance over Garrett's shoulder: "How are

24

you, Morris? I've been wanting to see you for the past week. I——"

Sheldon Garrett withdrew himself. So soon as he decently could he went to his hostess and made adieu. She said:

"So awfully glad you could come. . . . Lovely having you. . . . Do hope I shall see more of you. . . . I should love you to meet Roger. You and he would have such a lot in common. . . . You must dine with us quietly sometime; then you and Roger can have a real heart-to-heart talk. Roger's awfully keen on criminology too. . . . Goodbye, Mr. Sheldon, good-bye. I haven't seen your play yet but I've made up my mind that I'm going to at the very earliest possible moment. . . . Good-bye. . . . And do give my love to Maureen."

Garrett went out into the air. His temper was bad; his head ached; and he wondered, savagely, who on God's earth or below it Maureen could be.

He considered the hour—eleven-thirty—and bed. But he foresaw sleeplessness and thought of the club to which, by Brooks-Carew's efforts, he had been elected a visiting member.

2

He entered the club, having walked there, at exactly midnight. It was nearly empty. He made his way to the big bar whose windows overlook the river. Two men were there—Jack, the bartender, and one member who sat upon a high stool with his head in his hands.

Garrett ordered a whiskey and soda and, as he was drinking it, looked more closely at his one fellow drinker. He saw with delight that this was a man he knew, being none other than Jamieson Phipps, journalist and playwright and political firebrand.

Garrett went over and announced himself. Phipps took one hand from his head and looked up. For a moment he stared blankly and then a smile split his round pale moon of a face. He waved to a stool. He said:

"Siddown. Glad see you."

"And I," Garrett said, "am glad to see you. Very glad indeed! It seems to me that, although I know I'm wrong,

25

you're the only person of sense in this city. That's the sort of day I've spent."

"Too bad," said Phipps. "Too bad. Have a drink?" He made a sign to the bartender.

Garrett was looking at the floor. He suddenly said, without raising his eyes: "Look here, Phipps, I want your advice. . . . I want you to tell me, seriously, what you'd do in this place—London, I mean—if you had reason to know that a really serious—well, crime was going to be committed but you didn't know against whom?"

The bartender put down two glasses: in front of Garrett a whiskey and soda, in front of Phipps a tumbler half full of something darker. Phipps turned his head towards Garrett. He said: "Whassay?"

Garrett looked down at the floor again. He was trying to get muddled thoughts in order. He said after a pause:

"Let's put it another way. If you heard two men, that you couldn't see, talking about a serious crime they were going to commit and then you followed them and lost touch with them without seeing their faces, what would you do?"

Phipps turned fully round upon his stool. He looked squarely at Garrett. His eyes were screwed up as if in concentration of thought. He stretched out a hand for his glass and picked it up and drank. With his round, thin-haired, pale-faced head and his long and very thin body he looked, as he perched upon the stool with his heels over its topmost rail and his long arms hanging down at his sides, like an intellectual hobgoblin.

Garrett looked at him, awaiting an answer.

"What would I do?" said Phipps suddenly in a great voice so many times exceeding in volume his previous mutterings that both Garrett and the bartender jumped. "I'll show you what I'd do."

Slowly he unfolded his legs and lowered them to the ground and stood, revealing himself as even longer and more emaciated than Garrett had remembered him. He bellowed:

"I'll tell you what I'd do. I'd—I'd—I'd sing a song of sixpence, a pocket full of rye . . ."

On the word "rye" his voice went up to a cracked shriek and now, while Garrett stared in aghast astonishment and the bartender scurried for the gate at the end of the bar,

Jamieson Phipps threw up his hands, gurgled twice and fell as a tree falls.

Garrett, staring in incredulous wonder, saw the white-coated bartender kneel beside the prostrate body. The man said:

"If you'll just help me, sir ..."

They picked him up and laid him upon a sofa. He was surprisingly and even a little pathetically light.

"He's been on that stool," said the barman, "ever since eleven this morning except for one or two little trips like. Brandy, it's been. But I *was* hopin' *this* time he wouldn't get like this!"

"Good *Lord!*" said Garrett.

"I've been wondering, sir," the barman said, "whether it was something you said to him that upset him like."

Garrett smiled. The smile started as a light twist of his mouth but ended in a gust of laughter which struck even his own ears as almost maniacal. ...

3

He was back at the Savoy by a few minutes after one. He entered the lift frowning and preoccupied. He came out of the lift smiling and intent upon a purpose. He had achieved an idea, and a good idea. As he almost ran along the softly carpeted corridor to his little suite he joyously cursed himself for a fool. There was one man who would tell him what to do; tell him at once whether he was being a quixotic fool or a normal being—and a man, moreover, who most certainly would not be in bed at this time and would not mind being called even if he were.

He opened his door and slammed it behind him, hurrying into his sitting room. He looked in his notebook and found a number and asked for it.

There was a long pause, broken by the voice of the hotel operator. It said: "There doesn't seem to be any answer from your number, sir."

"Try again," said Garrett and waited.

Another and longer pause and then, just as he had given up hope, an answer. A man's voice; a very sleepy voice.

"Bill!" said Garrett.

The voice said: "Beg pardon, sir. Do you want Mr. Akehurst?"

"Yes!" said Garrett.

The telephone said: "I'm sorry, sir, but Mr. Akehurst is away. He is in Vienna."

"Hell!" said Sheldon Garrett and then: "When's he coming back?"

The telephone said: "The time of his return, sir, is uncertain. This is Mr. Akehurst's valet speaking, sir. Is there anything I can do?"

"No!" said Garrett and slammed back the receiver.

4

He got to bed at quarter to two. He tried to read but could not. He put out the light and tried to go to sleep and thought that he could not but did.

He then dreamed. Unpleasantly. He was running down a long narrow street. Upon each side of him rotting houses of grey brick reared themselves up like skyscrapers. None of their windows was lighted and the man-made canyon was dark save for a whitish effulgence which seemed to come from the low walls separating pavement from mouldering garden. In front of him, as he ran, were two other figures. From behind him, as he ran, came the sound of other running feet. He did not look round but he knew that these feet belonged to an enemy of whom he stood in deadly fear; an enemy who carried over his shoulder like a vanquished enemy a long slender sack. Before him the hurrying figures ran on. Behind him the pursuing feet drew nearer. His whole being was absorbed with a desire to reach some sanctuary which he felt he did not know now but would know so soon as he should set eye upon it. And then, immediately, he saw it. It was upon a corner. It was a small place. It was surrounded by Chinese paper lanterns. He ran towards its entrance, cringing as he came into the light of the lanterns. He plunged through a door and was in temporary safety. It was a vast hall in which he found himself, but a hall which he seemed to know. Over the floor of it were scattered, higgledy-piggledy, little eating booths, each containing a table. He plunged into one in a far dark corner like a frightened rabbit diving into its hole. He crawled under the little table and made himself small and lay there panting, his heart thudding as if it would break its way out of his body

28

through his throat. And then the others came. And they crowded into all the other booths which were all around him. There seemed to be hundreds of them, all talking at once and all talking in whispers. But he could hear their whispers and he knew what they were saying, even when some of the words were inaudible because of the thumping of his heart in his ears. They were talking about him. His name was like an obligato to the rise and fall of their hissing voices. They were going to do something to him. But that was not all. There was suddenly another note introduced into the sibilant choir. They were going to do things to him. That was bad. But they were also going to hurt someone else; someone whom he was suddenly surprised to find mattered to him more than himself. Who was it? The name was clear enough in their whisperings but, although he could hear it, it was as if it was in another language and he could not translate it. Not that that made any difference. It did not. That they were going to hurt *her*—so it was a woman!—was much worse than that they were going to hurt him. And then, like a thunderous bass to the foul music, came yet another name. And that was the worst of all, because if they were going to hurt this one then it would not only be worse than hurting himself but worse than hurting "her." He wanted to get up and shout. He wanted to crawl out from his silly little hiding place and defy them. His mind felt suddenly as strong as God's mind, but when he tried to make his body obey it would not, but lay there cringing and trembling as before. And then he was conscious of something new: he was conscious that somewhere in one of these places near him—perhaps in another little hiding place near his own—there was Someone Else; Someone Else who did not know him or the others, the whisperers; Someone Else who *could* help him against them. But would he? *Would he?* ...

He waked, sweating. The bedclothes were on the floor. All the muscles in his body were quivering and his throat was parched. He got up and switched on lights and drank water and roughly made his bed again. But there was no more sleep for him.

CHAPTER III

Sheldon Garrett moved abruptly in his chair; so abruptly
that his elbow, which had been resting upon the table,
knocked over his coffee cup. A waiter came hurrying and
busied himself with repairing damage.

"By God, I *will!*" said Sheldon Garrett.

The waiter stared. "Beg pardon, sir!"

Garrett started. He looked down at the white napkin
which the waiter was spreading over the brown stain. He
said:

"Sorry! Very clumsy of me! Don't know what I was
thinking about!"

Which was a lie.

2

He took a taxi from a rank in the Strand. For some
reason, which he admitted to himself was foolish, he did
not want to give his destination in the hearing of the Savoy hall porter. It was a salmon-colored taxi, very smart.

"Where to, sir?" said the driver, who, astonishingly, was
not only as smart as his taxi but was civil.

Garrett said: "Scotland Yard, please. And as quick as
you can."

"Lost Property Office, sir?" The driver was brisk.

"No," said Garrett.

"Which entrance then, sir?"

Garrett got into the cab and slammed the door behind
him. He leaned out of the window and spoke. He said:

"I don't know. Any one."

"It won't be Inspector Michaelson that you need after all, sir!" said the sergeant.

Garrett looked at his watch. "Who then?" he said, it is to be feared a little shortly.

The sergeant smiled ruefully. "Sorry to have kept you waiting, sir, but Inspector Andrews will be free in a very few minutes."

4

Detective Inspector Andrews looked past his visitor and out of the window. His visitor, looking at him, thought that he detected certain twitchings about Detective Inspector Andrews' mouth which might denote the beginnings of a smile.

"And that, sir," said Andrews at last, "is all that you have to tell me?"

Garrett moved uneasily in his chair. He said irritably:

"Yes. Isn't it enough?"

"In one sense, yes sir. In another, no." Andrews looked at a pad upon which, during Garrett's recital, he had from time to time been scribbling. He said with a briskness which seemed to presage dismissal: "Now let me see. I think we have everything. The address of the shop. Your description of these two women. Your own address and particulars. And the clerk has shorthand notes of what you recollect of the conversation in the shop." He looked up at Garrett. "That all?"

"Yes!" said Garrett firmly. As he spoke it seemed to him that the folded glove in his pocket and two small pieces of paper in his wallet were smouldering.

Andrews rose. In this small hutch of a room whose walls—and even part of whose floor—were covered with dusty, orange-covered files, he seemed disproportionately large; like a Saint Bernard who has outgrown his kennel.

Garrett, a sudden feeling of furious obstinacy surging over him, sat where he was. Behind him a door opened and a voice said:

"I want to see you when you get a minute, Andrews."

Andrews looked from the door to Garrett; from Garrett to the door. He said to the door:

"Shan't be long," and then waited.

But still Garrett did not move. He crossed one leg over the other and folded his hands upon his lean stomach and looked up at the towering policeman. He said after a pause:

"What are you going to do about it?"

Andrews put up a hand and rubbed reflectively at his long, smooth-shaven chin. He said heavily after a heavy pause:

"That, Mr. Garrett, is for my superiors to say. You understand that all—er—matters of this kind I make a written report about."

"When?" said Garrett.

The eyes of Detective Inspector Andrews opened more widely. He said:

"The report will be on my superior's desk this evening."

"Good!" said Garrett. "I'll call tomorrow at noon." He rose and with his rising the little cubbyhole of a room seemed suddenly filled with men beyond its capacity. Somehow Andrews slid round him to the door and held it open. He said:

"Don't bother to do that, sir. We'll communicate with you if——"

Garrett turned on the threshold. "It won't be any trouble. I'll call tomorrow at noon."

He turned on his heel and walked away down a stone-floored corridor. As he walked he took himself to task. His tone, he knew, had been wrong. But he had not been able to help it. Telling his halting story to the flat, expressionless face of the man he had just left, he had felt a fool—and there is nothing that makes a man more angry. More, having felt a fool, he had proceeded to justify the feeling by behaving like one. He twitched his shoulders angrily and walked out of the Yard itself and thence onto the Embankment.

5

At nine forty-five upon the following morning Chief Detective Inspector Horler came to the following passage in a report from one of his inspectors. He read:

2. *Thomas Sheldon Garrett.* This man called here this

afternoon and was interviewed. He is an American citizen visiting this country on a six months guest permit. His passport is in order. He states that he is of independent means and also a writer of dramatic works. A dramatic piece of his, entitled *Wise Man's Holiday,* is now showing at the Apollo Theatre. He is residing at the Savoy Hotel, Strand. He states that on Sunday last, the eighteenth inst., he was walking in the neighbourhood of Notting Hill. At about five-twenty he entered a teashop on the corner of Houston and Wilberforce streets, W.3 (name of teashop: Ye Willow-Pattern Tea Shoppe). He was served with tea, being on his entry the only customer. At five thirty-five approx. two women entered the shop and sat at a near-by table. He did not see them, owing to the disposition of the furnishings. He states that he then overheard a conversation between these two women (who were unaware of his presence for the reason given above) which seemed to him to denote that they were discussing some criminal undertaking involving possibly the abduction of a child and the execution of bodily harm upon some other person. When questioned as to what led him to suppose this, he stated, "The general tone of the conversation." Questioned further, he stated that one of the women seemed in fear of the other, who was threatening her by references to a man named Evans. Asked whether he could give any of the conversation verbatim, he endeavoured to do so. Notes of what he said were taken but are not included here as they did not seem to indicate anything serious. In fact, there was nothing in his statement which could not be explained by ordinary circumstances. Upon this being pointed out to him he grew excited and lost his temper.

I am of the opinion that there is nothing in this. The man being both a writer and a stranger to this country, it seems likely that he has let his imagination run away with him.

A frown creased the usually cheerful face of Chief Detective Inspector Horler. For a moment he regarded this paragraph with narrowed eyes; then shrugged broad shoulders; then went on to the end of the report; then turned back again to its second paragraph.

He said something under his breath and touched a bell. Five minutes later he was reading:

33

THOMAS SHELDON GARRETT
Statement re Alleged Conversation
in Willow-Pattern Tea Shoppe.

The women came in. They couldn't see me or I them. I knew there were two because of their voices. They sat in the next booth. The waitress came and they ordered their tea and she went away to get it. They had very different voices, so it was easy to tell which one was speaking. One had a deep harsh voice and the other a high soft voice. As soon as the waitress had gone away the one with the deep voice said something and the other one got nervous about whether anyone could hear them. The one with the deep voice told her that there was nobody in the place but all the same one of them made sure by looking over into my booth—the only booth they couldn't have seen into. As it happened I had dropped my wallet just at this minute and was under the table looking for it when this was going on. I heard them sit down again and then one of them said that there wasn't anybody. There was something very strange about the way they were talking—the deep voice bullying and the other frightened—and both being so particular about not being overheard. I got back into my seat without making any noise and, as it were, against my will, settled down to listen. There was something so underhanded and—"furtive" is the only word I can think of— about them that I was deeply interested right from the start. When they were settled down again the first thing that happened was that the one with the deep harsh voice asked the other whether she had made up her mind. She apparently hadn't because she said she was frightened and then—I think I can remember her exact words here—she said: "I want to do it but I can't help thinking that if I do terrible things will happen to me; because when all's said and done it's not *right!*" I should say that at some time just about here their tea came and they stopped talking. I was frightened that the waitress would speak to me and thus give my presence away but luckily she didn't. As soon as she went away they went on. And now the bullying one seemed to get angry. She said she was disgusted with the other for being frightened! She wanted to know what there was to be frightened about when there was no danger and a lot of money coming if whatever they were talk-

34

ing about was put through properly. Then she seemed to put on the screw a bit by pretending she'd accepted no for an answer and saying that she supposed she'd "have to go and tell Evans." I think I can remember some more of her exact words here. She said: "He won't like it with you knowing everything." This mention of Evans seemed to put the other woman into a real panic. She began to stall and say she hadn't meant anything and—let me think—and it was then, I believe, that they went into a real fight, because the one with the deep voice said something that seemed to get under the other's skin and *she* got angry too. She said something like this: "Of course I want the money and I know there won't be any trouble but that's not it! The trouble is that I might get *fond* ..." and then the other one interrupted her and she said something that gives the cue to the whole thing. She said: "You make me sick. Nobody's going to hurt it." Please mark the "it." And then the other one—the gentle voice—she got madder still and said: "Even suppose they didn't. It's still wrong." And then she said, right on top of that: "Anyhow, what about *him!*" She accented the "him" strongly so that I could tell that this "him" wasn't the same as the "it." And I should say, too, that she said this in a voice I can only describe as being heavy with threat; she said it as if she were playing a trump the other woman didn't know anything about. It certainly scared the other one, who said—damn roughly: "What are you talking about?" And the gentle one, still mad, said something like: "You know what I'm talking about! If I did take the position and follow instructions and then get paid that would be all right if that was all there was to it. But I'm not going to be mixed up in what amounts to ..." and then, before she could say the last word, the other one must have reached over the table and grabbed at her because she gave a little sort of scream and said: "Don't! You're hurting me." The other one told her she must be crazy and demanded to know what fool idea she'd got hold of. It was obvious that the gentle one had acquired some knowledge she wasn't supposed to have. It was equally obvious that she wished she hadn't said anything but was so terrified by the other woman and references to this Evans that at last she admitted to having heard something not intended for her "the last time she was at the house." She said she'd been waiting in the par-

35

lour while the other woman and some other people were
in a room and she'd accidentally overheard something they
were saying. She said "the other man was talking very
loud" and she couldn't help but hear. She then tried to
make things better for herself by saying that she hadn't
heard anything *definite* but it was obvious that she had,
though she was too frightened to say what it was. That
seemed to be her crisis, as it were, because after that, and
after some more bullying by the other one, she surren-
dered completely. It was clear that she was so frightened
of the other woman and "Evans" that she wasn't going to
give them any more trouble. By the end of the conversation she had agreed to do anything they wanted. She was
then congratulated by the other, who again referred to
easy money or something of the sort. And—oh yes!—the
other woman dinned it into her that—I remember the exact words—"that nobody was going to get hurt." I can
only tell you, about that remark, that it was said in such a
way as to convince me that it meant the very reverse.
That was all they said in the shop. They then paid their
bill and went out, still without seeing me. Then, as I've
told you, I followed them. On the way to the subway station where I lost them I caught one more bit of talk. It
was from the boss woman—the deep voice. She said
something about if someone could see the other woman tomorrow they could get on with things. And then she
said—I remember these words: "You should be there in
under a fortnight." That's all, I think. Oh, wait though,
there *was* something else. At one stage—it was after the
one with the soft voice had got really docile—she asked
how long everything would take, and then the boss one
said it couldn't be longer than six months but would probably be "a damn sight shorter." And that *is* all.

Horler set down the sheets. He stared at them for a
moment; then picked up a desk telephone.

6

Chief Detective Inspector William Horler looked genially across his table at Mr. Thomas Sheldon Garrett. The
geniality of the look must go down to Horler's credit, for

he had spent, of a busy day, nearly two hours with his visitor; a time not made lighter by his visitor's manner.

Horler tilted back his chair, rested his elbows upon its arms and placed the tips of ten broad fingers nicely together. He said:

"So you see, Mr. Garrett, when we examine your statement piecemeal the way we have this afternoon we find that there's absolutely nothing to act upon. No definite statement of any kind was made by either of these women and—at least so far as you can tell us—neither of them said anything that couldn't refer to—er—perfectly ordinary matters. What I think——"

Sheldon Garrett twisted in his chair. "But, look here! *I* heard that conversation. I *know* that there was some—something devilish that those two women and the man they were talking about were going to do. I don't think I'm quite a lunatic, and I'm absolutely *sure*——"

"One moment, Mr. Garrett, one moment!" Horler's voice was unexpectedly loud and he held up a vast hand for silence. Behind him Garrett's mind could see, ranged in orderly, passive ranks, the ratepayers of Great Britain.

"I must ask you to understand, Mr. Garrett"—the voice was normal again—"that this matter has been very fully considered. Possibly even more fully considered than if you had been a native of this country. We like to do all we can for strangers and above all we like to show that we're grateful to those who try to assist us in our duties. On the other hand, you must allow us the superior knowledge and experience. We're extremely obliged to you for bringing to our notice what you thought was the planning of a criminal action. . . ."

Sheldon Garrett stood up. It is to be regretted that he said, "Nerts!"

Chief Detective Inspector Horler rose. He said politely: "I beg your pardon!"

Garrett said: "Nothing! Nothing! Sorry if I seem rude, but this business, and trying to explain it to you people, has got me a bit edgy."

Horler came out from behind his table. He said:

"Believe me, I quite understand, Mr. Garrett. And, if I may say so, I appreciate the spirit in which you have come here. But I'd like to put it to you that you're worrying yourself needlessly. Between you and me, I shouldn't be a bit surprised but what one of the women had got into a scrape of some kind—you know the sort of thing—and the other was trying to help her out of it. That would explain the—what you called 'furtiveness' of the conversation. But nothing criminal. I don't think that for a moment. And, if I may say so, I've had a great deal of experience at this game. I can smell a crime ten miles away and I get no scent here." He laughed with heartiness. "Not a trace of scent."

"I see," said Garrett dully.

CHAPTER IV

Avis Bellingham let herself into her flat. She did this, as indeed she did everything, with little noise. Her maid, therefore, did not hear her. She put down a small parcel and her gloves and her bag upon the small table in the small hall. She crossed the hall and went into her drawing room. It was evening and the room was dark save for a fire which sent little flickers of light softly over pleasant furnishings. She took off her coat and threw it over the arm of a chair. She took off her hat and put it on top of the coat. There was a mirror over the mantelpiece and to the left of the mirror a light switch. She crossed to the fire and stood before the mirror and pressed the switch and two soft lights above and to the sides of the mirror sprang into life. She looked into the mirror and put her hands to her hair.

But she saw something in the mirror as well as her own reflection. Her hands dropped to her sides and she turned and stared, her eyes even larger than nature had made them.

"My God!" said Avis Bellingham and for a moment continued to stare.

She was looking down at a large, low chair which stood to the right of the fireplace, half in and half out of the soft light cast by the right-hand lamp. This chair should have been empty. There was no excuse for it being filled. And yet it was. And, astonishingly, by the body of a man. Dark-trousered legs sprawled out into the light; but above the waist the body was in shadow, merging its darkness into the darkness of the enveloping chair.

Avis Bellingham moved. She crossed the room towards

39

the door but did not go through it. Instead she pressed the light switch beside the jamb and the lights inside the bowl which hung from the middle of the ceiling sprang into life.

She stood where she was, looking towards the chair. She could see now that its occupant was lying back. One arm was crooked across his face, hiding not only this but all the head. Still he did not move. Crazy and unpleasing thoughts shot unbidden across the surface of her mind. She repressed them and concentrated her gaze upon the chair. Was the body motionless? Or was there a slight movement which told of breathing? . . .

"This is absurd!" said Avis Bellingham and found her voice strange in her own ears. Again she was forced to apply the curb to imagination fed by bookish memory.

And then the man stirred—a definite movement; a movement which, even in its inconsequentiality, put dread imaginings to ludicrous flight. Consumed now by the relatively pleasant sensation of curiosity, she moved across the room again. She stood in front of the chair and once more stared down at it and its occupant.

"Hey!" she said.

The arm came down; but the eyes in the now revealed face were still closed in deep sleep. The man twisted in the chair and a thick, somnolent voice came from him. It said:

"Lot o' saps! *Is* some way! Must be!"

"Tom!" said Avis Bellingham. A smile of pleasure curved her large and charming mouth. She bent down and set a hand to the sleeper's shoulder and shook it.

Thomas Sheldon Garrett awoke. He sat bolt upright, his arms stretched out upon the arms of the chair. He looked once wildly round the charming little room and found it strange. He rubbed a hand across his eyes and looked up at the woman.

He shot to his feet. He said, seeming and feeling like a small boy caught jam-handed:

"Avis! I—I—how—they said—I hope you——"

She went on smiling at him. She said: "Sit down. And stop making noises."

Twenty minutes later she looked at him over the rim of a glass. He was no longer tousled but from beneath sleek blond hair his face looked at her, haggard and drawn. She said:

"Finish that drink and get yourself another. And then tell me."

Garrett laughed; a laugh which she did not remember. He rose and obeyed her and came back and sat once more to face her. He said:

"Tell you all about what?"

"Everything. What are you doing in London? How long have you been here? Why haven't you been to see me before? How did you get in? And, much more important, what's the trouble?"

"I'm in London because Brooks-Carew has been fool enough to do a play of mine. . . ."

"Tom! And I never knew! But I *won't* read the papers."

"I've been here two weeks. I haven't been to see you before because—as you might guess—I didn't know you were here. I found out yesterday, accidentally, from Dorothy Brooks-Carew. When I got here this afternoon your maid said you were out so I gave her a long hard-luck story and got in. I didn't mean to go to sleep but I did mean to see you—even if I waited here a couple of days. . . . That's all, isn't it?"

"No sir, thank you, sir. It's not even the beginning! What's the *matter?*"

"Should I only come to see you because there's something the matter?"

"Don't be a donkey. But there *is* something!"

"What makes you think that way?"

"You ought to be beaten. You're more like a small boy than any small boy ever was. Sit back, relax, sip at your goblet of some amber-coloured fluid and—tell me what's the matter! In order to avert further procrastination on your part I'll tell you that you look, though distinguished as ever, like hell. You're nervous, you're jumpy, you've lost weight, you've got that reversed look about your eye which tells of an idée fixe . . . and, finally, you haven't been sleeping. . . ."

Garrett said: "Haven't been *sleeping!*" and laughed.

"*And* your laugh's about the worst imitation of one that I ever heard. . . . Don't be silly, Tom! Tell me!"

Sheldon Garrett looked at his hostess. For a long moment his eyes were caught in the great blue pools of her eyes. There flowed into him, like salving oil upon an angry

41

wound, a sense of sudden ease; the relaxation of a strain whose tension he had not known until it was lessened. He said:

"You're right. But then I suppose you always are. There *is* something—only I'm beginning to think it's so damn silly that perhaps I'm going haywire. But it's got me, though I tried not to let it. When I'd done everything I could about it and got nowhere I told myself to forget it. But I didn't succeed. Not a bit. It's been eating with me and trying to sleep with me and making me behave so oddly that everybody's thinking I'm qualified for a lunatic asylum. And I can't get rid of it. . . ."

"Tom! Will you stop beating round all these bushes!"

"Listen!" said Garrett and began. . . .

2

"And that," said Garrett thirty minutes later, "is what's the matter. Now say I'm a fool with an overheated imagination! Tell me the world goes on much better when people mind their own business! Tell me that by going to Scotland Yard I've done everything possible! Tell me to forget the whole thing! Show me—oh, so reasonably!—that I read into a conversation a lot of stuff that wasn't there! Tell me——"

Avis Bellingham stood up. "What I do tell you," she said, "is to shut up!" She went to the door. With her fingers on its handle she turned. She said:

"Wait here. And be good." She opened the door.

"Here! Wait a minute!" Garrett jumped to his feet. "What you going to do?"

"Telephone," said Avis.

He crossed the room towards her. "About—about my—idée fixe?"

She pulled a face at him. "Don't be egotistic!" she said and was gone.

She was with him again after five minutes or less. She was smiling and there was a sparkle in the blue eyes. She looked at her watch and then at Garrett. She said:

"It's half-past six. How long to go and put on a dinner jacket and get back here?"

He looked at her curiously. "Forty-five minutes. Why?"

"You're dining out. With me. So hurry!"

"But I ..."

"But nothing! You—are—dining—out—with me!"

"Oh," said Garrett, "I see."

CHAPTER V

The taxi bumped and jolted. Garrett said, breaking a silence:

"And where are we going?"

"Didn't I tell you? How stupid of me!" She did not look at him. "To some great friends of mine. You'll like them. I hope they'll like you. I——"

"The name?" said Garrett.

"Gethryn. Lucia Gethryn and her husband."

"Oh!" said Garrett in a different tone. And then: "You don't mean Lucia Gethryn and her husband. You mean Anthony Gethryn and his wife!" He leant forward in his seat with hand outstretched to tap upon the driver's window.

But gloved fingers, surprisingly strong, caught his wrist and a voice said softly:

"Don't be a fool, Tom!"

He dropped his hand and turned in his seat and stared through the dimness at a profile which said:

"And, if you *must* be a fool, don't be an ill-mannered one!"

He said: "Sorry, Avis! But I won't be dragged into a busy man's home as a poor sap with a bug in his head and——"

She said: "I don't like to think that coming out with me is being *dragged*. And at the moment Anthony's not a busy man."

"But . . ."

She drew a deep breath. "*And* I've said nothing about your bug! Nor will I until you tell me." She looked at him without turning her head. "And I thought it wouldn't do

44

your bug any harm for you to know the one man who might——"

"Stop!" said Garrett. "I'm sorry. And you're a darling."

"That's better," said Avis Bellingham.

2

"Something tells me," said Lucia Gethryn, "that the hostess now collects the women with her eye. Come on, Avis!"

Garrett opened the door for them. As he shut it, and before he turned back towards the table, the left eye of Anthony Gethryn closed momentarily. Spencer Hastings[1] nodded.

Garrett came back to the table and sat. The port went round. There was desultory talk. Hastings began the inside story of the informal cabinet meeting which had led, two days before, to the abrupt resignation of the foreign secretary.

Upstairs in the drawing room Avis Bellingham and the friend who was her hostess sat and smoked and stared at a fire of logs.

Lucia said: "I smoke too many of these things. I like him. But why did you say he wasn't much to look at?"

Avis lit another cigarette. "I wonder whether the stories are over yet?"

Lucia said: "They don't, not much anyhow. In fact, not nearly as much as we do."

"That's not what I mean," said Avis Bellingham.

Lucia said: "I know."

Avis said: "D'you think they've got to it yet? ... Lucia, you didn't tell Anthony ... ?"

Lucia said: "Of course I did! At least I told him that Mr. Garrett wanted advice about something. I even said a bit more. . . ."

"*Lucia!* You *promised.*"

"*But* I also told him that you thought it best not to let Mr. Garrett know that you'd said anything at all about it."

"Oh!" said Avis Bellingham and then, after a pause: "How's the heir?"

Lucia smiled. "Magnificent. He asked after you yesterday, at great length. So you've got two fervent admirers at

[1] See footnote on page 62.

least; and at the moment both under the same roof. Must be nice."

Avis Bellingham said: "Alan's adorable."

Downstairs Hastings filled his glass and pushed the decanter, to complete its circle, towards Garrett. He said to his host:

"But that doesn't say that, theoretically, the whole basis of police work is wrong. . . ."

"Of course it's wrong," said Anthony Gethryn. "But then, it never could be right. Because in no state of civilization will there ever be enough public wealth to establish the only sort of police that a Utopian would tolerate."

Hastings said: "That sounds clever. Unfortunately it doesn't mean anything."

Anthony grinned. "Put in simple words for the young, Spencer, what I mean is that the ideal police force is not an organization for the apprehension and punishment of criminals but an organization for the *prevention* of crime."

Garrett started. He looked sharply from his host to his fellow guest—but neither was looking at him.

Hastings said: "A foul idea! The only way it could be run would be to make every man a spy on his neighbour. We haven't much privacy left as it is; for God's sake, let's be alone sometimes—even if it leads to rape and murder."

"Thereby," said Anthony, "giving Spencer Hastings—and the rest of Fleet Street—a continued and lucrative existence."

Garrett stared at his host. "Look here!" he said suddenly and loudly. "D'you *mean* what you're saying? Or are you just taking the thin end of an argument?"

"He doesn't know," said Hastings.

Anthony said: "It's a theory; but a sound one. Unfortunately, however, progress is the enemy of sense."

Garrett still stared at him. "But you *do* mean that you believe that crime should be prevented rather than punished?"

"Naturally," said Anthony. "Don't you?"

Hastings said: "Deprive man of his time-honoured occupation of shutting stable doors after horses have been stolen and you take a good deal of the salt away from his daily food."

"Yes! Yes!" Garrett said. "I see all that." He spoke hastily and with a lack of politeness most foreign to him.

46

And he did not look at the man to whom he was speaking but continued to gaze at his host. He said suddenly, his eyes narrowing: "Did Avis Bellingham say anything to you? About me, I mean?"

Anthony's slight stare of bewilderment was admirable. He said:

"Sorry! I don't quite understand."

"All I meant," said Garrett, "was—well, skip that! I was just going to say: It's most extraordinary that we should get on a topic like this. Because only a few days ago I ran right into a living example of it. I . . . But perhaps it'd bore you. You must get your belly full of crime and criminals."

Spencer Hastings laughed.

Anthony said: "I was born suspecting the doctor, I shall die indicting the priest. Go on."

3

Garrett came to the end of his story. He smiled, more than a little wryly. He said:

"So I suppose I'm crazy, or at least feeble minded."

Anthony smiled. It was a preoccupied smile and the crease which had come between his eyes did not leave. He said:

"Only if you go on thinking so. . . . Who did you see at the Yard, the second time?"

"Man called Horler," said Garrett. "Chief Detective Inspector Horler."

Anthony said: "Not a bad fellah. Find him a bit short on imagination?"

Garrett said: "If he'd got any he certainly hid it someplace. But he was very civil, which I'm afraid I wasn't."

Anthony said slowly: "And you never once saw even a profile of either of those women?"

Garrett shook his head. "Not even half a cheek. I saw 'em from the back first, last and all the time. If it hadn't been for that goddam elevator I'd——" He broke off, lifting his shoulders in a small, helpless gesture.

Anthony seemed absorbed in the little puddle of dark wine at the bottom of his glass. He said without looking up:

"And you didn't hear where either of them booked to?"

Garrett stared at him. "Booked?"

"When you got to the tube station you weren't close enough behind them at the ticket office to hear where they took tickets for?"

"Oh!" said Garrett. "Sorry. They didn't get tickets at the window. They got them out of one of those machines."

Anthony looked up sharply. "Both out of the same machine?"

Garrett nodded. "Yes. Why?"

"If you went back to the station could you point out the particular machine?"

"Yes," said Garrett.

Anthony said: "That helps. Or might."

Garrett looked at him. "I don't see how."

Spencer Hastings said: "Nor, with all due respect to Master Mind, do I. What you mean, I take it, is that if Garrett showed you the machine you would at least know within half-a-dozen stations where they went to."

"Magnificent!" murmured Anthony.

"But," said Hastings, "you wouldn't know whether any of the stations represented the district either of 'em lived in. One doesn't always go home after tea—even in Notting Hill. Particularly on a Sunday."

Garrett looked at his host. But Anthony's gaze was still down bent and he did not raise it and no sound came from him.

Garrett said: "I hadn't thought of that. . . ." His voice trailed off into silence but he was conscious of a vast relief, for here at least were intelligent men who were not treating him like a frightened small boy who must be humoured but were actually applying their minds to this business which obsessed his own.

Still Anthony did not speak nor raise his head. But Hastings said:

"It's like Sawing through a Woman."

"Eh!" said Garrett.

"Or the rope trick," Hastings said. "I mean, it's damned interesting but impossible to work out."

"Oh!" said Garrett.

"Think!" said Spencer Hastings. "Think! In greater London there are roughly eight million people. There is nearly, I believe, a two-to-one preponderance of women.

48

That gives us at least five million women. ... God, what a thought! ... And out of these five million you've got to find two backs. ..."

"And two voices," Garrett said. "Don't forget that." His tone was heavy.

Hastings said: "That's not really a help. It's like Sawing through a Woman again. You know there must be two women in the box but you can't see how the devil they got in there."

"Backs!" said Anthony suddenly. He lifted his head and looked at Garrett. "Ordinary backs? No shoulder higher than other shoulders? No humps? No limps? No odd gaits? No real peculiarity of dress?"

Garrett shook his head.

"Wait!" Hastings leaned forward suddenly, nearly upsetting his glass. "They might go back to that tea place again."

Garrett smiled without mirth. "No one in their senses would. ... And, anyway, they hadn't up to yesterday. I went back there."

Anthony looked at him. He said slowly:

"You're pretty sure about this, aren't you, Garrett? I mean, sure there was what you'd call dirt in it?"

Garrett said: "I *know* there was! I've told you, very badly, what they said. But there was more—far more—in the way they said it."

The other men looked at him curiously. They saw that his face was suddenly pale and that there were new lines in it.

Anthony said as if to himself: "If only there were *something* else!"

Garrett moved suddenly in his chair. He looked first at his host and then at his fellow guest. He was frowning in concentration. His eyes seemed to be trying to push vision beyond faces. He suddenly stood up and they stared at him, surprised by the suddenness of the movement. He leaned his hands upon the table and again looked at them both. He said:

"You're interested in this—this thing. That's plain. But how far is your interest going? Is it academic only? Or is it—*real*?"

He hesitated a little; then added in a different tone: "I

know I'm being the worst kind of nuisance. But I want a real answer to that."

Spencer Hastings spoke first. He said: "You want the truth, I gather. My interest, so far, is purely academic. It's got to be—because I say that your problem's impossible to solve."

Anthony said: "I'm interested. And not academically. It's time somebody's old governess joined this party to tell us there's no such word as 'can't' in the dictionary."

"Right!" said Garrett. He put a hand to his breast pocket and took out a wallet. He laid this on the table and flipped it open and from it took, with great care, two envelopes. From the first and larger envelope he drew a woman's black kid glove; from the second, two small pieces of paper. He said:

"Here are the only things I didn't tell you about. As far as I can see they don't make matters any easier, but they are 'something else', and you were asking for that."

Anthony pushed back his chair and rose and walked round the table to stand beside his guest. He looked at the exhibits with his head cocked to one side. Garrett said:

"When I went back to the teashop just after I'd lost the women in that subway station I pretended I knew them. The waitress swallowed the story and told me that one of the women—she didn't know which—had dropped a glove. She said would I take it and I did. Inside the palm of the glove were those bits of paper."

"Hmm!" Anthony grunted and pulled his chair towards him and sat. He picked up the glove by its extreme edge and looked at it and laid it down. He bent over the two scraps of paper, flipping them towards him by their edges.

Spencer Hastings rose and sauntered round the table and stood by Anthony's right shoulder. Anthony said without looking up:

"Show these to anyone at the Yard?"

Garrett shook his head. "No. Not when I saw what sort of reception my story was going to have."

Hastings peered over Anthony's shoulder. "One cheap glove; best bargain-basement style. One numbered bus ticket. One—what's that—oh, one shopping list. *Very* enlightening! All you've got more, Garrett, is handwriting. Problem: if there are five million women in London how can you find one when you've never seen her face, you

50

don't know where she lives, you're not even sure she's a Londoner, *but* you've heard her voice and seen her handwriting and know she knows a man called Evans? The answer, I'm afraid, is nohow!"

Tea
Slt Bttr.
P. ons.
Gt. Shrmps
½ lb. Ssgls
Matches
L Lamb.
1 lb Str

"Why her own handwriting?" Anthony spoke without looking up. "Might be her mother's. Or anyone's."

"The glove," said Garrett. "Is there any way of analyzing . . . ?"

Spencer Hastings laughed. "Shades of Thorndyke!"

Anthony said: "You mean, have the dirt extracted from it and examined and see what combinations you get. That's been done. It works, too, *if* you're lucky enough to have subjects which belong, for instance, to someone who lives with a starch factory behind him, a flour mill in front of him and a pencil manufacturer's at the end of his road. But it *doesn't* work if the owner of your subject's just an ordinary person living in an ordinary neighbourhood with ordinary soot and ordinary mud and ordinary dust."

Hastings said: "Anthony, you can't do it! What's the matter with you? Can't you see——"

Garrett said: "You don't *have* to discourage him, do you?" His voice was harsh.

Hastings looked at him quickly; then smiled. He said:

"I'm sorry. Didn't mean to be a wet blanket. But, anyhow, you can't stop Carlton Howe[2] when his nose is to the trail."

Garrett said: "It's I who ought to apologize. I'm——"

Anthony said: "For God's sake, shut up! Both of you." His elbows were on the table now and his chin was propped on his hands. Immediately in front of him, now tidily arranged, were the little scrap of paper which was the shopping list, then the bus ticket and then, half full of air and thus rather horribly caricaturing life, the black glove of cheap kid.

There was silence in the room for a long moment while six eyes gazed at the little miscellany upon the table edge; and then Anthony pushed back his chair and stood. He said, looking at Garrett:

"That ticket machine. Did you notice the value? . . . I mean, was it a twopenny machine? Or a fourpenny? Or——"

Garrett said: "Couldn't say. You see, I was——"

Anthony said: "But if we go there now you can point it out to me?"

"Yes," said Garrett. . . .

4

"But how long will they be?" said Lucia Gethryn.

Spencer Hastings smiled. "Anthony's driving. They've been gone five minutes. They'll be back before I want another drink."

Three minutes after this Garrett opened eyes whose lids for the last mile of his journey had been screwed tight shut. He sighed a small sigh of relief and turned down his collar and got out and stood on the pavement and found himself facing the arched entrance to Leinster Terrace underground station. Anthony joined him and they walked through the archway and into the booking hall. It was almost deserted.

Garrett pointed. "That one," he said.

[2] See *The White Crow.*

They walked towards the machines and now Garrett saw that at the top of his choice was a large plaque bearing the sign "3d." and underneath this a printed list of stations. This list, he saw with disappointment, was a long one. He said:

"Seem to get everywhere in the world from here."

Anthony did not answer. He took out a pen and a small red notebook and began to write rapidly. He finished writing and put pen and book away. "Come on!" he said and started with long strides for the street.

But once on the pavement he did not make for the car. He halted and looked about him. He said:

"Just a minute. There should be one somewhere here."

Garrett wondered what the "one" might be and then saw, as Anthony moved towards it, a flat-capped, blue-uniformed figure standing with broad back to a tobacconist's window. As they drew close he read, up on the badge above the cap peak, the words "London General Omnibus Company."

CHAPTER VI

Anthony Gethryn and his wife were alone. Through the library windows came faintly to their ears the sound of the starter of Hastings' car mingled with a grinding of gears from the taxi in which were Garrett and Avis Bellingham.

Lucia sat upon a corner of the big writing table and looked across the room at her husband.

"And now," she said, "perhaps you'll tell me what it's all about."

Anthony crossed the room and stood to face her. He said:

"Young American, solitary, hears two women, unaware of his presence, talking in a teashop. For him the conversation, being largely allusive, is vague in detail and indefinite in statement; but is sinister in purport, tone and atmosphere. It conveys definite impression that there is a scheme afoot which will make money through a child and may also bring injury to a male adult. The only name mentioned is that of an ally and is the disconcertingly ubiquitous one of Evans. Young American decides to make himself able to identify the women and unobtrusively follows them when they leave the shop. They get to Leinster Terrace tube station and he loses 'em, never having managed to see their faces. He goes back to the teashop and has his first piece of luck, getting one of the women's gloves, inside which are a bus ticket and a scrap of paper bearing a pencilled shopping list. These leave him no wiser. After much thought and abortive search for advice he goes to Scotland Yard, which, not unnaturally, is civil but unimpressed. The thing gets on his mind but there seems nothing he can do about it until he finds a charming friend who knows us. Finish."

A small and worried frown creased Lucia's white forehead. "But . . ." she began.

"And here," said her husband, interrupting, "we have exhibits A, B and C." He went to the front of the table and opened its centre drawer and took out the glove, the bus ticket and the scrap of buff-coloured paper. He said, half to himself:

"Here are some things and some very pretty things. Now who is the owner of these very pretty things?"

Lucia got to her feet and came round the edge of the table and stood beside him and put her hand upon his shoulder. She said:

"Listen, darling! I'm—I'm worried."

Anthony raised his head sharply to look at her but he did not speak. She said after a pause:

"That's a very nice man and this thing seems to have eaten right into his mind. To you it's just a new sort of puzzle—new because instead of being asked to find out who *did* something you're being asked to find out who's *going to do* something. And—and . . ."

"Well?" said Anthony. He looked at her with the beginnings of a smile pulling down one corner of his mouth. She said:

"It's—it's . . . Oh, damn! It's just that I can't help thinking you've given the boy too much encouragement. Didn't you see how different he looked when he left—after you'd told him to come to lunch tomorrow and hinted that you might be further ahead? You *must* have seen. And I just thought it wasn't . . ."

Anthony said: "All right, Officer, I'll talk!" All vestige of the smile had left his face. "I liked Garrett. And you know what I think about Avis. In any case I'd help any friend of hers. But in this business I'm not being actuated by friendship. . . . If you go up our stairs, madam, to the third floor and open the second door on your right, what do you find?"

Lucia stared at him.

"The night nursery, of course."

"And in a corner there's a natty small bed, isn't there? And what's in the natty small bed?"

"What *are* you talking about, Anthony?"

55

"What's in the natty small bed? Answer me!"

Lucia said: "Alan, you fool!"

Anthony said. "Yes. And, thanks to God and despite the treasury, I'm a moderately rich man. Suppose, then, that when we left this room, in about an hour, we walked together up to the third floor and opened the second door on the right, very quietly so as not to wake the occupant of the natty small bed. And suppose we found the french windows on to the balcony there wide open and the natty small bed entirely empty. And suppose that, earlier in the evening, downstairs here, we'd heard some sound from above but hadn't thought anything of it. And suppose——"

"Stop! Will you stop!" Lucia was white faced and her breath came quick.

"Suppose ..." began Anthony again and then put his hands upon his wife's shoulders. Beneath his touch he could feel her body shaking. He kissed her and smiled and said:

"Sorry. But I wanted to make you understand. I believe, not only what Garrett heard, but what he felt and feels. And if this is a long business I want you to understand it because you've got to feel like that too. You see, my dear, you didn't hear him tell his story after dinner. He told it damn badly but it was the more convincing for that."

Lucia stood on tiptoe and returned the caress of a moment ago. And then, turning, she was gone from under his hands and crossing the room. Her gait showed desire for haste cloaked by simulation of leisure.

Anthony stood where he was, looking at an open door. There came to his ears a series of soft, swift, ascending sounds.

2

Lucia came softly down the stairs. She was smiling but behind her upon the third floor the nursery door stood wide. She reached the foot of the stairs and crossed the hallway and went into the library.

Anthony, seated before the writing table, did not turn as she came in. She crossed the room and stood beside him. Now the glove and the bus ticket and the scrap of paper were at one side of the table, their place taken by two maps, one overlapping the other—a folded map of the Central London Underground Railway System and a bus chart headed, "Route 19H."

"Anthony!" said his wife and he turned his head to look up at her.

"I've been thinking!" she said. "Those things don't happen in England."

"Everything happens in England," said her husband.

The dark head was shaken. "No. Not kidnapping."

"It has," Anthony said. "And it will again."

"It's American!" said his wife. "It's American!"

"And England," said Anthony, "in common with the rest of the world, is becoming more Americanized every day. In the main not a bad thing. Very clean. In some specific instances like this . . ." He shrugged.

"These women," Lucia said. "Were they American?"

"Don't think so. Why should they be?"

"But, Anthony, are you seriously trying to tell me that you believe that this might be—well, a sort of beginning to a kidnapping whatd'youcallit?"

"Racket, d'you mean?"

"Yes. . . . But, after all, why should it be kidnapping at all? Did these women say anything about *stealing* a child?"

"How can you make money—big money—through a child unless you kidnap it? I could think of other things but I'd rather not . . . and anyhow, they wouldn't fit."

Lucia pondered. "What I don't see is why this worries Sheldon Garrett so much. After all, it's not even his own country. And even, according to him, the women didn't say anything *definite*. Why doesn't he just forget it? Or are all playwrights public spirited?"

"I'll tell you," Anthony said. "I got it out of him on the way back from Leinster Terrace. He has a sister with a child. And she married Barry Hendricksen——"

Lucia interrupted. "Hendricksen! Not . . . ?"

"Yes," said Anthony.

"But they got the boy back, didn't they? Not that it wasn't terrible, but I mean, it wasn't like that awful Lindbergh thing."

Anthony smiled at her. "If you'd wait a minute, woman!" His smile went. "It was only given out to the world that the child was sent back after the third ransom payment. What was omitted from the news was the fact that when it came back it left half its mind behind it."

Lucia stared at him, the colour ebbing from her face. Her lips opened as if to speak but no sound came from them. Her husband turned his chair and once more stared down at the maps. He said almost briskly:

"Now watch ye and wait, for ye know not at what hour the Answer cometh. . . . Two feminine voices; two feminine backs; one feminine glove; one feminine shopping list; one neuter bus ticket; the knowledge that both women booked from the threepenny machine at Leinster Terrace . . . Problem: find the owner of the glove."

Lucia perched herself upon the arm of the chair and, one hand upon his right shoulder, looked down over his left at the maps. She said:

"It's impossible! You can't do it! . . . Oh! And you forgot that one of the voices knew a man called Evans."

Anthony said: "There's no such word as 'can't,' missie, in the English language. Listen! We discard the voices as being useless. Likewise we discard Evans and the glove. Contrariwise we hang on, first of all, to the bus ticket plus the knowledge of that threepenny machine." He opened a drawer and took from it a pencil and with the pencil made a ring round one of the black dots upon the railway map. He said:

"That's Goldhawk Market. And it's the last station but one of the longest possible threepenny rides from Leinster Terrace, going west. Why do I choose it when I could choose any of sixteen other stations reachable for threepence from Leinster Terrace? The answer to this minor problem is to be found in exhibit B." He pointed to the bus ticket. "See what I mean?"

Lucia said: "I don't and you know I don't. I've——"

" 'Ush, 'ush! I will have 'ush. Why do I choose Goldhawk Market, I say? I choose it because the owner of the glove took a threepenny ticket from Leinster Terrace station and in the glove was found this ticket from an L.G.O.C. bus on the 19H route."

"But . . ." Lucia began.

" 'Ush again! This bus ticket, although it hasn't got any names on it, has numbers. And it is a twopenny ticket punched at Number 5. Now the western end of the 19H route is Gunnersbury. Station 1, which by no means strangely coincides with the beginning, is the Bald-Faced Stag in Iron Lane, Gunnersbury. Station 2 is the junction of Goldhawk Road and Jennifer Street. Station 3 . . . but why bother you with all this professional detail. Let it suffice to say that, being twopenn'orth and having been punched at Station 5, the ticket must have been bought by someone boarding the bus between the Goldhawk Road—Jennifer Street junction and the Shepherd's Bush Empire and intending to get off at the Notting Hill point. We thus have a good presumptive knowledge of the district where the owner of the glove lives. . . ."

"Why?" said Lucia quickly and drawing a deep breath. "She might live in Hampstead and 've been driven out to Richmond by a cousin to see an aunt and then driven back as far as Shepherd's Bush and then have got on a bus to Notting Hill to meet the other woman and then have been going out to supper with a friend *anywhere* on the threepennyworth from Leinster Terrace. . . ."

Anthony looked at her. "The Eighth Wonder," he said. "Reba the Reasoning Woman . . . We are going, madam—we've got to go—by probabilities; and I say, taking the threepenny train ticket in conjunction with the bus ticket, that it is eminently probable that the owner of the glove lives—or has constant association with someone who does live—within a radius of half a mile from a point midway between the Shepherd's Bush Empire and the joining point of Jennifer Street and the Goldhawk Road. . . ." His voice tailed off and he muttered as if to himself: "And he said these didn't help."

Lucia said: "Well, they don't much, do they? It's really just as impossible in that radius of yours as it is in the whole of London. I mean, to find a woman you've never even seen properly. Needles get lost in haystacks; I shouldn't think the size of a haystack would——"

"If you lost a thimble in a forty-acre field," said Anthony, "and God came down on a cloud and told you it was in the middle acre, you'd be nearer finding that thimble than you were at first? . . . And hold your jaw, woman!"

He pushed away the maps and picked up the glove and

59

the dirty little scrap of paper and set them before him on the blotting pad. He said:

"Three little articles belonging to Who. One gave a message and now there are Two."

"Whimsical, aren't you?" said his wife.

Anthony did not answer. He had turned away from her again. He propped his elbows on the edge of the writing table and dropped his head into cupped hands. . . .

3

The hands of the clock upon the table stood at a few moments after one. Lucia had long since gone to bed but her husband still sat and stared down at a piece of buff paper and a black right-hand glove. The smoke from his pipe hung above him in a blue cloud. Neither his head nor his body moved but the green eyes were alive. . . .

"Hell!" said Anthony suddenly and thrust back his chair and stood and stretched his long body. He began to walk up and down the big room; from balcony windows to door and back again. His pipe went out and he did not relight it. He went on walking—and his brain went on behaving like a squirrel on a treadmill.

He halted. He found himself opposite the writing table again and once more staring down at the paper and the glove. He took himself to task and opened a drawer and dropped into it the glove and the scrap of paper and the bus ticket. He locked the drawer and walked across the room and switched out the lights and began to make his way upstairs.

4

He was in his dressing room. As she had not called to him, he knew that upon the far side of the inner door Lucia slept. He pulled on pyjamas and stood for a moment motionless while his unruly mind insisted upon giving him, yet again, an orderly résumé of L'affaire Garrett.

Odd thing to happen to an American on a Sunday afternoon in Notting Hill. Odd thing for this kind of an American to be in Notting Hill at all, Sunday or no Sunday. . . .

"My *God!*" said Anthony Gethryn aloud. He tore open the wardrobe door and reached a long arm into its dark interior and snatched at a dressing gown. Pulling it on as he went, he left the room and ran downstairs. He opened the library door and switched on the lights and made for the writing table with long strides. He unlocked the drawer and opened it and took out the little scrap of buff paper.

CHAPTER VII

The telephone rang, and went on ringing.

It waked Thomas Sheldon Garrett from the first real sleep he had achieved since the night of Saturday, the seventeenth. He raised himself on an elbow and muttered thick curses and reached out a groping hand. He opened his eyes and his gaze fell, even as his fingers closed over the telephone, upon the travelling clock beside it. The time was ten minutes to eight.

He lifted the receiver and held it to his ear and growled.

The telephone said: "Garrett? Gethryn here."

"Oh!" said Garrett, anger leaving him.

The telephone said: "Sorry to wake you. Can you change that lunch appointment to breakfast?"

2

"Did I wake you?" said the telephone.

"Yes," said Spencer Hastings bitterly. "Get to hell! What d'you want?"

"Dyson," said the telephone. "And Flood."

"They're busy," said Hastings, now not so much himself as editor and half owner of *The Owl*.[1]

"What on?" said the telephone.

[1] *The Owl* is a weekly review of which Colonel Gethryn is half proprietor. His friend, Spencer Hastings, is half proprietor and editor. *The Owl*, besides its ordinary weekly edition, runs "special" editions whenever there is "scooped" any news sufficiently exciting to warrant these. In connection with the specials a special staff is employed. Description of the paper and its methods was first given in *The Rasp*. Dyson and Flood, who are the mainstay of the criminal side of the paper's "special" department, first worked with Anthony Gethryn in the case of Daniel Bronson described in *The Noose*.

The editor said: "Eh—oh—I——"

The telephone said: "Come out of the manger. I need 'em."

"Right!" Hastings was fully awake now. "What's on?"

"You should know," said the telephone.

"Good Lord!" Hastings was astonished. "You don't mean——"

The telephone interrupted. "So if you'd have 'em sent down as soon as they get to the office I'd be glad. G'bye."

3

Garrett stood before the writing table in Anthony's library. Upon the blotter there was now spread an inch-scale sectional map whose centre was the green of Shepherd's Bush. Anthony tapped with a forefinger upon a spot somewhat to the left of this. He said:

"I chose a point roughly halfway between the bus stop here and Goldhawk Market, which is *here*. I then took a compass and used this spot as the centre and drew a half-inch or half-mile circle." He looked at the studiously blank face of his guest and a little smile twitched momentarily at the corner of his mouth.

Garrett said with a stolidity of tone which did him credit: "I'm afraid I don't see we've got much further—except, purely presumptively, to narrow our search to a mile-wide circle of what seems to be a very densely populated part of this city. And as we still don't know—and how could we if you come to think of it?—what the woman looks like or what she's called . . ."

He let his voice trail off into silence and Anthony's smile became a laugh.

"I'm afraid I don't see the joke," said Garrett stiffly.

"There isn't one," said Anthony. "I apologize. But I'm pleased with myself. I've got something we can get any number of teeth into. And it's not only a new fact, it's also corroborative of *this* district"—he tapped the map with a forefinger, right on the inch-wide circle—"being the right one."

Garrett said: "Go on! Go on!"

Without speaking Anthony opened the centre drawer of the table. His right hand went into it and came away bearing a six-inch square of white cardboard. Garrett, looking

63

with puzzled eye, saw that in the centre of this was neatly pasted the yellow, irregularly edged slip of paper which bore the shopping list.

"You said your exhibits would tell us nothing," said Anthony and pointed to the list. "But *that,* my lad, shouts information!"

"Eh!" said Garrett and frowned and picked up the cardboard gingerly. He stared at the paper pasted to it. He said:

"But it's just a shopping list. We all——"

Anthony interrupted. "Read it out. And construe."

Garrett held the cardboard nearer to his eyes. He said hesitantly: " 'Tea.' That's easy. Then 'one slt. bttr.' I didn't know what that meant until you told me, salt butter. 'P.ons.' I remember you or Hastings said that was pickled onions. The next means a quart of shrimps. Then one half pound of sausages; then matches; then a leg of lamb and one pound of—of—I can't remember what you said, something——"

"Suet," said Anthony and grinned.

"That's it!" Garrett looked from the cardboard to Anthony's face and then back. He studied the list again, his lips moving as he repeated each item to himself. He said at last:

"Sorry, I don't see."

Anthony said: "I don't blame you. In your enlightened country any sort of foodstuff can be bought on Sunday. Here the only shops which are open on Sunday are sweet-stuff shops, occasional chemists, what you'd call delicatessens and tobacconists. There are some others, of course, but they don't matter here. . . . *Now* look!"

Garrett obeyed; only to glance up again after a moment. He shook his head and lifted his shoulders. He said:

"It's no use! I see what you mean but I don't see what the effect is. You mean that there are some things on the list—I suppose butter and meat and suet—that she couldn't have bought that day. But I still . . ."

Anthony said: "You're getting close. But the real point isn't so much the impossibility of buying certain things on Sunday; it's this—that whoever wrote this list *knew that impossibility.* A shopping list written on a scrap of paper torn from a magazine and thrust into a glove isn't a shopping list for the morrow; it is, almost inevitably, a shopping list for the same day and the same trip for which the glove is put on—because no woman, under normal circumstances, carries anything in a glove which isn't for immediate use. In other words we can assume that the woman of the glove was going to translate the list into commodities before returning home. We know that she put the list into her glove on Sunday and that therefore this was Sunday shopping—a fact borne out by all the list except the last two entries, for only those are impossible of Sunday purchase. She can't have been ignorant of the fact that it was Sunday, because such ignorance, in this still Sabbatical town, is impossible even to a half-witted child. Therefore this is, on all heads, a Sunday list. Therefore lamb and suet—particularly the first, are intruders and unbelievable intruders. Follow?"

Garrett nodded but between the eyes which were fixed upon Anthony was still a frown compounded of bewilderment and disbelief. He said:

"It sounds all right. But lamb and suet are there!"

"That," said Anthony, "is where you're wrong. They are *not* there!" He opened the middle drawer of the table again and from it took a reading glass. He said: "Take that and have another look."

"Listen!" Garrett said. "If you think I lived with that thing for days and didn't look at it under a glass you must be——" He checked himself. "You must think I'm dumber than I am! If what you're trying to tell me is that the last two items on the list weren't written at the same time as the others, or were written with a different pencil, you can save yourself the trouble." His tone showed him almost beyond pretence of civility. "I didn't happen to mention it when I gave it to you because I thought anyone could see it with half an eye."

Anthony looked at him. "I see. How d'you account for it then?"

Garrett said: "I thought it was simple. I thought it meant that at some period the owner of the list suddenly remembered the meat and the suet and added them on."

"And that roughness in those entries," said Anthony. "You can see what I mean with the naked eye, but better under the glass."

Garrett stared at him. "Written on a rough surface.

Against a wall, maybe. Or on anything which wasn't smooth."

"Say a handbag?"

Garrett laughed; a harsh little sound. "No. I've *thought* about this business, you know! Not a handbag. Because if she'd had a handbag she'd have put the list into that and not into her glove."

"Possibly," said Anthony softly, "someone else's handbag. And, also possibly, in a moving vehicle. If you look carefully you'll see that the letters—especially the *m* in 'lamb' and the *b* just before 'St'—are shakily made."

Now Garrett did look, bending over the card on the table and using the glass. He said grudgingly:

"It's possible." He straightened and turned once more to face his host "But it doesn't alter anything. It merely means that she may have written this in a train or a bus or a car."

"And on a Sunday?" Anthony's tone was meek.

"I don't . . ." began Garrett and then checked himself. His right hand rubbed reflectively at the back of his head. He said in a sudden little burst of words.

"Look here, *will* you tell me what you're driving at?"

Anthony smiled. "Sorry. I love to be mysterious and reveal all in the last chapter. . . . Let's recapitulate. First, the day the woman put this in her glove was Sunday. Second, the last two items on the list are the only ones not purchasable on Sunday. Third, she has no foreign accent and therefore knows the Sunday shopping laws. Fourth, she added the last two items to this Sunday shopping list in a moving vehicle and so had to press the paper upon a rough surface which, as there is nothing in a tube train or bus which will fill the bill, was most probably the outside of a woman's handbag. Fifth, she carried no handbag herself or she would not have put the list in her glove. . . . Add those five points together and I think you'll agree that the last two entries do *not* refer to a leg of lamb and a pound of suet. As a corollary to all that I'll add this—that once it had dawned on me that the last two lines were not what they seemed it also dawned upon me that, if they had been, they'd have been most curious. Because legs of lamb don't fit at all with the sort of larder that goes in for half pounds of salt butter and small quantities of pickled

66

onions. Further, it's unlikely that this sort of larder would buy, at one and the same time, sausages and lamb."

Garrett had picked up the card again and was looking at it. When he spoke his excitement was audible. He said:

"But what *are* these last two things?"

Anthony said: "Think. Our woman who (a) has no bag with her, (b) is unlikely to be buying legs of lamb and (c) wouldn't try to buy a leg of lamb on a Sunday, takes a bus to Notting Hill and while in the bus writes something at the bottom of her shopping list, using *someone else's* bag to write upon. But, since it cannot be shopping which she is adding to her shopping list, why should she write at all in the bus? Because it is something which she has suddenly thought of, and wants to remember, which has been brought to her attention while on the bus. Now, bearing all that farrago in mind, consider the actual words that she wrote. 'L. Lamb' and '1 Lb. St.' We thought, because we saw it in conjunction with a shopping list, that these last meant leg of lamb and one pound of suet. I maintain that what they really mean is: Miss, or Mrs., Lucy, or Letitia or Lettice or Lulu or Lola or what the L you like, Lamb, who lives at Number 1 'Lb.' Street."

"Great *God!*" said Garrett.

"You see," Anthony said, "it all fits. The bus, the bag and the Lamb. ... If you write something, on the only bit of paper you have, when you're on a bus, and you put the paper on a bag that you've had to borrow, I think it's a reasonable seventy-five-out-of-a-hundred chance that you're writing down the address of someone you've met in that bus. Now what sort of someone? It *might* be an acquaintance made during the bus ride but you're only having a twopenny ride and that doesn't seem long enough to get to the address-writing stage: it's more probable, therefore, that the address is that of a friend of other days and the same sex whom you've just met again."

"God!" said Garrett again. "It's grand. It doesn't matter a damn, Gethryn, whether it was a sudden woman acquaintance, a man she picked up or an old friend of either sex. It doesn't matter if it was a hermaphrodite! *Whoever* it was is going to be able to tell us *something*. If we——"

Anthony grinned. "Hold your horses! What sort of a street d'you think 'Lb.' stands for?"

Garrett stared at him. "I wouldn't know that. You have

67

damn funny street names anyway." Anxiety took the place of irritation in his tone. "Do you mean you can't . . ."

"I mean," said Anthony, "that I can't see Lb. as an abbreviation for any word likely to be the name of any London street. And if those two letters are Lb. we've got the devil of a job in front of us because it'd mean that we're dealing with an abbreviation which is unreasonable. I haven't yet looked through the London Directory but I'll bet you a pound to a dollar there aren't more than two streets beginning with *l* and ending *b*. And *no* street which *begins* with Lb. . . ."

"Hell," said Garrett, and two words more.

"Quite," said Anthony. "But look again through the glass at those two letters before the St. of 'street.' When our minds were on shopping we naturally saw Lb. But now I want to think that *b* is really another *l.*"

Garrett snatched up the glass and bent again over the card. He said almost at once:

"It might be! It might quite easily be. . . . Damn it, it's *got* to be. . . ."

"Zeal, all zeal, Mr. Easy!" Anthony crossed to the table and sat upon its edge. "But let's take it as a double *l* for a minute. And let's take something else. This isn't unassailable logic but I think it's fair presumption. If Miss X meets Miss Lamb on a bus near Miss X's home or place of constant visiting and writes Miss Lamb's address down in such extremely abbreviated form, it argues, both by reason of this extreme abbreviation and by reason of the coincidence of meeting on the bus, that Miss Lamb is living in the same neighbourhood as Miss X. If Miss Lamb were living in quite another district it would not only make the coincidence of their meeting on this bus far greater, but it would also tend, I think, to make Miss X write down the address more fully. I say, therefore, that our first step is to enlarge the circle which I've drawn on that map and then look inside it for all streets beginning with a double *l.*"

"But look here," said Garrett and then was cut short by sounds from outside the door—the closing of another door; men's feet upon parquet flooring; a rap upon the door of the room in which they were.

Anthony smiled. "Reinforcements," he said and then, raising his voice: "Come in!"

"Don't worry, we'll go right in."

The door opened to admit two men. The first was tall and thin and stooping and was clad in a stained and dirty raincoat from beneath which there came down two shapeless cylinders of ancient, maculate grey flannel. He carried a tortured bundle of greenish-grey felt which might have been a hat and around his neck was a woollen muffler of the colour of whole-meal bread. From the folds of this protruded a head like that of an eagle with a sense of humour and lank black hair. A pair of the largest horn-rimmed glasses which Garrett had ever seen bestrode the fierce beak, enlarging dark eyes which were at once heavy lidded and alert.

The second visitor was as different from the first as well could be; a youngish-looking man, clad with beautiful ease in brown, rich tweed, with a round and smooth and freshly coloured face, very sleek blond hair, rather prominent light blue eyes and a trim solidity of body which made him seem shorter than his real height—in short, what would have been a picture of healthy, pleasant, rather fatuous young English manhood save for the lines about the mouth and the gleam of tired and doubting humour in the light blue eyes.

"I want you two," said Anthony, "to meet Mr. Sheldon Garrett. Garrett, Mr. Dyson; Mr. Flood."

In that order the first man nodded his eagle's head; the second came forward and held out his hand and clasped Garrett's and shook it firmly.

"Dyson and Flood," said Anthony, "are going to help us." He looked at the two. "At least I think they are. Anything interesting on?"

Dyson shook his head, drawing down the corners of his wide, thin-lipped mouth. Flood said:

"There isn't anything interesting. Not any more."

"Sit down," said Anthony. "And I'll change your minds."

They sat, Dyson collapsed into a corner of the big leathern sofa chair with one hand hiding his spectacles, Flood neatly upright in a high-backed chair. Anthony addressed them. He was brief and lucid and extremely careful of details—but he came at last to the end. He surveyed his visitors and said:

"*Now* is there anything interesting? Have a drink?"

69

"Yes," said Dyson without taking his hand away from his face. "And yes."

Flood said: "So the first step is Ll Street? ... Thanks, I believe I will."

4

Dyson took a glass from his lips. "Need a street directory," he said.

Flood nodded.

"All done," said Anthony. "We've got five alternatives on the Ll line. Lloyd Street. Llewellyn Street and Llowndes Street—though what a name like that's doing down there is puzzling—and Lowell Street and Laval Street."

Dyson's collapsed length seemed suddenly to have received, from source unknown, a revivification; at one moment he had been lying back collapsed, at the next he was on his feet.

Flood rose too. He took out a linen handkerchief and neatly wiped his mouth and put the handkerchief away again. Dyson looked at him. Without a word they went towards the door, opened it and were gone. It shut behind them.

Garrett looked at his host with raised brows.

Anthony said: "We'll hear. . . . Come and meet my son."

CHAPTER VIII

A small neat motorcar with bright blue paint and gleaming fittings turned into the Hammersmith end of Lloyd Street. It hesitated at the corner, slid along the left-hand curb and then, after a moment, shot directly across the road and repeated the performance. Seeming to regain sanity, it crossed to its proper side and purred easily down the street. At the farthermost end it stopped and there emerged from it a young man in admirable clothes of brown tweed. He looked this way and that along the street and then up at the door of the first house; a door which once had been green but which now was of an indeterminate putty colour flecked by streaks of grey where time and weather had entirely removed its paint.

The young man ran up the steps. He looked upon each side of the door for a bell and, finding none, put his hand to a knocker of wrought iron which hung by only one screw. A hollow sound came and he waited. After a minute he knocked again; then again waited. He inclined his head towards the door and seemed to be listening. He straightened himself and knocked with considerable force, this time using the side of a gloved fist.

No sound had come from behind it but the door was suddenly opened with a violence which sent its inner handle crashing against the wall of the passage. Flood blinked and saw that there stood framed in the doorway a short square man clad in blue trousers too large for him and grey shirt too small. The trousers were held neither by belt nor braces, and their nether ends hung down in a series of elephantine folds. The shirt, buttonless, gaped across a

71

rufus-thatched chest and its sleeves were rolled up over a pair of abnormally muscled forearms. In the left hand was an open book whose large print afforded to Flood's quick eye a surprising glimpse of Latin verse. From the massive shoulders rose a short thick neck almost wholly hidden by the ragged edge of a bright red beard, and from beneath bushy brows of the same improbable colour two fierce little eyes shot fire.

With effort Flood kept upon his face the smile which he had prepared. He said:

"Is Mrs. Lamb in?"

Through the beard came a deep and distant voice.

"No!" it said.

Flood tried again, still smiling. "Miss Lamb, then?"

"No!"

Flood eased his aching mouth. He said with impressive courtesy: "Do I address Mr. Lamb?"

"No!"

Flood persevered. "Perhaps you can tell me," he said, "when Mrs. or Miss Lamb *will* be in?"

"No!" This time the sound was a bellow.

Flood stood his ground though many a man would have recoiled. But he no longer smiled. He said:

"Haven't you *any* idea?"

Flames seemed to dart from beneath the beetling red brows. The beard moved, this time enough to show teeth of extreme whiteness. From between them came one word.

"No!"

Flood, with the feeling of one who plays spillikens with shreds of ammonal, stuck to his tank. But he, too, became monosyllabic.

He said: "Why?"

The figure in the doorway moved. It took a step back and lifted a right hand as big as a cluster of plantains and set it to the edge of the door. The hirsute head was suddenly thrust forward and the bearded lips opened once more. From them came a roar.

"Because they don't live here!"

Then a shattering crash which made Flood fear for the very walls of the dilapidated house and he was left staring once more at the maculate, putty-coloured door.

72

A postman came down the steps of Number 9 Lowell Street. As he reached the pavement a large and loud and mud-splashed motorcycle slid up the gutter beside him.

"Oy!" said its rider and propped himself with one foot on the curb.

The postman stared into a pair of vast horn-rimmed spectacles. "Beg pardon!" he said.

"Where's Number 1?" said the rider. "Or did they pull it down?"

"Number 1 Lowell Street?" The postman pondered. "That's the Red Lion at the corner. Y'see, they don't——" He was left staring, his ears ringing with the explosions of an exhaust which did not comply with regulations. . . .

In the Red Lion's public bar, a lady of contours ministered with Olympian condescension to four casuals who sipped and chatted and were at ease. The scent of beer was over all and there was peace—which, with brutal lack of warning, was suddenly shattered.

"Mercy on us!" The goddess put a hand to the amplitudes of her bosom. "What's that?"

A thin man smiled beneath a moustache. "Like Vimy!" he said.

The swing doors crashed inwards and there marched up to the bar a tall and thin and stooping form wrapped in a stained raincoat. Beneath a hat of age showed horn-rimmed spectacles astride a fierce nose.

"Bitter!" said Mr. Francis Dyson and put down money.

The goddess served him. He picked up the glass and put it to his mouth and set it down empty. He said:

"Thanks! Name of Lamb?"

"Eh?" said the goddess.

Mr. Dyson repeated himself.

"Paget," said the goddess. "And the Christian name is Doris. Though what it's got to do with *you,* young man . . ." Her voice trailed off into silence, for Mr. Dyson was already halfway to the door.

"Well!" said Miss Paget, and the door swung shut behind Mr. Dyson's going.

There was no other customer in the Lion's saloon bar when Mr. Dyson entered.

"Bitter!" said Mr. Dyson and put down money and received his glass.

"Thanks!" he said and drank and put the glass down, empty. "Name of Lamb?"

He spoke to a large and corpulent and genial male whose every action and circumstance proclaimed him landlord.

Across the darkly gleaming mahogany of the bar this one looked benevolently at Mr. Dyson. He said:

"No sir. The name's Prescott. Alf Prescott. . . . No sir, there's no one 'ere of the name o' Lamb. There's the Blue Eagle in the Finchley Road, now! That's——"

He found himself regarding Mr. Dyson's departing back.

3

Llewellyn Street is very small, very shy and very neat. It contains, in all, twenty-two houses. It hides itself discreetly between the noisy bustle of Gunnersbury High Road on the one side and the clangour of the railway on the other. It is surrounded by other small and narrow streets which are of different character, being as untidy and blatant as Llewellyn Street is quiet and reserved. Something of an anomaly, Llewellyn Street, but an anomaly curiously common in the sprawling unreason of London.

The houses in Llewellyn Street are small, square brick boxes—but each is separated from the pavement by a narrow, railed-off strip and it is with these strips that the street expresses itself. Some are flagged with stone; some actually green with growing grass; some bright with neatly rolled gravel round which grow shrubs and even flowers. To come into Llewellyn Street, as Flood came in his little blue car, from the neighbouring squalor of Pettifer Road is to please the senses—both by contrast and intrinsic merit.

Flood, driving slowly along the curb and peering out at the neat doorways, saw a brass-knockered 21 and then a white-painted 19. He increased the pressure of his right foot and the little car shot forward, to stop at last before the corner house.

Flood wriggled out onto the pavement. He looked with pleasure at Number 1 and walked towards its little iron gate, between which and the white steps leading up to the door was a patch of vivid green grass. He passed through the gate and in two strides was at the white steps. He mounted them and pressed a bell whose surrounding brasswork gleamed gold in the sunshine.

From the other side of the neat door came the crisp tinkling of a bell; the sound of the opening of some interior door; quick footsteps.

The door opened. Flood raised his hat and smiled, this time without difficulty. He was faced by a young woman in pleasing accord with Llewellyn Street in general and Number 1 in particular. She was tall enough; and slim enough without angularity; and owned very blue eyes which looked straight into Flood's from a round face of cheerful comeliness. And the hair of her neat small head reflected the warm goldness of the sunshine.

"Miss Lamb?" said Flood in his best manner.

The blue eyes opened a thought wider; but they continued to rest without displeasure upon the visitor.

"That's me," she said. And her voice was good match for face and figure and the whiteness of her teeth when she smiled.

"Good!" said Flood with a heartiness easy of achievement. He thought quickly, rejecting two prepared stories and adapting a third in the space of a second. He said with a nice blend of camaraderie and diffidence:

"My name's Aston. Charles Aston. Of Aston, Sparks and Aston. I'm the second Aston. We're solicitors. . . ."

The blue eyes lost something of their friendliness. "What d'you *want?*" said the mouth beneath them.

Flood hastened to repair damage. "Don't think for a moment that there's anything unpleasant about my visit, Miss Lamb." His tone was judiciously chosen. "But if you *could* give me just five minutes of your time you might be able to do us a great service and—er . . ." The ingenuous junior partner of the mythical firm of Aston, Sparks and Aston became suitably embarrassed. "And—er—and what I mean is, the firm would be only too glad to—in fact . . ." Mr. Aston lost his thread and fumbled for a notecase.

The blue eyes of Miss Lamb were cleared of suspicion.

"You mean," said Miss Lamb, "you might make it worth me while?"

Young Mr. Aston was grateful. He laughed heartily. "Exactly! ... Exactly!"

Miss Lamb, her attractive head upon one side, went through a short parade of consideration. " 'Specs you better step in," she said at last. She stood aside and young Mr. Aston, removing an admirable brown hat, passed through the door.

"In here," said Miss Lamb and ushered young Mr. Aston into a small bright room completely filled with furniture.

"Jest a minute," said Miss Lamb and was gone, closing the door behind her.

Mr. Aston threaded short-stepped way between two occasional tables, a rocking chair and a harmonium. He stood before a crowded mantelshelf and looked with awe upon a glass case beneath which sea shells were cemented upon crimson plush. From some recess of the little house voices came to his ear—the sharp but pleasing tones of Miss Lamb blending with a lower but still feminine rumble which was beyond doubt maternal.

Miss Lamb came back. "Jest tellin' Mother," she said crisply. "Sit down. Make yourself atome!"

Mr. Aston made himself at home upon the edge of a chair of alarming discomfort. Miss Lamb arranged herself to face him. She folded her hands in her lap and looked at him.

"Now!" she said.

Mr. Aston began his story. It was, he could promise Miss Lamb, a rather curious combination of circumstances which had brought him here. A sort of coincidence. Miss Lamb was, in fact, a godsend, if she might be called that without offence—and Mr. Aston was sure she might. And so on and so on. ...

"But coming to the point," said Mr. Aston in suddenly professional tones, "do you recollect, Miss Lamb, travelling upon a Number 19H omnibus upon Sunday, the eighteenth of this month?"

"Quite the lawyer, aren't we!" said Miss Lamb. "Now, let's see. Sunday the eighteenth; that'd be a fortnight ago come next Sunday."

"That's it!" said Mr. Aston eagerly. "On a 19H, going east."

"East!" said Miss Lamb. "I don't take no truck with compasses and such. . . ."

"Towards Notting Hill," said Mr. Aston. "Surely you remember!"

"Yes!" said Miss Lamb. "Yes, I do. I was—but that's neither here nor there."

"The point is this," said Mr. Aston impressively. "Do you remember, Miss Lamb, meeting someone on that bus?"

"Aha!" said Miss Lamb. *"Now* I see what you're after." She regarded Mr. Aston with something like suspicion. She said slowly:

"Suppose I was to say that any of my friend's business was no business of mine. Suppose I was to say that I didn't——"

"My dear lady," said Mr. Aston. "I don't want you to suppose for a moment that you'll be doing anybody at all any harm by helping me." He smiled a candid, boyish smile which produced its answer upon the face of his hostess.

"In fact," continued Mr. Aston, "I can solemnly assure you, Miss Lamb, that you'll be doing your friend a good service. Now, you *do* remember meeting a friend on that bus, don't you?"

A moment or so passed before Miss Lamb answered—a moment during which, though she kept her gaze upon Mr. Aston's face, she seemed to be considering other things than Mr. Aston. And then the look of abstraction left the blue eyes and she became decisive. She said:

"There don't seem any harm in you. . . . Yes, I remember well enough riding on the bus and I remember meeting Janet. Couldn't very well forget. Y'see, we useter be great chums and I hadn't seen her for nigh on a couple of years. What about it?"

"This is excellent!" said Mr. Aston with enthusiasm. "Splendid! Now, Miss Lamb, I'll tell you exactly why I want to get in touch with your friend and you'll see where you'll be doing her a good turn. And—er"—Mr. Aston coughed—"possibly yourself as well."

Miss Lamb regarded him, her blue eyes entirely friendly. "Get it off your chest," she said.

Anthony Gethryn was deep in the largest of his library chairs. His long legs were crossed and fragrant clouds of cigar smoke hung round him. Through half-closed lids his eyes surveyed the nervous prowlings of his guest.

"Sit down, man!" he said, "and take it easy. We'll hear soon."

"Sorry!" said Sheldon Garrett and laughed. He threw himself into a chair and looked at his host. "This thing's got right under my skin." He jumped up and resumed his pacing. He said:

"D'you *really* think those two'll get anything?"

Anthony held up a finger for silence and cocked his head towards the door. The sound of footsteps came faintly from outside it; and then a knock and then White, who said, "Mr. Flood, sir." And then Flood himself.

He came slowly across the room, his face expressionless. He nodded to Garrett and walked over to the big writing table and took a cigarette from a box and lit it.

"Well?" said Anthony.

Flood's hand went to a side pocket and came away with an envelope in its fingers. He looked at the envelope and read aloud:

"Miss Janet Murch, care of Lady Ballister, 27 Roxburne Gardens, S.W. 7."

Garrett started forward. "Do you mean . . . ?"

"Look for yourself," said Flood and handed over the envelope.

Garrett looked at it, reading the words that Flood had read; words written in a round, schoolgirlish script.

"The address," said Flood, "of the owner of the glove."

"My God!" said Garrett and sat down.

"Turn it over," said Flood.

Garrett twisted the paper in his fingers. Upon the back was written in the same script: "Mrs. Bellows, 148A Iron Court, Stockholm Lane." He read the words aloud.

"J. Murch's aunt," Flood said. "And Stockholm Lane's right on the 19H route. And the shopping list 'd be for Aunt Bellows."

"Great!" said Garrett and smiled broadly. *"Great!"*

Anthony looked at Flood. "Was it Llowndes? Or Lloyd?"

"Llewellyn," said Flood. "Second shot. Heard from Dyson?" A smile threatened to divide his face.

Anthony shook his head.

"He'll call," said Flood and went on smiling.

Garrett said: "Who's L. Lamb?"

Flood said: "Girl. Name's Letty. Pretty. Early twenties. Good sort. Used to work with Janet Murch about three years ago. On the bus was the first time they'd met since then."

Garrett frowned. "Doesn't sound like what we're after, if it's true."

Anthony said: "My good Garrett, you didn't think we'd bagged both birds with the first rock, did you!"

"Well ..." Garrett shrugged. "It was possible."

Anthony smiled. "But damned unlikely. The women you heard talking hadn't just met, had they? They knew each other's addresses without writing 'em down, didn't they?"

Garrett nodded. "I was just dumb, I guess."

Flood said: "Lamb's all right. All aboveboard. And she wasn't in any teashop on Sunday: I checked up to make sure."

Anthony stood up and stretched his long body. "Lamb's out. We concentrate on Murch." He looked at Flood. "Where's that she's working?"

Flood said: "Janet's doing well. *Very* superior. She works for Major General Sir Charles Ballister—you know, big bug in the War Office."

Anthony went over to the writing table and from the shelves above it pulled down the red bulk of Who's Who. Garrett looked at Flood.

"How in the world did you do it?" he said.

Flood grinned. He told of Mr. Charles Aston's call upon Miss Lamb. "When she heard that the firm of Aston, Sparks and Aston were looking for Janet Murch in order to pay Janet Murch a legacy Letty was only too glad to help—*and* get the couple of quid which the junior partner thought was an adequate reward for helping his firm."

"Here we are," said Anthony from behind Who's Who. " 'Ballister. Major General Sir Charles Montague. b. 1870' ... Blah. ... 'm. 1910 Alice, e.d. of Mr. and Mrs. Fenton of Stoke Poges' ... Blah ... blah ... *and* blah ... 'one s. two d.' ... blah ... blah ... 'address 27 Roxburne Gardens S.W 7.' " He closed the book with a slam. "And there, in a manner of speaking, we all are." He looked at Flood. "Would they know at the *Owl* office?"

Flood looked at him. "Such as?"

"Age of children," Anthony said. "All three."

"Use the phone?" Flood said.

Anthony nodded.

"Look here," said Garrett, suddenly staring at Flood. "What I don't see is, how in the world you got the woman's name."

Flood smiled, not without complacence. "Letty gave it to me. The Christian name right away. I had a few nasty moments because I couldn't get her round to saying the surname without giving away that I didn't know it. She kept Janeting and made it a bit tough for poor Mr. Aston ..." He smiled reminiscently. "But poor Mr. Aston has a bad hand; sprained the tendons of his thumb and first finger. Too bad! But Letty didn't mind writing Janet's address on that envelope."

"Oh!" said Garrett and laughed. "Pretty good."

" 'One s. and two d.,' " Anthony murmured. "I could bear to know their ages."

"Sorry!" said Flood and went round the table and picked up the telephone. He was busy with it, cryptically, for a few minutes. He hung up the receiver and came back to the middle of the room. He said:

"Son thirteen; just gone to Charterhouse. One daughter, nine; second daughter, seven."

There was silence for a long moment. Anthony looked at the end of his cigar, Flood down at the floor and Garrett from one face to the other.

Garrett tried to keep silence; but could not. He was at once elated and obsessed with desire for action. He said, looking at Anthony:

"It's easy now. Isn't it?"

Anthony continued to look at the end of his cigar. He said: "Maybe. Nice delicate approach shot required." He put the cigar back in his mouth and went over to the table and sat upon it and reached for the telephone.

CHAPTER IX

Anthony Gethryn walked up the six shallow steps which
led, between the pillars of a portico, to the gleaming front
door of Number 27 Roxburne Gardens. As he reached the
topmost step the door opened and a man came out. He
was a little man who accorded ill with front doors in
Roxburne Gardens; a little man in dark nondescript
clothes and an ill-brushed bowler hat a size too small. He
had a large head whose pale sharp face was undistinguished in its foxy outline but whose carriage was peculiar
in a sideways tilt which implied its habitual averting from
any and every eye.

He passed Anthony and ran down the steps with a
quick pattering. Behind him the door started to close and
then, with a jerk, opened widely to show a portly manservant whose impeccable mask regarded Anthony with the
prescribed blend of doubt, deference and inquiry.

"Lady Ballister," said Anthony. "She expects me. Mr.
Gethryn."

The man stood aside. "If you would come in, sir. . . ."

In a spacious but cheerless hall Anthony removed his
hat. It was taken from him with a correct murmuring and
he followed the portly back down the length of the hallway and into a library.

"If you would wait here, sir, I will inform her ladyship.
. . ." The door shut discreetly and Anthony was alone.

He likes strange rooms. They interest him; and this
room was no exception to rule. Very much a library. A
few pieces of gleaming silver. Many hundreds of books,
probably unread and certainly uninteresting. A businesslike
writing desk of an ugliness quite supreme. Leather chairs
whose invitation was in inverse ratio to their apparent size

81

and comfort. A small fire glowing redly in an ugly grate. A pair of curtained french windows behind which could be sensed the usual grey Kensingtonian garden. A steel engraving of moorland and cattle; a surprisingly good water colour of a brigantine before the wind; a stiff, awkward bazaar scene in oils; a Sergeantesque portrait of a woman whose original might have been beautiful; a very bad hunting scene. On the writing table a large photograph, in a silver frame, of a woman who might be the original of the portrait. On the mantel, between two pieces of Benares brasswork, a photograph of three children—a lanky, bespectacled boy awkwardly posed between two round-faced and younger girls . . .

The door opened and there came towards Anthony the original of the portrait and the photograph. She was tall and moved well, though with a certain suppression of grace. "All my people are service people," thought Anthony and moved forward to meet her, manœuvring so that the light from the curtained french windows fell upon her face. It was a good face; better by far than that which artist or camera had shown him. He put her down, with an eye aided by memory of the Who's Who entry, as in her early forties. There was no trace of grey in the dark hair but there were deep lines from the corners of the nostrils to the mouth. She was very pale, with a sort of luminous greyish pallor possibly natural but possibly impermanent and recently caused.

She said in a voice so low that it gave the impression of determination to subdue unsteadiness:

"Colonel Gethryn? I—I had a message from Edith Carisbrooke . . ."

Anthony bowed and held out his hand. He said:

"Sorry to bother you like this but I'm sure you'll understand. . . ."

His hand remained outstretched. Its insistence could not be denied, and a slim, long-fingered hand was put within its grasp; a very cold hand which seemed to be shaking a little.

Anthony released it. It was clear to him that he was supposed to speak next and so he did not speak and there was a moment of silence, uncomfortably protracted.

"I'm afraid I didn't quite understand Edith," said the

82

woman at last. "She wasn't clear what it was that you wanted." Her mouth barely opened for the words.

Anthony laughed. "I was afraid you might be fogged. It's purely a domestic matter, but perhaps all the more important for that." He was genially fatuous. "Really, my wife should be seeing you. But she's in bed with a chill. Dreadful weather, this. . . . What I'm going to bother you about is the vitally important question of nursemaids. My son's nurse is leaving us. She's going to get married—awkward woman!" His laugh was a masterpiece. "And both my wife and myself, Lady Ballister, are almost morbidly careful about nurses. Now Edith Carisbrooke was talking to my wife the other day and happened to mention what an extremely good nursemaid you had for your two little girls. And so . . ."

He allowed his sentence to dissolve. He wanted once more to force those lips to make words; to watch the lips to see whether they would not at last defeat the will behind them and obviously tremble. He waited and wondered—and she spoke and the lips did tremble. She said:

"Oh! . . . A nursemaid? Yes, I see. Yes . . . Yes, Janet *is* very good." She stopped. She seemed to think that she had answered.

Half-formed ideas in Anthony's mind were forced into dissolution. It was plain enough that his hostess was agitated; had received, recently, a shock. But since it was plain that her mind was not on the conversation—and therefore not upon children—that shock was foreign to Colonel Gethryn's business. He said:

"What I really wanted, Lady Ballister, was a few words with this excellent nurse of yours. Really, Edith Carisbrooke was so impressive about her that we wondered whether the girl could put us on to a good thing, as it were. Very odd request, I know! But I always say, you can't be too careful!"

From beneath thin dark brows, eyes which were clouded with other thoughts regarded him. The brows bent themselves together, as if in effort at concentration, and a light came into the eyes beneath them.

"Talk to Janet?" said Alice Ballister. "Oh! . . . I see what you mean. You wish to interview my nurse."

Anthony nodded. "Yes. That's the idea. See if she's got a sister as good as she is, what? Ha!"

"I'm sorry," said the woman, "but Janet has left."

"Oh!" said Anthony. He experienced some trouble in maintaining pose. "I see. ..." He pulled himself together and achieved heartiness once more. "That's too bad! Too bad! So Edith Carisbrooke was wrong, what?"

"No!" said the low voice. "Janet was an excellent nurse. Excellent!" The voice showed the straining of the mind for concentration. "I'd no fault to find with her. She gave notice herself a few days ago. She left yesterday. I tried to persuade her to stay; offered her more wages. But her mind seemed made up. ..."

The voice died away. The pallor of the face was increased, as if fatigue had been piled upon horror.

"Too bad!" said Colonel Gethryn again. "Better job, I suppose. Or what she thought was a better job. Damn ungrateful, the servant class!" He was all sympathetic indignation.

The woman put up a hand to her forehead and drew long fingers across her brow as if to ease pain. She said:

"I've no idea." There was a desperate under-ring to the muttered voice; it was as if she were preparing herself for one effort which must be the last. She said in a louder tone than any she had used:

"I'm sorry I can't help you. I haven't even got her address."

"Thanks. Thanks!" Colonel Gethryn was taking his cue. He made the beginnings of a movement towards the door. "So sorry I've had to give you this trouble for nothing."

Her mouth made effort to twist itself into a smile. Murmurs came from it. She moved doorwards with Colonel Gethryn.

They stood a moment in the hall. From recesses appeared the portly manservant, bearing Colonel Gethryn's hat. Colonel Gethryn took it and bowed over it to his hostess. He said:

"Thanks again! And again apologies for having bothered you."

The woman stared at him with clouded eyes. She said:

"I'm sorry I couldn't be of more use." And then with a last attempt at courtesy: "If it's any use to you I know of a very good agency. Janet came to me from there." Once more the hand went to her brow and drew long fingers across it. "It's called the—the KJB. It's not far from here.

84

in Brabazon Road, behind the Naval Museum. I—I can't remember the number but . . ." Once more the voice died away with the passing of effort.

"Very kind of you!" said Colonel Gethryn. "Very kind!" He bowed again and through more apologies got himself to the door and out. He ran down the steps. Drawn up to the pavement, two houses away, was his car. He went to it with long strides and seated himself behind the wheel and beside Thomas Sheldon Garrett. The air was thick with the smoke of Garrett's cigarettes.

"Get anything?" said the smoker with eagerness. "Did you see her? Do you think . . . ?"

Anthony shook his head. "Check!" he said.

2

And "Check!" he said again, twenty-five minutes later, when the long black car stood at the curb outside the grocery shop which stands at the corner of Stockholm Lane and Iron Court.

"Hell!" said Garrett. "Why?"

Anthony settled himself behind the wheel. "Because Mrs. Bellows, who is Martha Bellows and the aunt of our Miss Murch, is no longer in residence."

A frown creased Garrett's forehead and there came back into his face something of the look which it had worn when Avis Bellingham had taken him to dine in Stukeley Gardens.

Anthony looked at him. "I said *check*, not checkmate. Remember KJB."

Garrett shrugged. "The agency. That's unlikely to be of much use." He put a cigarette between his lips but forgot to light it.

Anthony started the car, slipping into first gear and beginning to thread careful way through the narrow and encumbered unpleasantness of Stockholm Lane.

Garrett made a motion with his head towards the place from which they had come. "Wasn't there *anyone* there? Anyone who could tell——"

Anthony interrupted. "There were many and they could all tell. But not much. Iron Court's what you'd call a tenement. Martha had a two-room. At the beginning of last week, on Tuesday, Martha told her neighbour, Mrs. Petti-

85

grew, that she'd 'had a letter' and was going away. Mrs. Pettigrew says that Martha was much excited. The letter, it seems, had had money in it. The letter, Mrs. Pettigrew was inclined to think, had come from *relations*. It certainly entailed a visit to Scotland. Martha packed her traps, put her trunk in charge of the caretaker and went off with two bags in a taxi. The taxi stuck in the Pettigrew throat: taxis are rare in Iron Court." He fell silent, intent upon nosing the car out of Stockholm Lane and into the wider but no less grim thoroughfare of the Goldhawk Road.

"No address?" said Garrett. "No knowledge of even the part of Scotland?"

Anthony shook his head. "None so far. A sprinkling of ten-shilling notes and a day's work might produce something. But I say KJB first." He sent a sidelong glance at his passenger. "Cheer up. All good runs have a check or two."

Garrett smiled with noticeable effort. "I know," he said and fell silent.

The black car swung in and out of traffic. It reached Hammersmith Broadway; checked; swung round the circle and shot along the easier way of the broad Hammersmith Road, past St. Paul's School and Olympia; over the hump-backed bridge at Addison Road and so swiftly to the broad Kensington ways and the grey, ugly shapes of the museums. It swung left; then right; then left again and was in a narrow cul-de-sac whose eastern end was dominated by the looming bulk of the Naval Museum and whose northern and southern sides were lined with small Victorian houses of a shabby gentility.

The car slowed. Its driver looked out of the near side window while it crept up the northern side of the street. The car stopped. It was opposite the fourth house from the end. Over the door hung a neat sign in white letters upon a black board.

"Third hole," said Anthony and pointed.

Garrett, craning his neck to look out of the window, saw the board and read what was on it—KJB DOMESTIC AGENCY.

Anthony got out of the car and went to the door beneath the sign and pressed the button on the jamb. From within the house came the sound of a bell; but no other sound followed. He pressed again and waited, looking up at the sign. After a moment he looked at his watch and went slowly back to the car. He opened the door and once more sat beside his passenger. He said briefly:

"Sorry. Closed for the evening."

3

Brabazon Street, in bright, early morning sunshine, wore its shabbiness with cheerful defiance; there was about it a this-is-the-way-I-am-and-if-you-don't-like-it you-can-go-to-the-devil sort of air which was not offensive but friendly. It was a place impossible to any city but London and seemed to know this. It held itself, with a kind of gamecock perkiness, secure in the protection of the grey skirts of the museum. It was clean despite dilapidation and the windows of some of the little houses were brightly curtained and on the southern side a front door had been newly painted bright red. At the end of the cul-de-sac, just beneath the museum wall, two trees amazingly lifted their grace from the roadway and beneath the brown-gold of their branches a small white dog and a large orange-hued cat gambolled in amity.

Garrett, who had come by tube to Brompton Road station, turned into the open end of Brabazon Street as the museum clock chimed the quarter-hour before ten. He had, despite the disappointments of the day before, slept very well; the fast, short walk from the station had warmed him. He liked the morning; he liked the sunshine; he liked Brabazon Street—and he was aware of a pleasant excitement within him. Yesterday he had watched while other men worked upon this business which, after all, was his; his by right of discovery, by right of insistence, by right of anxiety and determination and devotion. But now, today, he was at work upon it while the others waited for what news *he* should bring *them!*

He lengthened his stride and swung the stick which seemed so natural to his hand in London and began to whistle, with soft and tuneful incongruity, "The Sidewalks of New York."

He came to the door, halfway down the northern side of the street, over which hung the black-and-white signboard. Beneath this he paused for a moment, making unostentatious parade of reading what it might say and in his mind running over the lines which his side of any coming interview must take.

He turned to the door and found that this morning it stood open. The word ENTER, neatly lettered in ink upon a square of white card, was tacked upon the right of the doorway. He obeyed it, to find himself in a dark, narrow hallway which smelt, not unpleasantly, of soap and and linoleum and floor polish. Facing him and the front door, past the foot of stairs which ran up to his left, was another door, having an upper half of ground glass upon which, in black letters, were the words: INQUIRIES: PLEASE STEP IN.

Again he obeyed. As he pushed open the glass door a bell tinkled above his head. He closed the door and looked about him and found himself in a thin room which stretched the width of the little house. It had a french window at the back, through which came sunlight and suggestions of a tidy little gravelled garden. It was barely furnished with filing cabinets, two typewriting tables and a few chairs. It was very clean. Upon one of the cabinets stood a vase of bright flowers. The walls were distempered a clear, primrose yellow and in a bright-barred grate a small fire blazed gaily. In the back wall of the room, at the opposite end from the french window, was another glass-topped door bearing in black letters the word MANAGER. At the typewriting table nearer to this door sat a neat and round-faced girl. She looked up as Garrett came in and flashed up at him a friendly but well-modulated smile.

Garrett cleared his throat. "Nursemaids," he said. "I—er—wanted to inquire . . ."

She rose and came out from behind her table and shifted the position of one of the chairs by half an inch. She said:

"If you'd sit down? I'll see if Mr. Hines is free."

Garrett sat looking about him at the bare, cheerful little room. To his American eye it was so little like an office—and yet so very definitely an office—that he found it of interest. The girl had disappeared through the door marked MANAGER. From behind it came a murmur of voices and then, through it, the girl again. She held the door open and looked across the room at Garrett.

He rose and crossed the room and found himself in another. It was smaller but by contrast almost luxurious. From behind a flat-topped mahogany table a little man rose and bobbed his head jerkily in greeting. He might have served as a model for one of the Cherryble brothers. He waved to a chair with courteous gestures.

"Nursemaids," said Garrett. "I wanted to inquire about one." He warmed to his work. "You see, I'm an American staying in London. My wife and small daughter are joining me next week and I have strict orders to get the best nursemaid procurable."

"Exactly! Exactly!" said the little man behind the table. "If I may say so, Mr.—Mr.——" Through the glittering spectacles a pair of bright brown eyes regarded Garrett with inquiry.

"Schumacher," said Garrett easily. "Leslie Schumacher."

"And you want a nursemaid, Mr. Schumacher?" The little man rubbed his hands. "If I may say so you couldn't have come to a better place. ... Now let me see! Let me see!" He reached out a neat white hand and pulled towards him a fat black ledger and opened it and began to turn its pages. From his lips there came a cheerful little humming sound.

"Just a moment," said Garrett. "I should explain ..."

The eyes behind the glasses twinkled at him. "I'm sure, Mr. Schumacher, that we shall be able to satisfy you."

Garrett smiled. He liked the little creature. He said:

"It's like this, Mr. Hines. I'm not after *any* nursemaid. I want a particular nursemaid—if you follow me."

"You mean ... ?" The small round head was cocked to one side.

"Just what I say," said Garrett. "You have on your books a particular young woman whom I'm very anxious to get. Her name's Murch. Janet Murch."

The mouth of Mr. Hines pursed itself and a frown of concentration creased his smooth brow. "Murch?" said Mr. Hines as if to himself. "Murch?"

"Janet Murch," said Garrett firmly.

"The name is familiar, Mr. Schumacher. Definitely familiar." The head was nodded decisively and a white thumb ran down the indented index letters of the ledger and flipped it open again.

"Murch?" said Mr. Hines. "Murch ... Murch ... Ah!" His forefinger stopped at the bottom of a page. "Here we

89

are. Murch. ... Yes ... hmmm ... Yes ... hmmm. Now in service with Lady Ballister. Wife of one of our most famous soldiers, Mr. Schumacher. I very much fear——"

Garrett frowned. A sinking sensation attacked his stomach. He said a little sharply:

"But she isn't. She gave Lady Ballister notice some time ago and left just recently. I thought ..."

The eyes behind the spectacles regarded him with wonder. "Left? A position like that! Are you sure, Mr. Schumacher? I——"

"If I wasn't sure," said Garrett shortly, "I shouldn't be here."

"Tsck-tsck!" Mr. Hines was perturbed. He pressed a bell upon his desk and after a moment the door opened and the round-faced girl stood at Garrett's elbow. She was given orders and departed.

She was back again in thirty seconds, bearing a card from an index-system drawer. She laid this before her employer, who studied it and frowned and made little cheeping noises.

"Nothing here! Nothing here!" said Mr. Hines and pushed the card away from him and sat back and regarded his acolyte. He said: "Murch has not telephoned, Miss Burns? You have not heard from her at all?"

The girl shook her head. "Nothing, Mr. Hines."

The little man was perturbed. "Curious!" he said. "Curious! Did you say ... ?" He looked inquiry and again the girl shook her head.

"No, Mr. Hines. Murch paid all the commission due as early as last March. There would have been another payment to come on the third of December."

"Tsck!" said Mr. Hines. "Tsck! Tsck!" His plump little hand waved the girl away. He looked across the table at Garrett with a glance of real concern. He said: "I am sorry, Mr. Schumacher. Very sorry indeed. But these things will happen. Every now and then girls leave us. ... Now, if you will allow me, I think I can find you exactly what you require even though Janet Murch is no longer in our hands. ..." Once again he pulled the ledger towards him and began running a forefinger down its columns.

"I'm sorry," said Garrett. "But I really do want Janet Murch."

Mr. Hines looked up from the ledger. He raised plump

90

shoulders and spread his hands. From behind the glittering glasses his soft brown eyes looked at Garrett sadly. He said:

"Once more I must apologize, Mr. Schumacher, but you heard what my secretary told me. Murch has thrown up a very good position without consulting us and, moreover, has not come back to us. We must therefore strike Murch from our books!" His kindly little mouth closed in a firm line.

Garrett shifted in his chair. "You mean that you can't even give me her address?"

"We-ll . . ." The tone was doubtful.

Garrett hastened to remedy tactlessness. He said hurriedly:

"Of course I should insist upon your taking a fee for the information." His left hand made a suggestive gesture towards his right breast pocket. "Should we say . . ."

"Tsck-tsck!" said Mr. Hines again but this time with a different intonation. "Very handsome of you, I'm sure! But really, Mr. Schumacher, might I suggest that we try and get you something else. We have many good girls on our books. Excellent girls. I do not wish to boast in any way but I think I may say that, particularly in the nursemaid line, we can do better for you than any similar establishment in London. I can say that with no fear of contradiction." Once more he turned to the still open ledger. "Now for instance, I see, purely by chance, that we have here—momentarily disengaged——"

Garrett interrupted "I'm sorry. But I *do* want Janet Murch."

The little man closed the ledger with a slam. He smiled a defeated but friendly smile. "Janet Murch's address? Very well, Mr. Schumacher." He pressed a bell and the round-faced girl came again and was bidden to bring back Murch's card and returned immediately with it. Mr. Hines adjusted pince-nez. He picked up the card and cleared his throat. He said:

"Murch's address, Mr. Schumacher, is care of Mrs. Bellows, 148A Iron Court, Stockholm Lane, W." He laid down the card and over it beamed at his visitor.

But Garrett did not answer the smile. Once more there had come to him that feeling of emptiness. Once more he was at a dead end. He said after a moment during which Mr. Hines gazed at him with concern:

"That won't do. I got that address from Lady Ballister. Yesterday. I went there but failed to get in touch with Janet Murch. Mrs. Bellows is her aunt and Mrs. Bellows left two or three days ago and the rooms have been given up."

"Tsck! Tsck!" said Mr. Hines and then, "Dear me!" He mused for a moment, placing his elbows upon the arms of his chair and the tips of his outspread fingers together. He said at last over the finger tips:

"Really, Mr. Schumacher, I don't want to appear pressing—it is a motto of KJB never to press a client—but I would like to suggest, especially in view of all the circumstances, that you let us try and provide you with some other young woman. Murch really seems to have been behaving in a most curious way and I think that perhaps someone *steadier* . . ."

Garrett shook his head. "No. I must try and get in touch with the Murch woman." He pulled himself together. "I'll go off and see what I can do." With effort he smiled across the table at the plumpness of Mr. Hines. "You've been very kind." He rose. "More than kind." He got himself to the door, followed by exclamations of distress from the little man. With his fingers upon the handle he turned. "Of course," he said with effort, "if I have to give up Murch I'll come back to you."

He closed the door firmly and a moment later was out again in Brabazon Street. But now, although the sun still shone, it seemed only a cheerless and dirty little backwater.

CHAPTER X

Mr. Sheldon Garrett walked rapidly across the Savoy lounge. His step was springing and his pace was rapid and a wide smile of welcome was upon his face; but Avis Bellingham, looking up from the chair in which she had been awaiting him, saw that the face itself was bloodless and drawn and that the smiling eyes were strangely glittering. She held up a hand to him and he took it in both his own and bent over it and raised it to his lips. The eyes of Mrs. Bellingham widened a little.

"Here we are!" said Mr. Sheldon Garrett. "Here we are! Here we are!" His tone was louder than was normal with him; and he still retained the gloved hand.

"Tom!" said Avis Bellingham and stared at him. "You're tight!"

He released the hand. He made a gesture in the grand manner. "You mock one," he said, "who has this day stared into the jaws of death."

Mrs. Bellingham continued to regard him with gravity. "I should like some lunch," she said.

They walked side by side out of the lounge and into the grillroom and Garrett went on talking. He was still in speech as they sat at his corner table and it was in a froth of words that he ordered their meal.

Avis Bellingham looked at the cocktails. She said: "I think I should have yours as well." Her tone was light enough but there was a faint frown between the eyes which still looked, with something puzzled in them, at her host.

"Beautiful," said Sheldon Garrett, "you can have as much to drink as you like; but you cannot have my drink.

93

No!" He drained his glass and set it down. "You see, darling, I am a shattered wreck! A bundle of nerves! Only an hour since, almost did I embrace the Grim Reaper——"

She said sharply: "Tom! What on earth are you talking about?"

He waved a hand towards windows through which showed, instead of the daylight which the hour should have brought, only a greyish-yellow vapor.

"Fog," he said. "London fog. The motorist's enemy, the doctor's friend, the stand-by of the American novelist. Observe Sheldon Garrett himself, at a few moments short of noon, clutching his stout staff, whistling to his dogs and plunging out into the perpetual night. Observe him making slow but valiant way across the Strand and then, by devious and dingy ways, coming at last to the theatre——"

"What theatre?" said Avis Bellingham.

Garrett stared. "What theatre! There's only one theatre. The rest are mere mumming booths. *The* theatre is that where Sheldon Garrett's masterpiece is now showing." He lifted the glass which the waiter had just filled and drank and set it down again nearly empty.

"We left our hero battling through the fog. We battle with him as he swings along, insouciant, and comes at last to the little alleyway down which he must plunge in order to reach the stage door of the one and only theatre. Does he gain the entrance without untoward incident? He does not—because Death tries to bar the way! Over the stage door is a scaffolding where large men in unseemly trousers have for weeks been endeavouring to replace three bricks and a beam. Today the large men were not working, for fog is bad for their chests. But during their absence something untoward happened upon the scaffolding—so much so that our hero, singing a snatch of Touranian melody, is just about to pass beneath the scaffolding when there comes from above him a tearing, rending, avalanche-like sound and there swiftly descends, from a height of about thirteen feet, an enormous balk of timber! ... Any ordinary man would inevitably have been annihilated. Not so, however, our hero: light-footed as a chamois, he let out a piercing shriek and jumped. The timber struck the place where he had been, knocking off his hat in the process and—yes indeed!—splitting the flagstone upon which it fell. . . . If you like this story please tell your friends.

There will be another adventure of Sheldon Garrett in our next issue. . . ."

Avis Bellingham looked from her own empty plate to Garrett's full one. "Will you please eat?" she said.

Garrett picked up knife and fork. "And that," he said with bitterness, "is all the reaction I get." But he began to eat and was at last silent.

Avis put her elbows on the table and her chin in her hands and stared at him. She said after a moment:

"I know what's the matter with you. I mean, as well as being tight."

Garrett set down knife and fork. "I am *not* tight! I never get tight! And there's nothing the matter with me."

"Eat!" she said. "I *think*, Thomas, that something's gone wrong with your—your puzzle. I've been with you nearly an hour and you haven't mentioned it. And I don't think that just because something nearly fell on you you'd drink so much in the morning."

Garrett looked at her in silence. He was smiling but the smile was awry. "There's nothing wrong with my 'puzzle' as you call it; nothing wrong at all! How could there be when the whole affair's in the capable hands of Colonel Gethryn? No, nothing's wrong at all—nothing beyond the fact that although we know the woman's name we can't find out where she is or get hold of anyone who can tell us anything! No, there's nothing wrong! And even if there was, why should I care? Like Mehitabel, my motto is Toujours gai!"

For the first time the half-searching, half-puzzled look left the blue eyes of Mrs. Bellingham. "Oh, Tom," she said, "I'm so sorry! But it's probably only a temporary check; and Anthony Gethryn's hands *are* capable. More than capable. Once he's started something like this he doesn't stop. I'll bet you he's doing something now, at this minute!"

The smile left Garrett's face. "What he's doing at this minute is to wait. That's all he can do. We've got one line and one line only. Somewhere in Scotland—*maybe*—there's an old aunt of the Murch woman. Gethryn's got lines out for her. . . ." He put the smile back upon his face. "They won't catch her of course. But what the hell if they don't! Toujours gai!"

They had coffee in the sitting room of Garrett's suite. Outside the windows the fog pressed, grey-yellow and heavy, unabashed by the lights within.

"Have some brandy?" said Garrett and from a cupboard brought two great bubbles of glass and a dust-smeared bottle.

His guest shook her head.

"It's good, darling!" said Garrett. He poured a liberal dark gold splash into each glass.

Avis Bellingham sat straight. She said:

"I don't want brandy. Nor do you."

Garrett sat upon the edge of the table. He took his glass in cupped hands and began gently to swirl its contents. He looked at her over the glass. He said:

"How wrong you are! But you look adorable like that: so few women can be angry and wrong *and* lovely all in one expression!" He lifted the glass and sniffed at its bouquet and put it to his lips.

"I don't *think*," said Avis Bellingham, "that I like you like this." Her mouth was smiling but her eyes were not. "I can only hope that whoever it was was wrong about in vino veritas. . . ." She leant forward. "Tom, do please be nice!"

"Nice?" said Garrett. "*Nice!* What a word! But I know what you mean. Haven't I been nice? Am I not now nice? Shall I not go on being nice? Nice, forsooth!" He drained his glass and set it down and picked up the other. He said:

"*Nice!*" and then, raising the second glass: "A toast; a toast! Your husband, God blast—I mean, bless him!"

She started. The smile that she had been striving to keep upon her face was wiped away. She looked at Garrett with a gaze he found it difficult to meet. She said with an odd inflection:

"That's the first time you've mentioned George. D'you know that, Tom? And since that evening you paid your first visit to the flat, we've——"

He took the glass from his lips and interrupted. "Let us not speak of the man! He cramps my style! Whenever I look at you his wraith rises gibbering before me! Whenever I follow the rustle of your skirts, my heart pounding, I feel him dogging my very footsteps! I am like one who turns no more his head, because he knows a Frightful Fiend doth close behind him tread! . . . That's apt! . . . How I dislike the man! My New England conscience gives him a power which my libido refutes! I am on the horns of a Dilemma—see under Zoo. I am a poor thing and not even mine own. My heart is yours to tread and I dare not—durst not!—put it beneath your number fives!"

"Tom!" said his visitor sharply. "Shut up!"

He reached behind him for the bottle upon the table and splashed more brandy into his glass and lifted the glass and drank.

"And that," said Avis. "is *not* the way to drink good brandy! If you must wallow, at least do it like a gentleman!" Her words came fast and her pallor was a match for his.

He set down the glass and dropped upon one knee before her in transpontine humility. He said, tripping a little over his words:

"Pour scorn upon me! Vilify me! Ridicule my hopeless passion! I love it, I'm a masochist!" He reached out his hands towards her in traditional supplication. "I love you, madame! I——"

Avis Bellingham got to her feet. Her face was very white and the blue eyes blazed fire through a sheen which glittered. She said:

"Damn you! I hate you!"

Garrett was left staring at a door, the echo of its slamming ringing in his ears.

3

Anthony Gethryn picked up his telephone.

"When you get him," said Lucia, "ask him to dinner."

Anthony spoke into the telephone; then over his shoulder. "They're getting him." He waited.

Lucia said: "And I *won't* ask Avis."

Anthony turned again. "Why not?"

"Fog!" said his wife. "*And* they're in love but aren't sure of it—at least, *he* isn't for some reason."

Anthony said: "Wrong, aren't you?" And then into the telephone: "Ah, that you, Garrett? . . . Gethryn here. . . . Dine this evening? . . . Yes, do. There's nothing yet but there might be. . . . What? . . . Yes, if the fog's still on, come by tube. Strand to Knightsbridge. When you get out of the station ..." He gave explicit directions and rang off and turned his chair to look across at his wife. He said:

"Sound picture of dramatist in dumps!"

And that was at five minutes past five.

4

It was a quarter to seven when Garrett left the Savoy, coming through the centre swing door and out into the court. The fog was worse; the air was chill and there was no breath of wind. The lights from the lamps and the windows of the hotel and the portico of the little theatre did not diminish obscurity; they merely thinned the greyish-yellow curtain of vapor, misleading men who had thought light means vision.

A cold and acrid stinging of his nose and throat made Garrett pull his muffler up about his mouth. He thrust his hands deep into the pockets of his overcoat and walked slowly along towards the lights of the Strand—yellow nimbuses behind the veil. He passed the portico of the theatre and, keeping close to the wall, reached the broad pavement of the Strand and turned left along it. His progress was now easier. The roadway, indeed, was crowded, with long lines of monstrous shapes crawling nose to tail westward and eastward but the pavement was almost bare of pedestrians. Counting the corners carefully and only twice having to halt to avoid collision with other humans, he got safely into John Street and then, by brushing the railings of the houses with his left shoulder, came with creditable speed down the hill and at last into Villiers Street and across it to the Strand tube station.

He found the booking office and bought his ticket and plunged beneath the surface of the earth. He experienced for the first time that sense of gratitude to the makers of the underground railway which is no uncommon feeling for a Londoner. The tubular, tiled warrens were brightly lit and evenly temperatured, and a man could see so far as his eyes would let him. And here, too, were men and women—many men and women—who were real and sure stepping, not dim and furtive and blundering wraiths.

At the end of the corridor leading to his platform Garrett found himself walking with small shuffling steps by reason of the pressure of his fellow creatures. He had a mental vision of a town beneath the earth; of men living, with the common sense and security of badgers, beneath the surface of an unfriendly world only to be entered in adventure.

He came out of the corridor and onto the platform. It was black with people. Of inclination and by reason of pressure behind him he went forward. In front of him was a little clear space at the edge of the platform. Beside him men and women were converging on it. He marked out the clear space for himself and with two long strides was there. He hoped that when the train came in it would have the grace so to arrange its length that there was a door immediately in front of him. Idly he glanced up and to his right at the hanging electric signboard. It would, he felt, be in keeping with this bad day if the next train proved to be omitting Knightsbridge from its halts; but when the letters of the sign sprang into life he saw that in this small thing at least he was lucky.

He waited. . . . From afar came the beginnings of a rumbling roar. . . . He was aware of a shifting and milling of the crowd about him. More people were flooding in from the corridors to the platforms. . . . He foresaw with a dim, subconscious foreboding that if there were no door opposite him when the train came in he would have a struggle to get to one. From the back of his mind there suddenly pushed its way forward to the front the barbed wish to be going, on this same train whose roaring was now louder, to a station which would lead him, not to the house in Stukeley Gardens, but to the great building of grey stone which contained, vividly real among a hundred unrealities, Avis' little house. . . .

In a crescendo of demoniac noise the train burst from the enclosing sheath of its tunnel. With a scarcely perceptible slackening of speed it slid shrieking into the station, its rows of lighted windows bulging out over the edge of the platform. Garrett, head turned towards its onrush, again speculated, with a corner of his mind, on the problem of doors.

There was a stirring among the crowd; a murmur; a preparatory shuffling. It was like a beast who rises from sleep and stands and stretches and makes ready for movement.

And then, as the two gleaming lights on the front of the train were almost level with him, there came from behind him, as it were, from *within* the general movement, a violent flurry: a short harsh cry; a little clattering; a sudden violent blow upon his shoulders and back. His toes were almost to the edge of the platform. There was nothing between him and the yawning trough along whose floor ran the rails. And right upon him, as he felt himself impelled downwards into that trough, was the front of the oncoming monster.

He does not know to this day—nor do the people who were round him—how his mind conveyed to his body, in such an infinitesimal fraction of time, the message which made him, with a racking of every muscle and sinew in him, resist the impulsion of his own weight. But somehow, semimiraculously, he twisted himself upon the balls of his feet and threw himself backwards and sideways. His arms flung themselves out. His hands clutched at the soft fur of an animal. He slipped to one knee. He felt the wind of the passing of the first carriage of the train. His ears were filled with the screeching of brakes. His eyes saw nothing save a black mist; a mist which had counterpart in his mind and did not clear until he found himself sitting in a corner seat of a long carriage crammed with humanity. All the seats were filled and down the centre of the long car men and women supported themselves against the swaying and bumping of the train by gripping leather loops depending from steel rods. He did not know how he had got in or how he had come to be seated. He looked down at his hands. In one of them was a tuft of greyish fur. He brushed it off with the other and saw that both were shaking and that upon the left was a long graze from which red blood oozed. He pulled out a handkerchief with the right hand and began to dab at the wound. Hearing came back to him. He was conscious that there was an excited muttering of voices all about him; from the seat next to his; from above, where two men clung to straps and swayed with the motion of the train. He turned his head, finding a curious difficulty in the movement. Beside him there sat, overflowing the seat arm between them, a large woman of middle age. Her face, which was round and by all laws should have been highly coloured, was grey and drawn. She was wrapped in a coat made from the beautiful fur of grey squirrels. She was talking stridently, shouting to make herself heard above the roaring of the train. She was talking, upwards, to the two men—one long and cadaverous, the other short and sanguine. They were talking too. All three of them were talking; all shouting their words; all trying to drown the noise, not only of the train, but of each other's voices.

He began to catch scraps of the talk. . . . *"Miraculous!"* . . . *"Somebody dropped a stick; first thing I know I was falling forward!"* . . . *"You must have pushed him right in the back!"* . . . *"Thought nothing could stop him from going!"* *"Good thing I'm not one of these thin women!"* . . . *"Nearly a terrible accident!"* . . . *"Nobody seemed to see it!"* . . . *"All's well that ends well, thank goodness! . . ."*

"I say!" said Garrett and was astonished to hear his voice as a strange croaking sound. "I say!"

The woman turned to him a face into which the colour was creeping back. It was a pleasant and good-natured face. She said:

"Feeling better? That's good! You're a *very* lucky man!"

Garrett looked fixedly at a place upon the sleeve of the grey coat. Near the shoulder was a bare patch. He remembered the fur upon his hand. He said:

"If it hadn't been for you I'd have been over."

She laughed, showing admirable teeth. She said: "I was saying, it's a good thing I'm not one of the thin sort! If I'd weighed a couple of stone less you wouldn't be here. . . ."

"Your coat," said Garrett. "I . . ."

"Don't pay any attention. It's old *and* insured!" Once more the friendly, chuckling laugh.

Garrett felt better. "What happened?" he said.

Now the two strap-hanging men joined the talk again.

"It was me who pushed you," said the tall cadaverous one.

"But he was pushed from the back," said his round and sanguine companion. "I was standing just beside *you*." He looked at Garrett. "Somebody somewhere behind this gentleman dropped a stick and it seemed to me like as if he made a grab for it and lost his balance and bumped into this gentleman and this gentleman, of course, bumped into you. . . . *Phoo!* That was a narrow squeak, that was!"

Garrett walked up the corridor towards the lifts of Knightsbridge station. He was annoyed with his legs. They felt unsure of themselves. As he walked he brooded. A bad day! Filthy weather! Balks of timber which fall near a man! Fools on crowded platforms who drop sticks and nearly push a man in front of a train! The obvious necessity of buying a grey squirrel coat—outsize! A permanent feeling of sick disappointment concerned with the blindness of the trails which had seemed so certain to lead to Janet Murch. Horrible memories concerning the little son of his sister, who was Barry Hendricksen's wife. ... All these—and something else; something which persisted in thrusting itself to the front of his consciousness against orders. Something to do with a fool of a man who lets disappointment and weather and unpleasing adventure lead him to unprecedented consumption of alcohol; a fool of a man who behaves like a boorish and conceited schoolboy to the loveliest woman in the world!

A crammed lift bore him upwards and he came out into the little arcade of Knightsbridge station where there struck him once more the foul and acrid reek of the fog. It was even thicker here than it had been in the Strand. The highway was choked with lines of stationary vehicles whose lights only seemed to increase their helplessness. The red flares of policemen's torches stung the yellow veil. There was sound but it was muffled and unreal. This city aboveground was dead and full of useless ghosts; only below ground were there light and comfort and purposeful movement. ...

He took three steps away from the arcade entrance and the fog closed about him. He pulled up his muffler over his nose and mouth and buttoned the collar of his overcoat tight and pulled down the brim of his black soft hat. He held his hand out before his face: at arm's length he could not see it. He halted. He thought of the warm, well-lighted warrens below his feet and half decided to plunge back into them.

A groping woman bumped into him; murmured half-scared apologies; veered off and was lost.

"Come *on!*" said Garrett to himself. He groped his way along, making his mind blank save for the purpose of this journey. He must keep on this pavement. Then second on the right. Then on until the first cross street. Then turn, cross the road and go down the continuation of this cross street and he would be in Stukeley Gardens. Then up to the first angle of the Gardens and immediately across to Number 19A.

He groped his way onward. He made one false turn but was lucky enough to bump into a policeman. He was put right and retraced his steps and this time found his turning. He came down to the cross street, fumbled his way across the road and was in Stukeley Gardens. He walked faster now. Either the fog was thinner or the bare pavement and the guide of the Garden railings made progress easier. He reached the first corner of the square, pushed himself away from the friendly iron, turned to his left and walked out into the road.

He shuffled across the roadway, his smarting eyes trying to pierce the yellow murk. Soon he must come to the curb—and if he came to the curb without seeing it he might fall. He did not want to fall. His whole aching body rebelled against the very idea of falling. He saw the curb. He sighed relief and lifted his foot and stepped up onto the pavement.

A faint sound came from behind him. And then something fell with dreadful, crushing force upon the back of his head.

Behind his eyes came a sudden burst of bright yellow flame and then darkness. A grunting sound burst from his throat and he pitched forward onto his face and twisted once and lay still.

6

White came out of the baize door at the end of Colonel Gethryn's hall. He crossed to the chest of Breton oak which stood against the right-hand wall, near the front door. He hoped that there were no letters. But there were—four of them. All stamped and addressed and crying for the dark maw of a pillar box.

White sighed. In his square, clean-shaven face the lips moved in the shape of a round and military oath. He picked up the letters and opened the front door and grimaced at the fog. He turned up the collar of his coat and went carefully down the steps and along the flagged path-way to the gate. He frowned as he went and screwed up his eyes against the sting of the fog and blew through closed lips as if he were grooming a horse. He came to the gate and opened it and stepped out onto the pavement. He thought with distaste of the hundred yards which sepa-rated him from the pillar box at the corner. He shut the gate behind him and turned to his right and began the walk.

He had not gone more than five yards before he stum-bled. His right foot had met something soft and heavy.

"What the *'ell!*" said White and stooped to see.

The body was lying on its face. It was crumpled, with one arm flung out straight beside its head and one leg twisted beneath it. It might, from the attitude, have been devoid of life. But White thought not: he had seen many dead men.

He knelt. The cold dampness of the flags was chill against his knees. With a grunt he turned the body over. It was heavy. The yellow fog was all round them, pressing down upon the consciousness like a foul blanket. White stooped lower. He could not see anything of the face save a white oval blur but he put his ear to the blur and felt lit-tle gasps of warm breath come from between the lips. He straightened himself, still on his knees, and fumbled in his pocket for matches. He found one and struck it. Shielding the little flame with his hand, he bent once more over the face. He started. The flame flickered but he saved it. He bent again.

"Kor bloody swop me!" said White. He stood up and threw away the dead match and for a moment strained his eyes uselessly against the fog this way and that. He gave up trying to see and instead, for another moment, tried to hear. But there was nothing to hear. He made up his mind and stooped over the body and caught one of its arms and, twisting his thick solidity, got beneath it to apply the fireman's lift. ...

CHAPTER XI

At five minutes to nine the fog was thicker than ever but at seven minutes past nine there was no fog. A gentle easterly breeze had swept it from every crevice of the city. Now a black, star-encrusted sky arched over the world.

Mrs. Bellingham sat in her drawing room. It was orderly; it was softly but adequately lighted and the fire glowed red and the book which was open upon Mrs. Bellingham's knee was by a man who can write and was a book to whose reading Mrs. Bellingham had been looking forward for weeks. And Mrs. Bellingham wore a favourite gown and had cigarettes within reach and had dined lightly but with excellence.

She should, therefore, have been content. But the book, though open, remained unread and the cigarettes tasted of nothing but smoke and the pleasant redness of the fire did not glow for her eyes and even the gown felt as if it sat awkwardly upon her body.

She looked over the book and into the fire with eyes which saw neither. There were little lines about her mouth which generally were not there. And her head was held too consciously erect and there was a look of pain somewhere in the blue depths of the unseeing eyes. . . .

There came to her ears the sound which told of pressure upon the bell of the outer door. She started, almost violently. The book slid from her knees and lay unheeded upon the carpet by her feet.

She took herself to task. It was plain to her that she had been *listening*. It was also plain to her that the sound she had expected was not that of the doorbell but that of the telephone. At the back of her mind there had been, ever since she had reached home, the thought of the telephone. . . .

The bell rang again, insistently reminding her that her maid was out. She got to her feet and crossed to the door and opened it and went out into her little hall. Through the ground glass of the upper half of the outer door she could see a man's shadow. In defiance of the stern orders of her mind her heart jumped. She crossed to the door and put fingers to its latch and opened it.

The original of the shadow raised his hat.

"Anthony!" said Avis Bellingham.

2

Anthony Gethryn stood with his back to Mrs. Bellingham's drawing-room fire. He looked at Mrs. Bellingham, noting the whiteness of her face. He said:

"You heard what I was saying. There's no danger." His tone was sharp.

The lids which had veiled the blue eyes were raised slowly. The blue eyes looked up and met the steady stare of the green. She said:

"You're sure? There can't be——"

Anthony interrupted. "No, there can't. He's unconscious but there's no possibility of his dying." His tone was intentionally brutal.

Her tongue came out and moistened her lips. She said with difficulty:

"How . . . what . . . Have they any idea how . . ."

Anthony said: "Blow on the back of the head. No bruises. Fairly advanced concussion. No means of telling how it happened. Might have been a fall—but he was lying on his face when White found him and it seems improbable that after a blow like that he'd have turned over. Possibly struck by something projecting from a car." He looked down at the woman. "Dozens of ways it might have happened," he said slowly. There was a slight emphasis on the fifth word of the sentence.

Avis Bellingham sat upright. She said: "I—I'm afraid I've been silly. But—but it was rather a shock. I——"

Again Anthony interrupted. "What you need is a drink. Thank you, I'll have one too. Don't move; I can find it." He reached the door in three strides and was gone.

He returned quickly, carrying a tray upon which were decanter and siphon and glasses. His hostess smiled at him as he set the tray upon a table near the fire. She said:

"Is there anything you're bad at?"

Anthony poured whiskey. "Golf and letter writing," he said and added soda water to whiskey and put a full glass into her hand. "Drink that."

She sipped.

"Drink!" said Anthony.

She drank and took the glass from her mouth and smiled up at him. She said:

"I'm all right. Give yourself one—and then tell me what you think."

Again Anthony busied himself over the tray. He said:

"About accident to prominent playwright?"

She nodded.

He took his stand before the fire and lifted his glass and drank.

"It's possible," he said at last, "that it *was* an accident."

From the depths of the big chair Avis Bellingham stared up at him. She said, her eyes widening:

"I don't . . . Has he said anything?"

Anthony shook his head. "He's unconscious. He'll probably remain so for quite a while." He was looking at her keenly. "What else do you know?"

She said: "What I was going to say was . . . that it's—it's sort of odd——" She stopped. White teeth bit her lower lip and a frown of concentration came between her eyes. She said:

"I lunched with Tom today. At the Savoy. He—he—he told me about an accident he'd had this morning——" Again she broke off.

"This morning?" said Anthony. "Tell me."

She said: "He went out before lunch. It was foggy. He went to the theatre to see George Brooks-Carew. Builders have been doing repairs over the stage door. They weren't working today but as Tom went into the stage door something happened to the scaffolding and a great beam fell and nearly hit him. It might have killed him." Her voice was deliberately flat.

"And then?" said Anthony.

She stared at him. "I was only thinking . . . that's *two*

accidents in one day. It's—it's rather frightening, some-how."

"You think, don't you?" said Anthony. He put a hand to his pocket and brought it away bearing a thin wallet of blue morocco leather bound with gold. Upon the outer side were the small stamped initials T.S.G. He said:

"This was all he had in his pocket. There's ten pounds in it; some cards of his own; a driving licence—American; and this." He opened the wallet and put his fingers into one of its compartments and brought them away bearing a woman's visiting card. He took a step away from the fire and held the card before her eyes. She read: Mrs. Claude Kenealy, 97 Stockbrook Road, Richmond, Surrey. In the bottom left-hand corner there was a pencilled telephone number—Richmond-0246.

"Know her?" said Anthony.

Avis shook her head.

There was silence. Anthony, after regarding the card for a moment, put it back into the wallet and returned the wallet to his pocket. He said:

"You saw it was crumpled. When I found it it was bent double. It had been shoved into the wallet in a hurry. Rest of the wallet shows neatness. . . . In the circumstances a call to Richmond-0246 is indicated."

She looked at him intently. "I don't know what you're driving at."

"Nor do I," said Anthony. "But we'll find out." He crossed to a corner table and sat by it and lifted the receiver from the telephone and worked the dial. Avis twisted in her chair to watch him.

"Hello!" said Anthony. "Richmond-0246? . . . Is Mrs. Kenealy there? Oh, I see! This is a friend of Mr. Sheldon Garrett speaking. Mr. Garrett has met with an accident and——" He was cut short by a perfect flood of talk from the telephone. The metallic cackle rang in Avis' ears. She rose and crossed the room and went swiftly to the table and stood by Anthony. He said into the telephone as she reached him:

"I see. . . . No, it wasn't anything to do with that. . . . He was coming to dine with me and he met with this acci-dent just outside my house. . . . What? Oh! Martin; Theo-dore Martin. I live in South Kensington. . . . Yes. . . . Yes. . . . Yes, I'm afraid it was a nasty accident. . . . Must have

108

been hit by a car which didn't stop in the fog. You know what these motorists are! . . ."

Again Avis was forced to listen to a cackling outburst from the receiver at her visitor's ear. Again she could not distinguish a word. Unconsciously she put a hand upon Anthony's shoulder; a hand whose fingers dug painfully.

"I see," said Anthony to the telephone. "Most extraordinary thing! . . . Yes, obviously his unlucky day! . . . Yes. . . . Yes. . . . I'm afraid I don't quite understand. . . . Oh, I see! Yes, I'll tell him. . . . Yes, by all means—my number's Flaxman-00123. . . . Yes. . . . Thank you. . . . Thank you. . . Yes. . . . Goodnight. . . ."

He replaced the receiver firmly. He turned in his chair and looked up at his hostess. He said, smiling:

"What long, strong fingers you have, Grandmamma!"

Avis Bellingham looked down at the hand which had been digging into his shoulder. She said, taking it away:

"Oh, I'm sorry! . . . What was that, Anthony! I couldn't get a word. I didn't——"

Anthony rose. He rubbed at his shoulder and smiled at her. He said:

"That? That was another oddity in a maze of oddities. Curiouser and curiouser! Mrs. Claude Kenealy says that she met Mr. Garrett for the first time this evening. On the Piccadilly railway. She hadn't known him before. She was standing beside him on the westbound platform when somebody slipped in the crowd behind him, just as the train was coming in, and very nearly pushed him in front of the train. . . ."

"*God!*" said Mrs. Bellingham.

"Quite," said Anthony, "but by an effort which Mrs. Kenealy thinks miraculous Mr. Sheldon Garrett saved himself. In saving himself he was forced to clutch at Mrs. Kenealy. In clutching he damaged her fur coat. They travelled together as far as Knightsbridge, where Mr. Garrett got out. Mrs. Kenealy insists that the damage to her fur coat doesn't matter but Mr. Garrett—always the gentleman—insisted that it did and exchanged cards with Mrs. Kenealy. Two men witnessed the near accident but Mrs. Kenealy doesn't know who they are. As far as she knows Mr. Garrett—who seemed shaken, but who in the circumstances was marvellously self-contained—did not exchange names and addresses with them. Mrs. Kenealy was

109

definite in the assertion that neither of these two men was the person who originally caused the near accident. Mrs. Kenealy thought that Mr. Garrett was a most prepossessing young man, though American. She wishes very much to be informed of his progress. . . . So I gave her the number of Mr. Theodore Martin who lives in South Kensington. It's actually the private number of a fellow called Gethryn. Message ends."

Avis sank into a chair. She said, and seemed to have some difficulty in saying it:

"That's *three!* In one day! And—and——" Her voice shook but she mastered it. "Isn't that—isn't that—well, queer?"

Anthony went back to the mantelpiece and retrieved his glass. He said:

"I don't think so. *Accidents* are queer; but if, in one day in London, when you are deeply interested in a business more than queer, you meet with three happenings, any one of which might cause your death, they cannot be accidents. Therefore they are not queer. At least, not queer in the sense in which you mean. For there's nothing irrational in desiring the obliteration of a person and setting out to cause that obliteration."

She stared at him but she said: "I knew you were going to say that. At least, I knew you were going to say that these things weren't accidents . . . that *someone* was trying to—to kill him. But . . ." Her voice trailed off into silence.

Anthony smiled down at her; a reassuring smile. "But you didn't know that I was going to suggest that the attempts were anything to do with Miss Murch, et omnes?"

She nodded without speaking.

"They must be," said Anthony. "Listen!"

3

And "Listen!" said Anthony an hour later into a telephone at the other end of which was Lucas.[1]

[1] Sir Egbert Lucas, K.C.B., etc., assistant commissioner of police and head of the C.I.D. Lucas is an old friend of Anthony Gethryn. It was through his acquaintance with Lucas that Anthony brought the difficult Hood case (recorded in *The Rasp*) to such a satisfactory conclusion; and his successful working with the police throughout all his other cases has been greatly helped by the friendship.

"I shall be in your office," said Anthony, "at nine forty-five tomorrow. Ack emma."

"Go to hell!" said the telephone sleepily.

At twenty minutes past ten the following morning Sir Egbert Lucas sat back in his chair and turned his head to look at Superintendent Pike. They both looked at the long and lean and recumbent form in the armchair beneath that window which, it is popularly supposed, has the best river view in all Scotland Yard.

There was a silence which Lucas broke. He said:

"Very interesting, Gethryn! A pretty story! A little forced, perhaps, but who can help that nowadays with so many people writing these things?" He was all irony. "But what, exactly, d'you think *we* can do?"

Superintendent Pike looked at Colonel Gethryn—but said nothing.

A voice came from the armchair. "It isn't so much what I expect, Lucas; it's what I hope."

Lucas smiled sourly. "Still the master of persiflage! Elucidate."

Anthony sat up. "I was hoping that for once you'd exercise your real function—or what should be your real function—and help me to shut a stable door before a horse is stolen."

Superintendent Pike continued silent; but he also continued to stare with speculative eyes at Colonel Gethryn.

Lucas lit a cigarette. Through smoke he said:

"I'm sorry but I can't see any door that wants shutting. I can see an overheated imagination at work; but that's all. I——" A telephone upon his desk rang shrill. "Just a minute!" He picked up the receiver and spoke into it and listened. He said:

"What's that? ... Who? ... How do you spell it? ... Oh! ..." There was surprise in the last ejaculation. "Who's the divisional surgeon? ... Oh yes. Good man! ... What did you say? ... Yes. ... Yes. .... That's something to be thankful for, anyhow. Well, get on to Andrews and get all the detail done and have the usual report sent. ..." He put back the receiver and looked once more at Anthony. "Sorry!" he said. "But that was business."

Pike looked at him with an eyebrow inquiringly cocked.

Lucas said: "No bother. Suicide. There'll be a fuss,

111

though. It was old Ballister's wife. Personally, no suicide in *his* family would surprise me. I once sat——"

He broke off to stare across the table at the suddenly risen form of his visitor. "What's the matter?" he said.

Anthony came up to the far side of the table and leant his hands upon it and stared across it at its owner. His face was devoid of expression but yet there was about him a certain tensity which a moment before had not been there. Superintendent Pike continued to stare, now with a deep frown between his brows.

"Alice Ballister?" said Anthony. "Wife of Charles Montague Ballister, major general et al?"

"Yes," said Lucas.

"When?" said Anthony.

"Found this morning," said Lucas. "An hour ago, to be precise. Divisional surgeon says she may have been dead three hours. Definitely suicide."

Anthony sat himself sideways upon the desk. He said:

"Well, well! And that's that! Now, Police, you'll *have* to help me with my stable door."

Lucas sat back in his chair. He said with rude clarity:

"What in the name of God are you talking about?"

Anthony said: "Alice Ballister was the employer of Sheldon Garrett's Janet Murch. I saw her myself."

The right hand of Superintendent Pike began to rub reflectively at his lantern-shaped lower jaw.

"What!" said Lucas. And then: "Must be a coincidence."

"You," said Anthony, "are one of these survivals who live by the application of old wives' tales; the sort of man who thinks that an albino can divine gold and that a right-footed sock from a left-handed man will cure the staggers! Coincidence my eye!" He looked down at Lucas with an air blent of tolerance and irritation. He said after a pause:

"Listen! You obviously need the whole thing again—only this time including the unfortunate Ballister woman. . . . Are you ready? We're off! A man hears two women talking. He is convinced they are planning a crime or crimes, part and parcel of which is the kidnapping of a child. He is a stranger to this town and country and has difficulty in finding anyone to believe he isn't just a scaremonger with a hypersensitive imagination. But he gets help at last and he and his helpers find that the only clue he had leads them to a friend of one of the women whom he heard but never properly saw. From the friend they get the woman's name—Janet Murch—and the information that Murch is working in the household of General Ballister. Helper Gethryn—by unprincipled use of a common acquaintance—calls upon Lady Ballister and asks to interview Janet Murch. But Janet Murch has left the Ballister service, of her own accord! Lady Ballister cannot tell Gethryn Janet Murch's address but she does tell Gethryn that she got Janet Murch in the first place through the KJB Domestic Agency of 14 Brabazon Road, South Kensington. Gethryn leaves with this information—and also with the knowledge, acquired by his observant eye and receptive personality, that, at the time of the interview at least, Alice Ballister is a harassed and extremely frightened woman. He does not—why should he?—associate this harassment and fear with the subject of his own search but merely files it in his encyclopedic brain for future reference, noting also the fact that as he entered the Ballister house a nasty little man, most unlikely to have been a social visitor, was leaving the house. Armed with the one piece of fresh Murch information—to wit, the address of the agency—he goes back to Mr. Sheldon Garrett. They decide that the next step is to go to the address of Janet Murch's aunt, furnished previously to another helper by Janet Murch's friend. But when they get there the aunt is flown! She has, most inconsiderately and indefinitely and suddenly, departed for Scotland—in great excitement and a taxicab. The next morning Garrett visits the KJB Domestic Agency—under the nom de guerre of Leslie Schumacher, a visiting and parental American in search of Janet Murch, said to be the world's champion nursemaid. The manager of the agency—a certain Hines—is cheerful and obliging but he cannot help his prospective client because Janet Murch has severed her connection with the agency. Mr. Hines endeavours, naturally enough, to induce Mr. Schumacher to let KJB procure him another nursemaid but Mr. Schumacher, also naturally enough, will not commit them to this course. This was on Saturday. On the following Monday Mr. Sheldon Garrett—about his own business—visits, in the fog, the theatre where his play is running. He then meets with the *accident* of the stage door which you will remember. In the evening he sets out to dine with Gethryn and is first nearly pushed under a tube train and then hit by a mysterious something—which I'll bet you a quarter's income to a sixpence was a sandbag—on the back of the head on his way to Gethryn's house. The next day Gethryn comes to Scotland Yard to tell his story and to use what appears to be an entirely mythical influence. After he has told it the would-be satiric gibberings of the assistant commissioner of Metropolitan Police are interrupted by a telephone call which announces the death, apparently by suicide, of Lady Alice-in-brackets Ballister."

He broke off, looking from one of his listeners to the other. He said:

"And that's that. And more than enough."

Lucas said: "It looks odd. I'll agree to that. But then, anything *can* look odd." He turned his glance on the third of the trio. "What do you say, Pike?"

Pike did not look up as he answered. He seemed to be regarding the tip of one of his shining boots. He said:

"I agree with both, sir, as you might say. What I mean: I see that the way Colonel Gethryn looks at it, it's a very queer business and one that could do with looking into and ought to be looked into. On the other hand, I know what *you* mean, sir. . . . It might just be coincidence."

"Yes, and again no," murmured Anthony. "Pike, you ought to be in the Foreign Office!"

Lucas said: "It's all conjecture." His tone was peevish. "What's more, it's not even complete conjecture. You want us to stop somebody from doing something but you don't know who's going to do it or what they're going to do. . . . Damn it all, Gethryn, it makes about as much sense as Lewis Carroll."

"That's saying a lot," said Anthony. "But you're not even right at that."

Pike said: "Gosh! I wonder whether. . . ." He looked hard at Anthony. "You mean to suggest, sir, that Lady Ballister didn't commit suicide?"

Anthony shook his head. "No. It's a possibility, of course. But then . . ." He turned to Lucas. "Who was the divisional surgeon?"

"Latrobe," said Lucas.

Anthony said: "In that case it's a hundred to one that it

was suicide." He looked at Pike again. "And it fits much better that way."

"Really?" Lucas was ironic again. "What fits what? What do you mean, 'fits'?"

Anthony said: "You remarked just now that I wanted you to try and stop an unknown human quantity from committing an unknown crime quantity and didn't know either of the quantities. Right?"

Lucas nodded.

Anthony said: "You meant, in other words, that I had no case against anyone. Right?"

Lucas nodded.

Anthony said: "I say that two cases lie. The first is against the absent Janet Murch. The second is against the present KJB Agency."

"Charges?" said Lucas. "Do you want me to find Janet Murch and put her in the dock on the charge of being such a good servant that her leaving caused the suicide of her mistress? Or do you want——"

Anthony interrupted. "What I do want is absolute 'ush! ... Rex versus Janet Murch: Janet Murch is overheard talking about a possible crime which entails a new job along the nursemaid line. She gives up her nursemaid job, voluntarily, with Lady Ballister. She does not leave any address with Lady Ballister. She does not go and stay at her only other known address and the other owner of that address, the aunt, also leaves mysteriously. Reasonable inference—Janet Murch has taken up a nefarious job: we have indications that she was going to and her behaviour strengthens and colours them. After Janet's leaving Lady Ballister commits suicide. A man attempting to trace Janet Murch is nearly killed three times almost immediately following his inquiries. Presumption: That Janet Murch and/or her associates are unpleasant and criminal persons with whom the police should make acquaintance."

Lucas and Pike exchanged a glance. Lucas frowned and picked up a pencil from his desk and began to draw horses' heads upon a blotting pad.

Anthony said: "Rex versus the KJB Domestic Agency. The KJB Domestic Agency furnish Janet Murch to Lady Ballister. Janet Murch leaves Lady Ballister. Lady Ballister commits suicide. The KJB Domestic Agency are approached in regard to Janet Murch and cause the attempted murder of the inquirer. Presumption——"

"Whoa!" said Lucas; and Pike stirred in his chair.

"Yes?" said Anthony politely.

Lucas said: "Even if we assume that the three—er—adventures of Mr. Garrett yesterday were not coincidental accidents but deliberate attempts to murder him we cannot assume that the attempts necessarily had anything to do with this agency."

"Well, well!" said Anthony and looked from Lucas' face to Pike's.

Pike nodded. He murmured: "That seems right enough, sir."

"And why?" said Anthony.

Lucas repressed a movement of irritation. He began to draw again.

Pike said after a moment: "Because although Mr. Garrett did go and ask about this Murch at this agency there's plenty of other people, according to your own story, sir, who've been approached about Murch and who *might*'ve been the people who were trying to do away with Mr. Garrett."

"No," said Anthony.

Pike stuck to his guns. "But surely, sir! F'rinstance, there's this friend of Janet Murch—the one that gave her address in the first place. And there's all the other people who were asked while you were trying to find the address——"

Anthony said: "I triumph; but it's a cheap triumph because I may not have explained properly. The attempts on Garrett *must* have been made by KJB, or by those in association with it, because none of the other inquiries were made by him. Further, no one of the other persons questioned can have associated Garrett with the inquiries because (a) they never saw the inquirers more than once, (b) were given—where names were used at all—false names *and* (c) had no means whatsoever of following the inquirers. You can take that from me as being not supposition but fact. How different with Garrett and KJB. He goes into their office, having walked from South Kensington station. He gives a false name and inquires about Janet Murch. He will not take any other answer but Murch. He walks away and it is a simple matter to follow

116

him back to the Savoy, inquire from a servant, entirely unsuspiciously, who he is and find out, not only that he is not Mr. Leslie Schumacher, but that he is unmarried. How simple, too, to follow the KJB line of reasoning when they have this information. Thomas Sheldon Garrett is a young American playwright. He has been in London for only a few weeks. Under a false name and on a false premise he is trying to find out how he can get in touch with Janet Murch. Though possible, it is very highly improbable that he needs a nursemaid—so wherein lies his anxiety? Janet Murch is engaged in nefarious business; why is anybody so interested in her? They talk it over and talk it over. They come to the conclusion that there is a possibility that Garrett has in some way come into possession of knowledge which has made him suspicious concerning the doings of Janet Murch. Anyone snooping about Janet Murch at the moment is most undesirable. It can do no harm to try and eliminate this sole snooper, providing the elimination is done in such a way as not to bring any suspicion to bear upon the eliminators. . . ."

"Wait!" said Lucas. "You're now trying to get us to believe that this KJB Agency is behind the Murch affair."

Anthony looked at him. "Oh, my dear fellow! Because I gave you two separate cases I didn't mean that the two affairs weren't bound up."

Lucas grunted.

Pike said: "If there's anything, sir, it's something big. They were taking a chance on this Mr. Garrett."

"*Big!*" said Anthony and laughed.

Lucas threw down his pencil. He leaned back in his chair and looked at Anthony. He said:

"I still don't see what we can do. If you want me to say that you've convinced me that there's something going on that oughtn't to be going on I will say it. But—what can we do?"

Anthony stood up. "I'll tell you," he said. "But later. . . . Good-bye and thanks for bearing with me."

Two men were left staring at a closed door. Lucas sighed and picked up his pencil and began upon another horse's head. He said without looking up:

"I suppose he's right. Damn him!"

CHAPTER XII

Big Ben was sounding the first stroke of noon when Anthony nosed his car out of the Whitehall entrance to Scotland Yard. It was six minutes past the hour when he pulled it up in Stukeley Gardens and jumped out and slammed its door behind him. Half a minute later he was seated at the writing table in the library. And then bodily activity ceased while his mind raced, swiftly but orderly tabulating those things which he must do. . . .

The door opened softly and Lucia came in. He looked at her and smiled and reached for the telephone and began to dial a number. She crossed the room and stood by his chair. He turned to speak to her but immediately was checked by an answer from the telephone. He said into the mouthpiece:

"Hello. . . . Dyson? . . . Gethryn here. . . ."

Dyson said: "Everything going by the book. We were all set just after ten. We missed one, while Harris was getting things fixed. But we caught all the others. He says the light's good. Any further orders?"

"No," said Anthony. "Carry on."

Dyson hung up his receiver and turned. He was in a small room whose furnishings proclaimed it as coming under the head "bed-sitting." There was a couch against one wall, spread with an orange-hued cover which incompletely disguised its nocturnal purposes; then a wardrobe of white-painted deal, one armchair, two ordinary chairs, a Jubilee Chiffonier, a table and an insecure-seeming bookcase containing old periodicals and a nearly complete set of the works of Bulwer-Lytton. These were the normal trappings; but today there were more—a tripod of black

118

wood and bright steel, set up in the one large window, and atop of it was what seemed a black rectangular box. Behind the tripod knelt a man. In a chair beside him, reading a pink paper, sat Flood.

Dyson came across the room and stood close behind the kneeling man and looked out through the window onto the cheerful, sunlit little stretch of Brabazon Road, South Kensington.

In the library of 19A Stukeley Gardens Anthony Gethryn twisted in his chair and looked up at his wife and saw that she was smiling.

She said: "He's been conscious. Nurse says that he suddenly came round and spoke to her. That was just after you'd gone out. He was in pain, so she gave him the injection that Doctor Holmes left. He's sleeping now."

"Good," said Anthony. "I could bear to see Avis."

Lucia stood up. "I've phoned her already. Nurse said he'd sleep for five hours at least. . . . But all the same I——"

Anthony said: "I do perceive here a divided duty. . . . Bring her in here as soon as she comes!" He smiled up at his wife again and reached once more for the telephone. "And now, woman, stand not upon the order of thy going." Once more he began to dial—the same number as before.

"Quite the Napoleon!" Lucia pulled a face at him and dropped a kiss upon the top of his head and was gone.

Anthony got his number. He said into the telephone:

"Mr. Flood, please. . . . Hello, that you, Flood? . . . Yes. . . . Yes. . . . I've got Lucas to take notice, *because* Lady——"

"Ballister has killed herself," said the telephone. "I saw that. I wondered——"

Anthony interrupted: "Don't, you're right. Here's your job: Shove a discreet paragraph into as many of this evening's papers as you can to the effect that Mr. Thomas Sheldon Garrett, distinguished young American playwright and author of *Wise Man's Holiday*, et cetera, so on and blah, had a severe fall in the street (locale unmentioned) yesterday. He was found by Samaritans and is now lying—concussed, unconscious and seriously ill—in the nursing home of Doctor Travers Hoylake in Welbeck

Street. Pitch it in as strong as you can. Give a definite impression that it's most unlikely that he'll live.... No visitors allowed of course.... That's all you've got to worry about. I've already fixed things with Hoylake and the nursing home will know what to do if there are any calls. Repeat, will you?"

The telephone cackled briefly.

"Right!" said Anthony. He put back the receiver and rose and crossed to a far corner of the room and stood looking down, with distaste, at a small table upon which stood a typewriter. After a moment he sat before the machine and put paper in it and began with great speed, considering the use of only one finger upon each hand, to type....

He sat back after thirty minutes and sighed relief. He picked up the five pages and put them into order and scanned them. He read:

DEAR LUCAS: Belated apologies for my intolerable manners this morning. But I had—or thought I had—to be rude before you would really give me your attention.

I know you well enough to be sure that your last remark to me meant that you were going to play. Therefore I send you this:

We know that the KJB Domestic Agency is not the innocent affair which it seems. However, so far, we have nothing which would be sufficiently concrete in the minds of the ordinary muttonheaded British jury (and the D.P.P. if it comes to that) to bring a charge against KJB and those behind it. Therefore, do not let us make the frightful mistake of warning them. This, as it is, is an upside-down case and must therefore be treated with upside-down methods. Whatever KJB (and those behind it) may have already done must be left for the moment, for we cannot stop that; but if we play our cards properly we may stop whatever they are going to do. Below I list some general and some particular lines for us to follow:

A. GENERAL

1. Do not by any overt act let anyone know, in connection with the Ballister case or otherwise, that there is any curiosity upon the part of police in regard to KJB.

120

2. Exercise your "influence" with the coroner to see that the above applies to him too.

3. To effect (1) and (2) above properly, insure that the routine inquiry at the Ballister house is handled by someone who knows what we are really after and *not* by some intelligent and pushful peeler who *might* stumble upon something accidentally.

4. Above all do not let any official body, under any pretence or for any reason, go anywhere near the KJB office.

B. PARTICULAR

1. Put a good man on the Travers Hoylake's nursing home in Welbeck Street and follow anyone who calls there to ask after Garrett. (Garrett is still in my house. He is recovering. But, following my policy of not frightening KJB at all, I am having a notice put in this evening's papers to the effect that Garrett is in the nursing home, unconscious, and is not expected to recover, his injuries being due to a *fall*.)

2. Get in touch with Hoylake (who knows what's required) and tell him who his operator is to call at the Yard directly she receives any telephonic inquiries at all for Mr. Garrett. Also, if possible, arrange with the Exchange to keep a record of the numbers from which calls about Garrett to the nursing home are made.

3. Put a good man onto Miss Letitia Lamb, of Number 1 Llewellyn Street. He should not approach her personally but should find out, if possible, whether she is as innocent of entanglement with KJB and/or Janet Murch as her name and appearance (*vide* Flood) would appear. Has she a good record? Has she ever been in any way connected with undesirable persons, employment or happenings? (A purely precautionary measure, this. I feel sure Lamb is all right; but we must double-check.)

4. The same in regard to Mrs. Claude Kenealy, of 97 Stockbrook Road, Richmond, Surrey—the woman whose bulk and fur coat, she says, saved Garrett from a tubular death.

5. Try and find the present whereabouts of Mrs. Bellows, of 148A Iron Court, Stockholm Lane. This is the reputed aunt of Janet Murch. A few days before we obtained this address through Lamb Mrs. Bellows went sud-

denly and excitedly and mysteriously to Scotland—or said that she was going to Scotland. I have had rough inquiries made at the possible departure stations and also in the neighbourhood but these have got nowhere.

6. Get someone (I hope it is Pike) who has been in on the official inquiry into the Ballister suicide to tell me about and/or present to me all the concrete collected evidence in the matter. As soon as possible.

7. Have a search made in Records (if you haven't already) for Janet Murch. (It will probably be abortive but should be done.)

8. Ditto for Evans—the man used as a threat in the conversation which Garrett overheard in Notting Hill teashop and which started the affair. There will, of course, be thousands of Evanses but it might be well worth while to see if any of these have been connected with any nefarious doings in any way bound up with the domestic agency business in general or domestic service in particular.

9. Similar inquiries about the KJB Agency itself, though these are almost certain to be abortive.

10. Send me as soon as you can (if possible by White, who will bring this to you) the reports of Garrett's two interviews at the Yard with Andrews and Horler on the nineteenth and twentieth of last month.

11. Try and find out, very discreetly, who the man was that left Ballister's house just before I saw Lady Ballister—i.e. at about three o'clock on Friday, the thirtieth of last month. What's his name and business? Whom did he see? Had he ever been to the house before? (I have no specific reason for wanting to know about this man except my favourite one of general oddity.)

12. If—but only if—you have a very good man making the Ballister routine inquiries get him to find out, without giving away interest in the concern, how many servants in the house within the last year came from KJB.

Thank you kindly, sir. Bear with me and get the quickest action possible.

Anthony came to an end of his reading and rose and took the sheets to the writing table and signed the last of them and pressed a bell.

Sheldon Garrett opened his eyes, for the second time this day, upon surroundings which were strange. The room was full of the grey-blackness of dusk about to turn to night but this melancholy pall was shot through with red and cheerful and flickering reflections which told of a large fire. He was barely conscious of his body. His eyes told him that he was in a bed but he did not feel the mattress beneath him nor the clothes above him. He was numb and glad to be so. . . .

He stared at the ceiling. His eyes saw what they looked at but they seemed heavy and sluggish and unwilling to move when his half-benumbed mind ordered them. But his ears were preternaturally sensitive. There came to them magnifications of every sound. . . . A very faint, very muffled rumbling of traffic. . . . A very loud, very sharp crackling of hot coals. . . . The creaking of wood as a body shifted its position in a chair. . . . A very faint sound of voices from somewhere beneath him in this house. . . . And then, imperiously imposing itself atop of all these sounds, the crackle of starched linen. . . .

His mind ordered his muscles to raise his head from the pillow and turn it to his right. But no movement resulted—only a stab of pain which, starting at the base of his skull, sent fiery fingers to every nerve in the whole of him. . . .

A mist came over his sight and he was dimly conscious that sweat had broken out all over him. He lay still. . . .

Preceded by a louder crackling of starched linen, there swam into his vision the upper half of a white-clothed woman. She bent over him, putting a dry hand, hard surfaced yet softly fleshed, upon his sweating forehead. Flickering rays from the fire struck sparks of light from the panes of glass which hid her eyes. She said:

"And how are we feeling?" Her voice was soft and devoid of all humanity.

He said, thick and low:

"Bit sick, eh? . . . Head hurts. . . . Where's this?" The words were not so much reflections of his thought as essays in the difficult exercise of speech.

She took the uncomfortable hand away from his forehead and straightened herself with another rustling and stood looking down at him. She said something; but his mind, wrapped up in its own affairs, did not trouble to interpret the words. He said:

"Mrs. Bellingham? . . . Where's she? . . . What house is this? . . . Call up Colonel Gethryn. . . ." The effort of so many words brought out beads of cold sweat upon his face. But he went on. "Colonel Gethryn . . . The number's—I can't remember. . . . Mrs. Bellingham—St. John-4383. . . . She'll tell . . ."

Another crackling of linen as once more she bent over him. Her mouth pursed itself and there came from it a *sshushing* sound. She said:

"Don't talk now! You'll only hurt yourself if you do. Lie quiet and everything will be all right!" She picked up his right hand, which lay outside the bedclothes. Her fingers fumbled for his pulse and, holding the wrist, she looked at a watch upon her own.

3

"You're sure," said Anthony, "that these are all we need to worry about?" He tapped with pencil butt upon the paper which lay upon the writing table before him. He looked across at the big chair in which his visitor sat.

Avis Bellingham nodded. "I don't think there can be any more. I used to know the whole family."

Anthony chewed the end of his pencil for a moment; then began to write. He came to an end and read aloud:

" 'Pay no attention reports seriousness of illness stop Perfectly all right stop Business reasons stop Telephoning by end of week love Tom.' "

He sat back in his chair and looked at his visitor. "All right?" he said.

She nodded again. She said: "If—do you really think he'll be able to telephone . . . I mean, that he'll be——"

Anthony smiled at her. "Of course. He'll——" A knock upon the door interrupted him. "Come in," he said.

The nurse made rustling entry. She stood just within the doorway and folded her hands and ranged her spectacles upon Anthony. She said:

"I am sorry to disturb you, Colonel Gethryn, but Mr. Garrett has awakened. He is in pain but I cannot give him

124

another injection until Doctor Holmes has been. I endeavoured to find Mrs. Gethryn but I am told that she is out. I must keep Mr. Garrett quiet, however, and he keeps on asking me to 'call up' Colonel Gethryn or someone called Avis. He keeps saying this latter name." She was silent for a moment while the eyes behind the glittering glasses flickered momentarily towards Colonel Gethryn's visitor, who had made a sudden movement but who now was still again. She said: "I could only keep Mr. Garrett quiet by promising to go. . . ."

Anthony had listened enough. "Quite," he said, "quite! This is Mrs. Bellingham, whom Mr. Garrett wants to see." He looked with deliberately expressionless face at Avis. "If you wouldn't mind going up. . . ?"

Mrs. Bellingham rose with admirable slowness to her feet. There was more colour than usual in her face. She looked at Anthony and smiled and moved toward the nurse and the door. She said:

"Good afternoon, Nurse. . . . If I can be of any help. . . ."

Anthony turned his chair back to face the table and picked up the draft cablegram and reached for the telephone.

4

The opening of the door sounded in Garrett's ears like a battery of artillery. But he had learned; he did not try to raise his head. He lay still and his breath came faster.

And then Avis was bending over him.

He looked up at her without moving his head. Slowly his eyes focused their sight so that every detail of her face was clear. Her eyes were very blue and very soft and they shone. Her lips moved as if she were going to speak but no sound came from them. They remained parted a little, so that behind the redness of their lovely curve he could see the whiteness of her teeth. He smiled, now heedless of the pain which the stretching even of these few muscles sent stabbing through his head. He was going to speak; to say her name at least—but he found, suddenly, that he was seized by a childlike and painful constriction of the breath. The smile stayed upon his face but, unbidden, smarting moisture came into his heavy eyes. . . .

Then a starchy rustling; a bump; and the unctuous, unnecessary voice of the nurse.

"Why don't you sit down, Mrs. Bellingham? And make yourself at home. But you mustn't let him talk too much or I shall be getting into trouble with Doctor Holmes." She had set down a chair behind Avis and was patting its back invitingly.

Avis sat. She did not take her eyes off the drawn face on the pillow.

Another rustling and the nurse stood beside her and herself bent over the pillow. She put her hand again upon the patient's head and held it there a moment. She said, drawing it away:

"Well, the excitement of a visitor doesn't seem to have done you any harm. But you must be good!" She wagged a distressingly roguish forefinger. "You mustn't be a bad boy and spoil this nice surprise I got for you!"

Garrett's lips moved, shaping themselves into a soundless and deplorable word. Avis choked. She took out a handkerchief and pressed it to her lips. She felt a strange desire to giggle and weep at the same time.

"And now," said the fat voice, "I'll leave you to yourselves." Once more the forefinger was raised in coy admonition. "But very little talking, mind!"

The starched linen creaked again and she was gone, to settle herself once more, with a determinedly tactful back towards the bed, in her chair by the fire.

Garrett's sluggish eyes moved themselves in her direction. Once more his lips soundlessly found a fearful word.

"Don't!" said Avis Bellingham in a choked voice. "Please don't, Tom!"

And then, suddenly, all desire for laughter left both their minds and again they stared at each other.

Garrett spoke first. From between his barely moving lips came thick words:

"Crack on the head.... Don't know how long here.... I wanted to say sorry for lunch the other day...." A groping look came into his heavy eyes. "When was it? ... Seems..."

She leaned nearer to him. She said:

"It was on Monday, Tom. Yesterday. And there's absolutely nothing——"

The thick, guttural voice interrupted her. "There is! ...

Behaved badly. . . . Too many drinks. . . ." His voice was laboured and each successive word came with more difficulty. She interrupted him, leaning forward and putting a hand upon the clothes which covered his shoulder. She said:

"Don't, Tom! It's all right; it's perfectly all right!"

His lips moved again. " 'Tisn't all right. . . . Very bad! . . . Fooled about things I—I—really meant . . ." The voice died away and his tongue came out in effort to moisten the lips which seemed so unmanageable.

"Oh!" said Avis Bellingham softly. "I——" She seemed to check herself, closing her mouth tightly so that further words should not escape.

There was a silence.

"I don't know . . ." began Garrett slowly and painfully—and then was interrupted.

A voice came to their ears from across the room. It was fat and efficient and obviously gloving iron in velvet. It said:

"Not too much talking for the patient, please!"

Garrett moved heavy eyes slightly in the direction of the voice. But this time his lips did not move; they were too tired to waste effort.

Avis leant closer to him. She smiled at him and it was as if an Olympian balm had been poured over his hurts. She said through the smile:

"I'll do it for you." And her lips moved soundlessly to form a word.

Garrett started to grin, checking the wideness of the smile only just in time to stop another stab of that agonizing pain. And then his smile went and he said with a curious sharpening of tone and words:

"How's the—what did you call it?—the *riddle?* Been having . . ." His brows creased themselves into a slow and painful frown and a cloud came over his eyes. "Been having . . . sort of dreams. . . . Barry and Edna and—and——"

Mrs. Bellingham stopped him. She said in an imperious whisper:

"You mustn't talk! And don't think about that sort of thing! It's not going to happen! . . . I've just been with Anthony. This is his house, you know. He's very busy. Very.

127

I'll tell you tomorrow, or he will. But lots of things have happened."

A light came into the languid eyes of the head upon the pillow and from the heavy lips came an eager croaking. It said:

"Found Murch?"

Avis said: "Sssh! I'm not going to tell you any details but you've got to believe me. All *sorts* of things are happening!"

Garrett said in a voice suddenly louder: "Please tell me——" And then with a determined crackling the nurse was at the bedside once more. She said in a voice from which everything save authority had gone:

"That'll do! No more now!"

CHAPTER XIII

There was amazement in the Gethryn household: its master not only appeared at the breakfast table but appeared bathed and shaven and clothed for the day. His son's joy and surprise were eagerly voiced; his wife's greetings satiric. He did not bow before the storm; he helped himself to food and sat down and began placidly to eat. He said:

"I'm a busy man. Great matters hang upon my every word and action." He drank coffee. "I might just be likened to the spider."

His wife looked at him with interest. "You've got that secret look on, Anthony! And you're excited about something."

He put down his knife and fork. "I say nothing, though I could say much. I will only say that in future I should be known as Semloh, the Upside-Down Detective." He reached for the paper and opened it and from behind it said: "When you come to think of it I *am* a spider—a subtle spider who doth sit in middle of his web which spreadeth wide."

"I don't like spiders," said his son. "But their webs are pretty."

Anthony lowered the paper. He made the face which never failed to draw a crescendo peal of laughter from his son. He said, looking at his wife:

"No brighter nor skilful thread than mine, my cabbage. If aught do touch the utmost thread of it I feel it instantly on every side."

He finished his breakfast to ribald chaff from his family.

He left them and went into his study and busied himself in thought.

At ten o'clock his expected visitor arrived. It was Pike, lantern faced and smiling and alert. He refused refreshment, took tobacco and sat in the big armchair close to Anthony's desk. He produced from his pocket a large and official-seeming envelope, and from the envelope a heterogeneous collection of paper bound with elastic. He said: "Well, sir?" and grinned.

"Well to you!" said Anthony and blew smoke rings.

Pike said: "I'll start, then. We did have the divisional plain-clothes inspector on the Ballister business, sir, but as soon as Mr. Lucas got your letter yesterday lunchtime he took him off. He asked me whether I'd go and I jumped at the chance, as you might say." He put his hand again to his breast pocket and brought it away bearing this time some folded sheets of typescript. He unfolded them and pressed out the creases upon his knee. He looked up at Anthony. "A copy of your letter, sir. How'd it be if I was to answer all the points right now?"

Anthony ceased to blow smoke rings. "All?" he said. "It would be magnificent. Can do?"

Pike smiled, not without pleasant traces of self-satisfaction. "Yes sir. Ready? . . . Taking the first paragraph of your letter, Mr. Lucas told me first of all to say that he hadn't taken any offence when you were there. Second, I was to say that of course we were going into it. Third, I was to say that he quite saw your point about not warning this KJB lot. . . . And now I can get down to your numbered points. Under the heading 'General', and taking them in order, I can tell you that *nobody* is going to get any idea that we're a bit interested in KJB. Second, we've sent Mr. Sparkes—you know him, sir!—to talk to the coroner—and *that's* all right: he won't show any interest in KJB. Third—well, I *hope* that's answered by my having charge of the inquiries personally. Fourth, I've taken good care that nobody in any way connected with the police is going anywhere near the KJB office."

He turned over a page of manuscript, sat back more comfortably, cleared his throat and began again. He said:

"Now, sir, for your heading 'Particular.' . . . One: I've put a very good man—you remember Howells?—onto the nursing home in Welbeck Street. He's an extra porter there now, in uniform and all. There's another man outside and if anybody comes to ask for Mr. Garrett, Howells will tell him and he'll do the necessary following. . . . Two: I've been onto Doctor Hoylake personally and told him his operator must call extension 232 at the Yard when she receives any telephonic inquiry for Mr. Garrett. I'm afraid, though, that we can't arrange with the Exchange for a record of numbers calling. This automatic business has beaten us in that way."

"Progress!" said Anthony. "Ourobboros!"

Pike stared politely. "Sir?"

"Swalloweth itself," said Anthony. "Go on."

Pike said: "I've put Dixon—I don't think you know him, but he's a good man—onto this young woman, Lamb. He's got some more work to do but I saw him this morning before I came here and I should say that from what he's got already there's no possibility of *her* being mixed up in this business at all. We've looked for her in Records and she doesn't appear there—nor anyone of the name. He's been into antecedents, as you might say, and everything's well aboveboard. . . . Now for Four: Last night I went after Mrs. Claude Kenealy myself. You can take it from me, sir, that *she's* all right."

He looked at Anthony with one eyebrow cocked.

"If you say so, Pike," said Anthony and meant it.

Pike beamed. "Thank you, sir. Number Five: Mrs. Bellows—I've got nothing to report on yet. We sent a man from Hammersmith Division down to Iron Court and he reports that she was very well liked in the neighbourhood. Very respectable body. All bills paid and that sort of thing. Lived there for quite a while. She told the neighbours she was going to visit relatives in Scotland. No address given. We may have some more on this later when we've been properly round King's Cross and St. Pancras. But at present I've got to confess we're nowhere."

He paused for a moment and tapped the bundle of papers on his knee. "In Number Six you asked for all the concrete evidence in the Ballister business. Here it is, sir, and we'll come to it in a minute. . . . In Number Seven you asked us to search Records for Janet Murch. We've done so and haven't got anything—as you expected. In Number Eight you asked for a similar search about Evans." He laughed. "You were right about there being

131

thousands of them, sir; *but* we haven't got any one of 'em who we can in any way hitch up with domestic service. . . . And it's the same for Number Nine—the KJB Agency. No record at all, and a very high-class character in the trade, as you might say. Number Ten was a request for the reports of Mr. Garrett's interviews at the Yard." He tapped the breast pocket again. "I've got those here. . . ."

He cleared his throat and shifted his position. Over the sheets of paper which he held he glanced at Anthony, noting, with a little smile, that Anthony's eyes were half closed. He said:

"With Number Eleven, sir, I can give you something definite. This man you saw leaving the house when you called on Lady Ballister on that Friday: I've found out about him. The butler knew about it. The man was a representative for some firm of central heating engineers. Lady Ballister had some idea of having central heating installed in the general's country residence—that's in Bucks, near Aylesbury—and this man was trying to interest her in his firm's system. I put a casual question to the old general about this, sir, and he confirmed it. They don't remember the name of the firm but if you want particularly to know I dare say we can find out. The man's been to the house on several other occasions: the butler thinks four. His name was Mr. Smithers. . . ."

For the first time during the recital Anthony interrupted. He said:

"Good name. Not so obvious as Smith."

Pike looked at him, frowning. "Beg pardon, sir."

Anthony said: "It doesn't matter. What about Twelve?"

Pike smiled. He said: "Maybe I've been too egoistic, as you might say, about this, sir. What you said was if we had a good man on the job he was to make inquiry about how many of the servants in the Ballister house, within the last twelve months, were from KJB. I took the liberty of assuming that I'd fill your bill and put out some discreet feelers—very discreet! I'm sure I didn't arouse any suspicion and anyway, sir, in a manner of speaking, there weren't any to arouse. Because why? Because none of the present servants in the house come from the KJB Agency! I checked on them. There are five all told, including the new nursemaid who took Murch's place. Four of them come from another agency and the fifth privately. But, sir,

132

not only Janet Murch came from KJB within the year, but one other—a housemaid by the name of Dillson—Doris Dillson. She came in February last. She left at the beginning of May, discharged for impertinence. . . . And that, sir, I think covers, as far as we can at the moment, all the matters in your report."

Pike sighed and sat back, relaxed. His small bright brown eyes searched Anthony's face.

Anthony came to life. He said:

"Sometimes I agree with American novelists when they ascribe superhuman powers to Scotland Yard."

Pike smiled widely. He picked from his knee the elastic-bound bundle of papers. He leant forward in his chair and proffered them to Anthony. He said:

"Here's what you asked for, sir, in your Number Six: the stuff from the Lady Ballister effects."

Anthony took the bundle and put it down upon the table and turned his chair and undid the elastic band. He found the stubs of five chequebooks; a passbook; an envelope, opened, addressed in a sprawling hand to "Charles"; a little red morocco-bound book marked "Diary."

He spread these out upon the table and looked around at Pike.

"That all?" he said.

Pike nodded. "Yes sir, except for something else which I couldn't bring and which I'll tell you about when you're ready."

"Hmmh!" grunted Anthony and bent over the collection.

Pike lit a cigarette and looked at his watch. The hands stood at eleven o'clock. . . .

2

The clock over the Naval Museum was sounding the last stroke of eleven when there came out of Number 14 Brabazon Road a young woman in the blue cloak and blue-streamered bonnet of a nursemaid. Drawn up to the wall almost underneath the KJB signboard was a perambulator. The nursemaid bent over the perambulator and peered at its occupant, who, securely tucked beneath his covers, slept, red faced and peaceful. With care not to make the process jerky the nursemaid eased the pram away from the wall, cautiously turned it and set off briskly towards the end of Brabazon Road and the main thoroughfare of Emperor's Gate. She was a slender-ankled, brisk young woman carrying her becoming uniform with an air and wearing upon her lavishly powdered and nicely formed face a look of supreme if unsympathetic competence.

She had not gone more than halfway between the door of Number 14 and the end of Brabazon Road when there emerged from Number 11, upon the other side of the street, a brisk young man in the dark cap and blue overalls of a mechanic. His overalls were fairly clean but his hands bore the black marks of his calling and in the right was a small leather tool bag. He turned sharply to his left as he reached the pavement and strode, whistling shrilly, towards Emperor's Gate. The pretty nursemaid and her perambulator were moving fast but the mechanic was moving faster. As the nursemaid reached Emperor's Gate and turned to her right she was barely ten yards ahead.

The mechanic ceased to whistle. Having reached Emperor's Gate, he turned to the right, too, crossed the mouth of Brabazon Road and went on his way, more slowly. It was a way which seemed to coincide with that of the nurse and the perambulator. . . .

She reached the top of Emperor's Gate and turned left along the broad road which divides Kensington Gardens from the brown masses of the houses which front it. Sometimes twenty, sometimes only ten, yards behind her came the mechanic. The maid and the perambulator took the third turning on their left. So, a few seconds afterwards, did the mechanic. As he turned the corner he looked upwards, as if in doubt of his whereabouts, at the street plate. He read the words, "Pierpont Gardens" and strode on.

At Number 17 the nurse halted. The mechanic was then opposite Number 11. He dropped his bag and the catch sprang open and his tools spilled themselves about the pavement. He swore roundly and stooped to collect them. He seemed in no hurry about the work.

Outside Number 17 the nurse busied herself. She took a strap from the foot of the perambulator and hitched its wheel to the area railings. She removed the covers from the still-sleeping occupant, gathered him into her arms and mounted the steps to the front door.

The mechanic collected the last of his tools from the gutter. He fastened the catch of his bag and continued upon his path. He was now merely strolling. He arrived opposite Number 17 just as the door shut behind a flutter of blue. He looked up at the number above the door. He put his bag between his feet and made great play of consulting a card which he drew from the pocket of his overalls. Then, whistling, he marched to the area gate of Number 17, pushed it open and ran, still whistling, down the steps and pounded upon the tradesmen's door. . . .

3

Anthony pushed away the last of the books of cheque stubs. He opened an envelope marked, "Letter Written by Lady Ballister(Deceased) to Husband." He read:

My dear Charles,

You must not think too harshly of me for what I am going to do and what I shall have done by the time you read this. I have told you, I think, of my headaches. But I have never told you how frightful they were. They have been periodic and getting steadily worse. And they have done things to my brain. I have kept myself under iron control, thinking that perhaps they would pass; but they never have! And *now* I know what is the matter: *I am going insane!*

I can bear neither the thought of being a thankless burden to you and to our dear children nor, for myself, of being a witless thing!

I am going to end it. I can only hope that you will forgive your loving wife,

Alice.

Anthony turned in his chair and looked at Pike. He said:

"And exhibit Three, that you couldn't bring?"

"Exhibit Three, sir," Pike said, "was a lot of charred paper in the grate of Lady Ballister's room. The fragments were analyzed. The report was—very think paper on thin pasteboard, with one highly glazed surface."

135

Anthony shrugged. "Whatever that means, a bonfire's in order. It all fits, doesn't it?" He flicked a finger at the cheque stubs. "A women spends about thirty-five pounds a month for years; then suddenly draws large cheques to Self, increasing in amount from a hundred to five hundred, every few weeks. She burns papers and kills herself, leaving an overwritten letter which doesn't ring at all true. It's all according to Cocker."

Pike nodded, his long face lugubrious. "Meaning the lady's suicide was caused by blackmail, sir? Yes sir."

Anthony looked at him. "What's the matter, Pike? Blackmail fits."

Pike said slowly: "What you want it all to mean, sir, is that this KJB Agency was behind the blackmail. Am I right?"

"Shades of Dupin!" said Anthony and grinned. "Pike, you're no policeman; you've got too much imagination."

"Am I right though, sir?" Pike was insistent.

Anthony said: "You are indeed! I was wondering when you'd make the sum of KJB plus Murch, plus KJB plus Ballister come out as KJB equalling blackmail." He looked at Pike and found no lightening of the gloom in the long face. "What I'm wondering now, Pike, is why you're so sad about it all."

Pike twisted uneasily in his chair. "For a whole heap of reasons, sir. And they make a pretty muddle in a man's head, if I may say so. First, there's——"

Anthony interrupted. "Hold those horses, Pike; they're getting away with you. Your only trouble's this: you feel—probably rightly—that however much we probe we won't be able to fix this Ballister blackmail on KJB and that, therefore, probing will only warn them that they're under suspicion and give them a chance to cover up l'affaire Murch so that we'll *never* get at it."

"That's it, sir. That's just it." Pike was animated. "You see——"

Again Anthony cut him short. "Wait. That's just half your worry. The second half's this: if we don't probe this Ballister case how are we going to get hold of anything at all against KJB which will serve as a handle for us in the forthcoming Murch business?" He surveyed Pike with benignity. "There you are. Your trouble in a nutshell. No fee."

Pike lost himself in frowning thought. After a moment he smiled, a little ruefully. He said:

"You're right, sir. That's all there was to it. But it's plenty, at that, when you come to look at it."

"So don't," said Anthony.

Pike stared. "Beg pardon, sir?"

"Don't come to look at it. Don't look at it. Don't consider it at all. Cancel the Ballisters, poor people. And incidentally, please Sir Charles, who certainly would fight tooth and nail to rebut all evidence of blackmail."

Pike got to his feet. He was fidgety, a most unusual state for him. He said vehemently:

"But then we've got *nothing* to work on from this KJB end. We——"

Anthony said: "Preserve absolute calm. We want KJB. First—forgetting the Ballisters—we need to prove to ourselves that KJB is nasty but without frightening KJB into being nice. Then we want to catch KJB red handed. Yes?"

Pike stopped the jerky walk with which he had been pacing from desk to window. He said almost savagely:

"All right, sir; I'll forget the Ballister case. That puts us back to where you said we weren't to go near KJB or do anything at all about them!"

Anthony nodded. "Exactly."

Pike almost glared at him. He said in a voice which came near to a shout:

"Then we can't do *anything!*"

"Exactly," said Anthony again. "You can't." There was the slightest extra emphasis on the pronoun.

"Eh?" said Pike sharply. And then: "Do you mean to tell me, sir, that you've got somebody onto KJB yourself?"

Anthony nodded.

"Oh!" said Pike. His face was expressionless but he stood still and very straight.

Anthony said: "Don't collect umbrage. Remember that I came in on this *after* Scotland Yard had refused to listen to Mr. Garrett. Therefore I had to be unorthodox. Stay to lunch and I'll show you the results."

CHAPTER XIV

Pike stayed. They lunched at one and after the meal went into the drawing room. They talked, but not at all of the matter uppermost in their minds.

At a quarter past three they were joined by Flood. He nodded to Anthony and grinned at Pike and shook hands.

Pike said with a sound akin to a sniff:

"I'm not surprised!" But he smiled.

Flood looked at Anthony. "All ready," he said.

They moved towards the door, Anthony leading.

Pike said: "And where's our Mr. Dyson?"

"Busy," said Flood. "Quite the bee!"

They went downstairs and into the library once more. Heavy curtains were drawn over the windows and the centre lights were on. Over the bookshelves at the end of the room nearer the door was hung a white sheet. At the other end of the room, by the french windows, stood a cinematographic projector. Beside it was a small, bald-headed man with the appearance and manner of the skilled worker. A few feet in front of the projector, facing the sheet, were three chairs.

"Walk up!" said Flood. "Walk up! See the Wonderful Movin' Pitchers! The most sensational fillum of the century! Man Huntin' in the Kensington Wilds!"

"Shut up!" said Anthony and sat himself upon the middle chair and motioned Pike to one side of him and Flood to the other. He turned and looked over his shoulders at the man by the projector. "Ready when you are," he said.

There was a click and the lights went out. There was a whirring sound from the projector and then a broad swathe of white light illuminating the sheet.

"Modern Detective Methods!" said Flood beneath his breath. "Collecting Clues with the Camera!"

Pike grunted. He settled himself in his chair and dug his hands into his pockets and stared at the sheet.

Upon it there appeared a picture. It occupied the centre third of the sheet. It had, apparently, been taken from very close to its subject. It showed bricks—the mortar between them considerably crumbled—surrounding the dark and rectangular mouth of an open doorway. At the top of the picture, in the middle, hung something which looked like a batten of wood. Upon the right-hand jamb of doorway, not quite halfway down the picture, appeared a card, enlarged upon the sheet to vast dimensions, upon which was lettered in black the word ENTER.

Anthony said: "Pike, you're looking at what is technically called a close-up of the front doorway of Number 14 Brabazon Road, South Kensington. That thing at the top is the base of the KJB signboard. Although the angle of the picture indicates that the camera was higher than its subject, it looks as if it had been close. Actually, however, it was in a first-floor window of Number 11 on the other side of the street—with a special telescopic lens on it——"

He broke off. There had come a sudden darkening of the picture and for an instant the little scene had been blotted out by a dark mass which had appeared on the left-hand side and then swept over. But at once the mass moved and diminished as it went away from the camera. It was the back of a man in the cap and high-collared coat of a chauffeur. The back vanished into the doorway and was swallowed up in the dark maw.

A flicker . . . and then, this time coming out of the dark mouth of the doorway, a figure again. The same figure, this time viewed from the front. The chauffeur's cap was at a jaunty angle. The bright buttons on the dark uniform coat glinted in the sunshine. Every feature of the clean-shaven, square-cut, hard yet youthful face was absolutely clear. The figure halted for a moment. The thin lips pursed themselves into what must have been a jaunty whistling and then hands were raised while big gauntleted gloves were drawn onto them. Then, giantlike, the figure surged forward. . . . The head was lost, the coat filled the screen. . . . Once more the doorway was untenanted. . . .

"Stop!" said Anthony over his shoulder.

139

A whirring and a click. The blade of light from the projector was cut off. Another click and the centre lights of the room went up.

Anthony looked at Flood.

Flood turned over the pages of a small red notebook in his hand. He read:

"Fourth October—that's yesterday. Ten forty-one A.M. Second visitor. Drove up in Rolls-Royce saloon, Number GW-8439Y. Time between entering and departing—seven minutes. Unable to follow owing to car. Car belongs to Lord Charles Montfort, 34 Lennox Street and Bickleigh Towers, Hertfordshire. Chauffeur's name Thompson. Been in service with Montfort four months. Finish."

Pike grunted.

"Right!" said Anthony over his shoulder.

Once more the centre lights went out and, following the whirring noise, the beam of the projector came again and once more the doorway was upon the screen.

The next figure, which showed first back and then face, was a woman. She was fat and middle aged and dressed, with a certain neatness, in the manner of a past decade of domestic service. Once more, at Anthony's order, the film was stopped and the room lights came on. Once more Flood read from his little book. He said:

"Yesterday again. . . . In fact, all these are yesterday's because today's won't be developed in time. . . . Third visitor. Eleven-three A.M. Time between entering and departing fifteen minutes. Not chosen as suitable for following."

"Right!" said Anthony again, over his shoulder. . . .

This time it was a nursemaid clothed in a uniform which seemed to be not quite large enough for her. The back was enormous, the face almost nauseatingly maternal. . . . Flood read:

"Fourth visitor. Eleven-thirty A.M. Time between entering and departing—seven minutes. Followed. She was alone. Walked back to Emperor's Gate and took a bus to corner of Morden Gardens and Fulham Road. Entered Number 9 Morden Gardens by servants' entrance. Ascertained to be nursemaid to the three children of Mrs. Charles Frampton. Been in place for seven months. No known prospect of leaving."

The next was a girl as small and trim as the last occupant of the screen had been stout and untidy. She was bareheaded and wore a dark coat which covered the white apron and black clothes of the parlourmaid. ...

Flood read: "Fifth visitor. Twelve-five P.M. Time between entering and departing, nine minutes. Followed. Walked round the corner into Emperor's Gate and entered Number 98. Ascertained to be parlourmaid in household of Count Feralli. Been in place for two months. No known prospect of leaving."

"Right!" said Anthony again ... and the process went on.

2

It was over. The library was normal again and the sheet taken down and the little man and the projector gone.

Pike said, speaking for the first time since the film had come to an end:

"That's very interesting, sir." He looked at Anthony with puzzled eyes: "But I must confess I don't see where it gets us. Particularly as I understand Mr. Garrett hasn't seen the pictures."

Anthony said: "He'll see them tomorrow."

"And you think ..." Pike began.

Anthony interrupted. "No. I'd bet that he won't recognize any of these backs."

"Oh!" said Pike and then, in a tone frankly bewildered, "Then I *don't* see what you're driving at, sir. I suppose the pictures might be useful—but only if we ever got to the point where we could *act* in regard to KJB. And we're a long way off that."

Anthony said: "Consider, Pike, and you'll find that those pictures *do* advance our knowledge." He looked at Flood. "Correct me if I go wrong. ... Yesterday there visited KJB thirteen persons. Four of these were in uniform and all of these four were followed and/or inquired into. In all cases we find that the persons are in good work, are not under notice and have not given notice. Four out of thirteen ... let's see ... that's over thirty per cent. Now I maintain that if KJB were only the respectable little business which it proclaims itself it would be impossible for it to have, in one day, thirty per cent of uniformed visitors *not* wanting jobs." He looked at Flood. "For further information we will apply to Agent X-13. He will tell us what happened today; the pictures won't be ready until tomorrow."

Flood grinned. He looked at Pike with a twinkle in his eyes. He said:

"I've got the details up to two-thirty this afternoon." He put a hand to his pocket and brought the little red notebook out again and opened it. "From nine forty-five this morning until two-thirty this afternoon there were fourteen visitors, seven of 'em in uniform."

"Fifty per cent today," said Anthony.

Flood said: "We followed four but missed t'others. They overlapped, you see. The four were a couple of parlourmaidish sorts, a footman——"

Anthony interrupted. "Footman?"

Flood said: "Something of the sort. Had a soft hat and light overcoat, but underneath a livery suit with metal buttons. You'll see tomorrow."

"Go on," said Anthony.

"And the fourth was another nursemaid. She had a perambulator, with a kid in it. I did her. Works in Number 17 Pierpont Gardens, South Kensington. Name's Jessie Brice. Very popular with the other servants. Been in the place six months and no one's heard anything about her leaving."

"Next?" said Anthony.

Flood said: "I only did one. Dyson had the others. Mine was the man. Works for Sir Harry Goodenough—that's the big steel man. Been in the place two months. Seems set. No discoverable question of him leaving.... Now Dyson's two women. One was a Fulham job—cook. The other was lady's maid to Nona Moon. Both been at the jobs three months. No talk of going."

Anthony looked at Pike. "So there!" he said. "On two ordinary days over forty per cent of the visitors to KJB are uniformed, in work and seem to have no prospect of being out of work. Why, then, do they go there? Normally servants only visit agencies to get jobs! When they're in work they try and forget the agency, often to the point of forgetting to pay."

Pike rubbed reflectively at his lower jaw. "Yes sir. Put like that, it's odd." He spoke slowly. "But it still doesn't get us anywhere. All we can say is, as I see it, that it's another queer thing to add to our list of queer things about

KJB. It certainly doesn't give what I think we want—something we can take action on."

Anthony smiled. "Wait, Pike, wait!"

Pike pulled down one side of his mouth in a half-rueful smile. He said: "You're up to something, sir, I can see that. I suppose you can't tell me what it is."

"God forbid!" said Anthony. "You're too respectable. And you're paid to uphold the law as she is rather than as she ought to be."

"Antiquated," said Flood and shook his head solemnly. "Antiquated."

Pike glared at him. "As for you, you've probably broken the law a dozen times in the last six hours on these inquiries. And as for your friend Dyson——"

"Messrs. Flood and Dyson," said Flood with dignity, "are citizens of unimpeachable virtue. You're referring to two mechanics from the gas company."

Pike looked at Anthony again. "So you won't tell me what you're up to, sir."

Anthony said: "You wouldn't countenance it. And the commissioner would have a fit. Into your private ear, though, I'll whisper two little words. French words. Agents provocateurs!"

CHAPTER XV

At 10:30 A.M. on the morning of Friday, the seventh of October, Miss Rose Parfitt was being taxi-borne from the heights of St. John's Wood towards Waterloo Station. Upon Miss Parfitt's round and homely face was a broad smile like that of a child suddenly elated by an unexpected treat. In Miss Parfitt's bag was a five-pound note which she had not earned and beside the driver of the taxi was Miss Parfitt's trunk of yellow tin. Miss Parfitt was entering upon an unexpected and therefore doubly delightful holiday.

At 10:45 A.M. Miss Ada Brent entered the vestibule of Lords' Mansions, St. John's Wood. Behind her trailed a taxi driver bearing a trunk which might have been sister to that of Rose Parfitt. Miss Ada Brent was of an age somewhere between twenty-five and thirty. She was of good figure and pretty, with a rather lavishly powdered face. She was neatly but soberly dressed in black.

Miss Brent had a few words with the commissionaire, who then superintended the setting down of Miss Brent's trunk and watched Miss Brent with approving eye while she paid the taxi driver.

"Fourteen A, is it?" said Miss Brent and made play with her large dark eyes.

The commissionaire said that it was 14A; that Miss . . . ?

"Brent," said Miss Brent and smiled.

"Ah!" said the commissionaire boldly and in military fashion twirled his fierce moustache and smiled. "Mine's Stubbs. Sergeant Stubbs. Eric Stubbs."

Miss Brent smiled, showing pretty teeth between very red lips.

144

"You'll see to my box then?" said Miss Brent and was assured and got herself to the lift and was raised rapidly to the sixth floor.

2

"I don't think you'll find it a hard place," said Mrs. Bellingham. "The man at the agency spoke very highly of you and, judging by your references, I think we'll suit each other admirably." She smiled. "I consider myself very lucky to get you on such short notice."

"Yes madam," said Miss Brent and allowed herself a civil answering smile which did not touch her eyes. "Thank you, madam."

She was then shown her room and made acquainted with her duties. She superintended the arrival of her trunk and in a space of time remarkably short was busy about her new employment, neatly and becomingly clad in black serge and white linen. . . .

She proved deft and quick and efficient and automatically courteous. She was even a good cook when occasion arose. She was, in fact, a far better servant in every way than the holiday-making Miss Parfitt. But, to a remarkable and sometimes almost abashing degree, she "knew her place." Round-faced Miss Parfitt made friends with her employers where she could and where she could not was unhappy and left them. Not so Miss Ada Brent, who never spoke unless she were spoken to and then from the wooden and soulless visage of the copybook servant. . . .

3

At seven o'clock upon the morning of the third day of her employment Miss Ada Brent switched off the bell of her alarm clock, got herself out of bed, bathed herself, dressed herself and set, with exemplary dispatch and efficiency, about her labours. By half-past eight the flat, except for the bedroom of her mistress, was ready to face the day. At nine o'clock punctually Miss Brent knocked upon her mistress's door and was bidden to enter and did so, bearing with her a tray upon which were coffee and croissants and a morning paper. . . .

Two hours later Miss Brent closed the front door behind her mistress. She was happy in the knowledge that her work was done; that her mistress would not be returning until after dinner; that she was not to wait up; that there was little chance of any of these arrangements going wrong; that all she had to do in the way of labour was to answer the telephone.

Miss Brent walked demurely along the narrow little passage and into her gleaming kitchen and sat down with her hands folded in her lap. Her face was masklike as ever. Upon a shelf over the stove, where Miss Brent could see it without turning her head, was a clock. There was silence in the flat and Miss Brent remained motionless and the minute hand of the clock moved with steady imperceptibility....

It reached fifteen minutes past eleven—and a change came over Miss Brent. She always allowed a quarter of an hour, and now this one had flown. She rose and plucked the cap from her head and threw it onto the table and ran her hands through her charming mane of black hair and, whistling cleverly a melody of the moment, passed out of the kitchen and down the passage and into the drawing room. From a silver box upon the mantelshelf she took a cigarette. Lighting it, she wandered out of this room and into the dining room. Here, from a decanter and siphon upon the sideboard, she helped herself to a whiskey and soda. Glass in one hand, cigarette in the other, she sauntered back into the drawing room and sat herself down by the telephone and crossed admirably stockinged legs and lifted the receiver and worked the dial. She said after due pause:

"Harry in? ... Well, wake him up.... Tell him it's Miss Brent.... Don't bloody well argue with me; you don't know who you're talking to...." She scowled at the telephone; then smiled; then alternately sipped and smoked and composed herself to wait.

The telephone cackled.

"That you, sweetie?" said Miss Brent. "Listen, the bitch is out. The whiskey's good. I might be persuaded, if you promise *not* to behave like a gentleman, to ask you up for a visit this afternoon...."

The telephone cackled excitedly.

"Listen!" said Miss Brent. "Cut that out! Until this afternoon! *Then* tell it to me!"

The telephone cackled, less exuberantly.

"No, I can't," said Miss Brent firmly. "No. You come at two-thirty—and not a minute sooner. . . . Yes, of course I've done my work. That's nothing to do with it. . . . Now listen, baby! Either you come when I invite you or you don't come at all! You don't want to get me wild, do you? Two-thirty and not a minute before. . . . And *don't* use the lift; walk straight in and come up the stairs. . . . Fourteen A. . . . S'long, ducky! And keep yourself good till this afternoon. . . ."

Miss Brent slammed back the receiver. For a moment she sat staring in apparently pleasant contemplation at the telephone; then rose and threw the end of her cigarette into the fire and finished her drink.

Whistling again, she took her glass out into the kitchen, rinsed it beneath the tap, dried it and took it back to its proper place in the dining room. And then she ceased whistling and there came over her whole demeanour a sudden change. Where she had been deliberately and pleasurably idling, she now was brisk and definite. She walked back into the drawing room with a gait as different from her hip-swaying stroll of a minute before as it was from the quick-stepped, demure walk of her servitude. Now she moved with a long and free and purposeful stride.

She went directly to the small writing desk in the corner of the drawing room. She pulled out the chair before the desk and sat herself down and began to search, obviously with some definite object, in the pigeonholes of the desk. The contents of some pigeonholes she passed over after a cursory glance but those of others she took out and set upon the blotting pad and methodically examined. It was notable that when she had finished each examination and put the papers back everything was not only in its proper relation, but the whole bore exactly the same appearance as before she had disturbed it.

She finished the pigeonholes and sat back and glowered at the desk. She said aloud:

"God damn it!" And then, on a sudden note of excitement :"Oh, p'r'aps . . ."

She opened the blotter. It was a parchment-bound thing of some sixty or seventy sheets and in the middle was what she sought—the letter over which her mistress had seemed to be so busy upon the night before but which, every indication had told Miss Brent, had not been completed.

And here it was! Seven sheets of it! And stopped in mid-paragraph. . . .

"*Bloody* fool!" said Miss Brent with ineffable scorn.

She began to read. Her eyebrows raised themselves after the first five lines of reading and when the avid eyes had devoured every line of the closely written pages she sat back in her chair and blew out her cheeks and there came from her pursed red lips a long subdued whistle of astonishment.

"And if that's not *hot!*" said Miss Brent.

4

It was on Tuesday, the eleventh of October—two days, that is, after Miss Brent had read the half-finished letter which had so much astonished her—that Mrs. Bellingham's maid answered a ring from the front doorbell, held colloquy with the ringer and then sought her mistress in the drawing room.

"If you please, madam?" said Miss Ada Brent.

Mrs. Bellingham set down her book. "Yes, Brent?"

"A man's called, madam. He says he wants to see you on very important business."

Mrs. Bellingham frowned. "See me? On important business?" She thought for a moment; then shook her head. "Did he give his name?"

"Yes madam. Jenks, madam."

"Jenks?" Mrs. Bellingham smiled. "I don't know anybody called Jenks, Brent."

"He said, madam, that I was to tell you that the business was very, very important."

Mrs. Bellingham shrugged her shoulders. "Possibly wants to sell me something. Tell him to go away, Brent. . . . Half a minute! What does he look like?"

Miss Ada Brent considered for a moment; then gave a ghost of a sniff; then said:

"Ordinary, madam. . . . Excuse me, madam, but I don't think he'll go away. I tried to tell him you couldn't see him unless he'd state his business. But he was very—well, insistent!"

Mrs. Bellingham made a gesture of irritation. "All right, Brent. All right, show him in."

"In here, madam?"

"Yes, yes." Mrs. Bellingham stood and closed her book and put it down upon a table and waited, facing the door.

The door opened. Miss Ada Brent came through it first and held it open and looked, with a sort of expressionless disapproval, at the figure which followed her. When it was well into the room she closed the door and could be heard walking back towards her kitchen.

Mrs. Bellingham faced her visitor. She saw a small man of indeterminate age whose clothes were as undistinguished as his appearance. He looked, indeed, like any lower-grade clerk beside whom one sits in bus or tube; but Mrs. Bellingham had observant eyes and saw, after a moment of scrutiny, that there emerged two peculiarities from this molecule of the ordinary: first, that the head, thinly covered with sparse sandy hair, was very large for the meagre body; second, that this head was carried with a peculiar sideways tilt which seemed to enable its owner to study faces without meeting the eyes in them with his own.

He carried a faintly dusty-looking bowler hat in his left hand and underneath his left arm was held, clamped to his side, a thin buff envelope of the largest size.

"Well," said Mrs. Bellingham, who stood with her back to the light which streamed from the four windows at the end of the pretty room.

The visitor bowed with a little sideways ducking of his head. He said:

"Mrs. Bellingham, I believe?"

Mrs. Bellingham inclined her head.

"My name is Jenks," said the visitor. His voice was in keeping with his appearance: flat, monotonous and flavoured strongly with the pinched vowels and strident inflections of the City.

Mrs. Bellingham appeared to be studying him. "Yes, Mr. . . . Jenks? And what do you want?"

Mr. Jenks coughed. He murmured: "With your permission," and laid his hat, with a gesture which told of its worth to him, upon the arm of a chair. He took the envelope from beneath his arm and held it in both hands before him. He said:

149

"I represent a firm of—er—photographers, Mrs. Bellingham." He took two small steps towards her, still holding the envelope in both hands. His head seemed to be carried more than ever to one side and it looked, suddenly, monstrously large. It seemed to Mrs. Bellingham, who had difficulty in not recoiling, that suddenly he was reptilian.

"I am not interested in photography," said Mrs. Bellingham sharply. "I'm afraid you're wasting your time!"

The large head of the visitor was shaken from side to side; an unpleasing gesture as it remained tilted the whole time. He said:

"I think you will be interested in these photographs, Mrs. Bellingham."

He undid the clipped flap of the envelope and withdrew from it, slowly, two large square pieces of what appeared to Mrs. Bellingham, who could only see their backs, to be thin sheets of pasteboard.

He was now standing very close to her, after an advance which had been somehow imperceptible; and Mrs. Bellingham did now, indeed, step back. She said, more sharply still and on a higher note:

"I don't know what you're talking about. And I don't like your manners. Please go."

Mr. Jenks advanced again, this time with an open step. It became patent to Mrs. Bellingham, all at once, that his face was not ordinary as it had at first seemed, but was vulpine—and with a peculiarly dead-white skin. He said:

"I'm not guessing, Mrs. Bellingham. I *know* that you'll be interested in these photographs which my firm has taken." He suddenly turned the pasteboard sheets so that the face of the top one was beneath Mrs. Bellingham's eye.

She saw that the foremost sheet was glossy and that it contained what were apparently reproductions of two photographs, one higher than the other, of line upon line of a script which was familiar to her.

"Recognize the writing, eh?" said Mr. Jenks and held his hand higher.

Mrs. Bellingham did recognize the writing, and for the best of reasons. Her eyes widened and she drew in her breath with a sharp hiss. Her hand shot out but Mr. Jenks, with the air and balance of one playing a familiar game, put the things behind his back.

"No!" said Mr. Jenks. "That's naughty now!" ...

5

Upon the following day, Wednesday, Mr. Jenks was again in the drawing room of Mrs. Bellingham and talking with its owner. He noted, with businesslike satisfaction, that Mrs. Bellingham seemed of the pallor appropriate to the interview and that the hand which kept raising the cigarette holder to her mouth was trembling.

Mr. Jenks laid his hat, this time without request for permission, in the same place that he had set it yesterday and from beneath his left arm, with yesterday's gesture, took a large envelope. He looked at Mrs. Bellingham and did not bow. He said with a most unpleasing affectation of heartiness:

"Good morning, good morning! And how are we this morning! Good girl, eh?"

Mrs. Bellingham did not speak. She was staring at him as if he were indeed a reptile. She continued to stare while Mr. Jenks went through curious evolutions which had not been part of yesterday's programme. He went past Mrs. Bellingham to the windows behind her and lifted each of the four long curtains which hung in folds beside every window. He peered behind each and dropped it and at last was satisfied. He went back to the centre of the room and stood, his big head more on one side than ever, while his eyes darted glances this way and that about the room. He crossed the big sofa which stood diagonally athwart a corner and peered behind and underneath it. Satisfied again, he rose and, humming, crossed to the door and opened it and looked out.

He came back to take up his stand again before Mrs. Bellingham. He said, still with the noxious simulation of heartiness:

"Well, everything's nice and aboveboard! Glad to see you're a good girl.... Now then, let's get down to business!" He took the envelope from beneath his arm and opened it and took out the two prints which it contained. He said:

"Now then. I hope you remember what I told you yes-

151

terday. My principal's very particular about these things and never likes to handle checks—so if you'll just give me the money I'll hand over these!" He waved the prints in his right hand with a horridly jocular little movement.

Mrs. Bellingham was holding, tightly clenched in her left hand, a silk bag. Now she undid this and slowly produced from it a thick packet of treasury notes bound with an elastic band. She kept her eyes fixed, with a wide stare of fear and horror, upon the tilted face of Mr. Jenks. She made a motion as if to give him the packet; then snatched her hand back. She said, in a voice which was very different from the voice which she had used upon his first appearance:

"You're sure it's all right if I give you this two hundred now and you give me those prints——" She broke off, her throat working.

Her visitor said: "That's perfectly right. Then in thirty days from now I'll 'ave the pleasure of calling upon you again with the next lot of prints. Then you'll pay me for those ... and so on, through all five prints, until we reach the sixth payment—which, you mustn't forget, is double, Mrs. B.—and *then* you get the negatives!"

Mrs. Bellingham opened her mouth as if to speak but no words came from it. Her tongue came out and moistened her lips and she tried again. She said at last:

"But—but—suppose I *can't* pay every time."

Mr. Jenks raised a monitory finger. He said:

"Now, now! We went into all that yestiddy. Business, Mrs. B., is business! You pay for these photographs on the date we arrange. If you don't ..." Mr. Jenks paused. For a moment his head straightened from its usual tilt and he looked squarely into Mrs. Bellingham's blue eyes. He said: "If you don't ... *then*, business being business, my principal will be reluctantly forced to send copies of these photographs to—well, you know who...."

Mrs. Bellingham gasped. She said in a high-pitched voice:

"All right! All right! Now take this and give me those. Take it, I tell you, and give those to me!"

With his left hand Mr. Jenks took the packet of notes but with his right he held the photographs behind him. He said:

"Now don't be alarmed, you're going to have these,

152

Mrs. B., but, business being business, I must count this little lot first."

He turned and went to the writing table at the far side of the room and set down the photographs and put the packet of notes on top of them and flicked it over with a rapid, practised forefinger.

Mrs. Bellingham stood where she was, staring across at him.

Mr. Jenks finished counting and got to his feet. He picked up the packet of notes and put them in a pocket and buttoned his shapeless coat firmly about him. He picked up the photographs and walked back across the room to Mrs. Bellingham and held them out to her and she took them in a slow and doubtful hand. He stepped back. He said:

"There you are! All square and aboveboard! You pay, we deliver the goods!"

Mrs. Bellingham stared down at the sheets of pasteboard in her hand. Without looking up she said in a voice so low as to be almost a whisper:

"Go! Please go!"

"Certainly!" said Mr. Jenks. "Certainly!" He stood for a moment regarding her, with his left cheek almost touching his shoulder; then turned on his heel and went across the room and picked up his hat and marched towards the door. Just before he reached it he turned again. He raised his voice and said:

"Don't forget, Mrs. B., I'll be around to see you again on the twelfth of next month."

Mrs. Bellingham did not answer.

Mr. Jenks turned, with his hand outstretched to open the door.

But it was opened for him. Mr. Jenks took three quick little gliding steps backwards and stood, staring, as if his feet were clamped to the floor. . . .

Mrs. Bellingham sat upon the arm of a chair and lit a cigarette.

Three men came through the open door towards him. One was a large and ponderous person in clothes which were very plain. One was a smaller, brisk young man with an air of authority and an excellent, if sober, taste in dress. One was a less emphatic edition of the first and carried with some ostentation a pencil and a reporter's note-book.

A sound came from the mouth of Mr. Jenks but it was not a word.

The second and authoritative young man walked smart-ly up to Mr. Jenks and tapped him on the shoulder. He said:

"I have a warrant here for your arrest upon a charge of blackmail."

CHAPTER XVI

Although only early afternoon, all the curtains of the library of 19A Stukeley Gardens were drawn and over the bookcase at the far end from the french windows there once more hung the sheet which served as cinematograph screen. In the shadows a small bald-headed man was packing tripod and projector into their neat containers.

Sheldon Garrett frowned at the now blank whiteness of the sheet. He was pale with the pallor of one who has spent recent days upon a sickbed and in the thinness of his face new lines seemed to have etched themselves deeply. He shook his head and a small sound came from his lips. Avis Bellingham, beside him, put an unobtrusive hand upon his arm. He turned his head and looked at her but did not speak.

The operator left the room, a black case in each hand. The door closed behind him; to be immediately opened again by their host, who surveyed them upon their chairs with amusement.

"You look," he said, "like two children in the ninepennies."

Garrett did not smile. He said:

"Even in dime seats one ought to get something for the money."

Anthony looked at him. "Meaning that you're no forrader. You didn't expect to be, did you?"

Garrett lifted his shoulders.

Avis said: "You've seen it four times, Tom. If the woman *had* been there you'd have recognized her at once. So——"

Garrett said: "I know, I know! I'm just a goddam fool!"

Anthony said: "I've come to cheer you." He put a hand to his breast pocket and brought it away holding a thin packet of neatly folded quarto sheets. "You might like to read this. Possible cure for those Bayswater Blues." He put the sheets into Garrett's hand. He said:

"Copy of letter to Lucas, delivered at noon. But before you read it the time has come, the sleuthhound said, to tell you many things—the first being that I am now in a position to report that, beyond the flock of social and friendly inquiries for you at Travers Hoylake's nursing home, where you're still supposed to be, there have been four anonymous telephone calls—in each case in a man's voice and emanating from various untraceable call boxes. Second, a young woman called in person this afternoon— a mysterious beauty of whom you will hear more in our next thrilling instalment. Further, you will doubtless be glad to hear that the police have at last succeeded in attaching a line to the elusive Mrs. Bellows, aunt to Janet Murch. . . ."

Garrett got to his feet. A wide smile took many of the new lines from his face. He said:

"Where is she? Have they got anything out of her? Does she know where Murch is? I always knew that if— —"

Anthony smiled. "All zeal, Mr. Easy! Hold your horses. So far they only have one end of the line on the old lady, the end that begins in St. Pancras; the other appears to be in a little Midlothian village called Brodie; we shall know for certain by this evening." He pointed to the sheets in Garrett's hands. "Now get to it." He wandered across to the writing table and sat upon its edge and lit a cigarette.

Avis Bellingham moved closer to Garrett. She looked over his shoulder and with him read:

My DEAR LUCAS: This for your files. It is a condensed record of my recent nefarious (and, of course, unsanctioned) activities in the matter of the KJB Domestic Agency and of the steps which today led to the arrest of Arthur Jenks or Smithers, Eustace Hines and Bella Barnes. With the kind and courageous co-operation of Mrs. George Bellingham the following series of events was brought about:

1. Mrs. Bellingham gave her maid a holiday.

2. Mrs. Bellingham informed the KJB Agency that she was without a maid and ordered another immediately.

3. Having been supplied with one (Ada Brent), Mrs. Bellingham, soon enough after Brent's employment, copied out—as if it were original—a letter drafted by me purporting to be for no less a person than Lord——,[1] who is actually an acquaintance of hers and therefore (if any suspicion were aroused in the KJ Bosoms) would not look like a trap. (This letter, had it been genuine, would have been the very apotheosis of blackmailing tools, consisting as it did of nearly a thousand words of red-hot and by no means soulful passion.)

4. Having given Brent ample opportunity to find this letter, Mrs. Bellingham informed me, whereupon I had Brent's movements carefully checked, finding that she visited KJB in the evening, on Monday, the tenth instant, after closing hours. She was admitted and remained in the house for twenty minutes.

5. On the morning of Tuesday, the eleventh instant, Mrs. Bellingham was visited by a man giving the name of Jenks. He did not tell her from whom he came but proceeded to blackmail her by selling to her a photostatic copy of the letter mentioned above. Mrs. Bellingham, admirably simulating a thoroughly blackmailable woman, was then blackmailed—by instalments, as it were—Mr. Jenks arranging to call for the money on the morrow.

6. Having made the above arrangements, Mrs. Bellingham notified me and I in turn got in touch with Pike.

7. This morning, acting on my advice, Mrs. Bellingham sent Ada Brent out upon an errand which would take her a couple of hours—and when Mr. Jenks called to receive his first payment he was overheard by means of a dictaphone and subsequently arrested by Detective Sergeant Sharples.

8. Brent returned to Lords' Mansions at exactly the moment when Jenks was being brought out in custody. She was in a taxi; she was seen and recognized by Detective Officer Manners, who had had the job of following her

---

[1] For obvious reasons this illustrious name has to be omitted from the text.

before. I also saw her, having just arrived at Lords'
Mansions myself to fetch Mrs. Bellingham. Brent did
not get out of the taxi. Neither Manners nor myself
gave any indication of having seen her. She has, naturally enough, not returned to Mrs. Bellingham's, but she
has been followed. Dyson was with me and, obtaining
another taxi, managed to keep hers in sight.

I should also put it on record that I have asked you,
and you have agreed, not to take any steps to arrest Ada
Brent but to have her watched. I understand that one of
Pike's men relieved Dyson shortly after noon and that,
therefore, we can assume that Brent will be kept under
continual observation.

And there, with an initialled signature, the letter ended.
But Garrett, even after he had read it, remained with gaze
down bent upon the last page. Avis eyed him with concern, for his pallor had given way to a dull red flush
spreading from collar to forehead. She saw his eyes close
and a little grimace which told of pain distort his face. She
said something and moved closer to him but he held her
off with outstretched hand as he looked at Anthony with
furious eyes. He said:

"Take a bit too much on your own shoulders, don't
you?"

"Why, Tom!" said Avis in astounded dismay.

Anthony said quietly: "Don't know what you mean."

Garrett's lips drew back a little from his teeth. "Just
this: you might've got Avis hurt by these bastards! That's
all! I suppose you didn't think of that! Next time try your
tricks with a policewoman or some of your own family!"

"*Tom!*" said Avis Bellingham; and then was silent at a
sign from Anthony, who said:

"Take it easy, Garrett. And get it straight." His tone
was sober but free from anger or even tension. "You think
I put Avis in danger because——"

Garrett interrupted, taking a step nearer to Anthony.
His voice was harsh and his words came fast. "I know you
put Avis in danger! Didn't these gorillas try and get me?
Hadn't they been following me? Wasn't it likely they'd
seen me with Avis and checked up on her? And then you
go and get her to hire a maid through them to work a
trap! Don't you see, they might've got onto it and——"

"Shut up!" said Anthony with a sudden force that made Avis jump.

Garrett glared but was silent. Unconsciously he put a hand up to his head.

"Listen," said Anthony in ordinary tone. "It *was* possible that they might connect Avis with you—*but,* if they did, all they had to do was to refuse the bait. *And* it was only a maid she engaged. *And* Dyson and Flood were in the next flat, always one of 'em there, all the time——"

"Anthony!" said Avis Bellingham. "You didn't tell me that!"

"*And,*" said Anthony, ignoring her, "the minute KJB took the bait it was perfectly certain that Avis wasn't in danger." He grinned suddenly. "So be good."

Garrett sat down suddenly upon the back of a chair. His hand was still at his head. He said after a moment:

"You're right. And I'm what's known as a B.F. Sorry, Gethryn."

Avis frowned upon him. "You ought to be ashamed of yourself, Tom!"

"Head hurts," he said. "Very pathetic case."

She smiled at him then and pulled round another chair and made him sit in it and perched herself upon its arm. He looked his thanks and spoke to Anthony. He said.

"Have to hand it to you. You're an ingenious devil!"

Anthony touched his forehead. "Thank 'ee kindly, sir.'

"We oughtn't to be long now," said Garrett. "Ought we?"

Anthony lifted his shoulders. "Quien sabe?"

"What I'm thinking," said Avis suddenly, "is how sorry I am for all the poor people who've really been blackmailed. Just think what they'll go through when this case comes on!"

Anthony shook his head. "Not nearly as much as you think. We have a habit of conducting trials for blackmail without publishing the names of the blackmailees; and another habit—carried as far as is possible—of legally forgetting the errors of the blackmailees. I'll hazard a guess that the only real mud stirred up will be for Jenks and Company." He stood up. "And now, children, I leave you "

Avis looked at him. "Wait a minute! Why do we have to wait for that second instalment about the beautiful visitor at the nursing home?"

Anthony smiled at her. "Because I belong to the Detective's Union; motto: Never tell."

Avis did not smile. She said: "Well, I think it's horrid of you!" Her gaze flickered for a moment towards Garrett.

Anthony said: "Among my nobler qualities, however, is that of admitting when I'm wrong. I will now, therefore, tell you that the beautiful unknown who called at noon today at the nursing home and inquired after the progress of Mr. Thomas Sheldon Garrett was none other than Miss Ada Brent!"

They stared at him wide eyed.

"And what d'you know about *that!*" said Garrett after a pause. "What's it mean, anyway?"

Anthony walked towards the door. "God knows," he said, "and *He* won't split."

2

There was silence in the room of Sir Egbert Lucas. Lucas looked at Pike; Pike at Lucas. They did not speak. A telephone bell rang and Lucas with impatient gesture picked up the receiver. He said after a moment:

"Send him in."

Pike looked inquiry and was answered by an affirmative nod. They waited.

The door opened and through it came the long and elegant person of Colonel Anthony Gethryn. He sat upon the arm of a chair and looked from one frowning face to the other. He said:

"Problem picture. After John Collier. Police, what ails you?"

"Cheerful, aren't you?" Lucas was sour.

"Why not? Our affair marches. Or doesn't it?"

"*Marches!*" said Lucas and barked a laugh without mirth.

"Obstacles," said Anthony, offensively oracular, "are made to be overcome."

Lucas looked at him. "Oh, quite! And all is for the best in this best of all possible worlds! And so on ad infinitum and ad nauseam! What you think you're——"

Anthony interrupted. "Whoa! And tell me why woe there is."

"Pike will," said Lucas, and fell to drawing horses' heads.

Pike cleared his throat. "What Sir Egbert means," he said, "is that we've come to what you might call a dead end; a blind alley, as you might say."

Anthony said: "Might, but won't. Elucidate."

"Try French," said Lucas with bitterness. "Cul-de-sac, Gethryn!"

"Irritable," said Anthony. "Peevish. Snaps. Refuses food. A pinch of sulphur in the drinking water works wonders." He looked at Pike. "Am I seriously to understand that you can't make a case against KJB and Company? After all the trouble I've taken?"

Pike stared, "Oh, *that's* all right, sir! Our trouble is that, after netting this lot, we can't get any further with what I might call the Murch affair."

Anthony stood up. Once more he looked from one to the other of the two men. He said:

"History in the making. Tableau Number 14, English Policemen at Last Interested in Shutting Stable Doors...."

"Shut up!" said Lucas savagely.

Anthony sat down. "Sorry. Seriously, though, what's the matter? Won't any of the birds sing?"

The point of Lucas' pencil broke and he threw it down on his desk with a little clatter. "That's just it!" he said. "Damn you, Gethryn: you get us all stewed up about this case and just when it begins to be interesting we're forced back to where we started."

"No," said Anthony. "No. At the beginning of the case it wasn't a case at all." Once more he looked at Pike. "What did Hines say?"

Lucas answered him. "Nothing. Wouldn't make a statement; insisted on getting his solicitors first. And the solicitors, my lad, are none other than Dunkle and Abrahams. And Hines is getting Dunkle himself!"[2]

Anthony whistled. "And Jenks? No statement from him?"

Pike said: "A long one, sir. But——"

[2] For many years this firm of lawyers has been a thorn in the flesh of English justice: and they do not act for petty evildoers.

"All hot air," said Lucas. "Two thousand words meaning abracadabra."

Anthony pulled at his lower lip. "H'mm! What about the office girl—Barnes?"

Pike shook his head. "Nothing, sir. For the very good reason that she doesn't know anything."

Lucas looked at Anthony. "Pike's dead sure of that. He wants to let her go; but I think we'd better have her up and then get her remanded."

"That young woman, sir, has no more to do with any crooked business than—than the Archbishop of Canterbury." Pike's tone was resolute.

Anthony said: "Pike knows."

Lucas said: "If I let her go I'll put a man on her." He scribbled a line or two on a memorandum form and pressed a bell and gave it to the secretary who came in answer. Pike smiled at Anthony.

The secretary went and there was silence in the room for a long moment.

"I sometimes long," said Lucas meditatively, "for the—ah—wider questioning powers of my American colleagues."

Anthony grinned. "I'd love to see you giving Master Smithers-Jenks what I believe is known as the 'works.' I can see it all. Scene One: An Underground Cell in Scotland Yard. Characters: Police Captain Egg Lucas; Snipe Jenks. Uniforms by Office of Works. The piece of hose piping used in this scene supplied by Messrs. Dunlop."

Pike, shocked, studied the shining toecaps of his boots.

"But why the despair?" said Anthony. "You've had plenty of prisoners who wouldn't talk at first. They will later—after we've got on to Mother Bellows and——"

Lucas interrupted. "Show him that wire, Pike."

Pike got to his feet and crossed to Lucas' table and took from a tray upon it a pink telegraph form. In silence, his long face seeming more lantern shaped than ever, he handed these to Anthony.

Anthony read:

A.C.I. SCOTLAND YARD—LONDON | NO TRACE ANYONE BY NAME BELLOWS IN BRODIE STOP NO RESIDENT THERE THAT NAME AND SO FAR NO RECORD ANY RESIDENT HAVING CONNECTION THAT NAME STOP IN CIRCUMSTANCES YOUR DE-

"H'mm!" said Anthony and again pulled at his lower
lip.

"And now," said Lucas with relish, "to quote a line
from your friend Sheldon Garrett's play: 'How do you
like them onions?' "

Anthony shook his head. "Not so well. What've you
done?"

Pike said: "Sent a man down to Iron Court to get the
fullest description we can. See if he can get a photograph;
all that. As soon as he gets back I'll send MacFarland another wire."

"You know what we *should* do." Lucas' tone was reflec-
tive. "Take in this Brent woman and see whether *she's* got
anything to say."

Anthony shook his head. "Not unless the third degree's
come to town. Listen, Lucas: that woman, imagining herself free, is the only chance we have to get something on
the Murch line quickly." He looked at Pike. "I hope to
God you've got a good man on her."

"The best I've got, sir."

Lucas said: "I still think we ought to take her in. How
do we know she'll lead us to anything? What she'll probably do——"

Anthony interrupted. "She's already done something,
Lucas. About a half-hour before your men took over from
Dyson our Miss Brent called at Travers Hoylake's nursing
home, asking for news of Garrett." He looked from Lucas
to Pike and back again. "You'd have got that from your
own men tonight but I thought I'd be first with the news."
He surveyed Lucas' expression with pleasure. "And how, if
I may ask you, do you like *them* onions?"

3

Miss Ada Brent, walking briskly, came out of the arcade of Knightsbridge station. She was first of the attenu-
ated little crowd which had left the same underground
train. Miss Brent turned to her right and, evenly maintain-

ing her pace, pursued her way. About ten yards behind her, separated from her by other pedestrians, came a man whose size and clothes, gait and features, colouring and manner were so ordinary as to render him—as indeed they had on many an eventful occasion—practically invisible.

Miss Brent bore, except in feature, no resemblance to the quondam maid of Mrs. George Bellingham. Admirably, though perhaps in some subtle details oversmartly, dressed in severely cut and laudably tailored clothes, she was a sight to give pleasure to the eye of any young man and to arouse hope in the breast of those of their elderly brethren who like their woman dominant. But, on this morning at least, Miss Brent did not so much as note the many glances cast at her. The V-shaped lines of a frown drew her slender brows together; the corners of her mouth were down turned and about her eyes was a fixed look telling of concentrated thought which was difficult or unpleasing or both. Miss Brent looked worried; could not, indeed, have looked more worried even had she known that, at the moment when she turned into Stukeley Gardens, she was the subject of a conversation then taking place in the office of the active head of the Criminal Investigation Department.

Miss Brent slackened her pace. So, behind her, did the apotheosis of the ordinary, Detective Officer C. D. Fields. Although melting, as it were, into the townscape and not by look or action deviating from his paradoxically intense normality, he kept his attention upon Miss Brent and neither saw nor noticed—as why should he?—that behind him, at a distance approximately equal to his own from Miss Brent, came another man. . . .

Miss Brent was looking at the numbers upon the stone pillars of the gateways. She came to Number 19A; hesitated; seemed for a moment about to pass—and then, with a squaring of her slim shoulders, set a hand to the latch of the gate, thrust it open and marched up the path leading to the steps and the front door.

4

It was a quarter to four in the afternoon when Miss Brent set her fingers to the doorbell of Anthony Gethryn's house.

Ten minutes earlier, in Lucas' office, Anthony had got to his feet and said:

"I'll be off. Pike, be a good fellah and call me if there's anything new. See you both in the morning."

"Where're you going?" Lucas' tone was not free of suspicion.

"Home," said Anthony and smiled. "Only home."

Pike said: "I'm sorry, sir. I was hoping you'd come with me to have a look around Hines's house and Jenks's place."

Anthony looked at him. "Haven't they been gone over yet?"

Pike said reproachfully: "You know me better than that, sir. Search warrants were out before one o'clock, and a couple of men have been in each place ever since. But I was going to go round now and see what they'd found. Or missed."

Lucas said: "I wish all the department were as keen on everything as Pike always is on your affairs."

Pike looked at Anthony: "You might as well come along, sir."

"I suppose," said Anthony, "I might."

And so it was that instead of reaching his house at the moment when Miss Ada Brent was talking to White, Anthony, with Pike beside him, was changing the whole course of this history by driving through Hyde Park on his way to the solemn wastes of Bayswater.

5

At ten minutes to four Avis Bellingham sat in the bay window of Lucia Gethryn's drawing room.

Lucia bent forward and laid a hand upon the arm of her friend. She said:

"Avis, I think that for an intelligent woman you're a perfect idiot. Why don't you tell him?"

"I can't!" said Avis Bellingham.

Lucia said almost angrily: "That's the most ridiculous thing I've ever heard!"

Avis shook her head. "No, it isn't. Don't you understand? It's a sort of new angle on the 'love me for myself alone' idea."

"But he doesn't *know!*"

"Exactly. But suppose I told him and then found that he

didn't—didn't——" Avis cut herself short. "What's the use of talking about it anyway!" She turned her head and looked out of the window and down across the front garden to the broad straight sweep of Stukeley Gardens.

Lucia said: "Listen to me! I think that if you don't tell——"

She was brought to an abrupt stop. The whole pleasing frame of Avis Bellingham had suddenly stiffened and now her right hand grasped Lucia's arm with fingers which dug painfully into the flesh.

Lucia said, staring: "What's the matter?"

Avis was looking straight down into the garden, her eyes wide with astonishment. She said as if to herself:

"It's—it's *impossible!* What on *earth . . .*" She stared fixedly down.

"What *is* it?" Lucia bent forward and herself looked down. She saw beneath her, walking slowly along the path from door to gate, the slim and smartly dressed figure of a woman. She said:

"Who is it? Tell me."

"My *God!*" said Avis and leapt to her feet and ran. She wrenched open the door with such force that the handle crashed against the inner wall. She ran for the stairs and started up them. As she ran she shouted breathlessly: "Tom! Tom!"

6

Not Anthony nor Pike nor the men who had been in each place before them found anything in the small shabby house of Mr. Hines or the soulless, cheap flat of Mr. Jenks which might not have been there and these places sheltered humdrum and law-abiding persons.

It is no matter for wonder, therefore, that Anthony, upon returning to Stukeley Gardens at a little after six-thirty, should revile with lurid and choicely patterned cursings the ill luck which had led him to miss the phenomenon of Miss Brent's visit to his house.

White, with discreetly composed face masking his admiration of what he afterwards described to friends as "No more an' no less than an epic", maintained discreet silence.

"And why the frostbitten hell," said Anthony, "nobody

had enough sense to try and get in touch with me immediately is more than I can understand."

White coughed: "Excuse me, sir, that was suggested, but after the mistress and Mr. Garrett and Mrs. Bellingham had read the note the young lady left, sir, the decision was took to wait till you returned."

"Note!" said Anthony. "Where's Mrs. Gethryn?"

"In the drawing room, sir," said White—and was alone, watching the long legs of his master take the first flight of stairs three at a time.

7

The note, written in a curiously small, neat script, said:

Dear Sir:
Knowing you are interested re Arthur Jenks and therefore re a great deal more which I could tell you about, I think you might find it worth your while for us to have a quiet talk. Shall give you a ring re this later.

A. Brent.

"My God!" said Anthony and looked from the face of his wife to the face of Avis Bellingham.

"What is it? What is it?" The two women spoke in unison. Dark eyes and blue searched Anthony's face.

"*Re!*" said Anthony.

His wife said: "Beast! I thought you'd found something."

Avis Bellingham said: "What does it *mean*, Anthony? Her coming here like that!"

Her host lifted his shoulders: "Search me!"

Lucia said: "Haven't you *any* idea?"

Anthony looked at her. "Plenty. Not tidy, though. Either of you women see her?"

Lucia laughed. "I should think we did. I thought Avis had gone mad. We were sitting on the window seat there——"

"Exchanging confidences," said Avis, "all girlish."

Lucia said: "And suddenly Avis grabbed my arm and pointed down into the garden. I didn't know who it was. I only saw a girl. But Avis went hurtling out of the room and up the stairs like a mad horse. . . ."

Avis said: "I went to get Tom. I dragged the poor boy out of bed and got him to the windows just in time to get a good look at the back of Miss Brent. I had an idea, you see, Anthony. I thought it was brilliant! I thought that perhaps——"

"Miss Brent might be alias Murch!" said Anthony and smiled at her. "You think, don't you?"

Avis shrugged with a disconsolate lifting of her shoulders. "Not to much avail. As far as Tom knows—Miss Brent is Miss Brent. Her back certainly isn't the back of either of the teashop women. Not a bit like, Tom said. He was almost cross with me."

"He was, was he!" said Anthony; then broke off as the door opened to admit a White who exhibited unwonted signals of excitement.

"Sir!" said White. "A young woman, sir. On the telephone, sir. Gave the name of Brent, sir. Seems to——"

He never finished his sentence. He saw, for the second time within a half-hour, how quickly his employer could move.

In 19A Stukeley Gardens there are several telephones but the nearest to the drawing room is upon the little table in the alcove at the foot of the stairs. It was, therefore, to this that Anthony ran. Above him, at the head of the flight, White and Lucia and Avis Bellingham crowded, listening unashamed. Anthony's voice came up to them clearly. They heard:

"Yes, speaking. . . . No: there's no nonsense—this is Anthony Gethryn. . . . Yes. . . . Yes. . . . They told me that you'd called. I am sorry I wasn't in. . . . Yes, I certainly could, or would you rather come here? . . . I see. Give me the address then. . . . No, you needn't be in the least alarmed. I assure you that if I say I won't tell the police I mean it! . . . Thank you. You flatter me. . . . Are you speaking from home? Oh, you haven't a telephone—very wise! . . . One-six-three Swinburne House. . . . Yes; yes I do. Near Sloane Square. Yes. . . . Nine forty-five, then. . . . Good-bye."

The receiver clicked back upon its base.

CHAPTER XVII

There is a certain sedate and not uncomely cheerfulness about Sloane Square; but in the environs to the southeast this quality is stillborn at best; and in Daisy Street, which sullenly and most efficaciously belies its name, it has not been, is not and never will be existent.

A long narrow strip of dirty greyness flanked by frowning boxes of brick in which, presumably and unreasonably, certain human beings have their habitation, Daisy Street, born, as it were, out of nothing, culminates fittingly in the giant and frowning and prisonlike bulk of Swinburne House. Swinburne House is monument to the memory of a certain Joseph Hardcastle who—perhaps self-consciously influenced by his surname—inflicted upon a patient city half-a-dozen grim barracks known collectively as the Hardcastle Improved Homes for Workmen. Naturally enough, no member of the labouring classes has ever been known to inhabit a Hardcastle Home; the grim stone warrens—each with its hundreds of flats—are populated by all manner of other types of person. Here are clerks and harlots, typists and chorus men; nonconformist pastors and drunken pressmen; earnest female students; frivolous male students; struggling young doctors; lachrymose widows; parsimonious Eurasian demibarristers; retired merchant seamen; elementary schoolmistresses; and all the other thousand and one odds and ends of that drab gallimaufry known as the lower middle class.

If Daisy Street by day—even in rare sunshine—is grey and desolate reminder of the calculating bitterness of civilization, by night its hopelessness is abysmal. It is not clean enough nor rich enough to give any promise of hope; not poor enough nor dirty enough to achieve the lurid colourings of adventurous poverty. There is little enough life in Daisy Street during the hours of daylight—except when the flood of City workers from Swinburne House surges up its length to catch their morning train and down its length to snatch their evening meal—but at night, save for belated and momentarily high-living inhabitants of Swinburne House and an occasional empty taxi, there is no life at all. And so it was empty and dead and dark as the long black car of Anthony Gethryn nosed into it from Sloane Square. Upon the windshield of the car a fine drizzle had begun to settle and through the open window on the driving side came gusts of that soft yet painfully penetrating cold wind in which London winters seem diabolically to specialize.

"God-forsaken place!" said Anthony over his shoulder.

Dyson grunted.

Flood said: "Beats Poplar!" He peered out of the window. "Where's the place?"

"Here," said Anthony and slid the car to the left-hand curb and switched off the engine.

The three climbed out into the wet dim silence. The sound of the car doors slamming was like artillery. Anthony shivered, turning up the collar of his dinner jacket to protect the silk.

Dyson said: "Ought to have worn a coat," and buried his chin in the upturned collar of the oil-stained burberry which shrouded his own lank form. Flood tilted back his head to look up from under down-drawn hat brim at the lowering bulk of Swinburne House. He said:

"Looks like Dartmoor."

Anthony led the way, across the black and faintly shining surface of the road, to the frowning archway of the side entrance. He halted beneath the arch, peering out across the dark wastes of the concrete square around whose four sides rose the dismal walls of Mr. Hardcastle's memorial to ugliness.

Dyson said: "What's the number?"

"One-six-three." Anthony moved nearer to the far mouth of the little tunnel.

Dyson said: "Across, to the right. Fouth entrance on the far side."

"Datas!" Flood said: "The Man Who Forgets Nothing."

"Come on!" said Anthony and, head down, walked with long strides through the archway and out into the drizzle-swept darkness of the courtyard.

The sound of three pairs of feet rang out with a muffled echo sent back fourfold by the towering, window-pierced walls. There was no other sound.

They came to the far side of the rectangle and passed along it to the fourth doorless entrance. Over this, as over its fellows, there glimmered a feeble yellow gaslight encased in a lantern of dirty glass and cheap wrought iron. Dyson said:

"One-six-three'll be on the fourth floor."

Anthony said: "Thanks. You two wait here. And be inconspicuous." His voice was pitched low.

Flood said: "What about coming with you? We could go up to the next landing and wait. We'd be nearer."

"Too near," said Anthony. "If Brent's genuine you might scare her out of usefulness."

Dyson said: "If it's a trap we're too far away here."

"You stay put!" said Anthony and was gone.

"Theirs not to reason why . . ." murmured Flood.

Dyson grunted.

They stood looking into the darkness of the entrance. To their ears came back the sound of Anthony's feet on the stone stairs.

2

Beneath Anthony's shoes the shallow stone treads were hard and the iron of the baluster rail was cold beneath his fingers. It was very dark in Swinburne House. Upon each landing was only one light; a gas jet which flared and flickered and did little else. Upon the stretches of unkind stairway was no light at all.

Anthony went on climbing. He passed the second and then the third landing, seeing little and hearing nothing save the sound of his own footsteps. He achieved the fourth landing and—if Dyson were right—the end of his climbing. He went down the little corridor towards the door over which the gas jet flared and by its meagre flame saw the number beneath it to be 167. One-six-three, then, should be upon the same side, two doors off.

It was. He peered at the door and found a small brass

171

knocker and a bellpush. He put his thumb to the bell and pressed. From somewhere behind the door came a steady, tinny tinkling.

He waited. His ear anticipated movement from within but none came. He set his thumb to the bell again and again pressed and still was rewarded only by the burring tinkle. He took the little brass knocker between finger and thumb and with it beat a smart tattoo upon the door. There was no result save the sound itself and a devitalized echo.

"Hell!" said Anthony Gethryn and without hope tried the handle which projected below the yale lock. Surprisingly it turned in his fingers and the door gave.

There came over his lean face a new expression, curiously blent of wariness and not unpleasant anticipation. He lifted his right leg and with the sole of its foot thrust at the door. It swung inwards. He stood facing the rectangle of absolute darkness which showed where it had been. His arms hung loosely at his sides; his head was thrust a little forward in the attitude of one who listens for the faintest of faint sounds.

But no sound came. He took a step forward and stretched out a long arm and hooked its fingers round the doorjamb. They found a switch and pressed it and the rectangle was black no longer.

He went through the doorway. His eyes darted glances this way and that. He stood in a minute hallway. Facing him was an inner door. He opened it, repeating the procedure he had just now followed. Now light came from beneath a shade of distressing pinkness. It showed him a small room and plethora of unpleasing furniture whose coverings had a leering daintiness.

He threaded his way through the maze towards a door which stood ajar. He found a light switch and pressed it and passed through and was in a bedroom as unbeautifully spartan as the living room had been distressfully ornate. But, like the living room, it had no living occupant save himself. He looked about him at the furnishings. A single iron bed; a cheap chest of drawers with handles of white-chipped enamel; a tin washstand; a dilapidated towel horse; a wooden chair; across the corner by the window a green curtain dependent from a crookedly set brass rail. And, occupying nearly all the floor space, a large cabin trunk of good make and in excellent condition.

He went to the hanging curtain and pulled it aside and found clothes; many clothes—all a woman's; all good; some even beautiful. He probed among them and found nothing else. He turned back to the trunk and opened it. It was filled, to nearly a quarter of its capacity, with more clothes, obviously recently packed. He let the lid fall and stood straight and looked about him for a moment and then in two strides was back in the living room. Upon the other side of the window was another door still. He went to it and threw it open.

This time he did not have to grope for a switch. There was light already—from a single, unshaded bulb hanging from the ceiling.

He was in the narrow, cramped strip of a room which served this habitation as kitchen. And he saw, for the first time since his entrance to the flat, signs of humanity.

His eyes widened. He took two paces forward and stared down. He said aloud:

"God Almighty!"

3

Detective Sergeant Joseph Mather (C.I.D.) felt in his pockets for the new packet of cigarettes which should be somewhere on his person. He could not find it—for the excellent reason that it was not there. He cursed thickly beneath his breath, for the night now loomed long and black ahead of him. Outside the dark, cheerless shelter of the doorway in which he stood the drizzle was increasing to a steady fine rain beneath which the dark macadam surface of Daisy Street glistened unpleasantly. The rain did not come into the doorway but the wind—ever increasing in power and coldness—decisively did.

An all-night job and nothing to smoke! Sergeant Mather thrust his hands deeper into the side pockets of his frieze coat and tucked his chin down into his upturned collar. He glowered. He hated himself, his calling. Miss Ada Brent and Sir Walter Raleigh. He knew these jobs. Nothing would happen for the whole of a night whose every succeeding hour seemed double the length of its predecessor. And at the end of the night, in a cold and grey and probably rainy dawn, he would be relieved by another unfortunate and go back with a headache, a vile temper, a cold in the head and nothing to report.

It is to be regretted that Sergeant Mather said, aloud, a Chaucerian word. Perhaps he would have said more had his attention not been suddenly arrested by the sound of brisk footsteps which came from the courtyard of Swinburne House, whose arched entrance was immediately facing his lair.

These were beyond doubt a man's footsteps and therefore, in this particular job, not likely to be of official interest to Mather. But Mather was bored and disgruntled and ready for any distraction. He moved nearer to the mouth of the doorway and peered across the road towards the arch.

The owner of the feet came out and was for a fleeting instant visible beneath one of Daisy Street's few lamps. He turned to his left—and became simultaneously invisible and really interesting.

For as he passed out of the faint nimbus of light he ceased to walk and began to run. The sound of his feet— fast, long-striding feet—was a strange tattoo in the desolate silence.

Mather thought: "Bloody queer! Wonder what he's up to?" A fleeting wish crossed his mind that he were once more P.C. (M.X. 4321) Joseph Mather and in uniform. If he were still that Joseph Mather he could give himself something to do and keep himself warm by following the runner. But Detective Sergeant Joseph Mather (C.I.D.) must stay where he was, tobaccoless and futile, and watch a rabbit hole to see that one particular doe did not come out without being observed.

The sound of the runner's feet grew fainter; changed to the sound of walking feet; died away. Automatically Mather looked at his watch, seeing that its hands stood at ten minutes to ten.

Once more, now that there was no outside interest, his hands went to his pockets before his mind remembered that the shining, brand-new packet of twenty cigarettes was not there.

Again his lips formed the old word and again a wave of anger swept over his six feet and thirteen stone of solidity. To wrench his thoughts from tobacco he deliberately forced into ascendency the official part of his mind, trying

174

to concentrate upon this very dull matter of Ada Brent. . . .
But perhaps it wasn't so dull after all. There must be
something unusual to it for the super to have put a sergeant on the job: after all, it *was* one of Colonel Gethryn's do's. . . .

He began to feel less injured. He even smiled to himself
at the thought that only a few minutes ago he, unseen,
had watched Colonel Gethryn and those two journalist
blokes get out of the car which stood at the curb only a
few yards from him and go into Swinburne House. . . .

Perhaps something might even happen tonight, thought
Mather; for what else could those three be doing in a place
like this if their visit weren't somehow tied up with Ada
Brent? He felt better.

4

Flood stirred uneasily. He said: "How long's he been?"
Dyson grunted. "You're like an old woman!"

"I don't ..." began Flood; then checked himself as
there came to their ears, echoing curiously down the dark
cold shaft of the stairway, a shrill whistle of three notes; a
sound which they knew.

Dyson was first at the foot of the stairs. From a side
pocket in the old burberry he pulled a bulbous electric
torch and in the wavering white circle of its light began to
take the stairs two at a time. On the last flight Flood
caught him.

They saw Anthony's long figure standing just beneath
the gas jet on the fourth landing. They went to him and he
waved them through the open doorway of Number 163.
He said:

"Don't kick up a row," and led the way into the living
room and turned to face them under the pink light.

"Bird gone?" said Flood.

Anthony looked at him. "Yes," he said, "and no. Look!"
He turned to the door of the kitchen and pushed it open
and stood to one side.

Flood stopped on the threshold. He stared.

"*Christ!*" he whispered.

Dyson pushed by him and took two steps and was close
to the sink at the end of the room and looking down at
what was huddled beneath it. He said nothing but the lips

175

beneath his beaklike nose pursed themselves and there came from between them a soft, long-drawn-out whistle. Flood said suddenly:

"Look out for your shoes, man!"

5

Mr. Arnold Pike, a pipe between his teeth and a whiskey and soda at his elbow, bent happily over a chess table which stood before the fire in his living room. He had left Scotland House at seven-thirty—almost a half holiday for him—had shopped successfully; dined well; exchanged blue serge and shining black footgear for aged tweed and slippers, and now was waiting with placid expectation the arrival of an old friend and older opponent in the greatest of all games.

The bell of a telephone rang shrill. Mr. Arnold Pike started, turning to stare at the instrument with a look comically compound of apprehension and annoyance. He thrust back his chair and rose. The bell continued to peal.

Mr. Arnold Pike, of 78 Poindexter Mansions, lifted the receiver and made the usual noises.

"*What!*" said Superintendent Arnold Pike of the Criminal Investigation Department.

"You heard," snarled the telephone. "Dyson here. Speaking from Swinburne House. Porter's lodge. Ada Brent's dead. Gethryn found her. . . ."

Pike said: "Murdered?"

The telephone said: "Utterly. Listen: Gethryn's up there. Flood's gone out to find your sleuth. Gethryn says come right away."

"Right!" said Pike and slammed down the receiver; then immediately lifted it again to call Whitehall-4000 and give crisp orders.

That was at five minutes past ten.

6

At thirty-two minutes past ten Superintendent Arnold Pike came out of the kitchen of Number 163 Swinburne House. In the pink light of the living room his face showed very pale.

Anthony looked at him. "Well?" he said.

176

The corners of Pike's mouth twitched downwards. "It takes a good bit to upset me, sir. But *that* does! Whoever did that must be the worst sort of madman."

Anthony said: "Meet Mr. Evans? Or don't you agree?"

Pike rubbed reflectively at his lower jaw. "You do jump, sir, don't you?" He murmured apology and went to the further door and through it, to return after a moment followed by two men in very plain clothes. The first carried a long thin case of japanned tin; the second a tripod and two large cases of black leather. Pike pointed to the kitchen door.

"In there," he said.

The softly heavy footsteps of the pair crossed the little room. The man with the tin case opened the kitchen door; halted with a jerk; drew a little hissing breath between his teeth and went in. His companion followed stolidly. The door closed behind them.

Pike looked at Anthony. "Now, sir?"

Anthony said: "While you and I were abortively searching the kennels of Jenks and Hines this afternoon Miss Ada Brent called at my house. . . ."

"*What!*" said Pike.

Anthony said: "Quite. Hearing I wasn't there, she left a note. Here it is."

Pike's small brown eyes were glittering. He took the paper from Anthony's hand and read avidly.

Anthony said: "She telephoned. She wouldn't come to the house. Asked me to call here at nine forty-five. On condition that I wouldn't tell the police. So I didn't. But, having a nasty suspicious nature, I brought Dyson and Flood along. Up here I couldn't get an answer. But, oddly enough, the door was on the latch. When I'd looked in the kitchen I sent Dyson to phone you and Flood to find the Yard man on Brent."

Pike said: "That's Mather. He's a good man. Where is he, sir?"

"Out," said Anthony. "Wild-goose hunting."

Pike's eyes narrowed. "Meaning, sir?"

Anthony said: "At ten minutes to ten—that's a few minutes after Flood and Dyson and I came here—Mather saw a man walk out of this catafalque into Daisy Street. He turned left and began to run like hell. Mather's official instincts were sufficiently aroused for him to note the time.

A few minutes later Flood found Mather and brought him up here. Mather told me and I sent him out on a necessary goose chase. Agree?"

Pike nodded: "Of course, sir. Did he get a look at this man?"

Anthony lifted his shoulders. "For a split second. No use. Medium height; dark overcoat; ordinary build."

"H'mm!" Pike bent his head in his habitual gesture of thought; then raised it sharply as if offended by the sight of the battered brogues upon his feet. "He might have been running for a train; Sloane Square's up that way."

Anthony said: "And trains leave it every five minutes. Going both ways."

For the first time since he had been in this place Pike smiled. "He *might*'ve been running for a Hounslow, sir."

Anthony grinned. "Or exercise. Or a woman. Or just joie de vivre."

There was a small silence, broken only by the loud metallic ticking of a china clock and muffled stirrings from behind the kitchen door. Pike was the first to speak. He said:

"There's one chance. People are liable to notice a man running."

"Quite," said Anthony. "But he stopped running, Mather says, when he couldn't have been more than halfway up Daisy Street. Which was empty."

Pike shrugged his shoulders. "Well, we'll see." He looked about the room with little darting glances, his eyes resting at last upon the small writing desk. Upon its flap were some half-a-dozen tidy little piles of paper. He said:

"Been busy, sir?"

Anthony nodded. "Yes; no result. Nothing but junk anyone might have."

Pike said slowly: "What time did you say it was, sir, when you and Flood and Dyson came here?"

Anthony said: "Say nine forty-two. That's near enough."

"And Mather saw this man come out at nine-fifty; eight minutes later?"

Anthony nodded. "Quite. And we didn't pass anyone in the courtyard. And I didn't pass anyone on the stairs. And Dyson and Flood stood in the doorway all the time and nobody came out of this block."

Pike said: "So it comes to this, sir: if the man Mather saw *was* the murderer he must have left this flat and this block before you got here and then hidden somewhere until after you'd passed."

"There are a thousand and one corners to this place," said Anthony. "Perhaps he was inside one of the flats in another block. As a visitor—or even a tenant."

Pike said quickly: "You said *Evans* just now, sir. D'you mean . . . ?"

Anthony shook his head. "I'm afraid not. Dyson went through the list in the porter's lodge. There's no tenant called Evans."

Pike said: "Look here, sir. If he'd only just——"

Anthony interrupted. "If you're going to suggest that he was in this flat until he heard me coming and then got out some other way—fire escape, for instance—you're wrong. I've been round the windows. There's only one that even a cat could get out by. It's in the bedroom and leads on to the fire escape; but there's undisturbed dust an eighth of an inch thick all round it."

Pike's brows drew themselves together in a deep frown. He pulled at his lower lip and looked down at the tips of his shoes. He said after a pause:

"When you found—*that,* sir"—he jerked his thumb towards the kitchen door—"how long would you say— well, it had been like that?"

Anthony said: "I'm no doctor. And even if I were I couldn't give you any definite time. But if you want a guess, no more than fifteen minutes at the outside. Some of the blood hadn't even begun to dry. . . . Where's the divisional surgeon? And who?"

"You know him, sir—Hancock. He'll be here any minute." Pike was still looking down at his shoes; still pulling at his lower lip with his finger and thumb.

The kitchen door opened and the two plain-clothes men came out, closing it behind them. The one of the tin case was first; his round face, glistening with sweat, showed pallid in the pink light. Behind him, stolid, the photographer bore his tripod and cases. Pike looked at them. He said:

"All through? How many photos, Harris?"

"Dozen, sir," said the man with the tripod. "Not counting the prints for Johnson."

Pike looked at the other. "Any luck, Johnson?"

The man patted at his forehead with a large handkerchief. "As a guess, sir, no. Plenty of prints, but seems like they're all"—he gulped—"all hers."

From just outside the room came the cracked, burring tinkle of the doorbell. Pike said:

"That'll be Doctor Hancock."

7

Charles Grandison Hancock, M.R.C.S., L.R.C.P., was bending over a steaming tin basin which stood on a corner of the gate-legged table beneath the pink light of the living room. His work over, he was vigorously washing his hands. A strong odour of disinfectant rose about him.

Anthony came out of the bedroom with Pike behind him. Hancock looked up and nodded and bent once more over the basin. Anthony sniffed at the air. He said after a moment:

"Smells good—in here."

Pike said: "Anything special, Doctor?"

Hancock began to dry his hands. "Depends what you mean. Specially messy job."

Pike said: "Looks almost like the work of a madman."

"Who's sane?" said Anthony.

Hancock nodded. He looked at Pike. "If the man who did it is mad you wouldn't notice it if you saw him. Very tidy. Until I saw that overall and those gloves lying under the sink there I was thinking he must have been saturated in blood."

Pike said: "Any indication that he's had surgical experience, as you might say?"

Hancock shook his head. "No knowledge shown beyond the ordinary. Anyone knows that if you slit a throat and rip a stomach you'll kill. Any surgically trained person would be tidier."

"Probably," said Anthony. "Not certain."

Hancock smiled, showing a flash of white teeth beneath the small black moustache. "Still the stickler," he said.

Pike said: "Listen, Doctor. What I want to know——"

Hancock interrupted. "I know, I know. Time of death. Not more than a couple of hours; not less than—say three quarters."

Pike cocked an eyebrow at him. "Nothing more definite, Doctor?"

Hancock shook his head. "Not from me, nor from anyone else who knows his job." He crossed the room towards his bag, dropped his towel into it, snapped the bag shut and stood up. "If there's nothing else ..." he said and made brisk adieux and was gone.

Anthony looked at Pike. "Good example," he said. "Let's follow it."

Pike looked at his watch. He said: "I can't go yet, sir. Stephens and another man are coming down from the Yard. I've got to give 'em orders."

Anthony nodded. The tinny sound of the front doorbell rang sharply.

"There they are, sir," said Pike and went out into the little hallway to admit two solemn, solid men.

And that was at eleven-twenty.

181

CHAPTER XVIII

Thomas Sheldon Garrett could not sleep. Through his still sore head thoughts were racing willy-nilly. It was as though behind his forehead he had two treadmills of thought, both entirely different, both discomforting and, though so entirely different, each about a woman. . . .

"God damn it all to hell!" said Thomas Sheldon Garrett aloud and sat up in bed and stretched out an arm and switched on a light and began to grope in the miscellany of his bedside table.

He was searching for the little red box of opiate pills which, until this moment, he had determined not to use. It was not upon the table. In one movement he threw back his coverings, swung his legs to the floor and stood up.

He was rewarded by a giddiness so severe as to make him sit abruptly. His head whirled and his heart pounded and he felt a desire to vomit. He sat very still and little by little the seizure left him. He stood up slowly and began to cross the room towards a tall chest of drawers. He could see the red box leering at him from beside his cigarette case. And then, as he drew opposite the window, he heard the sound of a car coming to a stop before the house. Its doors slammed and he heard men's voices which he knew.

He realized, suddenly, that he did not want to go to sleep—and presently, clad in grey flannels and a sweater pulled over his pyjamas, was passing from his room to the head of the third flight of stairs.

He went down slowly and, as he went, heard voices. He crossed the hall and opened the library door and thrust his head round it. He said, a difficult smile creasing his drawn face:

"Any objection if I come in?"

And that was at eleven thirty-five.

2

"To sum up," said Anthony at one minute to midnight, "the state of the case is thuswise: Miss Ada Brent, an intimate associate of the Moriarty we are up against and whom, for want of a better name, I shall call Evans——"

"Are you sure?" said Garrett in excitement.

Anthony lifted his shoulders. "Don't get excited and don't get misled! We're not actually as near as that to Murch. I mean, we don't *know* that the murderer calls himself Evans and we don't *know,* whether he calls himself Evans or not, that he's the same man whose name was used as a threat to Murch. But everything in this unusual business points to one directing mind; therefore it's more than likely that the owner of this directing mind would be the threat."

Pike said: "No doubt, of course, he *might*——"

Anthony interrupted: "Don't be so subjunctive, Pike! If I want to call our Napoleon Evans, let me call him Evans."

Pike grinned: "Have it your own way, sir."

Garrett said: "How d'you know Brent was an intimate of—of Evans?"

Anthony said: "The proof of the pudding is in the eating. Wait for another slice and see what you get. Now then: Miss Ada Brent, an intimate associate of Evans and therefore more than the usual KJB blackmail operative, nevertheless takes on an ordinary operative's job in the case of Mrs. Bellingham. Why she does this we don't know but needn't worry about. What we do know is that Miss Brent sees confederate Jenks under arrest. She also sees that connected with the arrest is one Anthony Gethryn, whom she recognizes because—despite all his efforts—his photograph has frequently appeared in newspapers. Being quick witted, she does not get out of the taxi from which she sees all this but directs the driver to go on. Later, in at least temporary safety, she thinks things over and comes to a decision, one of the effects of which

183

is to tell us what we have already stated, namely, that she is a confidante of Evans. She decides that she had best save her own skin by double-crossing Evans—not by going to the police, who can only turn her into king's evidence and get her a reduced sentence, but by going to the Gethryn man. He is not an official policeman but he does have the ear of authority. With him she can bargain."

Garrett said: "Wait a minute! I don't follow you. How does all this prove that she's an intimate of the Big Shot's?"

Anthony smiled. "Special allowances made for recently cracked heads. Because, my good Garrett, her decision to talk—whatever the reason behind it—must mean that she knew something *more* than the general KJB blackmail activities. Brent was, you must admit, obviously a young person of shrewdness. Therefore when she sees Jenks arrested for blackmail she knows either that (1) by degrees the police will find out all about the blackmail and KJB, in which case she has nothing to bargain *with;* or she knows that (2) Jenks, Hines and Company are so well protected by and/or afraid of Evans that they will inculpate no one but themselves."

"Ye-es." Garrett's tone was doubtful. "It's *probable. . . .*"

Anthony said: "Think, man, think! Just like that it's so probable as to be almost certain. But it's *sure* when you add to this hyper-probability the facts (a) that Miss Ada Brent called at Travers Hoylake's nursing home this afternoon and asked for you and (b) that the second and third lines of Miss Brent's note to me read something like this: 'Knowing you are interested re Arthur Jenks and *consequently re a great deal more which I could tell you about.*'"

Garrett put his elbows on his knees and dropped his head into his hands. He said:

"Of course! Of course! I'm sorry."

There was a small silence, broken by Pike. He said slowly, looking at Anthony:

"Seems to me, sir, that whenever we think we've got anywhere in this case we come to a blind alley, as you might say. What do we know now about the Murch angle, as you might call it, that we didn't know at the beginning?"

"We know it's there," said Garrett without lifting his head.

"And we know it's big," said Anthony.

"Big!" said Pike. "It's more than that, sir. But what I mean is, where are we?"

Anthony grinned. "You mean, where's Murch. Oh, where is Janet, what is she, that we poor swine can't find her?"

Pike did not smile. "Lady Ballister might've helped us: she's dead. This Brent was going to help us: she's dead. And we don't look like finding this Aunt——"

Garrett said: "If only you people had put Brent in jail!"

Anthony looked at Pike. "And *that's* what Lucas'll say. But if we had, Garrett, she wouldn't've talked. She'd have taken her chance with Jenks and Hines. Turning king's evidence would only have got her a reduced sentence. That wouldn't have appealed. She'd've gambled, that girl."

Garrett raised his head. He stared first at Anthony; then at Pike. He said:

"Shan't we get Evans or whoever he is through this murder?"

Pike said: "If painstaking work will do it, Mr. Garrett, we shall. Two of my best men are in Swinburne House now, trying to get any line on Brent—habits, friends, anything. But——"

"You're not very sure," Garrett said.

Pike looked at him. "You don't want what Colonel Gethryn calls jam, do you, sir? . . . Well then, my personal feeling—my private opinion, as you might say—is that we'll get the murderer; but that it'll take us time. And plenty of it!"

"And in that time—the Murch affair will probably be finished." Garrett was despondent.

Anthony said: "That's if we regard the murderer as our only line on Murch."

"You know," said Garrett, "what we've got to do is get hold of the old Bellows dame. . . . We've *got* to! Don't you see that some hellish thing's going to be done?" His words were coming fast now; he sat bolt upright for the first time. "It was bad enough at the beginning. Now it's worse. At the start we just *smelt* crime—now we *know;* and know it's something bad enough to make the people behind it try to kill me and then butcher one of their own gang. And we sit here and gab and——"

Pike interrupted. He said stiffly:

"You can rest assured that the department——"

Anthony said: "Don't get official, Pike. This is Mr. Garrett's case. If it hadn't been for him . . ."

Garrett looked at Pike and essayed a smile. "Sorry, Superintendent. Didn't mean to knock. But this thing's got me. You see, I know, personally, what kidnapping means." His voice dropped; he looked down at the floor between his slippered feet. "It's—it's . . ." He checked himself. "But skip that! Just remember that this bunch tried to bump *me* off!" A hand went up to the back of his head.

Pike said earnestly: "Believe me, Mr. Garrett, I understand your feelings."

Anthony said: "Tomorrow's tasks: One: put more men onto the Brent murder. Two: ginger Midlothian about Mother Bellows. Three: go over Brent's chattels at——"

Garrett started. "For God's sake, haven't you——" He cut himself short. "Sorry, Gethryn!"

Anthony smiled. "We're not as bad as that. As far as the flat's concerned, Pike and I have been over everything—and found that it comes to nothing. What I was talking about was the trunk or what not she must have left at Avis'. We haven't got round to that yet."

Pike said: "It's being fetched tomorrow morning, sir."

Garrett said: "I don't suppose there'd be anything in it. She'd hardly take——" He broke off, staring at Anthony.

Anthony had got to his feet. A sudden frown was drawing his brows together and, although he was motionless, all ease had dropped from him. His face seemed leaner than ever and beneath the frowning brows the curiously green eyes were blazing.

Garrett said: "What's the matter?"

"What's Avis' number? Quick!"

Garrett stared, his eyes widening.

"Quick!" said Anthony. Now he was at the writing table, his hand outstretched for the telephone.

Garrett said: "St. John-4383." He found himself on his feet.

Anthony was working the dial. He said, his voice coming over the whirring little cackle of sound:

186

"We ought to be shot, Pike! He was running because he was in a hurry."

The dialing ceased. Pike, too, was now standing. Garrett went to Anthony's side and clutched his shoulder. He said:

"What's happened, Gethryn? Explain, for God's sake!"

"Wait!" said Anthony.

There was silence. Through it came, even to the ears of Garrett and Pike, a soft, intermittent purring from the telephone which told of a bell ringing at the other end.

Anthony listened. The purring went on. Then his face lightened. The purring had stopped, with a click which told of the removal of the far receiver.

"Hullo!" said Anthony. "Hullo!"

There was no answer.

He said: "Hullo! Hullo, there!" His voice was rising.

Garrett said: "Here, give it to me!" He snatched the instrument from Anthony's hand and put it to his mouth and shouted into it.

There was no answer.

Anthony looked at his watch. The time was twenty past midnight.

Garrett was shouting into the telephone. "Hello! *Hello!*"

Anthony said: "Shut up a minute, Garrett! P'r'aps she's out and someone else took off the receiver."

Garrett said: "Talked to her this evening. She was going to bed early. And there's the maid. Why shouldn't *she* answer if she goes to the phone!" He shouted again into the receiver.

Pike looked at Anthony. "Get another phone, sir?"

Anthony nodded. "Private line. My dressing room. Know the way?"

Pike was gone.

Garrett was shouting: *"Hello! Hello!"*

Anthony caught him by the left shoulder and swung him round and snatched the receiver and slammed it back on its hook. He said:

"Waste of time. Pike's onto Hampstead Police now. I'm going."

In three strides he was at the door. He wrenched it open and was gone.

It had stopped raining and the sky was clear; but the wind was now stronger and colder. And the engine of the Voisin was cold.

Anthony cursed and adjusted the choke and trod again upon the starter. The engine coughed; stuttered; burst into low, full-throated life.

The near-side front door was snatched open. Gasping, Garrett scrambled into the car.

"Damn fool!" said Anthony. "You're ill!" But he leaned over and clutched at the still open door and slammed it shut. He said:

"Hold tight!"

The black car shot down the length of Stukeley Gardens and swung right, with a pull which sent Garrett's body lurching against Anthony's shoulder, into the broad stream of Knightsbridge itself.

Garrett pulled himself upright. The needle on the speedometer jerked to fifty ... sixty.... Past Garrett's painfully straining eyes flashed the bulk of the Hyde Park Hotel. He shouted:

"The Park, man! The Park!"

But by the time the words had left his mouth the car was nearing the yellow nimbus of light opposite St. George's Hospital which guides the belated to the coffee stall known as the Junior Turf. Anthony said out of the corner of his mouth:

"Park's shut."

The coffee stall was passed; then the double gates of the Corner. The Voisin swung left into Park Lane. Garrett was hurled against the door at his left shoulder. He pushed himself upright. He said, almost shouted:

"What d'you think's happened! Tell me!"

Anthony was driving almost on the crown of the empty road. On the left the black railings of the Park streamed by. On the right loomed the dark mass of Dorchester House. From the turning just past it there suddenly shot out, right across the Voisin's path, a yellow taxicab.

Garrett involuntarily closed his eyes. A short breath hissed between his teeth and his right arm came up to guard his head. He felt the car swing violently under him and once more was thrown against the door. His ears were filled with the screaming of tortured tires. Suddenly, beneath him, came a bump which straightened his body and threw it off the seat. Then a lurching twist to the right, another bump—and once more smooth progression.

Garrett became aware of the arm across his eyes. With a little unreasonable pang of shame he took it down. He heard Anthony's voice. It said:

"Close one! Lucky the curb wasn't high."

And now they swung left, between the Marble Arch and the Park itself and were on the broad straight thoroughfare to Notting Hill Gate.

The needle on the speedometer dial touched seventy and passed it; the engine began to give out that low humming note which she achieves at high speeds. Then, as Lancaster Gate drew near, Anthony's foot was transferred from accelerator to brake. Garrett said:

"For God's sake, Gethryn! Tell me what you think has happened."

"Hold tight!" said Anthony.

Garrett clutched at the window and held himself steady while—it seemed on two wheels—the car swung right into Westbourne Terrace. Anthony's foot came down again upon the accelerator. In the comparative darkness of the terrace his headlights cut a white swathe. Garrett said:

"For God's sake, Gethryn! D'you think that devil has——"

The rasping, two-noted blare of the Voisin's klaxon drowned his next two words. They were approaching, at fifty miles per hour, the last cross street before the Marylebone Road, and across the blackness of the macadam, from the right-hand mouth of the cross street, was shining a single approaching headlight. Steering obliquely to his left, Anthony slammed his right foot down. The car seemed to throw itself forward. It flashed with an actually safe but apparently perilous yard to spare across the path of the owner of the headlight—a motor-police cycle and sidecar.

The Voisin roared on; but from behind her came the sudden and infuriated wail of a police siren.

"We're off!" said Anthony.

Over the Canal Bridge ... then right ... then left ... then right again and up to Westbourne Grove.... Left and on the straight again. . . . The needle on the speedometer hovered over the eighty mark. . . . The two-noted klaxon blared continuously. Behind, the police siren screamed its rage. . . . A bad tenth of a second with a van without a taillight. . . . A worse fifth with a careless or legally minded taxi driver. . . .

Then the long wall of the Lords . . . a squealing of brakes. . . . A sliding to the curb opposite the entrance to Lords' Mansions.

Anthony thrust himself out of the car, slamming its door behind him, the siren rang once more in his ears and he was bathed in the white flood of a single headlight. A deep, irate voice shouted at him. Coming through the sound of the voice was that of the far door of the Voisin slamming and those of men's footsteps as Garrett came round the front of the car at a stumbling run and two bulky, dark-clad, flat-capped forms detached themselves from cycle and sidecar and ran for their quarry.

Anthony, already halfway up the flagged walk which joins the portico of Lords' Mansions to the pavement, shouted back over his shoulder. To Garrett's ears, in which the blood pounded with a sound like the hammer of Thor, came two words: ". . . explain . . . card . . ." And at Garrett's feet, which persisted paradoxically in feeling as if they were made of lead and yet treading upon air, something landed with a little soft plop.

4

The flat of Mrs. George Bellingham is upon the second floor of Lords' Mansions. Anthony, knowing that there was no lift attendant after eleven at night, took to the stairs. As he reached the first landing he heard from beneath the sound of the swing doors and heavily shod feet running along the tiled vestibule.

He passed no one in his ascent and there was no one upon the second landing. He ran down it and with long strides to Avis' door. It was smugly closed. Behind its ground-glass, curtained upper half no light showed. He tried its handle but it did not give. With his left hand he beat a sharp tattoo with the knocker; with his right thumb he pressed the bellpush. But he did not wait for answer; knock and ring had not been appeal but admonition. His hands came away from knocker and bell. In one movement they had unbuttoned and ripped off his dinner jacket. He dropped it over his right hand, clenched this into a fist and wrapped about it, in a thick bundle, the soft black cloth and softer black silk. He thrust with a short stabbing punch at the pane of glass nearest to the lock. The tinkling crackle of the breaking glass mingled with the sound of heavy boots racing up the stairs.

He shook the coat from his arm and it fell and lay like a black stain upon the carpet. He thrust his shirt-sleeved left arm with swift caution through the broken pane and groped with long fingers and found the knob of the lock and turned it.

The door opened. He thrust his way into the darkness of the little hall. Inside, the memory of his only two visits to this place serving him well, he reached for the wall to the left of the door and found a light switch and pressed it. Above his head a softly shaded amber light jumped into life and flooded down upon a scene of perfect order. Nothing was out of place. To his right the drawing-room door stood closed; and closed, too, were all the other doors in the corridor which stretched away to the left.

The heavy running feet pounded close outside. The door creaked again and there came a fresh little tinkle of broken glass as it moved. Anthony swung round. He saw a policeman but not the policeman he had expected, for here was no motorcyclist but a helmeted sergeant with beads of sweat glistening on a round and red but shrewd-eyed face. Anthony sighed relief. He said sharply:

"From Hampstead Station? Superintendent Pike's orders?"

A hand went up to the helmet in salute. "Yes, sir. Colonel Gethryn?" The voice was jerky from recent exertion.

Anthony said: "Yes. Look in all the rooms on the right. Watch your step!"

Again the hand went to the helmet in salute. Anthony made for the drawing-room door and threw it open. The room was dark. He reached his arm round the door for a light switch and found it after groping. Into view sprang another scene of complete and charming order. He turned and went back into the hall. From the first door upon the right—that of the dining room—the uniformed figure of the sergeant came out. He looked towards Anthony and said:

"All right in there, sir."

"Get on! Get on!" said Anthony and himself ran to the first door upon the left.

What room this led to he did not know. He threw it open. It was dark like the drawing room. He reached his arm round the doorjamb but this time his groping fingers found no switch. He took a step forward, then checked himself. To his ear had come two sounds—or rather, one group of sounds and one particular sound. From outside the flat two or three more pairs of heavy running feet; from inside the flat, in the sergeant's briskly hoarse voice, words whose shape he did not catch but whose tone brought him back into the passage in a leap and sent him running towards the second door upon the right. This stood open and light streamed from it.

He was at it in two strides. A hand on the jamb, he swung into the room.

He saw the sergeant kneeling beside an inert, prostrate bundle which he saw, as he took a step forward, to be that of a woman.

She was lying on her back. She was fully dressed for the street in clothes of cheap but tidy black. A round blob of a face, the eyes closed, was pallidly upturned to the ceiling. The arms were flung wide. One leg was twisted underneath the body. Behind the head, still somehow attached to a mass of untidy but incongruously beautiful brown hair, was a hat of grey-black felt. From the right ear a thin chain dangled, at its end a pair of pince-nez from which broken glass had fallen to the floor and lay in small glittering stars upon the carpet.

The sergeant turned his head and looked up at Anthony. He said:

"She's alive, all right, sir. Had a bad crack on the head though." He pointed to a place on the forehead where a blue bruise lay like a shadow.

From outside came the creaking of the front door again; footsteps; a murmur of male voices; then Garrett's, which shouted:

"Gethryn! Gethryn!"

"Here!" called Anthony.

The sergeant, still on his knees, turned and pointed to the corner óf the room farthest from the door. He said:

"Look there, sir!"

But Anthony was already looking. Pulled out from the corner, its lid gaping, was a tin trunk and all around it, in appalling disarray, lay what had obviously been its contents. The sergeant said:

"Someone in a hurry, sir?"

Anthony turned back to the door. He said over his shoulder:

"Put her on the bed. Then go through the rest of the house and come back to her."

He went through the door and swung to the left and was brought into collision with a large blue-clad man in the gaiters and gauntlets and flatcap of the motor police.

" 'Ere!" said a brass rumble. "What's *your* business?" A gloved hand which seemed in itself to weigh a stone clamped itself upon Anthony's shirt-clad left shoulder.

Anthony's feet did not move; nor did his body. But his right arm came up and across, and its open, rigid hand brought its edge down in a short snapping blow upon blue-covered biceps. . . .

"Urch!" The rumble was, almost comically, now more baritone than bass.

"Out of my way!" said Anthony and thrust with a shoulder and was past.

The narrow corridor and the slightly widening rectangle which formed the little entrance hall seemed full of men. Under the amber light stood another motorcyclist constable. His thumbs were hooked into his belt and his feet planted wide apart and beneath the visor of his cap his long, boyish face showed blank and gaping and bewildered. Beside him, just entered, was a man in shirt and trousers; hair tousled from sleep. He, too, was gaping. From the doorway of the first room into which the sergeant had looked came Sheldon Garrett. He saw Anthony and stopped. He swayed and leant against the doorjamb. He said:

"Avis! She there?" His voice was harsh and laboured. He made a gesture towards the farther part of the corridor.

Anthony shook his head. "Hold on!" he said and stepped

193

past Garrett into the room. A woman's bedroom, delightful as its owner.

But its owner was not there.

The room bore signs of recent occupancy. There was no counterpane upon the bed. Upon its left-hand side was a pillow which still bore the impression of a head, and blankets and sheets were thrown back. It was a bed which recently had been inhabited.

Anthony took Garrett's arm and drew him into the room and thrust him gently backwards into a chair. The edge of the seat took the man behind the knees and he sat. Anthony said:

"Answer my questions."

"Yes," said Garrett. His voice was flat and dead and seemed to come from somewhere deep within him. He looked at Anthony with eyes which seemed to be set inches back in his skull.

Anthony said: "She told you she was going to bed early. When was that?"

The flat voice said: "Around eight-thirty. She said she was going to bed right away."

Anthony said: "There's a woman knocked out along there—in the maid's room. Short. Fat. Middle thirties. Sunday-go-to-meeting clothes. Lots of brown hair. Glasses. That the skivvy?"

"Yes. Name's Parfitt." Garrett stared unwinkingly.

Anthony said: "One more question. Is this Parfitt's usual evening off?"

Garrett put a hand up to his head, passing it in a squeezing movement across his forehead. Then, suddenly, he jumped to his feet. He said:

"What the hell am I doing, sitting here like a dummy!" He turned and took a quick step towards the door.

Anthony caught him by the shoulder and swung him round. "Damn you! Do as I say! This Parfitt's usual day off?"

"Yes," said Garrett. "And now, damn *you*, let me go!" He wrenched his shoulder free.

Anthony became aware that the murmur of voices from the passage had suddenly ceased. Now one voice spoke, a crisp, authoritative voice which he knew.

Pike was in the passage. Behind him were the gaping motorcyclist and the man in shirt and trousers. Before him

194

were the other motorcyclist, still rubbing ruefully at his right arm and, in the doorway of the servant's room, the sergeant. Pike was holding in his hands the thin morocco pocketbook which Anthony had thrown at Garrett's feet outside the building. Pike was saying:

"Lot of dunderheads! You *saw* this!" He waved the pocketbook at the arm-rubbing giant. "Inside it are Colonel Gethryn's own card *and* his special card from the commissioner! . . . Now get busy." He pointed at the arm-rubber. "Go get a doctor for the woman, quick!" He turned to the man in shirt and trousers. "What're you? Caretaker? Yes. . . . Get out into the corridor and wait. Don't go away." He turned on the gaping motorcyclist; then on the sergeant. Definite, brief orders came from him in a steady stream. . . .

Garrett came out of the bedroom, turned to his right and, pushing past the staring sergeant, blundered down the passage.

Anthony came out of the bedroom. He looked at Pike.

"Good man!" he said.

And that was at twelve forty-five.

CHAPTER XIX

By fifteen minutes past one much information had been brought to Pike in Avis Bellingham's dining room. He collated it—and found himself possessed of nothing. No one had seen Mrs. Bellingham since seven in the evening, when she had come in. No one had seen or heard any visitor to Mrs. Bellingham's flat. The caretaker, communicating over the telephone with Sergeant Stubbs, the day commissionaire, had discovered that Rose Parfitt had been seen to leave Lords' Mansions at half-past four in the afternoon but beyond this no one knew anything about Miss Parfitt, who still lay unconscious upon her bed, though now with a doctor tending her.

And no one of the dozen or more friends of Mrs. Bellingham to whom Garrett had telephoned had seen or heard of Mrs. Bellingham since the morning.

Pike, frowning, sent subordinates upon yet more errands of investigation, in none of which he had an instant's faith. In the servant's bedroom Dr. Harold Porteous bent over the inanimate person of Rose Parfitt, while behind him, in the corner by Ada Brent's open trunk, Anthony Gethryn knelt and probed ceaselessly into its past and present contents.

In the drawing room Sheldon Garrett, a white-faced automaton, sat with a telephone list before him and steadily called number after number. . . .

2

At precisely twenty minutes past one Avis Bellingham drove her car into the garage of Lords' Mansions, backed it neatly into place, left it and entered the building by the basement door. She had, indeed, gone to bed before eight o'clock. But by eight-thirty she had realized that she was wrong in assuming that bed was the place in which to think. She had, accordingly, risen at eight thirty-five and gone, in lone innocence, to a cinematograph theatre and thence, with an acquaintance encountered in the lobby after the show, for a drink at the Berkeley.

At twenty-two minutes past one she halted to face the front door of her flat and saw the broken pane of glass by its lock. The fingers which had been fumbling in her bag for a key withdrew themselves, for she saw that the door was not latched. Bewilderment making her eyes even larger than was their habit, she pushed at the door with a tentative little thrust. It gave. She became conscious of a murmur of male voices from the direction of her dining room. She frowned. She squared her slim shoulders beneath their covering of soft grey fur and marched into her little hallway. The voices from her left were clearer now. Her ear seemed to detect a familiar tone but before her mind could dwell upon this familiarity and name its owner she heard, through the half-open door of her drawing room, the rattle of a telephone dial and than the voice of Sheldon Garrett. It said:

"Mrs. Marshall? I'm sorry to disturb you but it's imperative that I should know whether Avis Bellingham . . ."

Avis Bellingham stared at the drawing-room door. The voice droned on. She did not hear all its words but the flat, deliberately emotionless tone made clear to her puzzled mind the fact that Tom thought that something had happened to her. . . .

She hurried to the drawing-room door and through it. Garrett sat with his back to her at the little table which bore the telephone. He was saying:

"You're *certain?* You see——"

Avis put a hand on his shoulder.

"Tom!" she said.

Garrett turned. As he turned he got to his feet. The light chair upon which he had been sitting fell to the carpet with a soft crash. In his hand the telephone cackled in agitation. His eyes, dark rimmed in an ashen face, widened in a stare of unbelief. The blood suddenly rushed darkly to his face; only to drain from it as quickly as it had come.

"*Tom!*" said Avis Bellingham again and took a step towards him and put a hand upon his arm.

There came an odd, constricted feeling into Garrett's throbbing and so recently maltreated head; his ears were filled with a roaring sound and everything in the sight of his staring eyes began to whirl about him.

He took a step towards the vision which had spoken to him. The telephone, cackling no longer, somehow slipped from his hand. It hit the leg of the table with a crash. He took another step forward and felt himself falling. . . .

3

He felt something wet and cold on his forehead and something wet and burning on his tongue. He opened his eyes but the light sent a stab of pain through his eyeballs into his head and he closed the lids again. There was a confused rumbling of voices all about him. He lay still and fought with his mind and steadied it until his hearing cleared. He heard, first, a man's voice which he did not know: a deep, slow voice with precise enunciation. It was saying:

". . . not to be wondered at. If the concussion, as you say, was serious, than all this excitement and agitation would be bound to leave——"

And then Avis' voice. "But, Doctor, there's no real damage, is there? I mean this won't——" Her voice broke off.

Then the deep, precise voice again. "Madam, there is nothing which cannot be rectified by that best of all specifics, a day in bed."

Then Avis again, only this time with a slightly different sound, as if her head were turned in another direction: "Anthony! Why did you let him——"

Then another well-known voice. "What was I to do, throw him out of the car? If I hadn't brought him he'd either have gone off his head waiting or——"

Garrett said without opening his eyes:

"Or done something equally damn silly. I'm—I'm all right now."

Cautiously he raised his eyelids, veiling sight with their

lashes so that the light did not send that stabbing pain back into his head. He looked up into Avis' face, now as white as his own, and saw eyes which were blue pools of pity and perhaps something else.

He closed his own eyes and felt soft hands on his forehead.

4

At twenty-five minutes to two the doctor pronounced Rose Parfitt as able to answer questions—"as few as possible, you understand, gentlemen, *please!*"

Rose Parfitt was luxurious in her mistress's bed, but shaken and nervous and filled with a feeling of pity for Rose Parfitt. Pike and Anthony surveyed her with compassion and friendliness and determination.

"Now, Rose," said Anthony, "we want your help."

"Y-yes sir." Brown eyes looked up at him from beneath snowy bandaging.

"And we don't want to bother you"—Anthony's tone was nicely blent of sympathy and command—"but we must know whether you saw the person who struck you."

"O-oh, sir!" The voice trembled and the sore head moved a little. "O-oh, sir!" Words ceased and a whimpering began.

Anthony sat upon the edge of the bed and picked up a pudgy, work-roughened hand and patted it. He jerked his head in an infinitesimal gesture and Pike withdrew softly from the Parfitt field of sight.

"Now, now," said Anthony. "We know how you feel, Rose. But you've got to be a brave girl and help us."

The eyes fixed themselves upon his with almost canine worship. She said:

"Y-yes sir. I—I did see 'im. For a flick of a second like. I—I come in all unexpectin' like an' goes along to my room an' opens the door an'—an'—o-oh!" Once more she began to whimper.

Anthony patted the fat hand again. "That's a good girl, Rose. That's a brave girl. Now take your time and tell us and we'll go away and the doctor'll give you something to give you a good sleep."

"Y-yes sir. Well, I opened me door an' thinks, 'ow did the light come to be on? An' then I 'ears a movement and out from behind the door comes a man an' 'e 'as something in 'is 'and an' ups with it an' 'its me." The voice began to falter; then grew stronger again as Anthony resumed the patting. "An' that's all, sir."

Anthony said: "Thank you, Rose. Thank you very much. We'll soon be out of here now. Just tell us what this man looked like. Just anything that you remember, however little it is. Anything."

The head moved a little. "There—there wasn't anything, sir. An' it was only the flick of a second before—before——"

Anthony patted. "I know. I know. Tell you what, Rose, I'll ask some questions. Then you won't have so much talking to do. Good idea, that, isn't it? . . . Now, was he a tall man?"

"No sir."

"Was he short?"

"No sir."

"I see—medium. Was he heavily built?"

"N-no sir. About—about medium, sir."

"I see. Did he have light clothes or dark?"

"Dark, sir. Oh, an' I remember 'e 'ad an overcoat on."

"Hat on, too, Rose?"

Her eyes flickered shut while she thought. "N-o sir. No, 'e didn't."

"Good girl, Rose. What colour was his hair?"

"No special colour, sir. Sort of—sort of—*medium*."

"I see. Now I'm nearly finished, Rose, so think hard for this one. Do you remember anything particular about his face? Anything at all, Rose?"

The eyes regarded him pitifully; then once more were closed in a not undramatic struggle for thought. She said at last:

"No sir. Not anything at all, sir."

"Did he wear glasses?"

"No sir. 'Is face was—was—sort of *medium*, sir. I'm sorry, sir, but it doesn't seem like there was anything about 'im *to* remember, sir. I—I don't even know as I should know 'im again if I was to see 'im, sir. I——"

"It's all right, Rose. It's all right." Anthony patted the hand again and stood up. He looked at the hovering doctor and nodded and bade Rose good night and went out with Pike at his heels.

In the passage they looked at each other.

"Nothing there, sir." Pike drew down the corners of his mouth.

"*Medium!*" said Anthony. "Well—back to the luggage." He led the way to Parfitt's own room and once more stood over the open trunk which had been Ada Brent's and looked down at it and the surrounding litter. Pike said:

"It's all very well, sir, but we aren't getting anywhere." He pointed to the trunk. "You've been through it already."

"Very perfunctory search," said Anthony and knelt. "If at first you don't succeed, Pike, pry, pry, pry again!" His head and shoulders were now so deep in the great box of tin that his voice came hollow and booming.

Pike said: "Can't see how we'll get anywhere this way, sir. We know this man—this Evans—came here to look for something. But we don't know what he came to look for—and either he found it and took it away with him or he didn't find it. But in any case we're none the wiser."

"Wait!" said Anthony and got to his feet, holding in his right hand a little collection of papers clasped together at their corner by a fastener of bent wire. He said:

"Taffy was a Welshman: Evans is a thief. Evans came to this house and stole ... Let's see whether we can't find out what he did steal!" His long fingers turned over the papers, disclosing a cheap dressmaker's bill for fourteen and elevenpence; a receipt from the KJB Agency for nine shillings; a printed notice from the Hammersmith branch of the Carnegie Library to the effect that the return of a work apparently entitled *Lady Wickmansworth's Folly* was much to be desired; a picture post card, with no message on it, of a particularly dreary stretch of the front of Torquay and an advertisement of bathing suits torn from a Sunday paper.

Pike frowned. Had his companion been any other person than Anthony Gethryn he would have sniffed. But he went on looking. Anthony had ceased to flick the papers over and now something was visible that had been hidden before—a small, jagged-edged piece of paper, wedged under the clip.

"Ah!" said Pike and made a movement with his hand.

"Yes," said Anthony. He slipped the clip sideways and

delicately picked out the scrap. It was of cheap, coarse paper; the sort of paper which will take only printer's ink or pencil. It was about an inch along its top, half an inch wide at its broadest and tapered down to a point where the tear ended. At the right-hand edge of the top was a mark in print—possibly the down-stroke of a capital letter.

"Here is a thing," said Anthony. "And a very pretty thing!" He turned his head to look at Pike. "What the hell is it? I should know. It tells me that I know. But I'm damned if I do."

Pike took the scrap between finger and thumb and looked at it this way and that and finally held it up to the light. He said at last:

"In such a hurry that he tore it." He looked at Anthony. "That's about the first bad slip he's made, sir."

"It's only a slip if we find out, quickly, what this is." Anthony's finger pointed to the morsel of paper.

Pike said: "Some sort of cheap notice. In the morning, sir, we'll get Summers onto it. He'll find out."

Anthony groaned. "That's too late." He looked at Pike and a sudden gleam came into the green eyes. He said softly:

"You know, we're not thinking. Because we're hurrying Evans, we mustn't let him hurry us. Think, bobbie, think!"

Pike said, smiling a little:

"Thinking won't do much good, sir; not at this juncture, as you might say. What I mean, sir: *after* Summers has found out what this is"—he waved the scrap of paper—*"then's* the time to start thinking. Until then—well, we *might* hear something from Scotland about the Bellows woman."

Anthony did not seem to be listening. A frown was drawing his eyes together. He said in the voice of a man talking to himself:

"Vile paper which could only take pencil or print ... A form of some kind ..."

Pike looked at him intently: he knew this voice; he said nothing. Anthony said:

"Intrinsically of no possible value. But he did one murder and half another to get it ... it's extremely important to him but it can't be in *itself*. Ergo, it *stands* for something important."

Pike's small brown eyes were bright now, like a bird's. He said:

"By gosh! A safety-deposit ticket, by jing!" The schoolboy oaths—a trick of his when excited—rang with all the brazen fervour of profanities. Again he held the slip to the light.

Anthony took it from his fingers. "Possibly, yes. But the vile quality of the paper is much more——"

"By *cripes!*" said Pike. "Cloakroom ticket! 'Scuse me, sir!" He brushed past Anthony and reached the door in two strides and was gone.

Anthony followed leisurely. By the time he crossed the threshold of the drawing room Pike was already talking on the telephone, to the Yard. On the sofa lay Garrett, his head propped by cushions; on one of the arms to face him sat Avis Bellingham. There was more colour now in Garrett's face and he wore the sheepish look of a man who has been so supposedly feminine as to faint.

Pike was saying to the telephone: "... yes. Now: get men on this right away! Understand? At *once!* Inside an hour I want a specimen cloakroom ticket from every railway company with stations in London."

Garrett looked at Anthony. "Cloakroom ticket?"

"Baggage check," said Anthony. "That's what Evans took from Brent's trunk ... I think."

Pike said to the telephone: "*I* know they're shut. But I want a specimen from every line inside an hour. I'll be in my office by then." The tone, most definitely, was a superintendent's.

Anthony grinned. "They'd better get 'em!" he said to no one in particular.

5

It was some minutes after three when Anthony, once more in his own house, answered a telephone whose ringing was insistent.

Pike's voice came to him. "We've done it, sir!" The tone was one of sternly suppressed elation.

"Congratulations!" said Anthony. "What is it?"

"A corner off a London and Great Eastern cloakroom ticket," said the telephone.

Anthony said: "And so ... ?"

The telephone spoke at length.

"Yes," said Anthony. "Yes. Neat arrangement. Very good indeed, Pike. . . . There's one thing, though. Make absolutely sure that each man understands that he's not to arrest the person presenting the ticket. Just follow him, and then——"

The telephone interrupted. "I made sure of that already, sir. One man inside; one out. They follow the person presenting the ticket; they don't take any further steps without calling here."

"Good!" said Anthony and meant it.

CHAPTER XX

Despite the needlecraft of his mother his father's trousers were still too large for James Widgery, which explains why, at a quarter of nine on the morning of Thursday, the thirteenth of October, James fell heavily to the pavement at the corner of a street in Lambeth.

The morning was cold, with a grey sky and an east wind which hurt. And the pavement was hard. James Widgery, for all his thirteen years, began to weep.

A hand came from nowhere in particular and helped James to his feet. He continued to blubber and looked up at the owner of the hand and saw a man and heard a voice which said:

"Hurt yourself, sonny?"

James, who had stopped blubbering, began to blubber afresh. He scented consolatory copper.

"Not 'arf!" said James through tears.

The gloved hand of James's rescuer went into the pocket of his overcoat. It came out again holding a silver coin which glittered.

James, having caught his breath, produced heart-rending sobs.

"You could earn this," the man said. "And another. They might make you feel better."

"Gotter go t' school," said James Widgery but without conviction.

2

James Widgery did not go to school. Instead he appeared—at nine thirty-five upon this cold, grey morn-

ing—outside the entrance to the East Dulwich station of
the London and Great Eastern Railway. One hand was
busy in holding up the trousers of Albert Widgery; the
other was firmly clutched about a small slip of paper in
the right-hand pocket of these trousers.

He looked up at the sooty façade of the station; then
made his way through the central archway into the dingy,
acrid-smelling booking hall. To his right was a line of
ticket windows. To his left, upon the far side of a heterogeneous row of telephone booths and slot machines, there
showed a lighted recess over which appeared the word, in
great yellow letters, CLOAKROOM.

Towards this James strode as manfully as he could in
his hampering garments. He halted with his chin only a
few inches above the outer edge of the counter and whistled between his teeth to attract the attention of the sal-
low-faced man behind it. He produced from the right-
hand pocket of the trousers a hot and grimy paw and
threw down its content upon the dirty, polished wood.

The luggage clerk surveyed James without approval. His
nose wrinkling, he picked up the crumpled paper slip and
unfolded it. He looked at it for a long moment with a lack
of facial expression wholly admirable in the circumstances.
He said sourly to James:

"Jest a minute," and was gone, disappearing behind bag-
gage-filled racks.

3

At exactly twenty minutes to ten James Widgery, still
holding up his trousers with his left hand, but now carrying in his right a flat leather portfolio of a certain quiet
elegance, made his way across the station courtyard
towards the bus stop outside the railings. He whistled as
he walked. There was in him—despite the certainty of a
thrashing for having played truant from school—a great
glow of satisfaction, for did there not repose in his pocket
a whole half crown? And would there not, when he had
delivered the little bag to the gentleman, be another added
to it!

Five whole shillings! James caught his breath and ceased
to whistle and passed out of the courtyard and took his
stand on the curb to await a westbound bus.

As he did so a young and burly man came out of the station and strolled, with every appearance of leisure, over the way taken by James. As he walked he read, absorbedly, a *Racing Special.*

A bus came. James climbed inside it and, finding it practically empty, ensconced himself luxuriously in a front seat. He congratulated himself that, having still twopence of his mother's shopping money in his pocket, he need not, as yet, break the half crown. He sat forward, the bag balanced on his bony knees, and looked out of the window with the alert curiosity of the gamin. He did not know—nor would he have cared if he had—that the man who had just entered the bus and was now seated by the door reading a racing paper was what his father would have termed a "busy."

The bus began to move—and just as it did so another passenger swung himself aboard; a large, thick-looking man in blue serge. James Widgery did not know—nor would he have cared if he had—that here was yet another "busy."

4

Strictly speaking, the fare from the East Dulwich station of the L & G.E.R. to Piccadilly Circus is fivepence. Wise, however, to the ways of conductors, James made the journey for less than half of this sum. At Swan and Edgar's he alighted and, after dealing with the refractory trousers, dived like a rabbit down the more southerly of the stairways to the tube station. Close on his heels, but exhibiting no interest in him, came the two men of the bus trip.

Although the time was not yet ten-thirty in the morning there were, as always in this great underground clearing-house of humanity, many people hurrying this way and that, upward and downward, round and about—with all the fussy speed and apparent aimlessness of ants. James Widgery, at the foot of the stairway, turned to his right and, swinging the incongruous portfolio, began to walk briskly round the circle. Behind him Detective Officers Frawley and King quickened their steps. Though not now attempting to conceal their companionship, they did not speak, each occupied in keeping in view the small, red, capless head of their quarry.

James moved through the thin crowd with the speed and precision of an eel—and, slipping behind a newspaper kiosk to avoid the oncoming surge of a crowd of uniformed schoolgirls, was momentarily lost to the eyes of King and Frawley.

"Where the hell . . .?" said King, blowing out his cheeks.

Frawley said: "Right there! Behind that newspaper stall!" He saw the boy again as he spoke.

King stopped dead in his tracks. A puzzled frown, showing the beginnings of alarm, creased his bucolic face. He said urgently: "Come *on!*"

James Widgery was standing still, looking about him with quick dartings—strangely reptilian—of his red head. His face was agonized, the mouth half open, the eyes glaring as they shot their glances in every direction.

And James Widgery was empty handed.

CHAPTER XXI

James Widgery stood upon the soft grey carpet in the room of Sir Egbert Lucas in Scotland House. He felt afraid and important and dirty. He had, it seemed to him, been answering questions for countless hours but the clock upon the mantel showed only eleven-thirty.

There were several men in the room and they all, at one time or another, spoke to James Widgery. At intervals they tried to persuade him to sit down but this he would not do—so they went on questioning him as he stood. Though asked in many ways, and with plethora of subsidiaries, the questions came down, really, to two: What was the man like who had given James the job and the half crown? And what was the appearance of the person who had snatched the leather portfolio from him in Piccadilly Circus station?

James said, many times, with as much variation as was allowed by his vocabulary, that the man who gave him the job and the half crown wasn't tall and wasn't short; wasn't smart and wasn't shabby; wasn't dark and wasn't fair; wasn't thin and wasn't fat—was, in short, medium.

He was obviously attempting, with effort which brought sweat to his young brow, to tell the truth—both when he said what had gone before and when, in reply to the second question, he averred that he'd no more idea than the man in the moon who it was—or what—that had grabbed the bag away from him at his appointed meeting place with the first man. One minute the bag was in his hand; the next it was gone, pulled away from behind like. When he'd whipped round there had been so many people he

couldn't tell and none of them *seemed* to have the bag.
. . .

At ten to twelve they let him go, the tall man who had
questioned him most following him to the door and giving
him a florin.

James Widgery clattered down a stone staircase and out
of this history, while Anthony Gethryn went back into Lucas' room.

2

In an office three floors below two large and sheepish
men bore, with assumed stolidity, the imprecations of
Chief Detective Inspector Horler.

"In Frawley's case," said Horler, wiping his forehead,
"there *might* be some excuse! He's only been on this job
for six months. . . . But as for *you*, King"—he jerked his
head round to glare at his objective—"all I can say is—
the only thing I can say—well, if this sort o' thing's going
to go on, *you* won't!"

Detective Officer King played with his hat.

Detective Officer Frawley said in a very small voice:

"Excuse me, sir . . ."

"And what's more," said Horler, "if anything of the
same sort happens again I'll have to send you up direct to
the super."

King said, clearing his throat:

"Very sorry, sir!"

Frawley said in a still smaller voice:

"Excuse me, sir, but I've——"

"It's not as if it was a *difficult* job!" Horler was plain-
tive now. "Just tabbing a little kid!"

King said: "With all joo respect, sir, it might of 'ap-
pened to anyone. This boy, 'e just ducks be'ind a newspaper stall and ain't out of sight more than twenty seconds
at the very most but juring them seconds *someone* comes
up and snatches this bag right out of 'is 'and. Not seein'
the boy, it's on'y natural that Frawley and meself didn't
see 'oo snatched the bag from 'im——"

Horler interrupted: "That's enough! There's no excuse!"

Frawley coughed. He said in an ingratiating whisper:

"Excuse me, sir, but——"

Horler said: "That'll do! Excuses only make the thing

worse! Now get out, both of you! And for the love of all that's holy, don't fluff like that again!"

"Yes sir!" said King smartly and turned towards the door.

But Frawley stood his ground. Frawley said:

"Excuse me, sir, but——"

Horler, who was now opening a blue-covered file upon his desk, looked up with a savage jerk of his head. He said:

"Get *out!*"

The young and cherubic face of Detective Officer James Davenport Frawley lost much of its ruddy glow. He said with a sort of hurried meekness:

"Yes sir. Thank you, sir." And obeyed.

3

In Lucas' room was a haze of tobacco smoke through which were visible Lucas himself, Anthony, Pike and a pale-faced Garrett. Lucas' voice, giving to Pike in more polished periods what Horler had just finished giving to King and Frawley, was the only sound.

Lucas came to an end, drew a deep breath and sat back in his chair.

Pike said: "Yes sir. I know, sir. If I'm not mistaken Horler will be dealing with the men right now, sir."

"Which," said Garrett bitterly, "is a hell of a lot of satisfaction!"

Anthony uncurled himself from the depths of Lucas' biggest chair and stretched. He said:

"Children! Children!"

Garrett said: "Shut up! I'm sick of all this suavity! All I can think of is that an hour ago we were on the point of getting our man and that *now* we're further away from him than we ever were! And just because somebody puts a couple of utterly incompetent flat feet on a job which should have been done by your best men! That's rude and I know it but I'm not going to apologize!" He was sitting very straight in his chair. His eyes blazed angrily, shooting challenging glances from one to another of the Englishmen.

Lucas looked at him, not too pleasantly; but was silent.

Pike looked at the floor or, perhaps, at the tips of his brightly polished shoes.

"'Tis true, 'tis pity," Anthony murmured. "And all we can do is to hope for Bellows."

The bell of a telephone on the desk blared imperiously. Lucas lifted the receiver and spoke. He said:

"Lucas speaking. ... Yes. ... What? ... Yes, read it out." He took a pad of paper and a pencil and began to scribble as the telephone stuttered into his ear. He said quietly as he finished writing:

"Thanks. ... Yes, I'll tell him." With exaggerated care he put the receiver back upon its hook. He pulled the pad upon which he had been writing towards him and looked at his companions. A smile in which there was little mirth crossed his face. He said slowly:

"Pike, that was from your office. A wire has just come in from MacFarland, of Midlothian. I'll read it to you. It says: 'Reference your AC-42 and my reply stop Body answering description Mrs. Bellows found on moor near Kinmarnock stop Death due strangulation medical opinion three days ago post-mortem today stop Further information follows MacFarland.'"

There was a long silence.

"And that," said Anthony, "is that! You've got to admit they're thorough."

Sheldon Garrett stood up. He was very white and looked like a man tired out. He walked across to a small table by the door and took his hat from it. He said with his fingers on the door handle:

"That finishes us, doesn't it? If they'd trailed the boy properly they'd've caught the man or someone who could have led us to him. But they didn't. And now this poor old woman's been killed too. ... And so we've just got to say that he's won." He paused for a moment and looked at Lucas. He said rather hesitantly:

"If I've been overofficious and uncivil I can only apologize."

He opened the door and went out, closing it quietly behind him.

After a moment's stillness Pike sighed and got to his feet and wandered over to a window. He said without turning:

212

"I can't help sympathizing with Mr. Garrett, if you know what I mean."

4

Downstairs in the small waiting room allocated to plain-clothes men of their division Officers Frawley and King were in mid-conversation, the former loquacious, the latter staring open mouthed.

". . . so when he said 'Get out'," Frawley was saying, "I got."

It is to be regretted that the reply of Detective Officer King is not printable. But it resulted in Frawley's immediate return to Horler's office.

5

Upstairs in Lucas' room its tenant spoke. He had listened to Pike and then to Anthony without a word. Now he said suddenly:

"I don't know what's got into you fellows. Because, for the moment, we've let this unknown quantity of a murderer get away you seem to think we've failed utterly. But really all we've had's a setback. A few days ago we didn't know anything about our man except what you'd guessed. But now it's very different: we've got two starting points to work from—the murders of the girl Brent and the old woman Bellows. Scotland Yard, you know, *has* been known to catch murderers!" He sat back in his chair and looked at Anthony.

But Anthony shook his head. "It's no good, Lucas. Specious enough, but signifying nothing." His tone was flat and sombre.

Lucas became indignant. "Meaning that this fellow's too clever for us?"

Anthony opened his eyes. "No. Meaning simply that Master Evans is too far ahead of us. We had an object in this thing, you know. We wanted to stop a crime—possibly involving kidnapping—in committing which a woman called Murch was involved, working under a man called Evans. We wanted, for once, to shut a stable door before a horse was stolen. This morning, through that cloakroom ticket, we *had* a chance of doing it. But that chance was, quite literally, snatched away from us. Possibly you will catch Mr. Evans and hang him! But unless something uncomfortably like a miracle happens you won't do it until after he's done whatever it is we've been trying to stop him from doing. . . . E. & O.E., that's the situation. Ask Pike if he doesn't agree."

Pike, his long, lantern-shaped face lugubrious, looked at Lucas. He said:

"I'm afraid Colonel Gethryn's right, sir."

"Colonel Gethryn," said Lucas bitterly, "always is! According to you."

Anthony slowly uncoiled himself and got to his feet and flung his arms wide and stretched. He said:

"Well . . . what about some lunch? I suggest that, wrapped in sackcloth and reeking in ash, we visit a pub and eat tepid mutton and watery boiled potatoes. Then we might toast each other in coffee essence and lukewarm water, thereby signifying the unflattering end of that epic tale, *The Upside-Down Murder Mystery.*"

Lucas looked at him. "Very whimsical! And what the hell is upside down?"

Anthony said: "Basically, your fallacious idea that a police force is for the purpose of punishing effected crime rather than preventing projected crime. Secondarily and consequentially, this 'case' itself, because instead of discovering a crime which *has been committed* and trying to find out who did it, we've discovered that a crime *is going to be committed* and are trying to find out not only who's going to do it, but what it is that he's going to do!"

Lucas said: "Well, I'll be damned!"

Anthony smiled. "Oh, my prophetic soul. . . . Of course, my dear fellah, I'm only theorizing. And theory's far more difficult than practice—a truism amply illustrated here. In an ordinary 'case'—shades of Quiller-Couch!—there's only one *essential* unknown quantity to be proved: who did it? But in this instance there are two essential unknown quantities to be proved: (a) what's going to be done, *and* (b) who's going to do it? . . . In the first example—Police Work As It Is—fifty people would be a very high number of possible suspects; but in this business the most modest computation of possible suspects is the population of Greater London which is, I believe, about eight million. . . . All of which goes to explain why you're very wise to

214

stick to the ancient and well-established conviction that you're here to *shut* the stable doors."

Anthony drew a deep breath. He turned and walked across the room and took his hat from where it lay upon a chair.

Lucas looked at his back and said:

"Extremely entertaining! As to the concrete value of the speech, however, I won't venture to comment."

Anthony turned. "Don't worry. I'll be on the air again next Friday at two-fifteen, probably speaking from Daventree."

"Correct pronunciation," said Lucas nastily, "is Daintry. . . . Where're you going?"

Anthony halted, his hand upon the doorknob. "To find Garrett. He really oughtn't to've gone alone. He should be in bed." Once more his voice was flat and sombre. He opened the door and was gone, closing it behind him.

Lucas and Pike looked at each other in silence. Outside the window a leaden-grey sky hung over the river and the city. Inside the room there was grey discomfort. Pike said at last:

"Well, sir . . . I'd better get busy."

Lucas said heavily: "Yes. On the usual lines. Who did you put onto the Brent affair?"

"Murchison, sir. Shall I take over?"

"Yes," said Lucas slowly. "Perhaps you'd better."

Pike made a move towards the door; then hovered. He said:

"Too bad about those men, sir."

Lucas lifted his shoulders. "Spilt milk, Pike."

Pike rubbed at his long chin. "Sort of feel as if I'd let Colonel Gethryn down . . . if you follow me, sir."

Lucas said bitterly: "I'm ahead of you. But I still say 'spilt milk.' . . . Now cut off and get some lunch."

"Yes sir," said Pike gloomily and made for the door.

"And, Pike!" said Lucas suddenly in what doubtless was meant for a cheerful tone.

Pike turned. "Yes sir?"

"You never know; we *may* have a bit of luck!"

Pike tried to smile. "Thank you, sir. We need it." He turned again towards the door, which before he could reach it was flung suddenly open, narrowly missing his face.

215

Anthony stood on the threshold. He said:

"Ran into Horler as I was going out. He's on the way up. Says it's something new."

There appeared in the open doorway behind him the figures of Horler and Detective Officer Frawley.

Lucas looked at them as Anthony stepped aside. He said irritably:

"Come in! Come in!"

Horler came into the room with Frawley, a large and crimson-faced and youthful shadow, at his heels.

"Who's this?" snapped Lucas and looked at Frawley.

Anthony shut the door and stood leaning against it.

Horler cleared his throat. "Thought I'd better come right up, sir. This is D.O. Frawley, who was at Dulwich station cloakroom this morning."

"Oh," said Lucas and looked again at Frawley, who sweated.

Horler said: "Yes sir. But when I had him and the other man in my office just now to tell 'em—to reprimand them, sir, Frawley omitted to tell me something that he's just told, and in the circumstances, sir——"

"For God's sake!" said Lucas. "Get it off your chest!"

Horler said: "Well, sir, Frawley here acted in excess of his orders, which were the same as those given to all the men in all the other cloakrooms—to follow anyone notified as having presented a cloakroom ticket with the lefthand corner torn off."

Lucas flung himself back in his chair. He said between his teeth:

"*Will* you tell me what he did?"

At the tone Frawley wilted visibly; but Horler, who knew his Lucas, went stolidly on.

"Yes sir," said Horler. "When the clerk brought the ticket round to where Frawley was sitting in the back office of the cloakroom, sir, Frawley got the notion, seeing that the bag was a small one, that he might exceed his orders by opening the bag, if it was unlocked, and making a list of what it contained."

Anthony came away from the door. He said:

"Three cheers for Frawley! Where's the list?"

Lucas, disregarding this most unofficial interruption, transferred a steely gaze from Horler to Frawley, who quivered.

216

Lucas said: "Well, Frawley?"

James Davenport Frawley tried to speak and found that no words came. He coughed and tried again but, instead of the well-modulated tone which he had intended to produce, emitted a sort of roaring squeak. Appalled by this strange sound, he swallowed. He said at last in a hoarse whisper which fortunately was audible:

"Here's the list, sir." He took from his pocket a folded piece of slightly begrimed paper.

"Oh," said Lucas. "Let's look!" His tone was noticeably less barbed.

With growing courage but still profusely sweating, Frawley advanced towards the desk, treading the carpet as if it were eggshell. He laid the paper down before Lucas, snatching his hand away as if the blotter were red hot.

Lucas lifted the soiled sheet and opened it. Almost simultaneously Anthony and Pike reached his shoulders.

They read, written in round and childish hand, the following words:

> One gent's cap. Dk. brown.
>   (Maker's name cut out)
> One gent's cap. Bk. and white check.
>   (Maker's name cut out)
> One travelling chess set.
> Six gent's hkfs.
> One pr. tort.-rimmed glasses.
>   (With plain glass)
> One pr. gent's leather gloves.
> Three pkts. £1 treasury notes.
>   (About £100 in each pkt.
>   Bound with paper tape. Notes
>   not new. On binding of one
>   packet pencil notation—
>   "L 10-5 A 10-11")

Lucas looked up at last. "All right, Frawley," he said. "Thanks. Good work."

Frawley made gratified noises.

Lucas looked at Horler. "All right. Thanks."

Horler made a movement towards the door, shepherding Frawley before him. As they reached it Lucas spoke again. He said:

"Oh, Frawley!"

Frawley turned. "Yes sir?"

Lucas said: "Another time, don't lose sight of your man!"

Horler opened the door and, pushing Frawley before him, went out. The door closed behind them.

Lucas looked at Pike, who was looking at his shoes; then at Anthony, who had picked the paper from the desk and was scanning it. Lucas said:

"Well . . . 'fraid it doesn't get us much further."

Anthony said without taking his eyes from the paper in his hand:

"Illuminating bagful! Nothing like changing the headgear in case you're followed. Nothing like horn rims to change the expression. Nothing like playing chess to take your mind off bigger schemes." He was mumbling, speaking more than half to himself. "Nothing like having a few quid in your pocket."

Pike said: "Wonder what he wrote the note numbers down for if they were old ones?"

Now Anthony did look up from the paper. He shook his head. "These aren't note numbers. That's what makes 'em interesting."

Pike grew suddenly alert. "On to something, sir?"

Anthony shrugged: "God knows! And, as I'm fond of remarking, *He* won't split. I could bear to know what these figures *mean*. That's all."

"Let's look!" said Lucas and took the paper from Anthony's hand and once more himself studied it. He read aloud:

"L ten hyphen five A ten hyphen eleven . . . no, they're not note numbers. They might be anything. Want to send 'em to a cipher expert?"

Anthony shook his head. "I don't think it's a cipher. It keeps being about to mean something and then doesn't. . . . Blast it!"

CHAPTER XXII

It was a quarter to one when Garrett rang the front door-bell of 19A Stukeley Gardens. He had left Scotland Yard a full forty minutes earlier; but the taxi which clattered away just as White opened the door had borne him, not direct from Westminster, but by roundabout way of St. John's Wood in general and Lords' Mansions in particular.

He reflected as he stepped through the door which White held open for him that if he had had any sense whatever in his aching head he would have telephoned Avis before going so fruitlessly to her flat. He could have saved time this way and, more than possibly, quite a deal of this feeling of nausea and malaise which held his over-driven body in thrall.

White took his hat and helped him out of his coat. Garrett said to him:

"Seen Mrs. Bellingham this morning, White?" His tone reeked of the casual.

White looked at him with some concern.

"Yes sir," said White.

A little colour came to Garrett's cheeks.

"For a few minutes, sir," said White.

"Oh," said Garrett with what he meant for indifference. He felt tired again and sick and his head was swimming.

White said: "Mrs. Bellingham went out with Mrs. Gethryn, sir. About half an hour ago. They said something about shopping, sir."

"Oh," said Garrett again. And then with a determined smile: "Tell you what: I think I could take a scotch high-ball."

"Pardon, sir?" White cocked his head to one side.

219

Garrett said: "Sorry, whiskey and soda. With a bit of ice."

White looked at him. "What you *should* 'ave, sir," said White, "is a glass of sherry and a nice cup of soup."

"Pr'aps you're right." Again Garrett essayed a smile. "I'll be in the library." He turned and went slowly across the hall.

The library was empty but a fire blazed in the grate and the big leather sofa was plumply inviting. He sank into its depths and closed his eyes.

White came in with a tray upon which were a decanter, a glass, a bowl which steamed and a gleaming little toast rack, half full. Garrett opened his eyes and murmured thanks and closed his eyes again.

White set down the tray upon a small table which he lifted to the side of the sofa. He said:

"Your soup, sir. And sherry." In his tone was some reflection of the qualities which had once made him—so Anthony Gethryn has often been heard to say—the best sergeant in the allied armies.

Garrett drank the soup, ate two pieces of toast and lingered over a glass and a half of the sherry.

White picked up the tray and left the room and Garrett let his head drop back upon the soft leather.

He fell, slowly and floatingly, down into a deep black cavern. It was soft and warm and enticing in its utter restfulness. It was death, his mind told him dimly, and he welcomed it and felt, through his absolute relaxation, a small pang of triumph that death was so exactly as he had, alive, always imagined it would be.

He lay in divine, barely conscious torpor. He was dead and knew it and was happy. Then with a sudden and searing stab vivid consciousness returned. He was sitting. He was bound to the thing which was serving him as a chair. It felt like metal but although there was no movement from it he knew sickeningly that it had life. He thought: I wish it wasn't so *dark*—and thus became aware of the frightful quality of this darkness and tried to scream. He racked himself with the effort but no sound came from his swelling throat. He strained at his bonds and they grew tighter. The frightful certainty that life—though of a form unknown—was in these bonds clutched at his entrails. A wave of terror shook him almost to nausea—and was forgotten as a voice, quite close to him, came to his ears. It was a child's voice, shrill and shaky with fear. It said one word which went through him like a sword.

"Don't!" it said.

Garrett made a tremendous effort. He must get free and help the child. But his foul bonds grew tighter yet— and something like a huge hand clamped down upon his shoulder and shook it, gently, yet with the power of God.
. . .

2

The hand which was shaking him turned, suddenly and happily, into the normal and long-fingered and entirely real hand of Anthony Gethryn.

Garrett rubbed at his eyes and sat up, wallowing with joy in all the matter-of-factness of the room and the reassuring existence of other men cast in the same mould as himself.

Anthony and Pike looked down at him, noting the greenish tinge of his colouring and the great beads of sweat which stood out upon his forehead. Anthony said:

"Damn fool! You ought to be in bed."

Pike nodded.

"O.K. in a minute," said Garrett and mopped at his forehead. "Had a ghastly dream!"

Anthony smiled. "All about hobgoblins and a futile police force and Sheldon Garrett struggling to prevent some disaster from happening and failing. Something of that sort?"

Garrett stared at him through narrowed eyes.

"Something," he said.

"Well, don't dream any more!" said Anthony. "Just listen. After you left the Yard we had a bit of luck. We got a list of what was in that bag!"

"Go on!" Garrett began to get to his feet. "Go *on!*"

"Sit down!" said Anthony. "On a paper in the bag was a pencilled note—some letters and figures. At first we couldn't make them out, then I realized what they were. Pike still isn't convinced, so——" He broke off, taking from his pocket a small notebook and pencil. Opening the book, he scrawled some figures on it and held it under Garrett's eyes. He said:

"Oblige the Court by saying, at once, what those figures convey to you. Don't stop to think!"

Garrett said, staring perplexedly:

"Tenth of October."

Anthony turned to Pike. "And there, sir, I rest my case!"

Pike rubbed at his chin. He smiled and said:

"It's a bit of luck and no mistake!"

"If somebody," said Garrett, "doesn't tell me what all this is about I shall commit something or other."

Anthony looked at him with contrition. "Sorry," he said. He took from his pocket a slip of paper and put it into Garrett's hand. "Here's the puzzle."

Garrett read what was written: "L 10-5 A 10-11."

Anthony said: "Right from the beginning those figures meant something that I knew—but I couldn't think what it was. I thought of dates but they didn't make sense. I was just giving the whole thing up when the register turned somewhere and I realized that they *were* dates, but written as Americans write dates, with the number of the month first instead of second."

Pike said, half to himself: "So our man's a Yank!"

Anthony shook his head. "Not necessarily. For instance——"

Garrett said: "What the hell does it matter whether he's an American or an Irishman or an Eskimo!"

Anthony looked at him. "Nothing. Only I think that Pike, knowing that whatever we're trying to stop is probably in part kidnapping, wants to feel assured that the patent isn't being infringed by an Englishman."

Pike smiled a little wryly.

Garrett was studying the slip of paper. He said without looking up: "Suppose these things *are* dates—so what?"

Anthony said: "Oh, my dear fellah! One: assume that the figures mean the fifth and the eleventh of October, this present month; two: realize that even though Evans himself may not be an American these dates are stated in an American manner. Throw into saucepan and stir well and see what 'L' and 'A' *must* mean!"

Garrett shouted: "Leave and arrive!"

Pike looked up sharply.

Anthony smiled. "Exactly! The steps are easy. Kidnapping equals American; American dates with six days between them equals a voyage across the Atlantic."

Garrett, the pain in his head momentarily forgotten, jumped to his feet. "My God!" he said. His eyes blazed with excitement. "But what're we going to *do!*"

Then, as suddenly as it had come, the light died out of his face. A frown drew his brows together and he dropped down to sit once more upon the sofa. He said:

"What the hell am I getting so het up about! We haven't got anything really; not a thing!"

Anthony looked at him but did not speak. Pike said:

"You're wrong there, Mr. Garrett. You're wrong there!"

Anthony walked over to the fireplace and pressed the bell beside it and kicked the flickering logs into a blaze.

Garrett said to Pike: "Well, *I* can't see it!"

Anthony came across the room and stood by the sofa and looked down at its occupant. He seemed about to speak but broke off as the door opened.

"You rang, sir?" said White.

Anthony nodded. "Bring some whiskey. And a siphon and glasses. Oh yes, *and* ice. And when a man comes from the Green Star Line bring him straight in here."

"Yes sir," said White and was gone.

Garrett looked at Anthony. "Well, what is there?" There was weary challenge in his voice. "Pr'aps I *am* a fool—I've certainly gotten into the way of behaving like one—but I fail to understand why we should all make whoopee because there's a note in our man's bag which *may* refer to a ship sailing from New York to Southampton or vice versa! It doesn't necessarily mean a thing!"

Anthony grinned. "Because it ain't got that swing. Not the way you put it. Try this instead: Eliminating all but essentials, we have (1) the hypothesis that Janet Murch, under the direction of X (Evans-for-short), is to take part in the commission of a crime or crimes of which the whole or part is probably kidnapping; (2) the certain knowledge, lately acquired, that X-Evans *is* a dangerous criminal; and (3) the certain knowledge that X-Evans, or a confederate, noted down figures which *might* refer to the voyage of a ship across the Atlantic." He paused for a moment and looked steadily at Garrett. "Right?" he said.

Garrett, lying back against the arm of the sofa, nodded but did not speak. His eyes were fixed on Anthony's face.

"Thuslywise," said Anthony, speaking slowly now, "we come to (4) the certain knowledge that—*if* we find that a ship left New York on the fifth of this month, arrived here on the eleventh and carried a child, of wealthy parents, whose nursemaid answers to the description of Janet Murch—we have such an overwhelmingly presumptive case that we can act on it."

Garrett stood up.

Pike chuckled. "And prevent a stable door from opening, sir." He rubbed his hands and a wide smile split his long face.

Anthony bowed with courtliness. "I thank you, Superintendent!"

Garrett said slowly: "That's right enough! ... By God, it *is* right! I got all muddled." He put an unconscious hand to his throbbing head. He said quickly: "It's the thirteenth. That boat's been in two days!"

"Hold your horses!" said Anthony. "Evans has been pretty busy for the last two days."

Garrett said: "Yes. Yes, he has. But *now* ... we've got to hurry!" His dream came back to him with a dreadful clarity. He sweated.

Pike looked at him curiously.

Anthony said: "Zeal, all zeal, Mr. Easy!" He took Garrett by the arm and gently pushed him down onto the sofa. "Everything, in the words of Mrs. Eddy, is going to be all right!"

The door opened and a parlourmaid came in with a laden tray which tinkled.

Garrett said: "But we've *got* to find out about the ship! And get passenger lists and check——"

He broke off as White opened the door and admitted a neat, small person with an attaché case.

"Mr. Perry!" said White and held the door open for the departing maid and closed it behind them both.

"The answer," said Anthony, "to the Playwright's Prayer." He went across the room to where, just inside the door, there stood the subject of White's announcement. He said:

"Mr. Perry? Very good of you to come so promptly." He waved a hand. "Mr. Sheldon Garrett. Mr. Pike ..."

Mr. Perry, of the Green Star Line. Have a drink, Mr. Perry?"

The firelight glinted upon Mr. Perry's pince-nez. "Thank you," said Mr. Perry with surprising promptness. "I will."

3

"You see, therefore, Colonel," said Mr. Perry neatly, "that it must be the *Gigantic*. It is true that the Cunarder also docked on the eleventh but *she* left"—a little cough of pride was tidily inserted in the speech—"a day earlier than our ship."

"Yes," said Anthony. "Got a passenger list?"

"Indeed, yes." Mr. Perry's capable little hands set down his tumbler, unlocked the attaché case and brought forth papers.

"Good!" said Anthony and gently eased away with his shoulder the crowding body of Garrett. "Now, could you tell us whether there were any children aboard? First class, of course."

Mr. Perry coughed, firmly but without any undue noise. "Let me see now . . . that *may* be possible, to an extent." He settled the pince-nez more firmly on his nose and flicked over the pages of a neat loose-leaf book.

Garrett started to say something but Anthony's elbow took him in the ribs. He was quiet.

"Abel, Mrs.," said Mr. Perry as if to himself. "Aaronson, Miss . . . Arden, Mr. and Mrs. . . . Axel, Herr." His white fingers travelled swiftly through the leaves of the book, their rustling making subdued accompaniment to the rapid murmuring of his voice. Every how and then both fingers and voice would stop as Mr. Perry neatly and swiftly jotted down certain names. Except for his voice and the flicking of the leaves there was no sound in the room.

". . . Witherspoon, Sir Guy," said Mr. Perry. ". . . Wessex, Mr., Mrs., and Miss . . ." Again Mr. Perry stopped to make a swift note upon the pad beside him. "Walters, Mr. . . . Wyatt, the Honorable Mrs. Jeffry . . . Yoland, Mr. and Mrs. . . . Yeomans, Miss . . . Yule, Miss . . . and," said Mr. Perry, shutting the loose-leaf book with a tidy little slam, "Prince Zeffatini."

He picked up the pad upon which at intervals he had been writing and studied it for a moment. He said:

"You'll at once see the major difficulty, Colonel Gethryn." He looked at Anthony over the rims of his pince-nez. "I can tell you definitely that there was one first-class passenger who was a child—namely, *Master* Kenneth G. Lester, travelling with Mr. and Mrs. Lester, presumably his father and mother. That was, obviously, the only boy on the ship in the first class. But when it comes to *girls,* we're in a different pair of shoes."

"Quite," said Anthony.

Mr. Perry regarded him with some signs of severity. "Because, in the case of girls, we can't tell whether 'Miss' indicates maturity or the reverse."

"Quite," said Anthony.

Mr. Perry pursed his lips and, picking up his half-emptied tumbler, set it precisely to his lips and drank.

"Look here ..." said Garrett violently and was once more cut short by Anthony's elbow.

There was a small silence while Mr. Perry finished his whiskey and soda. He took the glass from his lips and set it down upon the tray. He said: "To ascertain speedily how many young *girls* were travelling first class on the ship, Colonel, there's only one thing we can do: Get in touch with some member of the ship's company who would be able to enlighten us."

"Quite," said Anthony. "Have another drink?"

"Thank you," said Mr. Perry firmly. "I will."

4

When Mr. Perry, having made much play with Anthony's telephone, finally left Stukeley Gardens the time was a quarter past six. He left behind him an empty decanter, a profoundly irritated American, a memory of one hundred per cent efficiency and the name and address of the chief steward of the *Gigantic,* who, it must be known, was on leave in London.

At ten minutes to seven Anthony's Voisin drew up outside Number 27 Elmview Crescent, Brixton. A thick, white mist, marked every here and there by the orange nimbus of a street lamp, hung over Elmview Crescent. Anthony got out of his car and shivered and turned up the collar of his overcoat and opened a small iron gate which dismally whined. He went up a narrow path flanked by sorry shrubs which loomed uncouth through the misty half-darkness. He came to a door and discovered to one side of it an iron bellpull at which he dragged. From somewhere inside the house came a ghostlike tinkling, almost immediately followed by the sound of footsteps and the illumination of a glass transom above the door.

The footsteps drew nearer and their maker opened the door. Immediately, as if destroyed by the wind of a Merlin, the ghoulish and decaying atmosphere of Elmview Crescent was dispersed. Standing in the doorway, her head thrust a little forward, the better to see her visitor, stood a tall plump woman whose smile and carriage seemed to Anthony, in this uncertain light, to tell her age as somewhere in the thirties.

Anthony raised his hat. "Is Mr. Lawes in?" he said. "Mr. Peter Lawes?"

The neat head was shaken and Anthony saw with surprise that its fairness was white and not blonde. "I'm sorry. He's out for the evening," said a round and reassuring voice.

Anthony said: "That's very disappointing. I'd some urgent business with him. They sent me here from the Green Star offices."

"I'm Mrs. Lawes—Peter's mother," said the woman. "Was it very important?"

"Very," said Anthony and gave the word full value.

Mrs. Lawes looked intently at her visitor with an eye which, for all its pleasantness, saw deep. She said at last:

"Well, Peter won't like it; but I'll tell you where you might reach him." She gave the name of the largest moving picture theatre south of the river. "He's taken a girl there. He's that fond of pictures you wouldn't believe!"

"Thank you!" Anthony smiled at her. "You're very kind."

He left a card upon the back of which he scribbled a message in case he did not find Peter. A clock somewhere in the house began to chime seven. The front door closed and the light behind its transom went out and once more the darkness of Elmview Crescent closed in upon him.

He went quickly down the path between the shrubs and out through the gate to his car.

A horde of Bedouin horsemen surged irresistibly up the slope. Captain Dick Gordon, his teeth bared in a grin of desperation, pulled his revolver from its holster and, turning back into the cave mouth, dropped to his knees and looked down at the golden head of the exhausted girl.

And then, cutting through the hoarse, feral shouts of the advancing Arabs, there came to his ear the high sweet notes of a trumpet playing "The Charge."

"The regiment!" whispered Dick Gordon—and gently lifted Alice to her feet. Below them, on the hillside, the charging lancers—gallant men of the 35th—took the Arabs on the flank, utterly routing them.

The girl's arms stole about Dick Gordon's neck and their lips met—just as, from somewhere close at hand, came the high sweet notes of a trumpet playing "The Rally."

To a sudden orgiastic blast of apparently divinely inspired music *Star of the Desert* reached its final fade-out, to be immediately replaced on the screen by a roughly printed notice which read:

"If Mr. Peter Lawes is in the theatre will he please communicate with the manager at the box office."

That was at a quarter to eight—and produced no result! It was repeated after the three short pictures which, with *Star of the Desert*, made up the program. It still produced no result. There was then another hour and a half to go before it could be shown again, and Anthony, leaving his card with the manager—a genial and helpful and courteous person happy in the name of Aaronson—set out for home.

As he drove away from the glittering portico of the Colossal Theatre the hands of the clock on his dashboard stood at eight-forty.

6

Lucia, deciding not to wait for Anthony, dined in gloomy triumvirate with Avis and Garrett—and then, on circumstantial pretext, left them in the library.

But to no purpose. She had been gone a bare five minutes when, descending from a nursery which, every night now, she was wont to visit an inordinate number of times, she went into her drawing room and found there half of the pair she had left downstairs.

Avis Bellingham was curled, a picture of beauty and apparent comfort, in a chair near the fire. There was an open book upon her knees in which she seemed engrossed.

"Hu*llo!*" Lucia was momentarily startled into surprise.

With some effort Mrs. Bellingham took her eyes from the book.

"Oh, hello!" she said vaguely and dropped her eyes to the book again.

Lucia perched upon the arm of another chair. She lighted a cigarette and studied her guest, who went on reading.

Lucia bent forward. "Try it this way," she said. "It's not so difficult!" She twitched the book from Avis' hands and turned it the right way up and gave it back.

"*Oh!*" said Mrs. Bellingham.

"Quite," said Lucia Gethryn, rather in the manner of her husband. "What's it all about?"

Avis closed the book with a slam. She said abruptly:

"I'm unchristian! *I cannot* suffer fools!"

Lucia repressed all trace of amusement. "Who's a fool?" she said.

"Mr. Thomas Sheldon Garrett!" Avis spoke without opening her teeth. "A *damn* fool! . . . If he'd mind his own business, instead of interfering with other people's and nearly getting killed and *still* going on being a busybody, pr'aps he *might* have the intelligence to realize the obvious and stop being so—so bloody noble!"

Mrs. Gethryn whistled; then broke into a laugh—which would not be denied.

"Anyone," said Mrs. Bellingham bitterly, "can laugh! . . . But I tell you——" She did not, however; before she could, the door opened upon the belated Anthony. . . .

7

Garrett was packed off to bed and Anthony, besieged by questions, ate a scratch meal.

"That's all there is to it," he said and set down a glass. "Lawes'll catch the message somewhere."

"Isn't there *anything* else we can do?" There was concern, even agitation, in Mrs. Bellingham's voice.

Lucia looked at her and smiled. "Busybody!" she said.

The door opened and White came in. He said to Anthony:

"There's a Mr. Lawes to see you, sir. Mr. Peter Lawes. He hadn't got a card."

8

Mr. Peter Lawes was young and ruddy faced and inclined towards social nervousness. He had, however, a well-developed sense of humour which made this rather naïve gaucherie amusing even to himself. He also had, very fortunately, an observing eye, a retentive memory and a quick intelligence.

He sat upon the extreme edge of one of the straighter chairs in the library and nursed a glass of whiskey and soda and replied quickly and clearly to questions. He frequently blushed and then laughed at his own embarrassment.

Anthony said, smiling at him:

"So you can say, definitely, that in the first class there were only two children?"

Mr. Lawes nodded his blond head. "That's right, sir. Mr. and Mrs. Van Renseler's little girl. And Mrs. Lester's boy."

On the couch Avis stirred. She seemed about to speak but was checked by the pressure of Lucia's fingers upon her knee.

Anthony said: "Good. Now, Mr. Lawes, how much d'you remember about the two families? Tell it any way you like. But everything."

Peter Lawes dared a sip from his glass. He swallowed and coughed and shifted still further forward upon his chair. He said:

"I had more to do with the Van Renselers, sir. So I'll start with them. Pr'aps you know the name, sir. Mr. Van Renseler's one of the richest men in New York. And Mrs. Van Renseler must have near as much money herself, being old Cresswell Graham's daughter. But they're a very nice lady and gentleman. Very nice indeed! Very quiet like and yet plenty of life and always with a civil word. And

230

Mrs. Van Renseler's a very beautiful lady. The little girl—she's a sweet kid if ever there was one—would be about nine. Just like her mother. A real happy family. Kept themselves to themselves on the voyage but still very popular—you know the sort of people I mean."

"Exactly," said Anthony.

"That seems to be all about the Van Renselers," said Mr. Lawes slowly. "Unless you'd like to ask me some questions. Sort of draw it out of the witness." Mr. Lawes blushed and smiled.

Anthony smiled back. "Any nursemaid?" he said with an admirable appearance of casualness.

On the sofa Avis Bellingham sat upright with a sudden movement.

"Yes sir," said Peter Lawes. "Nice sort of quiet girl. English, I believe."

"Oh!" said Avis. "I——" She cut herself short at the renewed pressure of Lucia's hand.

Anthony said: "Happen to remember her name?"

Mr. Lawes, holding his glass with his left hand, scratched his head with his right. He said:

"I *should* . . . it's on the tip of my tongue. . . . Got it! It was Barnes. Mabel Barnes."

Avis sank back against the padded leather of the sofa.

Anthony looked at Mr. Lawes. "Sure?" he said.

"Quite sure. It only just slipped my mind for the moment."

Anthony said: "English, you said. What sort of a girl?"

Mr. Lawes pondered. "Just an ordinary sort of a girl," he said at last. "Pleasant faced; not ugly, but not much to look at. Any age between nineteen and twenty-four. Very nice and quiet, she was, with the little girl. Just a good nursemaid, you know."

"Was she tall?" said Anthony. "And slimmish, with a good figure?"

Mr. Lawes laughed; then blushed at the sound. "Oh, no sir!"

"I see," said Anthony slowly. "All right. Now what about the people with the boy. Lester, wasn't it?"

"Yes and no. The boy's name was something else. I'm afraid I don't know what. He was around ten years old and a nice little chap. His mother married this Mr. Lester about a couple of years ago. Least, that's what I'd put it at. They weren't such a pleasant family as the Van Renselers. Mr. Lester was very short tempered. Mrs. Lester was all right but seemed sort of crushed like. She and the little boy seemed real fond of each other, but—well, they both seemed sort of scared of Mr. Lester. Nothing out of the ordinary, you know, sir; but just a case of a bad-tempered man with what they call a strong personality."

Mr. Lawes took another swallow from his glass; coughed; found that he was unable to move further forward on his chair and so sat a little further back.

Anthony said: "The old stepfather story?"

Mr. Lawes nodded.

"Two questions," said Anthony. "Are they rich? And, if so, who had the money?"

Mr. Lawes pursed his lips. "They're rich, all right. At least they had that sort of way with 'em and I'm sure it was genuine. But as for who the money belonged to— well, I wouldn't like to say."

"Any nursemaid?" said Anthony.

Mr. Lawes nodded. "Oh yes. Nice sort of girl! Very superior!" There was a personal warmth in Mr. Lawes's tone. "She was English too."

"Name?" said Anthony.

"Matthews, sir. Jane Matthews." Mr. Lawes exhibited no hesitation whatsoever.

"I see," said Anthony slowly. He did not look towards the sofa. "D'you happen to know how long both these girls—Barnes and Matthews—had had their jobs?"

Mr. Lawes blushed. "Couldn't tell you about the Van Renselers' girl, sir," he said gallantly, "but Jane—Miss Matthews had only been with the Lesters a little while. She was talking about having done two trips across the Atlantic within a couple of months."

"I see," said Anthony again.

There was a little silence. A log in the fireplace crumpled and sent up a shower of sparks. Avis Bellingham, to whom a startling thought had obviously occurred, was breathing fast, her eyes flicking quick glances from Anthony to Lucia. Mr. Lawes shifted uncomfortably in his seat and finished his drink. He sat and nursed his empty glass in the manner of a small boy playing with his cap.

Anthony said at last: "What sort of a looking girl is Miss Matthews?"

Mr. Lawes hesitated. His face scarlet, he stared straight at Anthony with very blue eyes. He said:

"She was *good* looking, sir! Sort of dark with big brown eyes—almost black, they were—and one of the prettiest skins you ever saw!"

"Short?" said Anthony. "Or tall?"

"Tallish, sir. And sort of a slim figure." Mr. Lawes's tone became reminiscent. "She looked real nice in her uniform. *Real* nice!"

Anthony rose and took Mr. Lawes's glass and, not heeding murmured protest, refilled it and brought it back.

"Thank you, sir," said Mr. Lawes and then, carried away by desire to do the right thing, raised the tumbler in the direction of the sofa. "Ladies," said Mr. Lawes, "your very good health!"

He then blushed, vividly, and put the glass to his lips. Anthony said, looking down at him as he drank:

"Just one more question, and I won't bother you any more."

The visitor took his glass from his lips. "No trouble at all!" he said.

"I just want to know," said Anthony slowly, "whether *you* know where the two families were going from the boat?"

9

A desk lamp cast a bright circle of light upon the desk of Superintendent Arnold Pike. In the aureole was an open file and, just outside and above it, the long, lantern-shaped face of Pike himself. He was gazing down at the typewritten sheets; but his eyes were unseeing. He was thinking, not of the bloody business—so drily dealt with on the official paper—of the minor canon whose body had been discovered in the cistern of his own house, but of the strange and inverted case in which the American friend of Colonel Anthony Gethryn had so thoroughly enmeshed him.

It all went round in the shrewd brain behind the long face. Ye Tea Shoppe ... the shopping list ... KJB ... Lady Ballister's suicide ... the disappearance of Janet

Murch ... the trailing of the blackmailer ... the messy death of Ada Brent ... the sense of Evans being just out of reach ... the portfolio at Dulwich station ... Master James Widgery ... the contents of the portfolio ... the possibilities of the passenger list of the *Gigantic* ... the narrow escapes of Sheldon Garrett ... the strangling of the shadowy Mrs. Bellows ...

A lot! The dickens of a lot! And yet, so far as it concerned what they were trying to do, nothing at all!

The proverb concerning the horse and the stable door came into Pike's mind for perhaps the fiftieth time this evening. He smiled a little wryly; he was remembering a recent interview with Sir Egbert Lucas. ...

He was wrapped so many folds deep in thought that he started violently at the shrill pealing of one of the telephones beside him. He stretched out a hand for it and lifted its receiver and answered the voice of Anthony Gethryn.

"The chief steward of the *Gigantic's* just gone," said the voice. "We're getting somewhere. Ready?"

"Yes," said Pike and reached for pad and pencil.

"Two children only," said the telephone. "A girl—Van Renseler—with mother and father; rich; New York; believed to've come straight to London from Southampton. ... Got it?"

Pike finished scribbling. "Yes," he said.

"The other kid's a boy," said the telephone. "Surname unknown at the moment, travelling with his mother and stepfather; name, Lester; American; rich. Believed to've come up to London, like the Van Renselers, direct from the boat."

Pike scribbled fast. "Anything more, sir?"

"There's little; but how much it *might* be, Pike! Both families had English nursemaids. The Van Renselers' was called Mable Barnes and seems nondescript. But the Lesters'—the Lesters', Pike—the Lesters' nursemaid bore the name Jane Matthews. Jane Matthews: you'll note the initials?"

"Janet Murch," said Pike without knowing he had spoken.

"Exactly!" said the telephone. "And she was tall and slim and—according to the impressionable Mr. Lawes—of certain attractions. Also the Lester family—as compared

234

with the Van Renselers anyhow—wasn't so happy! Stepfather's unpleasant! . . . And if you put that all in your pipe, how long before we get any smoke?"

Pike grinned. When he spoke there was in his voice a reflection of the excitement in Anthony's. He said:

"It's a matter of luck, sir. I'll get right onto it. I gather that you want the present whereabouts of both families with more particular attention paid to the Lesters."

"How right, Pike!" said the telephone.

"How late can I call you, sir?"

"At any time, Superintendent!" said the telephone. "At any time at all. And if you're waking call me early, call me early, Super dear, for tomorrow I *might* be Queen of the May!"

The click of a replaced receiver sounded in Pike's ear. He put down this telephone and reached for another and became, on the instant, very busy indeed.

CHAPTER XXIII

The bedside extension of Anthony's private telephone—the one which is listed nowhere—began to ring, its insistent trill cutting through sleep like a sharp sword.

He sat up, awake with that instantaneous awareness which has so often served him well. He made a long arm and took the receiver from its hook and spoke into the mouthpiece.

"Pike here, sir," said a voice harsh with fatigue. "The Van Renselers are at the Alsace Hotel, Suite 306. The nurse is with them and the little girl. That's easy enough. But the Lesters—well, they're a different matter, sir."

"Haven't you got onto 'em at all?" Anthony's tone was sharp.

"Only in a manner of speaking," said the weary voice. "They came up to town straight from the boat and stayed at the Milan. But they left yesterday morning."

"Where for?" Anthony's voice was still sharper.

"That's just it. We don't know—yet. All I can get from the hotel is the address of Lester's bank and the information that he told several people that he and Mrs. Lester and the boy—the boy's name is Barris, by the way; Kenneth Barris—were going on a motor tour."

Again Anthony interrupted. "Motor tour! At this time of year!"

"Yes sir; it does sound fishy. But I've got the number of the car. And I've sent out an all stations call. I should hear something within the next hour. . . ." He hesitated, then added: "Sorry, sir."

Anthony said with a cheerfulness which he was far from feeling:

"Don't be an ass! Been to bed?"

"No," said the tired voice.

"Well, I have," said Anthony. "You ought to come round and kick me. But don't; go and have some breakfast instead. In the meantime I'll just do a little private check on the Van Renselers. We mustn't miss anything."

2

At twenty-two minutes past eight Pike, newly shaven and fed and with most traces of vigil gone from his face, re-entered his office.

Sitting upon a corner of his table, he reached for the telephone and spoke into it. It said in answer:

"No sir—nothing yet." And then: "Just a moment, sir, there's a call just coming in from York. . . . Hold on, please. . . . Here it is, sir."

3

At eight-thirty Anthony's private telephone was answered by White.

"Colonel Gethryn there?" said a familiar voice.

White said: "Colonel Gethryn's out, Mr. Pike. He said if you called I was to take a message and tell you he'd be back by nine-thirty."

"H'mm!" Sounds of cogitation were borne along the wire. "Tell him just this, will you: the Lester car's been seen in Yorkshire. Near Stagby. It was going north and—er—just say everything's all right, so far."

4

At twenty minutes to nine Miss Patricia Van Renseler came out of the bathroom of Suite 306 in the Alsace Hotel. Outside the window in the little lobby a pale winter sun shone with almost silvery brightness. Miss Van Renseler stood upon tiptoe and looked out of the lobby window at the river. There was a barge with a russet sail and the water glittered and cohorts of sea gulls changed formation against a hard blue sky.

An exclamation of pleasure escaped Miss Van Renseler—to be immediately replaced by one of surprise at a sound which had come from behind her. She turned to see that she was not alone. A long man in overalls lay upon the floor near the outer door. With tools he was doing something to the bell box of the telephone.

Miss Van Renseler, her hands deep in the pockets of a blue dressing gown the same colour as her eyes, walked towards him. He looked up, showing a lean, dark face—slightly grimy—which smiled at her.

Miss Van Renseler liked the smile. She smiled herself. She said:

"Who are you?" in an accent whose transatlanticism was only delightful.

"Telephone man, missy." The man in overalls was sharply Cockney; but he smiled again.

Miss Van Renseler chuckled. "You talk like Whosit in the movies," she said. "But I like you." She surveyed him with her head on one side. "Why've you got green eyes?"

The man on the floor opened the black box of the telephone bell. He said:

"So's I c'n spot the 'obgoblins!" He twisted his head and peered into the box in a manner which brought a bubble of laughter from Miss Van Renseler's throat.

A door opened and there was a rustling of starched skirts and a woman's voice, high pitched yet soft and pleasant. It said:

"Your mother wants you, Pat——" And then broke off the sentence suddenly. "Oh! Is there something wrong with the phone?"

The telephone man was tinkering with a screw driver. He looked round and up at a dumpy woman in the indoor uniform of a nursemaid of the higher sort.

"Fix it in a couple o' seconds, miss," he said.

From behind a door came another voice. A woman's.

"Pat!" it called. "Pat darling!"

"Bunchy!" said Miss Van Renseler to her nurse. "*You* talk to him! He's sort of nice!" She suddenly raised her voice and shouted "Com-ing!"

The man on the floor heard a thudding of running feet; a door opening; greetings in a deep woman's voice and a laughing man's; the sound of a small boy leaping onto a bed; squeals of merriment from Miss Van Renseler mingling with the other voices.

The nurse shut the door. The telephone man got to his

feet and picked up his tool bag and towered over the nurse and looked down at her pleasant, placid face.

"Nice little nipper," he said. "Pretty too!"

"Oh *yes!*" said the nurse. "Is the phone all right?"

"Yes miss," said the telephone man. "*Everything's* all right here!"

He went out of the suite, ran down the stairs and, out on the Embankment, took a taxi for 19A Stukeley Gardens, a bath and breakfast.

5

At nine-thirty Master Kenneth Barris came out of the ground-floor lavatory of the Bull and Bear in Cloughton and made his way into the coffee room.

It was cold in the coffee room, which somehow was like a roller-skating rink which has missed its vocation. At the far end was a fireplace in which a recently lighted fire fought against its draughtless construction and poured out into the room intermittent streams of greyish-black smoke.

Near the hearth, coughing at the smoke, Kenneth's mother and his stepfather sat at a table covered with the preliminary dishes of what the Bull and Bear considered breakfast.

His mother smiled at Kenneth cautiously—a thin woman of indeterminate age whose pleasant face bore traces of past beauty. Kenneth, with a glance of mingled defiance and apprehension at the paper behind which his stepfather was entrenched, returned the silent greeting. He approached the table and sat, making as little noise as possible.

But the paper rustled and was lowered. Over it appeared the heavy-featured face of John Lester. A thin but virulent jet of smoke shot from the fire and, it seemed, straight into his lungs. He coughed with rattling violence and glared at his stepson and spoke angrily. He was, it seemed, burdened beyond endurance by the inability of his stepson to come to meals in time. He told what he thought of his stepson, and what—if the stepson were not very careful—he would do to him. He switched attention to his wife at her almost whispered intervention, and then was himself interrupted in midspeech by the appearance of a slatternly waitress.

John Lester stared at her. She should have been carrying a tray laden with the sorry best that the Bull and Bear could provide: instead she was empty-handed. John Lester glared his unbelief.

The waitress sniffed. "Some'un askin' see tha," she announced.

Her speech was North Country at its broadest, and therefore, to John Lester, completely incomprehensible. He said, between his teeth:

"Where is our breakfast? We've been waiting nearly an hour." He articulated every word clearly, in the manner of a tourist in a foreign land striving to make the aborigine brain find meaning in a strange tongue.

The waitress sniffed. "Some'un askin' see tha," she said again.

Kenneth Barris stared at his stepfather with uncowed eye. He said curtly:

"She means someone wants to see you."

Mrs. Lester looked at her small son with an almost imperceptible shaking of her head.

John Lester looked at his stepson—but before he could speak the sound of a heavy, measured tread made him look towards the door.

A man was coming across the room. He was a burly, stolid person in tweed clothes of the pattern known as pepper-and-salt. His boots squeaked a little and he carried, in a hand of approximately the shape and almost the size of a leg of mutton, a hat which Kenneth would have called a derby.

The waitress sniffed. " 'Ere 'a be!" she said, and was gone.

The visitor loomed large over the table. John Lester stared at him. So, with varying expressions, did the woman and the small boy. Of their existence, however, the visitor seemed unaware. He said:

"Mr. Lester? Mr. John Lester?"

Lester nodded. He said with heavy sarcasm:

"You have the advantage of me, sir."

"My name's Bull," said the newcomer, his gaze fixed and oxlike. "Inspector Bull of the Yorkshire Constabulary."

At twenty minutes to eleven Anthony Gethryn, now in clothes of normal elegance, sat upon the edge of the bed in the largest spare room in 19A Stukeley Gardens and surveyed its occupant.

Sheldon Garrett had slept, and well. There was some colour in his face and last night's look of gauntness had lessened. He had eaten a large breakfast with pleasure and said so. His cigarette tasted of tobacco. He began upon expression of gratitude and was cut short.

"The Van Renselers," said Anthony, "are all right. I went to the Alsace myself. As a telephone man. Nice child; apparently pleasing parents. Excellent atmosphere. Nothing ominous."

"Nurse?" said Garrett.

"All right," said Anthony. "Nothing like your description. Kid's on very good terms with her."

Garrett crushed the cigarette in his saucer. "It must be the others, then—what's the name?—Lester."

Anthony nodded. "Definitely. But unfortunately, *they* aren't staying put. They're on a motor tour."

Garrett sat upright. "Odd time of year," he said.

"Exactly," said Anthony—and there was a silence broken by a knocking upon the door and a parlourmaid who said:

"Mr. Pike to see you, sir. He's in the library."

"I'll come down," said Anthony; then looked at Garrett. "No. Ask him to come up."

They waited, and Pike came, smiling. He said, after greetings:

"Well . . . we're on to the Lesters!" He looked at Garrett while he spoke. "They stopped for breakfast at an inn in Cloughton. Inspector Bull of the Yorkshire police interviewed the man *and* the nursemaid."

Garrett sat forward. "What's the setup?" he said.

Pike stared. "Beg pardon, sir. . . . Oh, I see . . . well, it seems they must be our people. I spoke to Bull on the phone and got the story direct from him. He's a good man; very sound. What he says, in brief, is that there's something odd, as you might say, about the whole—er . . ." He hesitated, groping for a word.

"Setup," said Garrett.

Anthony laughed. "Say it, Pike. Don't be insular!"

Pike grinned; then grew immediately serious. "It's this way, sir: Bull didn't know what he was looking for because my instructions carefully omitted anything definite; he simply knew, like the other officers all over who got the orders, that under some pretext he must interview the Lesters, if they stopped their journey in his district, and then communicate with me after he'd got all the information he could about where they were going and cetera—a general picture, as you might say, of the family *and* servants."

"And," said Anthony, "Bull no likee setup. Why?"

Pike, aware that he was being kept up into his bridle, repressed a fleeting smile. He said:

"Just coming to that, sir. Bull—and don't forget he knows nothing—didn't like the nursemaid!"

Garrett threw back the bedclothes and swung his legs to the floor.

"Passport?" said Anthony.

Pike looked at him. "Seemingly all correct in the name of Jane Matthews, sir. Bull got all the particulars and I've started a check."

"The little more," said Anthony, "and how Murch it is!"

Pike smiled dutifully. "But, as you can see, sir, the check's going to take time. Quite a time."

Garrett said: "You say this inspector didn't like the girl?"

Pike nodded. "After he'd finished with Lester, Bull made opportunity to talk to the girl and—well, he didn't cotton to her. Nothing definite, you know, but her manner wasn't right. He said she seemed a bit too quick to resent police inquiries."

"What *were* the inquiries?" said Garrett.

"Very tactful, you may be sure, sir." Pike looked slightly pained.

Garrett was putting on a dressing gown. "Why's tact necessary?"

"Well, really, sir!" Pike's tone was mildly astonished. "We've got to be careful. As it is, Bull had to trump up some question about Alien Registration even to have the right to speak to them. You see, there's nothing against these people: not yet."

242

Anthony said: "Pike: shake your sleeve!"

Pike laughed like a small boy, proud of an uncle's shrewdness. "Well, sir, there's a funny thing—Bull didn't like Lester any more than he did the nurse. Not so much, in fact. 'Superintendent,' he said to me, 'if there's anything rum about that lot, there's two of 'em in it—Lester himself and the nursegirl.' "

Garrett was lighting a cigarette from a box on the dressing table. He turned and walked across to Pike and stood facing him.

"And so what?" he said harshly.

Pike stared. "I don't quite follow you, I'm afraid, sir."

"Mr. Garrett," said Anthony, "is wondering what action the police are taking. What he'd like is to have these people detained."

"Yes," said Garrett. "Hold 'em—*and* give 'em the works!" He dropped into a chair.

Pike drew in his breath with a reproving little hiss. "We can't do anything like that here, sir." He shook his head slowly, in a movement of absolute negation.

Garrett stood up suddenly. A half-muffled groan of exasperation escaped him, but no words came.

"What we *have* done," said Pike, "is to issue general orders that the Lester car's to be watched for and reported on everywhere it goes. When the party stops for any reason, we shall know at once and a watch—though unobtrusive, as you might say—will be kept to see that nothing goes wrong. When they stop for the *night*——" He broke off and glanced towards Anthony, who now stood at the window. "Well, even if there's no *official* action, I'll wager that Colonel Gethryn and yourself will probably be at the place before morning."

"Very nice!" said Garrett savagely. "All very nice—unless something happens at some place along some road where there aren't any policemen! Which doesn't seem a bit unlikely!"

An angry light came into Pike's eyes and in his long face the mouth became a narrow line. He said stiffly:

"Mr. Garrett, this isn't the United States! Rightly or wrongly we've got what you might call a cast-iron legal system. . . ."

Garrett said harshly: "I know all about fhat! But don't you realize that if somebody doesn't *do* something——"

243

"Shut up!" said Anthony suddenly. He came from the window and stood looking from one angry face to the other. "Pike, Mr. Garrett's got some cause to be worried, and what's biting you is that you know it and can't do anything about it. Garrett, it's no good snapping at Pike; he's done everything that can be done—and a bit more! I'll do plenty of unofficial stuff—but we mustn't go chasing blindly all over the north of England when our people may be doubling back for all we know. So there's nothing for it but to wait until they're set for the night. And there are worse things to put your trust in than Scotland Yard. . . . Now, be good little men and make up!"

Garrett smiled, the angry light fading from his eyes. "Sorry!" he said.

Pike's mouth appeared again. "And me, sir."

"Bless you!" said Anthony and surveyed them benignantly. "Dear kiddies!"

7

The morning crept on and became noon—and still the sun, as if determined to make fools of the Air Ministry and those unsung necromancers, Zambra and Negretti, went on shining from a sky of impossible blue.

It shone, with what to Avis Bellingham seemed delightful partiality, through the french windows of Lucia Gethryn's drawing room and made of that charming chamber a place in which, thought Avis, a man could not be otherwise than happy—not even a man who, like the man with her now, was suffering from an idée fixe and a broken head.

She did not *think* this, she found; she *knew* it, although for ten minutes no word had passed between them and she could not, as she sat at Lucia's piano, even see her companion.

From her fingers—long slender fingers whose looks were so much at variance with the controlled strength of their touch upon a keyboard—flowed the last, rippling, sweet yet discordant notes of Ravel's "Fountain." She sat motionless for a moment—and then caught her breath as a man's hands fell upon her shoulders.

"Tom!" she said—and twisted from under the hands

244

and turned and was caught up by arms whose strength appalled and delighted her.

She found herself upon her feet, but the arms were still around her. A voice said her name and lips fastened upon her own lips and the world went away.

Then the lips went away and the world came back and was focused in Garrett's eyes. She put her hands upon his shoulders and heard herself laugh—a little, shaky sound. She said, in a voice which sounded to her own ears far away:

"Mr. *Garrett!* This *is* sudden!" And was immediately horrified at the banality of the attempted jest.

He smiled down at her, the old smile which she had known when they first met; the smile which made his eyes almost disappear; the smile with which she had fallen in love—how many years ago was it?—and which she had been forced, until she had found its owner so improbably asleep in her London flat, to put out of her mind as completely as she might. He said:

"It's time I talked to you. Sit down!"

He put his hands upon her arms and she found herself again seated upon the piano stool. He said:

"I haven't been myself. I've been—well, you know how I've been. I ought to apologize—and I do! I——"

Avis interrupted him. "Of *course* I understand!" she said and smiled up at him and set a hand upon his arm.

"How could I help but understand!" she said—and got to her feet, closing the fingers of the hand.

"You see," she said, "I've something to tell you; something I ought to have told you weeks ago!"

She moved the hand from his arm to his shoulder. She stood very close to him. She said:

"You mustn't be angry with me. I——"

She broke off, abruptly. Her eyes clouded, losing their blueness behind a veil of steely grey. They had seen the thought of her and the bright gleaming of happiness go from the man's eyes. She said:

"You're not *listening!* You're not even thinking about—about us! You're——"

There was misery in Garrett's face, and a puzzled wonder. He strove with evil-shaped, misty thought and wrenched his mind back to this room and this woman whom he loved. He said:

"Darling, forgive me! I was ... I suddenly had ..." He struggled painfully for words. "Look here, I *know* there's something wrong with this business! There's a *mistake!* I—I feel it! It's something wrong and twisted. There's something, somewhere, going on *now,* that we ought to be stopping! I——"

He cut himself short. He was looking at a back which receded.

"*Avis!*" he said—and took a step in pursuit and found himself alone, the sound of the closing door ringing in his ears. ...

The grandfather clock in the corner by the french windows came to life. It whirred and struck. Its hands showed the time as fifteen minutes past noon.

8

At thirty minutes past noon, a woman entered a sitting room on the seventh floor of the Alsace Hotel. She was laughing at something said to her in the bedroom which she had just left. She was neither short nor tall but most pleasingly in drawing; and of an age which might have been anything between twenty-eight and thirty-one. She walked to the high windows and stood looking out, over the green of gardens and the grey of the Embankment, at the sunlight playing upon the river. Stray rays of this light picked out gleams of gold in her neat dark head and bathed with hard radiance a face which had no reason to fear it.

A man came into the room and stood with an arm about her shoulder. He was tall and heavy and moved with the sure, easy smoothness which tells of conditioned muscles. His clothes looked like an Englishman's, but in his clean-shaven face was something pleasantly and essentially transatlantic. He held the woman close and they stood in silence, studying the river and the roofs beyond it.

"*This* isn't London!" said the woman at last. "Oughtn't it to be foggy? Or at least raining? This is a sort of New York day."

The man's arm tightened its grip about her shoulders. He said: "What time's Brat coming in?"—and would doubtless have been answered had not the bell of a telephone begun to ring.

The woman crossed the room and picked up the instrument. She said into the mouthpiece:

"Hello? Who is this?"

A man's voice came along the wire, but it did not answer her question. It was a flat, toneless voice with no accent in particular. It said:

"Mrs. Van Renseler?"

"Yes," said the woman. "Speaking."

"Mrs. Theodore Van Renseler?" The flat voice was insistent, an unpleasing sharpness somewhere concealed within it.

"Yes," said the woman. "Who *is* this talking?"

"Are you in the sitting room of the suite?" said the voice. "Or the bedroom?"

Helen Van Renseler looked up at her husband, who now stood close. Her face was screwed up in a deliberately comic—and extremely attractive—expression of histrionic bewilderment. Into the telephone she said icily:

"If you won't say who you are I shall hang up!" She winked at her husband.

"You'd better not," said the flat voice. "For your own sake!" It went on at some length, while Van Renseler studied his wife's changing expression at first with amusement, then with curiosity and finally with anger.

"Give me that!" he said at last and held out his hand for the telephone.

But the owner of the flat voice had rung off, and Van Renseler spoke into a dead instrument. His wife was frowning. She said:

"What an extraordinary ..." and let her voice trail off into silence.

"What's it all *about?*" said Van Renseler angrily; then laughed at himself.

"Must've been *crazy!*" said his wife; but the frown was still etched into her forehead.

Van Renseler took her by the shoulders. "Shake the life out of you!" he said. "What—is—it—all—about?"

He was smiling; but the woman was not. She said:

"It was a man's voice. It was sort of—well, beastly! And he said there was a letter in the Railway Guide." She pointed to a small corner bookshelf. "What do they call the things? ... Bradshaw."

247

She twisted away from her husband's hands and crossed the room.

"Some publicity stunt," said Van Renseler, and followed and stood beside her as she stooped and pulled the heavy Bradshaw, in its stiff leather case, from a shelf. She said, speaking as if to herself: "Page two-o-two-three ..." and began, with fingers that seemed a little uncertain, to flip over the leaves.

Van Renseler said: "I tell you it's some advertising trick!"

Helen Van Renseler turned a page—and a piece of note paper, covered with typescript, fluttered to the floor.

She was upon it before her husband could move. She began to read as she was straightening her body—and as she read the colour drained from her face.

"My *God!*" said Van Renseler, watching her. He put an arm about her and felt her body sag against the support. Over her shoulder he read:

To Mr. and Mrs. Theodore Van Renseler:

At 12:15 P.M. today we took charge of your daughter Patricia. If you wish to have her returned to you unharmed you are to carry out the following instructions *to the letter:*

> 1. Make no communication whatsoever to the police—or to anyone—concerning the situation. (You may be sure that if you fail to observe this instruction you will not see your daughter again.)
> 2. Obtain fifteen thousand pounds (£15,000) in one-pound currency notes.
> 3. Place this money (which must not be marked) *and* Mrs. Van Renseler's emerald necklace, earrings and pendant in a plain suitcase.
> 4. Mr. Van Renseler will bring the suitcase to Cromwell Road station at nine-thirty o'clock this evening.
> 5. He will then purchase a ticket and go down to the westbound platform by the *stairs.*
> 6. Someone will approach him within a few minutes of his arrival. This person will say, "Have you a safety match?" which is a signal for Mr. Van Renseler to hand over the suitcase.
> 7. The person taking the suitcase will then leave the

platform. Mr. Van Renseler will stay where he is for five minutes.

If these instructions are fully and personally carried out, and the contents of the suitcase are found to be in order, Patricia Van Renseler will be returned to you before to-morrow evening.

CHAPTER XXIV

Within a stone's throw of Victoria underground station there is an underground cocktail bar. It is, perhaps, the most pleasant of its kind in London and known only to a sufficient clientele. It is open during the usual hours; it is never empty and desolate, nor full and discomfortable. It is always quiet, unfailingly cheerful and invariably soothing. The liquor it stocks is of the best and its staff are expert craftsmen.

Here, at seven o'clock in the evening, were some eight or nine regular customers who set about at tables—and Sheldon Garrett, who stood at the bar.

He was doing what, out of respect to his battered skull, he should not have done—drinking his third martini. It was a good martini, but to Garrett it tasted like water tainted by the dissolution of a slate pencil.

The barman watched him with anxious eye. "How's that one, sir?"

Garrett sipped and essayed a smile of appreciation. He said the right things in a poor imitation of the right voice—and let his glance flicker towards the archway at the end of the bar.

Here, in the nearer of two telephone cubicles, Anthony Gethryn spoke urgently into a mouthpiece set immovably three inches too low for comfort. He said:

"Well, that's that. But they'll *have* to stop somewhere soon!"

"Yes sir," said Pike's voice. "And where shall I call you when they do?"

Anthony said: "If I'm not here—Victoria-84328—call

250

the Buckingham Theatre. I might take Garrett there. Anything to get his mind off this hunch of his."

Pike's voice said: "You sound worried, sir."

"I am. Garrett's no fool, and hunches aren't always to be despised. He says there's something wrong—and *I'm* beginning to feel it. . . ." Anthony's voice tailed off into silence.

"It's very trying, sir, waiting like this." Pike's tone was soothing. "Especially when, as you might say, our hands are tied."

"Yes, Auntie; yes *indeed!*" An antidote for oil was noticeable in Anthony's voice. "Jet is black, and the clouds over the mountaintop are the purest white. . . . In other words, Pike, call me either here or at the theatre the minute you hear where the Lesters lodge."

"Yes sir," said the telephone.

Anthony went back to the bar and his unfinished drink. He said:

"Just spoken to Pike. Lesters last noticed as having tea in Burtonbury. Then drove on. Pretty soon they're bound to put up for the night. Then we'll fly up——"

Garrett drank more slate-pencil water. "God!" he said. "I wish they'd hurry."

"Yes," said Anthony, and concealed irritation behind his glass.

Garrett said: "I wish we could *do* something! . . . Pike going to call you here?"

Anthony set his glass down on the bar—so hard that he experienced relief that it did not break. He said:

"No. At the Buckingham."

"The what?"

"The Buckingham Theatre," said Anthony. "It calls itself a Palace of Variety. In your tongue—a vaudeville joint."

"Oh!" said Sheldon Garrett. "But I——"

"But nothing!" said Anthony. "We're going."

2

Patricia Van Renseler waked. Her head hurt badly, worse than it ever had in all her ten years. And something had happened to the sheets, so that the blanket was scratchy against her chin. And she ached all over the way

251

she had when scarlet fever had made her so ill. There was a bad taste in her mouth, too, and she was so thirsty that she could not think of anything but water.

She opened her eyes upon darkness. She closed them again, quickly, because with the lids lifted a funny, burning pain shot through them.

She opened the parched lips. She tried to shout "Bunchy!" but only a croaking sound came from her mouth.

This frightened her—and, opening her eyes again in spite of the pain, she made as if to sit up.

But she could not. There was something around her body, outside the bedclothes, which pressed her down. And now she could see a little—and she did not know the room she saw!

Her aches were forgotten, and the funny pain behind her eyes, and her thirstiness, and the scratchiness of the blanket—all swallowed up in a great, unreasoning, comprehensive wave of terror.

"Mummy!" she screamed.

The sound, though roughly edged from the dryness of the small throat, was high and sharp and piercing.

A door opened, showing a rectangle of yellow light and a tall slim woman's figure, which advanced.

Patricia screamed again. But this was only half a scream, cut short by something soft which fell across her nose and mouth and was then pressed down by a hand whose weight made no concession to the youth of the face it crushed.

"Quiet!" said a voice which Sheldon Garrett would have recognized among thousands. "Quiet!"

It was a deep, harsh voice and had in it a definite ring of masculinity which accorded strangely with the ultrafeminine grace of the woman's body and movements as she sat upon the side of the bed, still pressing down upon the cloth and what was beneath it.

"Quiet!" she said again. "Understand me?"

Desperately Patricia's small head was nodded. Air, now, was her one desire; a necessity more vital even than water had seemed.

The pressure was eased; the cloth pulled away. Patricia drew in shuddering draughts of air. Her small body

252

shook—but beyond the gasping of her breath no sound came from her.

"And *now,*" said the woman, the deep voice even deeper, "you'd better go to sleep again."

With one hand she took the child's right wrist, drawing the whole naked arm clear of the blankets.

Through Patricia's dry, bruised lips came a whisper of sound; a shaking whisper which was inadequate gauge of the terror which gripped her.

"Please!" said the whisper. "Please, I——"

"*Quiet!*" The deep voice was savage in its harshness.

The woman's free hand came from her side as she spoke. It held something which faintly glittered.

"*Oh!*" said Patricia on a high note of pain. Something had pricked her arm just above the elbow. It hurt.

She tried to pull the arm away, but the woman's hand about her wrist was like steel. . . .

"A-ah!" sighed Patricia on a low note of drowsiness. And then: "Theo . . . Helen . . . I . . ."

The voice died away—to be replaced by heavy, laboured breathing.

Once more Miss Patricia Van Renseler slept. . . .

3

The first performance at the Buckingham was in full swing.

There were two acrobats and a girl in tights who handed them things. There was a performing seal who applauded himself and his self-satisfied trainer. There were a "Whirlwind" dance team; a Lancashire comedian; a family on stilts called the Stargays Brothers, and a remarkable person who wrestled and fought with a dummy.

And then there was Eustace Vox—a name which minimized the surprise of finding that he was a ventriloquist and a good one. Billed as THE MAN WITH THREE FRIENDS, he presided at a dinner table for three, his two guests being life-size dummies.

The audience, held silent for nearly two minutes by the skill of the one human on the stage, began to titter, then to laugh uproariously. For the dialogue, said by many to be the work of Mr. Vox himself, was excellent.

And then the third friend of the title made her appearance. It was another life-size dummy, operated by ingenious mechanism. It wore the neat uniform of a parlourmaid.

It spoke—and somewhere in the middle of the third row of stalls a man stood up, clapped a hand to his head, and in no uncertain voice called upon a traditional power.

He was a tall man who, by accent, clothes and bearing, should have known better. And he did not improve upon his first inexplicable *gaffe* by his subsequent actions—which consisted of seizing the arm of the man sitting next to him and dragging this person—heedless of the shoes and knees and comfort of others—out of his seat and the auditorium.

4

Garrett blinked in the sudden light of the exit corridor. He was breathing hard and his head hurt him. Behind him the laughter from the packed house dwindled in volume as the door through which Anthony had dragged him swung shut. He said irritably:

"What's the big idea!" and then suppressed further speech as he saw his companion's face.

Anthony said: "The women in the teashop: there was a short square masculine one?"

Garrett nodded.

"And a tall, willowy, feminine one?"

Garrett nodded.

"And the short masculine one had a deep harsh masculine voice as she bullied the tall willowy one, who had a high soft feminine voice?"

Garrett nodded.

"How do you know," said Anthony slowly, "which voice belonged to which woman?"

Garrett stared. "Damn it! I was there and ..." His voice tailed away, and he looked at Anthony with open mouth. He said in a whisper:

"My God! I *don't* know! I just assumed——"

"Come on!" said Anthony—and was gone.

CHAPTER XXV

In the sitting room of Suite 306 in the Alsace Hotel Helen Van Renseler sat in a straight-backed chair. She was motionless and rigid. Her face was blank and on her cheeks the dustings of rouge showed angry against the surrounding pallor. Every now and then the pupils of her eyes would narrow to pin points; then gradually widen until they well-nigh covered the irises.

She was trying, without success, to keep these eyes from looking towards the clock upon the mantel. Its hands stood at five minutes past nine. It seemed to her that they would never move. She wished passionately that they would and prayed desperately that they would not.

They did. They reached the sixth minute; then the seventh.

A soft knocking came upon the outer door of the suite. A scream welled up in Helen Van Renseler's throat, but she forced it back—and found herself standing.

The knock came again; a little louder—and she found herself just beside the outer door, her fingers on its handle.

• • •

The fingers turned the handle, and their arm pulled back the door.

A tall man stood upon the threshold. Her eyes took in a picture of him which told her mind nothing. He said:

"Mrs. Van Renseler?"

Her head nodded. The man stepped over the threshold, taking the handle from her grasp and shutting the door.

Through the grey mist which seemed to swirl about her mind she was aware of his eyes. They were green eyes, hard with purpose.

255

"Mrs. Van Renseler," he said, "is your daughter with you?"

The grey fog was ripped apart. She said in a strange, shrill voice:

"Who are you? I——"

The man interrupted her. He said:

"Mrs. Van Renseler: Is your daughter here with you—*now?*"

She breathed through distended nostrils. She said:

"Of course. She's been asleep for hours. Who are you?"

For a moment the man looked at her; then moved quickly past her to the first of the inner doors and through it.

She stood bewildered—amazement and fear bemusing the exhausted mind. She clasped her hands and wrung them so that the physical pain made her gasp a little. She thought:

"What shall I *do?* What shall I *do?*"

The man came back. Helen stood where she was. Even if she had wanted to move she could not have done so. He opened the outer door and put his head out into the corridor and spoke to someone invisible. He said:

"Get over to the Yard. Tell Pike to drop the Lesters and stand by."

He pulled his head back and shut the door and turned once more to Helen. He said:

"My name's Gethryn—Anthony Gethryn. You can consider me a policeman." He moved closer. "When did you discover that your daughter had been stolen? And have you heard from anyone claiming to hold her?"

She said harshly:

"I don't know what you're talking about. I must ask you to go."

Anthony took her by the arm. Under his fingers the bare flesh was cold and the muscles beneath the soft skin set like iron. He said:

"I can help. Come in here." He moved towards the living room.

Helen Van Renseler swayed. The fog was back in her mind now . . . swirling . . .

She found herself in an armchair in the living room. Anthony stood over her, a glass in his hand. He held this to her lips in such a way that she was forced to sip.

Brandy burned her tongue and throat, and she coughed and fought away from the glass and sat upright. She said, choking:

"Don't! Don't! ... I'm all right!" Her eyes shot a glance towards the clock, whose hands stood now at twelve minutes after the hour.

Anthony watched her.

"So there's a time limit!" he said, and sat in a chair to face her and set the glass on a table beside him. He looked at her steadily. He said after a long moment:

"I think that a little while ago you engaged a nursemaid who crossed from England to America to work for you. I think that at some time today this woman took your daughter out—and did not return. I think that since then you've received some sort of message from the kidnappers. I think, as you're alone, that your husband has gone to get in touch with these people as a result of the message. Am I right?"

Her eyes were wide as they stared at him, and their whites were visible all round the irises. Her throat worked and her lips moved, but there was no sound.

Anthony stood up. He said:

"And I think you won't admit that all this is right because you've been threatened that any interference will mean that you won't see your daughter again. . . . *But,* Mrs. Van Renseler, you'd better tell me all about it."

She got to her feet with a sudden jerky movement which sent her chair crashing to the floor.

"I won't!" she said in a flat voice which cracked. "I don't care who you are!" Her words began to come fast and faster. "In this country you don't know about ... about this sort of thing. We Americans do!" A sobbing gasp shook the voice again. "My God, how we do! After I've got Patricia again I'll tell you anything—*everything!* I'll spend every minute of my life with you until these devils are caught! But I won't say another word until she's back! If I did, you might make everything wrong, and then . . . and then——"

Her voice ceased abruptly. All numbness had gone from her now; all control. She was a distraught woman whose child was lost. Her face worked and her breath came in hard, irregular gasps. Her eyes flickered yet again towards the clock.

Behind an expressionless face Anthony's mind was racing. She must tell; must be forced to tell. But how, when her every instinct told her that to tell might cost her the child? How, when ...

A sudden light came to his eyes. Into the racing mind words had flashed; a sentence from the report of Detective Inspector Andrews, C.I.D., upon Garrett's first visit to Scotland Yard: ". . . some criminal undertaking involving possibly the abduction of a child and the execution of bodily harm upon some other person. . . ."

In one long stride he was close to her. He took her by the shoulders with hands which were not gentle. He said:

"Tell me! Unless you want to lose your husband as well!"

She was very still under his hands. Her eyes stared up at him. She said:

"Oh, God! I can't stand this! I——"

Anthony tightened his grip. "From the beginning of this case as we know it there's been this suggestion—that a child was going to be kidnapped *and* that someone else—a man—was going to be killed."

The shoulders twisted in his grip. Hands thrust vainly at his chest. She panted:

"Let me go! Let me go!"

Anthony said: "Tell me where your husband's gone!"

She struggled with desperate strength. The fingers upon her shoulders bit into her flesh. She shouted: "It's a trick! That's all I see! Let me *go!*"

Anthony said: "Listen to me! These people who have your daughter are going to hurt your husband—perhaps kill him. He's probably got ransom money with him; don't you see that if they take that and put him out of the way, they can still hold your daughter, for *more* money? Think, woman!"

She broke. The struggling fury became a limpness which needed his arms to uphold it.

He picked her up bodily. He set her upon the sofa by the long windows and stood over her. Tears rained from her eyes—helpless, hopeless tears which rolled unchecked. And sobs tore at her.

Anthony dropped to a knee beside her. He did not touch her, and he did not speak. ...

The sobbing grew less.

"Tell me!" said Anthony—and suddenly she was on her feet.

Anthony rose to face her; and now it was she who touched him. Her hands gripped his arms, just below each shoulder. Her eyes fixed their gaze upon his eyes. Her face was ravaged, but the new fire in her burned bright and steady. She said:

"I'm going to tell you. If it turns out wrong, I shall kill myself. My husband has gone to see—these people. He has the money with him, and my emeralds. He has to wait for someone on the westbound platform of a subway station. Cromwell Road. He has to be there at nine-thirty."

Her eyes went to the clock. Its hands were at nine twenty-one.

She said in a sort of dead whisper:

"There's not time! There's not time!"

She swayed and fell. But Anthony did not catch her. He was already at the telephone.

CHAPTER XXVI

A taxi sped down the grey, interminable length of the Cromwell Road. In the back of it Theodore Van Renseler sat huddled. His face was a dull mask, but behind drooping lids his eyes were alive. Upon his knees was a large dispatch case of dark leather—and his hands gripped it with a strength in odd contrast to the limpness of his body.

Upon the right of the cab the tall ugly houses gave way, with a sort of sullen enmity, to a row of small bright shops which nestled about the glass-canopied, brick façade of an underground station.

The cab stopped. It had barely ceased to move when Van Renseler was out of it. He thrust a ten-shilling note into the driver's hand, muttered something and was gone.

In the station vestibule the clock over the lifts showed nine twenty-five. A ticket collector lounged and yawned, and, save for Van Renseler, was the only human visible. At this time and in this place there is always lack of life; the workers are at home, the pleasure seekers already carried to their goals.

Van Renseler's step was heavy; without elasticity. He walked like a man who has to give thought to the business of movement.

At the only open booking window he bought a ticket for Piccadilly Circus—the only station his aching mind could remember. The clerk looked curiously at the white, expressionless face of his customer and was a little slow with his giving of change.

Van Renseler forced himself to wait: nothing, *nothing* must be unusual in his behaviour.

He took his change and turned and glanced at the clock. Nine twenty-seven ... Three minutes ... Then, the ransom paid, a frightful, sick waiting. "Patricia Van Renseler," that letter had said, "will be returned to you before tomorrow evening." The wait—the nightmare, agonizing interval—might, then, be twenty hours!

He checked the groan that rose to his lips. The liftman threw open the grilled gate and stood aside.

Van Renseler shook his head. "No," he said between lips which barely moved. "Can't stand elevators. Where're the stairs?"

The liftman pointed. "Over there, sir. Past the bookstall."

"Thanks," Van Renseler said. He walked away—very erect, very deliberate in gait, the black dispatch case at the end of a long right arm.

The liftman looked after him, a flicker of puzzled interest momentarily lighting his bored young face. "Looks queer," he thought, and once more leaned and yawned and waited for his shift to end.

The stairs were iron and sharply spiralled. The sheer, tubular walls were unrelieved grey-white, harshly lit by shadeless electric bulbs. The iron was slippery and rang hollow as Van Renseler's feet descended.

He plodded down ... around and down ... around and down ... around and down. ... The shaft seemed endless. He looked up and saw nothing but the circular sheathlike wall and the awful regularity of the twisting iron. He looked down, still plodding, and saw the same pattern inverted.

Sick fear caught him by the stomach in a sharp, new wave. Jagged irrationalities flashed through his mind. Suppose "they" didn't keep the date! ... Suppose this iron and this sheath *were* endless! ... Suppose his mind had gone and this iron-lined shell had no existence and instead of saving his child he were useless to her!

He began to run. His feet made a great clattering. His breath came hard. Beads of icy sweat started out upon his white face. ...

The stairs ended. There was a door. He went through it. He drew in a great breath and jerked back his left cuff and looked at his watch. It showed twenty-nine and a half minutes past the hour.

He was in a cross passage, blue-and-white tiled. The

261

roar of a passing train shook the earth. He turned and went towards the sound and came out upon an empty, gaily-postered platform. Panic seized him as he realized that he did not know whether ... Ah! he had seen a lighted sign which bore, among others, the word "Eastbound."

It was the other platform then. He turned sharply and went back down the cross passage, passing a uniformed porter as he did so.

He came out upon the westbound platform. There was no train nor anyone awaiting a train. And no official.

Again he looked at his watch. Half a minute past the time now. He walked with slow, heavy steps along the platform. He must wait; must wait; wait; wait. ...

He had reached the extreme end of the long, echoing platform when, from the last of the cross passages, just behind him, came brisk footsteps.

He turned. His heart beat with terrific force. He saw a man coming towards him.

2

Anthony's black Voisin screamed down the Embankment, its horn sounding almost continuously. It slid in and out of the variegated traffic like a snake through undergrowth. It achieved, even in this crowded, tram-strewn thoroughfare, an average speed beyond belief. Unscathed, it reached the Westminster Bridge corner, swung right and, writhing tortuous way between cars, drays, cabs and omnibuses, reached St. James's Park.

As it turned by Birdcage Walk a motorcyclist policeman leaned from his sidecar and gripped at the arm of his colleague astride the saddle. The Voisin, its horn playing an insistent, raucous fanfare, receded at terrific speed. ...

The policeman in the saddle shook his head. He had seen the unobtrusive sign (not to be mentioned here or elsewhere) which tells guardians of the law that here is no speedster but a colleague upon vital business.

The clock upon the Voisin's dashboard read nine thirty-two.

Two dark blue limousines of sedate appearance made their way, at a speed far from sedate, down an astonished Knightsbridge. Their horns, like the Voisin's, blared without cessation. And no policeman looked more than once at them without knowing them—as no civilian could—for what they were.

In the back seat of the first were Pike and Garrett and two others—quiet and burly men who spoke not at all.

Garrett twisted in his seat. He said:

"Wonder if Gethryn's behind us?"

Pike smiled thinly. He shook his head. "Not *behind* us, sir!"

Garrett said: "D'you think your people have done that phoning yet?"

Pike lifted his square shoulders, very slightly. "If they're not through yet, sir, they will be at any minute."

The clock on the dashboard stood at nine thirty-three.

A through train—eight out of ten go through Cromwell Road between eight-thirty and eleven at night—came roaring out of its sheathlike tunnel, rocketed past the long platform and hurled itself into the black mouth of the interrupted tube.

Van Renseler stood, trying not to look at the man who had seemed to be about to speak to him until a porter in uniform had come onto the platform and, by means of a portable ladder, had mounted to the direction board and begun to tinker with it.

That had been, it seemed to Van Renseler, an endless time ago: actually it was three minutes, for the clock now said nine thirty-four.

The porter came down from his ladder, folded it up, lifted it and walked off through the centre cross passage, his footsteps echoing shrill and metallic in this empty man-made warren.

Van Renseler, his heart pounding until to draw breath was conscious effort, watched the other man.

It was, primarily, an *ordinary* man. Of medium height

and build; of indeterminate clothing; of briskly inconspicuous gait.

The hollow reverberations of the porter's footsteps grew gradually less. Van Renseler, unable to move, stared dumbly at the sauntering back of the other man.

The echoing footsteps died away.

The man turned—not sharply, not hurried; just the ordinary turn of a platform loiterer.

But now he was walking directly towards Van Renseler.

He came on and on. Van Renseler ceased to breathe. Now the man was close. Now he halted, less than a full pace away.

His face was, at first sight, as commonplace as the rest of him. Neither round nor oval, sanguine nor pale, it was a face which a man might look at every day for a moment and never remember. But Van Renseler looked for longer than a moment. Moreover, this face and its owner were to him of paramount importance. And he saw that between cheeks of indeterminate shape and brows of indeterminate hue were eyes the like of which he had never seen.

For they were without colour, iris and pupil blending into one another through indeterminate shades of drabness, and the whites not white but merely a grey lightening of the utterly indeterminate shade of the cores.

The man spoke. He said:

"Have you a safety match?"

Van Renseler tried to speak but did not succeed. He proffered the black dispatch case.

The man took it. He shifted a little as he did so. He now stood with his back to the wall of the platform and facing the rails. Van Renseler had waited at the extreme end of the platform, close to the tunnel mouth. Shifting in sympathy with the other's movement, he now had his back to the edge of the platform just where it merged into the horseshoe wall of the tunnel. He was some three feet from this edge.

The man snapped open the lock of the dispatch case, which he took by its handle in his left hand. He looked full at Van Renseler with his colourless eyes. He said, in a voice which was neither deep nor high pitched, round nor thin:

"I've got a message for you."

He put his right hand into the inner pocket of the inconspicuous overcoat. Van Renseler's tongue came out in a vain effort to moisten dry lips. The man was groping in the pocket. He said, after a glance down the empty length of the platform:

"Here it is!"

His right hand came out of his pocket. It came very fast. In it was something dully black, like a long pantomime sausage. . . .

Van Renseler jerked his head aside—but it caught him a heavy blow on the temple, glancing down to his shoulder.

A flare like that of a Verey light soared inside Van Renseler's head. . . . He was falling. . . .

As he began to crumple his assailant thrust out the hand with the sandbag in it and caught him in the chest.

There was nicely judged power in the thrust; enough power to jerk Van Renseler's buckling legs into three staggering backward paces.

The fourth pace carried his senseless body beyond the edge of the platform. He fell like a limp sack. His body was in the darkness of the tunnel mouth—and directly across the passive, deadly, shining riband of the live rail.
. . .

Before the body had completed the bare four feet of its fall to certain cindered destruction by thousands of volts of electricity the man with the bag had turned and was walking—with brisk, unhurried, commonplace gait—towards the first of the cross passages. . . .

And the clock over the direction board showed a few seconds before nine thirty-five.

5

"Yes sir!" said the inspector in charge at Drayton Street police station. "Yes sir, I understand, sir. Right away, sir . . . five minutes at most."

He set back the receiver of the telephone and began to give curt, concise orders. Over his head the clock upon the wall showed nine thirty-five. He said finally:

"Got that, Sergeant?"

The sergeant stood rigid at attention. Out of a wooden face came sharp, metallic phrases. "Yes sir. Ten men. Surround Cromwell Road station, covering all hexits. Let no one enter or leave station till officers arrive from the Yard. Then take their orders."

The inspector nodded. "Get at it. Quick!"

6

"Yes, I will," said the little man in charge of the Cromwell Road tube station. "Yes, at once!"

His eyes were bright with excitement: here were happenings indeed.

He stood up and locked his desk: he was a neat little man. He started towards his office door, glancing at his watch as he went.

The time was nine thirty-six.

Some two seconds before he opened his office door a man carrying a black dispatch case crossed the vestibule from the direction of the stairs. An ordinary-seeming man, with a brisk yet unhurried walk. He went out into Cromwell Road and turned to his left.

7

The underground station faces Cromwell Road, but its eastern side is in a dismal Kensingtonian backwater called Illingham Street. At nine thirty-seven the black Voisin penetrated the gloom of Illingham Street like an angry bullet. . . .

Exactly at this moment the little stationmaster, accompanied by two uniformed porters, hurried onto the westbound platform.

The stationmaster looked up and down the platform.

"No one here," he said. "I——"

One of the porters drew in his breath with a sharp hiss. He was staring at the gleaming lines near the tunnel mouth at the far end. He shouted indistinguishably and began to run.

"What in the . . ." began the stationmaster; then himself saw and ran too.

At this moment, up above upon the surface of the earth, two blue limousines drew to a stop opposite the front of the station. Quiet men came from them and walked into the vestibule between the glowing windows of the shops. Pike was among them, and Garrett. To meet them, cutting through from the side entrance past the lifts, came the long form of Anthony Gethryn.

Across the wide straightness of Cromwell Road policemen in uniform—eleven of them, all at the double—came towards the station.

Pike saw them and glanced at his watch. "Not bad," he said, and turned to meet the sweating sergeant.

Anthony, who had merely nodded to Garrett, turned away again and went back towards the lifts. The movement gave Garrett a clear view of the roadway, and he saw, receding across it, a figure which had apparently come from one of the shops upon the same side of the street as the station, some twenty yards from the entrance.

It was a man's figure, of medium size and inconspicuously clad. It walked with brisk yet unhurried gait. And it carried a black bag in its right hand.

There was, in this figure, nothing at all out of the ordinary. Its movements were anything but furtive; it had not come directly from the station; in movement, stature, pace and appointment it had probably ten thousand counterparts in London.

Yet Garrett could not take his eyes from it. Perhaps it was the fact that the figure carried a bag; perhaps it was something far less simply explicable, but in the twentieth part of a second he made up his mind that he must know more of this man who was so calmly walking away. With a sudden feeling of breathless weakness in his stomach he turned to speak to Pike.

But Pike was not near, nor was anyone. They had all moved across towards the ticket office and lifts. . . .

8

Standing at the extreme edge of the platform, near the tunnel mouth, the stationmaster looked down and shook his head. His small face was pinched and white under the yellow radiance of the lights.

"Bad business!" he said, and made a ticking sound with his tongue. "Bad business! Must've died instantaneous."

The elder of the two porters was scratching his head and looking down in bewilderment at the sprawled body upon the gleaming rails. He was not perturbed like the

267

stationmaster; he was not fixed in bovine curiosity like his mate; he was all bewilderment.

The stationmaster jerked himself into bustling semblance of activity. "Come on, now!" he said busily. "Got to get him moved before the next train."

"Ah!" said the bovine porter.

But the other porter still stared. He said:

" 'E ain't dead!" He pointed with black-edged finger. "W'en they gets burned they goes all twisted like. An' there's a stink. An' . . . *look!* You c'n see 'im breave!"

"But—but the current," stammered the little stationmaster.

The bovine porter came to life. " 'E *is* breathin'!" he said firmly. "Cummon!"

9

A dark blue taxi, very new, very discreet and extremely shiny, sped westwards along Cromwell Road. One of a new fleet, it was a most superior taxi. It was smooth running, excellently sprung and admirably driven. It had—unusual for a London cab—shining bumpers at front and back. It also had, between the rear bumper and the body, a luggage grid.

Within it carried one passenger: a composed and ordinary-seeming man who held upon his knees a black bag.

The taxi slowed; then turned off Cromwell Road to the right. The turn completed, it was about to accelerate when there swerved in front of it a small boy upon a bicycle. Any onlooker would have given odds upon the boy's death—yet he was passed unscathed. The driver, as already has been said, was a good one. He braked, swerved, skidded, accelerated—and very nearly shook Garrett from his prone precarious perch between rear bumper and grid.

He felt himself going. His legs swung sideways and one foot actually scraped along the road surface. With a terrific effort he clenched his grip upon the bars of the grid. The muscles of his back and arms seemed to be tearing loose. And then, the swerve over, the taxi righted itself and he was once more safe. . . .

He put his head down upon his arm and wiped away the sweat which streamed from his forehead. He prayed—as he had been praying since that fantastic mo-

ment when, seeing the taxi begin to draw away with his
uncertain quarry, he had run blindly after it and swung
upon his perch like an oversized gamin—that somebody
would see him. Surely, surely, they must soon—in this
best-policed city in the world—pass a constable who
would catch sight of him and stop the taxi. Surely, if they
persisted in escaping the eyes of the law, another motorist
would see him in his headlight beam and overtake the taxi
and tell the driver. Surely, stopping at an intersection of
streets, some curious loiterer would shout to the driver
concerning his extra passenger. Surely something must
happen to stop this cab before the end of its journey.
Even a smash, he reflected, would be better than nothing.
Once stopped by some outside agency, and he would at
least—although under suspicion himself—be able to delay
matters for long enough. . . .

But the cab went on unchecked, through these dark and
frowning and always deserted Kensingtonian streets. Not a
policeman met Garrett's eye . . . not an observant busybody of a passer-by . . . no overtaking car. . . .

10

The lift gate opened with a rattling clang. The stationmaster was kneeling by the body of Van Renseler. He was
looking down into the still face and shaking his head. He
was talking to himself.

"No current," he was saying. "Can't understand it at
all."

Brisk men came and tapped him on the shoulder and
moved him aside. And uniformed policemen bent and
raised the unconscious man. In the back of the lift the two
porters, swelling with a delicious sense of importance, began unanimously to talk to a burly person in the plainest
of clothes.

The stationmaster, blinking, got to his feet and stepped
out of the lift. Now the inert body of the man who should
have been dead was being placed upon a stretcher held by
more policemen. Over this bent a tall man in clothes of
easy elegance.

The stationmaster was drawn irresistibly towards the
stretcher. He said timidly:

"Is he—I can't understand how—he was lying right across the live rail. . . . He——"

The tall man straightened and turned. He said brusquely:

"He's all right. Crack on the head. And the current was cut off from Lot's Road."

The stationmaster's eyes were wide and wondering. "But I don't . . ." His little bleat died in his throat as it became plain to him that he was unnoticed.

The tall man had turned to another. "Where's Garrett?" he was saying.

11

The blue taxi, having threaded tortuous way through gloomy frowning streets of shocking similarity, turned into another which, although no better lit, was wider and longer and flanked by more portentous buildings.

There were lights in many windows of the tall brick houses, but they were yellow, dismal lights which served not at all to relieve the dank atmosphere of disuse and decay. They were allies, it seemed, of the dirty-paned and infrequent street lamps.

The taxi stopped.

Garrett, who had been wondering what he would do when this thing happened, now made up his mind. He lay motionless. Thus he could not see anything save the roadway. But he heard the door of the cab open . . . feet alighting . . . a curt murmur of voices . . . the chinking of coins passed from hand to hand . . . and then brisk feet crossing the pavement and the whining of a rusty iron gate.

What he had not heard—because this man wore heels of rubber—was the taxi driver's descent from his driving seat. So that, rolling himself with caution off the unkind iron, he was shocked to find himself, as he rose to his feet and began painfully to ease his aching muscles, regarded by a burly person with arms akimbo and menacing stance. . . .

12

The two dark limousines from Scotland Yard sped westward down the Cromwell Road. Anthony sat beside the driver of the first and spoke to Pike over his shoulder.

"Five minutes start," he said. "Too much."

Pike said: "Maybe, sir." And then, uneasily: "And how do we know Mr. Garrett's on the right tack?"

Another exploded: "God damn it, man! Isn't it enough that he's on a tack at all! *We've* got nothing—except Van Renseler with his head bashed in and a broken collarbone!"

"That's all very well, sir." Pike was stubborn. "But I'm afraid it's a wildgoose chase, as you might say. Don't forget, Mr. Garrett had that crack on the head himself. And if he'd been—well, *normal*—why should he go running off and taking a whip-behind ride on some taxi without telling anyone? If that young constable hadn't happened to see him——"

Anthony interrupted. "Yes, yes! Quite, and all that! ... But don't forget, his hunch was right and we were wrong. What he probably did was to see something that we didn't—and have no time to do anything except what he has done." He went on, half to himself: "Hope to God enough people've seen him."

Almost as he spoke the driver swung the car into the curb and pulled to an abrupt halt with a screeching of brakes. At the curb stood a tall and massive and helmeted policeman.

Pike was out of the car almost before it had stopped moving. He ran round the front of the car and talked to the policeman. He ran back again and got into his seat and snapped at the driver:

"First to the right. Cranbrook Street. Keep your eyes open for constables." He said to Anthony: "That man saw him. Said he couldn't believe his eyes. Only hope, sir, we can *keep* on the trail."

The police cars—for the second had halted beside the first—moved on, swinging to the right at the next corner. London—even off the Cromwell Road—is not so lawless as it had seemed to the Garrett who had clung to the back of a taxi.

13

"But I tell you," said Garrett between his teeth, "that it's a police matter! Scotland Yard——"

The driver interrupted. His hands had come away from his hips and turned themselves into fists. He said:

"P'lice matter, is it? Tell yer what, cock, that's the first bleedin' truth that's passed your bloody mouth." He came closer.

"Aw, the *hell* with it!" said the Sheldon Garrett, once the best light heavyweight his university had ever produced.

His right foot drew back; his left foot went forward. His right fist, moving not more than nine inches, met the chin of the driver with a crisp and smacking sound.

The man's knees buckled and he fell forward—a sure sign of complete unconsciousness.

Garrett jumped away from the falling bulk; and then, without so much as a glance at it, stepped onto the pavement. He glanced apprehensively up and down the length of the dismal street. But no one met his gaze and there was no sound of footsteps. He looked next up at the house into which the man with the bag must have gone. There was one light visible—from a small window on the second floor. There was no sound.

On tiptoe he crossed to the spear-shaped railings of rusty iron which bounded the patch of mildewed garden before the house. His eyes strained upwards at the lighted window. He tried to see whether or not it was open and could not. He was obsessed by the fear that his quarry had heard his altercation with the driver.

His heart beat fast, with irregular thumps. His head hurt him, but he did not know it. His mouth was dry—and in him was ever-increasing certainty. On tiptoe still he went along the railing to the gate whose hinges he had heard creaking. He set his hand upon this to open it; then changed his mind.

He thought: "If I go in and ring the bell and spin some sort of a yarn—well, I won't be any place. They'll either get me—or I won't find out anything. Maybe I ought to scare up a bobbie. But if I leave *he* may get out while I'm gone—and then where are we?"

He took his hand from the gate and once more looked up and down the road. One way it stretched on interminably; but a hundred yards away in the other direction was a turning with a lamppost at its corner.

With long, loping strides he ran silently towards this

corner. As he went he counted the houses so that, when he was behind them in the next street, he could tell which one was his goal. . . .

14

The two quiet police cars surged in file up the dark, straight inevitability of Derby Street.

The leading car came to a crossroad and stopped. A street named Paignton ran off to the right; to the left there curved away into obscurity something called Biddlecombe Avenue.

Again Pike shot out. He ran back to the second car. He said:

"Take the left. We're going right. Ask all constables."

15

In a drab, unfurnished, dirty room upon the second floor of Number 17 Paignton Street a man and a woman talked. The woman knelt. The man sat upon a carpetless floor with his back against the wall and fumbled over a black bag upon his knees.

The woman, looking into the bag, drew in her breath with a sharp and sensually gratified hiss. She said after a moment:

"So we've done it!"

The man nodded.

He closed the bag, snapping its locks. He looked up at the woman over his shoulder. His mouth smiled and he said:

"Yes. And we've only just begun." He got to his feet, the bag in his left hand. "But we're not taking any chances. We're going, *now!*"

The woman looked at him. "Chelsea?" she said.

The man nodded, turning away.

The woman put her hand upon his arm. She said with a backward jerk of her head to indicate a room behind her:

"How do we take it? Open or trunk?"

16

"Easy there!" said Anthony to the driver, and pointed.

The police car lights swung a little to the right—and in the white beam there showed clearly the back of a shining dark blue cab. And something else—the huddled figure of a man who lay upon the road behind the cab.

The light seemed to rouse him. He stirred. His eyes opened. Groaning, he struggled to a sitting posture and put a hand to his head. Like a sleepy, peevish child he turned his head away from the white glare of the lights. He mumbled to himself and set a hand upon the edge of his cab's bumper and tried to pull himself to his feet. He was aware of the car with the lights stopping, and men getting out of it. He tried to stand without support and his knees buckled.

He would have fallen had not the adequate arm of Superintendent Arnold Pike come about his shoulders. A voice said to him, seeming to come to his ear from far away:

"Take your time and tell us about it."

His strength coming back to him with every moment, the man began to talk. . . .

17

Roughly, efficiently, the woman pulled down the single garment which she had slipped upon the inert body of the child. Now she began to pull stockings onto the straight small legs. This done, she looked down for the shoes—and saw only one. She frowned and called over her shoulder in her deep, harsh voice:

"Bring in that other shoe, will you?"

She was answered immediately—but not in the way she had expected. The man to whom she had spoken came swiftly through the door. His movements were tight and quick and soundless. There was that about them which made her look suddenly into his face, the colour ebbing away from her own. She would have spoken, but he silenced her with a quick movement of the hand. His strange eyes, normally colourless, seemed now to have a reddish glow behind them. He said:

"Quick. Back way. There's a car in front. Looks like police."

The woman's hand flew to her mouth. She said hoarsely: "But how . . . ?"

The man paid no attention. With an ease which told of strength not promised by his build, he picked up the flaccid, stertorously breathing body of the child and hung it like a sack across his shoulder.

18

The street which runs parallel with Paignton Street, to the south, is called Beckford Place. It is like Paignton Street but, incredibly, yet more dismal.

The house which backed onto Number 17 Paignton Street was, by divine grace, untenanted. In its weed-choked patch of back garden Garrett stood beneath a seven-foot wall of brick which now was all that separated him from his goal.

At some time or another, for some reason quite possibly disreputable, someone had made a door in this wall. It was, as he stood, some few feet to the right of him. He had tried its handle but with no success. Now, crouching, he suddenly sprang upwards—and his crooked fingers caught the top of the wall. With an ease which would have been greater had he not for the past days been a sick man, he levered himself up to sit astride the rough brick-work.

It was very dark. Above, the black vault of the sky showed no moon; and such stars as were visible at all could only be seen through the high, dark grey pall which London so often throws around herself. In the gloom the twisted shapes of drab persistent trees seemed to Garrett's straining eyes to thrust themselves upward like ugly hands. In the windows of houses to his right and left showed occasional dingy lights—but the house which he watched was unrelieved black.

He swung his right leg over the top of the wall so that now both his feet hung over the terrain of 17 Paignton Street. He made ready to slip down; then suddenly checked.

He had heard a door—or perhaps it was a window—being softly opened. It seemed to him that the sound had come from the blank black face of the house he watched. But he could not be sure.

He lay now along the top of the wall, flat upon his belly. He made himself small. And he held his breath as he listened.

He heard the door again; definitely it was a door. It was, he saw with that inner eye which translates sound into pictures, being opened more widely than before. Something came through it. There were scraping footsteps and a sort of soft, shuffling bump as if something heavy had struck against the doorjamb.

And then, waking thunderous and unexpected echoes, came the sound of a door knocker. It thundered against a door in Paignton Street; the door, it seemed, of Number 17.

The sound ceased, and Garrett heard other and nearer and softer sounds—footsteps which ran softly over the neglected garden; ran towards the wall.

Other footsteps followed. They were lighter yet less feline. They were short striding and quite definitely a woman's. He strained his eyes down into the darkness and saw indistinguishable shapes approaching, one some fifteen feet in advance of the second.

And then the knocking began again.

But he had no time for wonder. Below him the first running figure had arrived at the wall and was stooping beside the door. Even through the darkness, he could see that this figure was a man's; could see also that over its right shoulder another, far smaller figure hung limply. . . .

In one movement Garrett got to his knees and leapt downwards. He landed, as he had hoped, upon the left shoulder of the man.

They fell and rolled. And the small figure which had been over the man's other shoulder fell away from their struggling bodies. . . .

In the darkness, on the dank, dead soil, Garrett and his adversary fought in silence.

There was a strength entirely unexpected, Garrett found, in his enemy. But he himself was the heavier, and though his breath came in hard rasping gasps and there was searing pain in his head, he found himself at last astride of the other's body and caught the throat with his left hand while he drove short, heavy punches at the dimly seen face.

A savage flush of victory warmed him—and a pair of arms locked themselves about his neck from behind. They were soft arms, but there was a steely core to their softness. Garrett, choking, was forced to take his hands from the man beneath him. As he flung them up and backward in an attempt to snatch at this new assailant there was a violent heave beneath him and an upthrust knee came with sickening force into the pit of his stomach. He was flung backwards and sideways. He rolled in agony, fighting for air. . . . Two figures stood over him, and the small pointed toe of a woman's shoe cracked against his cheek.

The man was fumbling at his pockets. He said hoarsely: "Take the kid and get out. Quick! I'll be with you!"

Like a guardsman the woman obeyed. In a stride she was beside the small, motionless bundle and had gathered it into her arms.

Garrett conquered the momentary paralysis of his lungs and drew in a whistling gasp of air and started to struggle to his feet.

The child in her arms, the woman reached the door and, after bending over its lock, swung it open.

Something shone with a dull gleam in the hand of the man who stood over Garrett. He raised his arm.

With her burden the woman ran through the door in the wall.

Garrett, sensing a descending and fatal blow, put up a weak arm—and from the other side of the wall came a high-pitched scream, long drawn out. In the darkness it was animal, filled with panic and rage and frustration.

The upraised weapon of Garrett's enemy was checked in its movement as the man turned involuntarily to look in the direction of the sound. Garrett flung himself with his last ounce of strength at his adversary's knees. . . .

And now came more sounds from the other side of the wall . . . men's voices . . . running footsteps. . . . And then the white, knifelike beams of electric torches as men came running through the door and threw themselves upon the struggling pair and tore away from Garrett a man who snarled at them and raved and fought—and was at last subdued.

Garrett felt a strong arm about his shoulders and found himself looking into the face of Anthony Gethryn. He giggled weakly.

"Attaboy!" he said and giggled again. "That you knocking?"

"Take it easy," Anthony said. "Take it easy. . . . Yes, knock at the front and you push 'em out at the back. . . . It's a rule of nature. . . . Here! Where're you going?"

For Garrett, with a sudden twist, had pulled himself away from the encircling arm and now, on legs which were a little unsteady, was moving at a shambling run towards a group who knelt beside something upon the ground.

He, too, threw himself upon his knees and found himself shoulder to shoulder with Pike. He tried to say something, but only a foolish little rattling noise came from his throat.

Pike said: "All right, sir. All right. Just doped, that's all."

Garrett shouldered him aside and, still on his knees, shuffled to the little body and raised its head and shoulders in his arms. He looked down at the small white face of Patricia Van Renseler.

Its eyes opened, very slowly. In them, even through the darkness, Garrett could see the sudden fire of panic, and against him the body stirred with a quick constriction of every muscle. He held it tightly, and words came from him.

The fear went out of the eyes and the tenseness from the limbs. The eyelids began to droop again and the head fell against his shoulder.

"Oh," said Patricia Van Renseler. "You're *nice!*"

EPILOGUE

Paignton Street by daylight is no less dismal than at night. Indeed, it is more so, as was apparent to Anthony as he stood in a bare room upon the ground floor of Number 17 and looked out at a street bathed in remorseless sunshine. He saw dusty pavements; squalid gardens whose untamed, soot-stained growths seemed more unnatural than any brick; blistered paint and peeling stucco and windows of grimy glass. . . .

He shuddered and turned to Pike, who sat at a table set in the middle of the room and pored over tidy little piles of such ill-assorted matters as ancient envelopes, tins of foodstuffs, cheap and dirty and unmarked handkerchiefs, an incongruous—and empty—magnum of Perrier Jouet '29, a heap of newspapers.

Pike looked at him. "Not much here, sir." His tone was dejected, and a corner of his mouth pulled down.

Anthony stood over the table, looking down at the heterogeneous mixture. He said after a moment:

"What did you expect? Pretty good worker, Evans. Not the sort to leave his card."

Heavy footsteps sounded overhead, and others upon the stairs. A large man in clothes of the plainest came into the room and set down upon the table a blanket and some shreds of sacking. Pike looked at them; then at their bearer.

"That all?" he said.

"From the bedroom, sir? Yes sir."

Pike grunted. "All right. Keep at it."

Anthony moved the magnum and sat upon the edge of the table. He said:

"Anything new since yesterday?"

Pike shook his head. "Not a thing, sir. I don't mind admitting it's got me sort of baffled, as you might say. Over twenty years in the force and I've never struck anything like it." His tone was lugubrious.

Anthony said: "Clever man, Mr. Evans. Medium, you know." He looked at Pike and smiled. "Cheer up. You've got enough to hang him on. Twice."

"If we hadn't, sir, I'd—I'd *resign!* But it's not *that* that worries me, it's the sort of professional viewpoint, as you might say. Here we are, having laid our hands on the worst criminal I can remember, and yet it looks as if we're going to hang him without even knowing his real name. We go back and back, along every line we've got, and where do we end up? Nowhere! Why, even the KJB lot don't really know any more about him than we do. I questioned Hines myself and I know he's speaking the truth when he says that. Their blackmail business has apparently been going for years, and Evans must have horned in on them somehow."

"Poor Pike!" said Anthony. "What's his woman's name, by the way? You never told me."

Pike passed a hand across his forehead. "Believe it or not, sir, but he's even fixed her the same way. With the landlords of this place she passed as Mrs. Evans. And that's all the name we've got!"

Anthony lit a cigarette. "You know what Garrett'd say? 'Give 'em the works!' Sometimes, Pike, one sees the reason for the third degree."

For a moment a light flashed into Pike's brown eyes; then was officially repressed. He said:

"That's as may be, sir. But I do know this—once I get hold of this Janet Murch, *then* perhaps I'll get somewhere."

"King's evidence?" said Anthony.

"Yes sir." Pike's tone was more cheerful. "I got the commissioner's permission this morning."

Anthony surveyed him with sympathy. "So you're really back, my poor fellah, just where we started: where's Murch? Where is Janet, what is she, that we poor boobs can't find her?"

Pike's jaw was outthrust. "I'll find her," he said. "She left

280

the Alsace Hotel with the child. She must've been seen by hundreds of people! And I've got a hundred lines out."

Outside the room four pairs of heavy feet could be heard descending the stairs, and the man who had brought in the blanket and sacking stood in the doorway.

"All through upstairs, sir," he said to Pike. "There's only the cellar left and Bruce and Piggott are going there now."

Pike got to his feet. "Well—that's that!" He looked at Anthony. "Coming, sir?" Together they strolled out into the bare hallway. At the far end of it two plain-clothes men were fiddling with the handle of a door beneath the stairs. One of them turned to Pike.

"Locked, sir," he said. "And there's no key. Break it in?"

Pike went towards him, Anthony lounging at his heels. Pike said: "Yes. And be quick about it."

The man who had spoken pushed his companion out of the way and kicked at the door, just below the lock, with the flat of his foot and tremendous force.

There was a crash of rending wood. ... The kick was repeated. ... Almost limply the door swung gently open, revealing a dark and cavernous little stairway.

The kicker pulled an electric torch from his pocket and stepped over the threshold. They heard his feet descending a little way; then come to an abrupt stop.

A muffled exclamation came up to them; then the man himself. He said to Pike:

"Look at that, sir!"

He swung the beam of his torch along cobwebbed walls and downwards. From the doorway Pike and Anthony could see, in the yellow pool of light, a figure which lay huddled upon the narrow stairs.

It was the figure of a woman. Her feet were towards them and her head upon the bottom step. She was, obviously and dreadfully, dead. The body was short and thick and square, and to its head there still adhered the long-veiled cap of the uniformed nursemaid.

"Meet Miss Murch!" said Anthony beneath his breath, and then, to Pike:

"That's game and set to Mr. Evans! But we *still* get the match!"

Patricia Van Renseler left the room in merriment. From the other side of the slammed door the sound of her laughter came back, mingled with imperious summons for her mother.

Anthony looked at his host. "Yes. She *is* all right," he said.

Van Renseler laughed. "All right!" he said. The sling which supported his broken collarbone seemed to hurt him, and he adjusted it with an impatient twitch of his free hand. He said:

"She's so much all right that you wouldn't think anything had ever happened to her!" He looked at Anthony with eyes grown suddenly sombre. "And it's all due to you that she——"

Anthony interrupted. "Cut that out! I warned you."

Van Renseler said: "I never realized before that a man can *suffer* from gratitude." He smiled a little, but his eyes were grave. "I'm sorry if it annoys you, Gethryn, but I must——"

Anthony again interrupted. "Hold those horses! If you must bubble over, don't do it on me any more. Because there are plenty of others."

"Tom Garrett, of course! And Pike. But they aren't here, so you'll have to take it."

Anthony shook his head. "No. Plenty more yet. Very important, although some of 'em don't even know they had anything to do with it."

Van Renseler looked at him. "Don't get you," he said.

Anthony smiled. "I'll elucidate. First, Miss Letty Lamb. If it hadn't been for her we should never have had even the name Murch to follow."

"Lamb?" said Van Renseler. "Lamb? Oh yes. The girl on the shopping list."

Anthony nodded. "I'm giving you these in order of importance. Then there's the unfortunate Ballister woman. If it hadn't been for her we'd never have got onto the KJB Agency, which was the first string that attached us to Evans. You can't thank her, poor woman; but you might like to consider an extra gravestone or flowers or something. Then, of course, we sewed up KJB and got nearer still to Evans through Avis Bellingham——"

It was Van Renseler's turn to interrupt. "I've already talked to her. And so's Helen."

Anthony said: "Growing more important with every step, we now reach a junior member of the Criminal Investigation Department. One Detective Officer Frawley."

Van Renseler sat forward. "Who's he?"

"A boy with one year's detective service," Anthony said. "But if he hadn't used his brains and exceeded his orders by opening Evans' bag when that kid called for it at Dulwich station—well, I wouldn't be here now and Evans wouldn't be in jail . . . and you can finish all that for yourself."

"Frawley," said Van Renseler to himself. "Frawley. Frawley." He looked across at Anthony. "I won't forget that. . . . But all this doesn't get you out of anything, Gethryn. If it hadn't been that you were behind——"

"Wait!" said Anthony. "Moving on, we come to the still more important case of Mr. Vox, the ventriloquist."

Van Renseler stared.

Anthony grinned. "I mean it. He's nothing to do with this business—*and* everything. Entirely everything! If it hadn't been for him, Garrett and I would still be chasing over the north of England after an unpleasant fellah called Lester."

Van Renseler fiddled irritably with the knot of his sling. "I suppose," he said, "that you'll eventually tell me what you're talking about."

Anthony said: "We were after this man Lester. Garrett had a hunch we were wrong. To keep him quiet I took him to a music hall. This man Vox had three dummies—and one of 'em was in cap and apron. The combination of the voice-throwing and the uniform jerked my mind back onto the voices Garrett had heard in the teashop, *plus* the fact that one of these voices was a nursemaid—Janet Murch. I suddenly saw that Garrett might have made a mistake in ascribing the voices to the figures. And he had. And in ten minutes I was talking to your wife."

"God!" said Van Renseler—and fell silent. His face grew grim, and much of the colour left it as memory took him.

Anthony said quickly: "Then there's Harold Mattock.

Garrett's arms closed about her once more. She found herself crushed against him so that breath was difficult.

"The hell with George!" he said between his teeth—and was amazed by her laughter.

He let her go. He stepped back and stared at her. She laughed still. She put out her hands and caught at him.

She said: "You should read your social news, my darling. *And* realize that women want to be loved for themselves alone!"

He took her shoulders in a grip which hurt. He said: "What are you talking about? Tell me!"

Her eyes were full of laughter still, a tender laughter which played havoc with him.

"Divorce," she said. "I was unmarried from George two years ago!"

"My *God!*" said Sheldon. Garrett.

ABOUT THE AUTHOR

Philip MacDonald, grandson of the Scottish poet and novelist George MacDonald, was born and educated in Britain. He wrote numerous novels, suspense stories and film scripts, most notably the classic *Rebecca*.